I0658271

Torch Day

John Windsor

CT Press

This book is a work of fiction. The characters, incidents, and dialogue are drawn from the author's imagination and are not to be construed as real. Any resemblance to actual events or persons, living or dead, it's entirely coincidental.

TORCH DAY © 2016 by John Windsor. All rights reserved.

ISBN 978-0-9981310-0-9 (Kindle)
ISBN 978-0-9981310-1-6 (EPUB)
ISBN 978-0-9981310-2-3 (Paperback)
ISBN 978-0-9981310-3-0 (Audio book)

To Katrin, for the extraordinary gift of time.

Vipers

They were late. Two hours late. In five minutes, Harry's bladder was going to explode. It had passed "painful" twenty minutes ago. The main room at Card City was huge, but Harry figured he could flood it at least up to the table tops. Damn! Twenty-seven years in the FBI, and it was the first time he'd been sabotaged by his body. Ellen would give him shit about this for months.

It never occurred to him that these creeps would be late. They had a reputation for being methodical, even militaristic. That was one of their hallmarks: strike with precision; move the goods rapidly; annihilate impediments; and always wash your hands after—

God, he had to keep his mind off his bladder. Of course, the bright lights and frenetic activity around him didn't help. All that twitchy gambler anxiety just energized his bladder even more. Card City was the biggest gaming hall south of San Francisco, attracting crowds from throughout the Bay Area.

It also attracted a certain criminal element, which is why Harry had landed there a month ago, posing as a computer executive with a weakness for gambling. Computer chip thieves preyed on that profile, a guy desperate for money who would hand over exotic silicon wafers to be relieved of his gambling debts.

And they bought into Harry right away. With his graying hair, rumpled clothes, big smile, and a face that was every bit of 53, Harry Harper looked nothing like an FBI agent. He had a certain roundness to his frame—"droop," his partner Ellen loved to say— but he wasn't fat, just not sharp or angular. Physically, he was still strong, even agile if he had to be, but he didn't look it. He looked like a guy who would go bass fishing in his spare time. It was the perfect cover.

All it took was a few weeks of him losing Bureau money at Card City and the chip thieves were hooked, particularly when he said he was from Century Systems, the hottest chip manufacturer in Silicon Valley. One might have expected these guys to be cautious, since Operation West Chips a few months ago had put so many of their friends in jail, but they practically jumped on him. Sure, the calendar said "1996," but it felt like the Wild West out there.

Who could blame them? Ounce for ounce, computer chips were more valuable than diamonds or cocaine, and a hundred times easier to fence. Chips could change hands a dozen times in 72 hours. It was a volatile, violent, and incredibly lucrative enterprise. Gangs formed and faded, and most had been hit in the West Chips raids, but one group consistently managed to avoid the law.

That would change tonight, if Frick and Frack ever showed up. Their real names were something in Vietnamese, but calling them Frick and Frack seemed to fit the character Harry was playing. While they may have looked harmless, however, they were said to be brutal, leaving Harry only slightly comforted by the fact that more than a hundred FBI agents and San Jose police were lurking in the shadows. It was five miles from Card City to a dark warehouse where the prized chips, and a SWAT team, waited; a lot could happen in that time.

Harry looked up from his cards, trying desperately to avoid excess motion, lest it set off his urinary bomb. He and Ellen had spent six months developing Operation Card Shark, and it would take all of twenty minutes to resolve, once those—

Finally! A furtive wave from across the room, by two Vietnamese vipers trying to blend in with the wallpaper. Harry set down his cards, pocketed his chips, and whispered "Showtime" into his concealed microphone. He chuckled ruefully to himself as he approached his handlers. They didn't look vicious, just edgy. But two years in 'Nam had taught him to not underestimate anyone.

"Man, where have you guys been?" he said. "I didn't know which would give out first, my bladder or my wallet. I gotta pee before we leave."

Frick and Frack exchanged looks—a strange reaction, after all their previous bravado—then Frick jerked his thumb toward the restrooms. Harry shrugged off the response and started toward the promised land.

It appeared to be empty, but he lowered his chin to whisper into the microphone. "Sorry, guys, but this is for real. They didn't follow me, so you can turn down the volume. I'll be done in a minute."

Ah, relief! At a time like this, the world stood still. It felt good, too, to be wrapping up Operation Card Shark. All those stories of guys cutting off ears and killing their cousins had not made Harry feel warm and cozy. Too bad Ellen wasn't doing this undercover bit. She'd been in the Bureau for several years; it was about time she tasted some of that action. Of course, not everyone was right for it, and these vipers would've had a hard time buying a blond, fit, thirty-two year old woman as a compulsive gambler. Nothing about her screamed "loser." In fact, she tended to stand out in a crowd; not by her height, but by her energy. She'd probably never be able to dampen that spunky manner enough for undercover—

There was a sound behind him. A scratching sound, very light, but moving toward him. Someone was slinking across the tile floor, and that wasn't a sound you should hear. Guys shuffled into a restroom, or stomped, or ambled, but no one slinked in. Harry's heart rate quickened.

He couldn't look around. That would be too obvious. A gun was out of the question for lots of reason, not least of which was that he wasn't armed. That's what the SWAT team and a hundred others were for.

"Are you stalling?" The voice was inches from Harry's ear.

"No, I'm recovering," Harry said. He finished up and turned

to face a middle-aged man, whose eyes were piercing through him.

"You're not calling the police? Double crossing us?"

The guy was new, not one of the ones Harry had met with before, or even seen in reams of mug shots. The face and inflections were Vietnamese, but beyond that, the guy was a cipher.

Harry held up his hands. "Just answering the call of the wild." He walked over to the sink. "How come I'm getting this special escort?"

The man smiled. "You're special. Tonight's special. Let's go." He nodded his head, obviously intending that Harry go first. Harry complied.

Up ahead, Frick and Frack waited at the door; their nervousness was palpable. They were riveted, but not on him. Their focus went past, to the cipher man trailing behind. Something about this did not feel right.

Harry began to whistle softly. It was his signal to Ellen to be ready for anything. He hoped his partner had the volume back up.

Special Agent Ellen King was not tracking Harry at the moment. From her seat in the command van, near the targeted warehouse, she was fighting for his life.

"What do you mean, you're pulling the force?!" she shouted into the phone. "You can't do that, sir! Yes, I know you're the— Yes, I understand that, but— Forgive me, sir, that's bullshit. We've got an operation going down right now and my partner is— These guys are ruthless! You can't leave him unprotec—"

She slammed the phone down. In the background, cars were racing out of the parking lot. No sirens, just a torrent of squealing tires.

"Sonia, did you hear that?" she said, to the other occupant of the van. "Morton is pulling everybody. Everybody except us, the SWAT team, and one San Jose black & white."

Sonia Taylor, the local office's electronics wiz, whipped her head around. "Yeah, but not why. What's going on?"

"Somebody just hijacked a semi, not far from here, filled with ATF contraband, ammunition, even their traveling exhibit. Morton made it sound like everything the Bureau of Alcohol, Tobacco, and Firearms ever owned was in that truck."

"So?"

"That's what I said. But Morton said D.C. is screaming for everyone, including the janitors, to be out there looking for that truck. He said he'd leave us the SWAT team, like it was some big favor."

"Fucking bureaucrats."

"Later. We've got to make sure no one exits along Harry's path. I'll cover that; you get the SWAT team reset and find a place for that black & white."

Harry's nervous system went into high alert. Two cars had just raced out of the parking lot in close formation, taking a sharp left turn and vanishing into the dark. There was no question who they belonged to. Harry was pretty sure that Frick, Frack, and Cipher Man hadn't noticed, but something bizarre was going on. God, he hated being the bait.

Meanwhile, Cipher Man was rattling on in a language that was vaguely familiar to Harry, and it was unnerving how quiet Frick and Frack had become.

Frack grabbed Harry's arm and shoved him toward a sleek, black Mercedes. "Get in back," he said.

"A black Mercedes?" Harry said. "Where's the van?" He knew it might not work that way, but he had to keep the field updated.

"Get in!"

Frick and Frack sandwiched him in the backseat, with Cipher Man and a driver in the front. The windows were heavily tinted.

Leaving the parking lot, the driver paused, then turned right.

"Wait a minute!" Harry said. "You've got to go left."

Cipher Man spoke over his shoulder: "We're not going to the warehouse. We're going to the research building. Partners promised you'd get us inside."

"What?!"

The man turned to look at him. "Get us inside. Get us that special Millennium chip. You'll be a very wealthy man."

Harry turned to Frick and Frack. "What's he talking about? That wasn't what we agreed to. You said the DX chips, untagged. It's all set. You can't change that now. I don't know if—"

"You *will* get us those Millennium chips." Cipher Man raised a gun over the seat back and aimed it at Harry. "Right?"

"Listen, Mr. Whoever-you-are—"

"Trong."

Harry's face froze. Fortunately, the darkness covered him.

Ellen bolted out of her chair. "We're in trouble. We're in big fucking trouble."

"What do you mean?" said Sonia.

"That name: 'Trong.' He's the most savage thing around. Nobody's come close to catching him. Shit, he shouldn't be on the scene. Something's wrong."

Ellen grabbed her keys off the desk and ran for the door.

"I'm going after them," she said. "Get the SWAT guys and that black & white over to the research building, wherever it is. I may need you to guide me. Channel 14?"

Ellen raced out of the van, across the lot, and into a standard Bureau car. She was gone in a heartbeat, praying she could find the Mercedes in time.

Harry was good at thinking on his feet, but he was in quicksand when it came to technology; that was Ellen's territory. He had heard something about the Millennium chip while they were developing the case, but beyond that he was lost. He didn't even know where the research building was, let alone how to get in or where these mysterious chips might be.

"Hey, those chips aren't ready for production," he said. It was a guess.

Trong looked at him and smiled. "That's the whole point."

"What?"

"Sell the *technology* to the highest bidder, not just the chips. Make huge margins. Crush Century. Make lots of people happy. Make me super rich."

Please let the microphone be working.

"Who are your bidders?" Harry asked.

"I could tell you," Trong said, "but I can't let you tell." He pulled out a switchblade and pressed the release. The blade flashed open. "Still want to know?"

Ellen was hurtling down a blacked-out road somewhere in the backwaters of San Jose, trying desperately to find both a black Mercedes and a way she could stop it without getting herself or Harry killed.

Her pulse was jumping. You couldn't train for this kind of situation, you just had to trust; that's what Harry always said. But he was usually around at those times! Where the hell was he now?

Somewhere up in the distance—half a mile?—she saw the lights of a car turning left off the road she was on. Out here, at this hour, could it be anyone else? She jammed the accelerator and the car leapt forward.

As the speedometer passed 100 mph, an idea hit her. She cradled the steering wheel with her knees and pulled off her black jacket with "FBI" printed on the back. She threw that out the window, then began yanking on her blouse. No time for scruples.

* * *

The car suddenly erupted with noise and the four thugs turned to look out the back. Harry did the same. Headlights were bearing down on them, weaving sharply back and forth as a car raced toward them. It was an ominous sight, and it punched up Harry's nervousness. The thugs seemed to be off the scale.

The car was less than 100 yards behind them now, flashing its lights on and off, and honking its horn incessantly. The driver of the Mercedes edged his car toward the side of the road and eased his foot off the pedal, but the demon car just kept honking and flashing and weaving. Whoever it was had no interest in passing.

The car came up alongside the Mercedes and slowly forced it to a stop. Instantly, the thugs had guns in their hands, the safeties clicking off in succession.

The door to the demon car flew open, and a woman lurched out, her path to the Mercedes only approximating a straight line. Her blond hair was a wild mess and her blouse was askew, more out of her jeans than in, unbuttoned halfway down, and crumpled throughout. It was the most startling thing Harry had ever seen.

Ellen pounded on the windshield until the driver rolled down his window. The guns were now hidden away, but Harry was sure they'd reappear if needed.

"Jesus, didn't you hear me?" Ellen blurted out the words. "I mean, thanks for stopping, but—God—I thought I was going to have to run you off the road or something. Look, how I can get back to the Silicon Square Hotel? I've got to be there at 11 PM sharp, which is like five minutes from now, and if I'm not there for my husband's call, he's gonna absolutely kill me. He already thinks I'm—"

"Lady," Trong said, "why are you driving a government car?"

Harry didn't need to look; of course it was.

"What?" Ellen said. "Is that a—" She turned to look at it, then turned back to Trong, her eyes wide. "Oh, my God. He didn't tell me he was with the government. I thought he was an insurance agent or something. I figured I could borrow the car to dash to the hotel, then go back and see him later. I mean, he was passed out anyway, and—Jesus, do you think they'll come after me? Fuck!"

She started pacing back and forth by the driver's door, wringing her hands. "Oh, God. Oh, God. You guys gotta help me."

Trong leaned over and pointed his gun at her. Ellen froze.

"Lady, get in your car. Now!"

Ellen let out a wail and skittered back to her car. She started to get in, but stopped and came back to the Mercedes, moaning the whole way.

"Which way?" she pleaded.

The driver's arm shot forward.

Ellen dashed back to her car, dove in, and spun the tires driving off.

Trong looked back at Harry. "You've got strange women in the States."

If the man only knew.

Ellen drove two hundred yards past the entrance to the research building of Century Systems, turned off the headlights, and spun the car around. She pulled off the roadway to wait.

God, what a rush! Her heart was still racing. If that's what undercover work was all about, she had found her calling.

She flipped on her radio. "Sonia, did you get all that?"

"Loud and clear. Can't wait to hear Harry's version."

"So where are the troops? The Mercedes will be at the gate any—Shit! I can see them now."

"The cop is two miles away. SWAT team is right behind."

"Tell 'em to run with lights off. I don't want any sign until they're right on top of us. I'm going back." She stomped on the accelerator and roared off.

The Mercedes had just turned into the parking lot and was moving toward the security gate. This was trouble if Harry couldn't get them inside, and Ellen's expectations were low on that.

She cranked her car into the entrance, then flipped on her lights and lined up on the Mercedes. With a stab on the brakes, she threw her car into a sliding turn, and pinned the thugs' car against the gate. The four Vietnamese poured out of the Mercedes, guns drawn.

Ellen leapt out of her car. "Oh, shit! Did I scratch it?" She hurtled over the hood, heading for Trong. "Look, I'm desperate. My husband will never believe me. If one of you came back with me—just for five minutes—you could convince him we've been working on an important new deal. Please help me!"

Trong began walking toward her.

"I'll give you a hundred dollars. For five minutes of your time?"

Trong was getting closer, forcing Ellen back.

"Two hundred? And a blow job! How can you turn that down? $200 and a blow job from a beautiful blond, all for five minutes of—"

Trong shoved his gun under his belt, grabbed Ellen's arms and began pushing her backwards. "Lady, get in your car!"

Ellen grabbed the gun out of Trong's pants and jerked it upwards, catching him squarely in the jaw and jamming his head back. Then she brought her fist down hard on his nose and sent him sprawling to the ground. Before he could recover, she had him pinned, with the gun pointed at his head.

"If any of you creeps move," she shouted, "this guy doesn't have a face. Tell 'em who we are, Harry."

There was no time. The driver was inching backwards; Frick, to Harry's right, was raising his gun. No one was watching Harry.

"Heads up!" he shouted, and grabbed Frick's jacket.

That caught Frick by surprise and Harry slammed him against the open car door. Harry knew, more than saw, that the driver was turning his way, so he hoisted Frick in front of him as a shield.

The car door slammed back into him, and Harry and Frick crashed to the ground. Harry's head hit the pavement and it took him a long second to snap his mind back into the moment.

Then a gun went off, followed by two more shots.

Please, God!

Harry yanked Frick back, landed a shattering blow to his face, and then twisted the gun out of Frick's hand.

He rolled to his knees, expecting to see a gun in his face. But the driver was moving around the front of the car, responding to the shots. Harry thrust his hands forward and ripped off four quick shots. The driver spun to the ground.

The air was suddenly still. Harry waited in a crouch, but sensed no movement. Finally, he heard Ellen's voice. "You can come out now, Harry. I think we won."

Harry got to his feet, grabbed Frick's arms, and dragged the limp body around the car. He dropped Frick next to the driver, then turned to Ellen.

She was slumped against the wheel of the Mercedes, looking more than a little dazed. In front of her was Trong, who didn't appear dead; ten feet away was Frack, who clearly was. There was blood all over the scene.

"God, I'm glad you're alive," she said.

"Likewise."

Suddenly, there were lights everywhere, as the SWAT team and one San Jose cruiser descended on the parking lot. Harry and Ellen left the clean-up to others and walked away, collapsing against a fence.

"That was quite a performance," Harry said. "Outrageous, but it worked."

Ellen grinned. "Thanks, teacher."

Harry's face darkened. "It's not something to repeat. I'm grateful for what you did, but you've got to watch that Superwoman streak. You can't stop bullets."

The smile faded from Ellen's lips. "I had to, Harry. I couldn't abandon you." She shook her head. "You never imagine something like this."

"What?"

"Morton pulled the force."

"What?! Why?"

She told him the story of the hijacked semi, of Morton's decision or orders or whatever the hell it was, and of her certainty that Harry's life was in danger. Harry's mood ripped from fury to relief and back again.

Finally, he patted Ellen on the arm and gave her as much of a smile as he could. "Thanks. I owe you."

"We're partners. You'd do the same."

Harry burst out laughing. "Not like that!"

Ellen grinned. "Pretty good, huh? We should do more of this."

"Get shot at? Slammed around? Nearly killed?"

"You know what I mean." Her eyes were gleaming.

He hated that look.

The Good Stuff

Above the usual din in the Sunny Seniors solarium, Barnett heard a commotion, bouncing off the polished linoleum floor to the tin ceiling high overhead. He looked up from his computer screen. Nothing different at first glance: the blue hairs doing marching drills with their walkers; arguments posing as card games; people shouting to visions in the air. Then, in the corner, he noticed a gaggle of ladies circling some unsuspecting grandson. Piranhas in support hose.

He stretched his long frame and smiled. The contrast was so bizarre, it was laughable. Here he was, surrounded by the nearly-departed, and he was launching big plans. Big, bold, blow-their-fucking-mind plans amid the gum suckers and incontinence bags. It had a certain symmetry to it.

He turned back to the screen. So much for the community service gig from Hell. Sure, the past four weeks had been annoying, trying to teach these biddies about the Internet. It took extreme control not to smack this one geezer in the head when he drooled on the keyboard. But it was tolerable, since Barnett was back in front of a computer again. Two years and six months at Grasslands Correctional Facility had felt like a lifetime, though if the Authorities had their way, a lifetime would pass before he could ever touch a computer again.

Thus it was quite a coup that the judge sent him to this land of rotting flesh, to "use that wealth of knowledge for more positive ends." Yeah, sure. And contrary to the judge's orders, most of his time at the Sunny Seniors Center in Oakland, California was unsupervised, which opened the floodgates to what had been brewing in his mind for over two years. It couldn't have been more perfect, unless they nuked his parole officer.

Barnett looked at the progression on his screen and grinned. This equaled anything he had done in his twenty-six years on the planet. Maybe not as dramatic as commandeering a global telephone network, which landed him in Grasslands Correctional Facility two and a half years ago. Nor as involved as the electronic funds transfer gambit, his first brush with the world of law enforcement. But in the grand scheme of things, this was more significant. Much more.

On the surface, it looked simple: the story of a man. Iowa farm boy; Medal of Honor and Purple Heart in Vietnam; bankrupted rancher; largest landowner in Placer County, California. That was the public face of George Pilkin, which anyone could find if they searched a bit. Quite a contrast to: disaffected youth from Grosse Pointe, Michigan; teenage runaway; college dropout; minor dope fiend; Hacker from Hell, if one believed press releases barfed out by the Authorities. Not a match made in Heaven, but if things went right, they would form a partnership to rock the world. The key was his discoveries about the private life of George Pilkin.

Finding the aliases that Pilkin went by had been child's play, even after all that time away from a computer. Checking out Pilkin's bank accounts had been more of a challenge, both from Barnett's rustiness and advances in computer security in the past several years. Credit cards, financial history, real estate, medical records; a snap for any hacker worthy of the name, and a snooze for someone of Barnett's skill. What was truly significant was the progression of reports now laid out on his screen:

1) Large payments out of Pilkin's alias accounts, through a trail of foreign banks, to companies in China. Digging further, Barnett found those companies to be state-sanctioned arms dealers.

2) Shipping manifests and U.S. warehouse records for those

firms, coinciding with payments from Pilkin's secret accounts.

3) Delivery invoices from those warehouses to an address in the Lake Tahoe area, not far from a town called Sutter Springs. Later, shipments from that address to sites around the country, followed by substantial deposits into those secret accounts.

Conclusion: George Pilkin was a weapons dealer.

The Authorities probably didn't know about it, unless they abused the same laws Barnett had to string the information together. And to most people, this news held little value. But in Barnett's hands, it was leverage, unbelievable leverage. The kind of thing he needed to turn a dream into a reality.

There was a tugging at Barnett's sleeve. Actually, it had been going on for more than a minute, but now it was becoming insistent. "Come on, come on!" said the balding man sitting next to him. "Let's go back to the good stuff!"

Barnett chuckled. "Relax Benny, you bag of bones." He closed down the Pilkin progression and brought up the encryption file he had been working on.

"Come on, let's see those pictures again, Jeff," said Benny. "You wouldn't want me to tell the Wicked Witch of the West would you?"

"Ben, leave my parole officer out of this. Remember our deal: keep your mouth shut and I'll show you the good stuff. If you say anything, they'll take me away and throw you in a dark room and feed you rats for dinner. Does that sound like fun?"

The old man made a sour face.

"Besides," Barnett said, "if you say anything, Officer Gnat will find out about the gambling and they'll tell your son. Do you want that?"

Benny's head jerked side-to-side.

"Then sit quietly for ten minutes while I finish this bit of code. Okay?"

Trying to create a bullet-proof encryption program or rummage through some bank's database with a wheezing geezer at your side was not Barnett's ideal scenario, but the alternative was something like flipping burgers. That's what the Authorities wanted, to waste a brilliant mind in a grease pit. Contrary to opinion, he was no danger to society, but tell that to Them. They seemed, without exception, to relish his plight.

After the telephone affair, when they finally tracked him down and by some fluke captured him, they battered him relentlessly, as if that would purge their lingering humiliation. Then they vilified him in the press, making him out to be some deadly digital pirate. And they cheered at his sentencing, taunting him about being washed-up and worthless.

By virtue of that alone—criminal harassment, assault and battery, conspiracy to deprive him of a future—they were marked for revenge. Their critical mistake, however, was consigning him to Grasslands Correctional Facility. What happened there changed the whole color scheme.

On the best of days, Grasslands was a vile place. Sterile, cruel, and populated with the worst vermin imaginable. Not the place for Jeff Barnett, nor the crowd for him either. If he'd had any lingering sympathy for humanity before he went in, it was reamed out of him there. Survival should never have been an issue in his life, but for two and a half years it was. Then they stuck him with a satanic parole officer, who seemed determined to send him back.

It demanded retribution, savage retribution like he had suffered. If he let himself think about it, if he wallowed in his fury, it ate him up for days at a time. So he learned how to channel it, to use that ulcerous energy to advance his plans. And if he could keep the Medusa-haired she-dog parole officer at bay, he just might make it work. George Pilkin and company would see to that.

But Natalie Weston, aka "the Gnat" and "the Wicked Witch of the Weston," was a problem. She could have him put away forever if she found out what he was up to, and she was very good with computers. The Gnat hadn't discovered anything yet, but her visits every other day made Barnett nervous.

There was a new commotion near the entrance to the solarium, as clucking residents heralded the arrival of a visitor. Barnett popped his head up, saw the source of the disturbance, and smiled. A young man was picking his way through a swarm of chattering geriatrics. He was powerfully-built, but with a goofy expression and a posture so apologetic it fit in perfectly with the old folks.

"Kevin! Over here!" Barnett called out. "And don't knock over any old ladies." He chuckled and elbowed Benny in the ribs.

The young man worked his way to the corner where Barnett and the old man were sitting, giving a wide berth to the residents with their walkers.

"Man, I can't believe you're here," Kevin said. "I mean, with all these old folks and stuff." He held up a hand to Benny. "No offense, old guy. Hey, Barnett! Look at you, man! You're out!"

"You are so fast, Kev. Why you've stayed a guard all these years."

"Hey, well . . ."

"So how is Grasslands these days?"

Kevin grabbed a nearby chair, spun it around, and plunked down on it, hanging over the back of the seat. "Oh, not the same without you around. You know, just boring stuff again. I haven't found any new recruits yet, not at Grasslands. But, hey, all this computer stuff you got us going on—Wow! We're getting e-mails and stuff from militia groups all over the country! People are really starting to notice the Sierra Sentries now. The Commander thinks —"

"Am I ever going to meet this guy? That's all you've babbled about the last two years: this mysterious 'Commander'."

"Well, that's why I'm here, JB. I told him all about you and he's real interested to meet you. I told him how you got set up by the government, and how you're a genius with computers and stuff. But you gotta come up to see him. He's just way too important to —"

"Did he say that?"

"Well, God, no! I mean, he just is. You'll see when you meet him. The Commander is, like, awesome. But he never comes down from the compound unless it's really important."

"So . . ."

"So, there's this meeting that he'll be in town for next week. I mean in Sutter Springs, not here. It's next Wednesday. He said he could meet with you then. Can you get away?"

Barnett shrugged. "Depends on what my parole officer is up to. The bitch is keeping me on a pretty short leash, and if she showed up at my place unexpectedly." He suddenly smiled at the muscle man next to him. "Of course, if her tires happened to get slashed or such."

"Food poisoning is good!"

"Down, boy. Is that what you guys practice up there?"

There was another flurry of activity near the entrance. Out of habit, Barnett looked up. His heart froze.

Wait—she was just here!

He turned to Benny. "Take Junior here over to Mabel and her friends. Act like you're introducing your long, lost grandson. And Kevin, whatever you do, don't look this way. We'll both be fucked if you do."

Barnett pushed them away and hunched back over the keyboard. He had about six seconds before his parole officer would break free from the gaggle of geriatrics, then maybe another ten seconds before she made it to the computer. His fingers battered the keys: close the secret encryption file; exit the editor; activate the conversion program; reload the—

Natalie Weston barreled up, looking as harried and harassed as ever. Her formless parka and drooping curls accentuated her shortness, but the determination on her face obliterated any hint of weakness. She whipped around to look at the computer screen.

It showed a deck of cards in the midst of a game of solitaire. She threw her papers on the table in disgust.

"Officer Gnat!" Barnett said. "What a surprise. Two visits in one day. Care for a game of Power Solitaire?"

"You're jerking me around. I know it."

Barnett sighed heavily. "You're right. I might as well confess. There's a hidden directory on this called 'ATF.' Check it out and you'll find my notes on how to steal that truck." His voice dropped to a whisper. "Know where I stashed it? In cyberspace!"

"You're a real piece of work."

"Hey, if you don't want to be a hero and solve that case, but I guess with your heavy workload, even slugs need a break, huh?"

"Barnett, it would give me such pleasure to send you back to Grasslands. Really. And I'm sure the evidence is here on this PC, so get out of the damn chair."

"Didn't we do this already today? Seems like harassment."

"You're a convicted felon. Twice. You don't get such rights. Now, move. I don't have time for this."

Barnett rose slowly, arching backwards to stretch out his spine. Too many years spent hunched over a keyboard had taken their toll. Unless he was standing, one would never know he was six foot-two. Maybe if he had some muscle mass around his spine, or at least some flesh. But weight, like friends, never seemed to stick. Fuck it.

He folded his arms and rocked back and forth on his heels, trying to hum as inanely and annoyingly as possible. No sense easing the Gnat's comfort quotient, as she probed the computer's depths.

There were different ways she might find the evidence: scrutinize file stats and directories; search the hard drive for suspicious words; check for hidden files; review dial-up logs for frequency, timing, and duration of Internet sessions. Barnett had taken precautions for every type of invasion he could imagine her running, and so far his work had gone undetected.

But the Gnat was good. It was obvious in the way she ripped through files, and the new search routines she kept coming up with. How had he ended up with the one computer-genius parole officer?

Barnett might have enjoyed the challenge if the downside risk wasn't prison.

He glanced at the clock in the corner of the screen and smiled. A minor change in display—from "P.M." to "PM"—told him that his conversion program had finished its task. Now his encryption file looked like indecipherable hieroglyphics, something he could explain as an errant download from the CyberSeniors Web site. Normally, this conversion was run before the Gnat's visit every other day, but she had caught him off-guard. Fortunately, she was a creature of habit and hadn't yet started her—

Suddenly, Barnett's heart went into overdrive. His eyes snapped back to the clock, then jumped to the big clock on the wall of the solarium. The computer clock was off, way off. Almost two hours different!

He had forgotten to reset the clock. The date would be wrong, too.

In addition to the hieroglyphics, he had changed the icon on his file to make it look like one of dozens of gardening files the ladies had downloaded from the Net. To help disguise his work, he made sure that the date and time on the file were anything but that day or time, in case the Gnat went looking for something "recent." Call it habit or stupidity, but he kept changing the date and time on the PC's clock manually, rather than just editing the file's stats.

If she noticed it, the Gnat would cart the computer away and tear apart every file until she found the prize. Barnett couldn't take that chance.

"Hey, Benny!" he shouted across the room. "Leave Junior there and come say hello to Officer Weston."

He leaned down to his parole officer. "He's showing his grandson around, but I know he'd be upset if I didn't tell him you were here. I think he's got the hots for you. Do you like older men? I hear they give great gum."

Natalie Weston shuddered visibly, but kept her focus on the screen. A moment later, Benny arrived—alone, Barnett was relieved to see—and gave a bobbing wave of his hand. "Hello again, Officer Weston."

Her eyes rolled up to study the old man. "You guys sure spend a lot of time together at this computer. Been doing anything besides playing solitaire?"

His response, should she ever ask questions, was supposed to be a loose shaking of his head. Barnett thought Benny was clear on that point. But the old man cleared his throat and took an unusually large breath, and Barnett felt a wave of panic roll over him.

"No, miss," Benny said. "He's been showing me something new. Something scandalous." A lecherous chuckle tumbled out of Benny's mouth.

The woman wheeled around, pushing strands of hair off her face as she glared at Barnett. "Have you been downloading porn for this man? That's strictly forbidden under the terms of your parole and you know it! Christ, Barnett, can't you—"

"Wait a minute!" Barnett said. "I haven't done anything to violate my parole. What our delusional friend here is talking about, who the hell knows? You want to elaborate, Ben?"

That same strange chuckle rumbled out of the old man and his hand snaked through the air, settling finally on the mouse. After a jerky series of point–and–click maneuvers, he threw his hands in the air and sang, "Ta-da!"

There was dead silence for a second, and then Barnett burst out laughing. The parole officer looked completely confused. On the screen was a picture of the head nurse, with horns scribbled on her white cap, a broom sketched in at the bottom, and two blood-red words dripping across the top.

"Nurse Ratched," Weston said, reading the words. "What's this?"

"Shhh!" Barnett whispered. "We were just playing around. I wanted to show Ben how he could liven up some family photos. Got to keep the geezer here occupied, and this scanner was collecting dust." With a shake of his head, he added, "You're a real character, Ben."

Natalie Weston got to her feet, but her eyes lingered on the screen. "Something's bogus here, Barnett, and I'll find it. Trust me on that." She snatched her papers off the table. "Remember, California is a 'three strikes' state, and you've got two already." She wheeled around and stalked off.

"What does that mean?" Benny asked. "Are you and Officer Weston playing baseball? I thought you hated her."

Barnett patted Benny on the shoulder, his eyes following the departing parole officer. "No, Ben, it means if I do something—if I get *caught* doing something they don't like, they'll send me away forever. Nice thought, huh?"

"Are we doing something bad?"

The visions that flooded Barnett's head . . . All he could do was laugh. "Depends on who you ask. We're having fun, aren't we?"

Benny's head bobbed vigorously. "Can we look at those pictures again? The good ones?"

"Oh, man, you gotta go easy on that. If you get too wound up, you'll do something we'll both regret."

One of the aides appeared. "I've got a box for you, Ben, but I didn't want to interrupt you while that woman was here." She handed him the parcel and walked away.

Barnett glanced at the label and said, "I think that's for me, sport." He took the package, about the size of a hardcover novel, and set it on top of the computer. Then he grabbed the mouse and cycled through the directories until he found the downloaded images Benny had been drooling over that morning, disguised for the Gnat's sake to look like files on canasta. He offered the chair to Benny and said, "Just don't get overheated, okay?"

He picked up the box with Benny's name on it and tore open the tape with his car keys. Inside was a small computer board, two inches square, crammed with chips and circuitry. Barnett slid it carefully out of the protective wrap and examined it, his pulse quickening. It was a modem, but not just any modem. This piece of brilliance could tap into the Internet from anywhere in the world. It didn't need a phone plug, didn't need cell sites. It used radio frequencies to transmit data back and forth. Barnett could be in Maui and still stroll through the Bank of England's electronic vaults. The modem in the Sunny Seniors' PC was a Brontosaurus in comparison. He didn't usually get so jazzed about technology, but this was something special. Now all he needed was a laptop computer to put it in.

Benny was percolating on the chair now, and Barnett couldn't help but smile. The old man was a real find, a goddamned gold mine when you got right down to it. For starters, Benny would sit for hours like a happy lump of cells, looking like he was involved in what was happening on the screen, while Barnett worked on his plan. Better yet, the geezer went along with each thing Barnett proposed, like ordering this special modem. There was no way Barnett could have the product sent to him; the Gnat had to be watching his mail. But Benny? No one monitored him.

Not even his family, it seemed, which made the other part of their partnership so easy. Barnett had learned that Benny loved gambling, though "obsessed" was more like it. Without much effort, thanks to the scanner, a copy of Benny's son's signature, and a few well-placed letters, they adjusted Benny's financial portfolio and freed up large sums of cash. Then Benny could play with the Internet bookies, while Barnett had a source of funds to tap that was totally hidden from view. He had his own pile stashed away, but he couldn't get to it yet without drawing suspicion. The Porsche had to wait.

A conga line of old ladies heading for the far corner of the room suddenly caught Barnett's eye. That was where he had last seen Kevin.

"Oh, shit, Benny! I forgot all about Kevin. Go get him, will you? It's getting ugly over there."

A minute later, Kevin reappeared and dropped into the chair

next to Barnett. "Whew, those ladies sure are gabby, and grabby, too! Heh, heh."

"So, listen, Kevin, about this meeting."

"Yeah, it's next week. Can you—oh, yeah, you said something about your parole officer. You want us to do something there?"

"No, first let me see if I can scam the evening off. How long will it take to get there?"

"Three hours or so, unless I'm driving. Then it's: Yee–haw!"

"You're a wild man, Kev. Which reminds me . . ." Barnett's voice dropped to a whisper. "Did you guys steal that ATF truck?"

Kevin's eyes got really big. "Can you imagine? Whoo-whee!"

"By the way, does the Commander really go by that name?"

"Yeah, everybody just calls him 'the Commander,' out of respect. Maybe three people in the world have called him George or Mr. Pilkin, and two of them are dead."

Kevin hopped up from his seat. "I'll call you Monday about details and stuff. And thanks again for getting us onto those Patriot bulletin boards. It's awesome what's out there. We are really gonna rock those bastards!"

Barnett gave him a Nazi-style salute. "To the New World Order!"

"JB!"

"Oh yeah, sorry. It's the bad guys who are the New World Order. I always get that mixed up." He nearly choked trying not to laugh.

Kevin gave him a more modest salute and marched out of the room.

Barnett was left shaking his head. It really didn't pay to get close to humans. And if he thought Kevin and Benny were loose cannons, imagine a guy who called himself "the Commander."

A Catalyst

On another day, he might have appreciated the glorious San Francisco morning. But Harry was oblivious to it as he stormed toward the office. He was trying to talk himself out of committing suicide, professionally at least.

This was going to be Harry and Ellen's first meeting with their new boss, James Morton, the Special Agent in Charge of the San Francisco field office. Morton had recently been installed as the SAC and was in the process of meeting all the agents. Harry and Ellen's appointment had been set for a week.

Okay, so first impressions mean a lot, and SACs are pretty high on the Bureau's food chain. But what do you say to a guy who left you for dead four nights ago? "Hey, thanks a lot"? More like: "Nice to meet you, boss" and then—pow!—a sharp one to the nose.

Harry stomped off the elevator and headed for his desk. His whole weekend had been one long festering sore of anger and frustration, and it was going to take a major effort to keep his emotions in check. It would feel so good just to: POW!

It wasn't a bright idea, considering this was a Special Agent in Charge. Three years ago, one SAC sent him off on trumped-up charges to Butte, Montana, which was Purgatory for FBI agents. A fall guy was needed when Harry's mentor was caught flaunting certain rules of propriety, and Harry was the designated chump. He cried "Foul!" but to no avail; internal politics ruled the Bureau as much as any other business, and Harry was a lousy politician.

He considered quitting, but that might have doomed him to life as a security guard, so he accepted his fate, hoping a change of scenery would clear his head.

Then a year ago, he was transferred to San Francisco, and the reigning SAC, Brendan Crowley, tore into Harry immediately. Not for any infraction, but as revenge for something years before. During a brief partnership in New York City, Harry discovered Crowley was taking bribes from mobsters they were investigating; Harry reported it. Crowley got a slap on the wrist and a transfer to L.A., meager punishment for such an offense and testament to Crowley's political connections within the Bureau. He was soon rising again, and vowing to get even.

Fortunately for Harry, their time together in San Francisco was brief. Crowley had been warned about his abusive management style, and his vicious attacks on Harry were the catalyst for Crowley's demotion to some nameless position in the bowels of the FBI's Hoover Building in D.C.

Still, that was a SAC Harry had tangled with, so an altercation with a third one, Morton, just might tag Harry with a label of being "difficult," no matter how justified he was.

He got to his desk, dropped his briefcase on the floor, and took three long breaths. He tried telling himself it wasn't that bad, but it was.

Beyond the fact he could have been killed, Harry was surprised at Morton's actions. The man was supposed to have a great reputation: a street agent at heart, not a rules-mongering bureaucrat; a guy with some balance, who didn't blindly wave the Bureau flag. The contrast with the last SAC, power-mad Brendan Crowley, was said to be stark. So how could Morton have done that?

A paper bag suddenly appeared in front of Harry's cubicle, swinging back-and-forth like a pendulum. Behind it was Ellen's face, in a wicked grin.

"You are in my power," she said. "You will take this bag of donuts and—"

"Don't mess with me right now." Harry grabbed at the bag.

Ellen pulled the bag away and continued swinging it. "You are in my power. And if you don't lighten up, I'm throwing this crap in the trash." She sat down in the extra chair and tossed the bag on the desk. "It's a bribe, okay? My donuts for your silence."

"Silence? You don't like those anyway, unless they have sprouts or something."

"I know you, Harry, and I'd like to keep working with you. So shove your face in that bag, stuff in as many of those donuts as you can, and try to keep your mouth shut for the next hour." She softened her voice. "We were lucky to survive, but you've got to let it pass." She brightened up again. "Hey, look at me, lecturing you."

Harry snarled at her. "Nice."

"Look, I had a lousy weekend, too. No matter how I tried, I couldn't get away from the image of that guy turning on me with his gun. But we need to just get on with it, bury ourselves in something useful."

The phone suddenly buzzed. Harry hit the intercom button and a tinny voice said, "He'll see you now." Ellen mimed zipping her lips and they got up.

It was strange to be back in the SAC's office. Not just because of the change in the furnishings, from Crowley's ostentatious decor to Morton's austere surroundings. It was the stench of Crowley's cologne, probably scrubbed out of the room, but still rancid in Harry's nose as he flashed back on so many altercations with the man, both recent and long past. Some wounds would never heal, and Harry quickly pushed the memories from his mind. Brendan Crowley was the last person on earth he wanted to think about, now or ever.

James Morton rose from his desk and walked toward them. "King. Harper. It's an honor to finally meet you." His sweeping gesture motioned them toward two straight-backed and decidedly un-plush chairs. Morton himself sat on the corner of his desk.

He began to speak, slowly and carefully. "I've spent all weekend trying to figure out what to say. Apologies aren't enough. Gratitude doesn't capture it, except maybe gratitude that you're both alive." He paused, shaking his head. "That was an extraordinary piece of work, and I am deeply sorry I had to put you in that position."

The honesty of that moment softened Harry's anger.

"What happened?" he asked.

Morton took a long breath. "The Bureau of Alcohol, Tobacco, and Firearms got burned, badly. If it was just a matter of ATF being humiliated in the press, as we're seeing, we would not have joined in the way we did. It was unconscionable to leave you alone like that. But Washington demanded we put every resource possible into that search, immediately and without question."

Ellen snapped. "For what? A truck full of guns and ammo and some illegal weapons? That's outrageous! Even if they could outfit a small army, it's barely a dent in the number of weapons stashed around this country."

"It's not that," Morton said.

"What, were ATF's parade uniforms on board?"

Morton leaned forward. "What was on that truck *could* outfit a small army: 500 automatic weapons; rocket launchers; anti-personnel devices; laser-guided surface-to-air missiles—"

"What's ATF doing with all that?" Harry said.

"Hell if I know. You think they confide in me?"

"Excuse me." Ellen clipped the words. "How does that justify abandoning us? Those weapons couldn't go far."

Morton shook his head. "If that truck fell into the wrong hands."

The man was hiding something, Harry could feel it. Fucking SACs and their power trips. His eyes burned into Morton's, looking for a clue. "What was really on that truck?"

Morton just stared at him.

Finally, Ellen said, "What about these 'wrong hands'?"

"Domestic terrorists," Morton said. "There's been a huge

increase in the number of extremist acts over the past few years. Bombings, church burnings, thefts from military stock piles, bank robberies to finance who knows what, and there's a lot of concern within the Bureau about it escalating."

He shifted uneasily. "Let me rephrase that. We're not as concerned about it escalating as we are about it coalescing. Most of what we've seen has been the work of individuals or small groups. Hell, look at the tragedy that only two guys caused in Oklahoma City. The potential for that lurks all across the country; we've got active investigations going in more than half the states. Most of the time we're scurrying to stop them before they jump: that group in West Virginia plotting to blow up the Bureau's info services facility; those militia guys in Arizona drawing up plans to wipe out the government buildings in Phoenix; all those guys in Idaho and Oregon and Washington with huge weapons caches and a rabid hatred of the government. Can you imagine what would happen if they ever got organized?

"And you think this theft could be a catalyst?" Harry said.

"It's possible," Morton said. "With the items on that truck, they could make the Oklahoma City bombing look like—"

"So what's the deal?" Ellen said. "It's been three days. Nobody's found anything?"

"Barely a clue. It was obviously a professional job; estimates are that twelve to fifteen people were in on the hijacking. But it happened so fast and was handled so cleanly that everyone is left spinning. It's a huge embarrassment for the ATF, but that's obviously not the biggest concern."

"What about the truck?" Harry said.

"Into thin air."

Harry wanted to say: "Impossible!" But the less he said right now, the better. If he opened his mouth, who knew what might come out.

"As you can imagine," Morton said, "this has become our top priority. I need your help on this, but I'll try to cut you some slack, considering what you've just been through. I've got something that should be right up your alley."

Harry didn't like the sound of that.

Morton reached across his desk to grab a stack of papers several inches thick, then looked at Ellen. "Your personnel file says you're a computer wiz. What do you make of these?" He handed them to her.

She fanned through the stack. "These are transcripts or downloads from the Internet. That or . . ." She stared intently at one page. "Whoa!"

"What?" Harry said.

Ellen's eyes raced across the page. "Listen to this: *When the Jews and niggers and other mud people are destroyed, when the politicians have all been slaughtered and the government is put out of business once and for all, only then can we achieve the freedom, happiness, and purity which Yahweh and the Constitution guaranteed us. This will only come about through your individual effort--every day, in every breath you take. The New World Order will soon be out-of-order. ZOG's days are numbered!"*

"Let me see," Harry said. He pulled the stack out of Ellen's hands and flipped through the pages, pausing occasionally, then shaking his head and continuing on. Finally, he looked up.

"That's quite a cavalcade. White Aryan Resistance, Posse Comitatus, Bruder Schweigen, Identity Christians. There's probably more I didn't see. But why do we have this material already? Who gathered it?"

Morton chuckled. "I figured you'd know this stuff. You had to do something while you were stuck in Butte."

"How would you know that?" Harry said. "I told everyone I spent two years fishing on Bureau time, which I did for the most part."

"Yeah, but you were probably up by Noxon or over the border in Idaho, all those hot-beds of militia activity. I mean, look at your personnel file. You can't leave a situation alone or just sit back and take orders. It makes sense that if Harry Harper was in Montana, he'd be checking out the scene, no matter how pissed off he was about why he'd been sent there. It's not like you to just go fishing."

Harry shook his head. "Thanks for the compliment."

Ellen grabbed the stack of papers back from Harry.

"So what's the story with these?"

"Maybe nothing," Morton said. "Short of catching someone with a bomb in one hand and a lighted match in the other, a charge of treason or sedition would be difficult to make stick. But anti-government forces are building up all across the country and we can't afford to let our guard down."

He got to his feet. "Much of that stack is from BBSes—bulletin board systems, Harry—in Northern California. Every other region is going through this same exercise. You'll see how sophisticated these extremists have become as you get into it. Go online for a while, too, and monitor what's new. The wires are probably really heating up after that hijacking. These guys love a conspiracy."

"I've got a question," Harry said. "Somebody's obviously been following this stuff for a while. Why?"

Morton shrugged. "Got to stay on top of things. In the absence of any help from Congress, we've got to be creative. And preemptive. I know they're trying again to pass an anti-terrorism bill that means something, but—"

The phone rang suddenly. Morton leaned over the desk and picked up the receiver. He did very little talking.

One long minute later, he hung up the phone.

"The Director of the FBI has been shot." He paused. "It may have been from one of those stolen weapons."

The Grant Street Grill provided no break. The atmospheric lighting, brick walls, and exotic food were no better than the stale coffee and fluorescent hell they had just left behind. Nothing permeated the fog in Harry's head. Or Ellen's, if the way she pushed her food around was any indication.

"I feel sick about this," she said, "like one of my own family's been shot. Why would anyone target the Director? The man's a saint."

"Who knows? Someone taking shots at the Bureau? A guy with an ax to grind? I just hope he pulls through."

"What are the chances there's a connection with the hijacking?"

Harry shrugged. "Very likely, if the weapon really was from that shipment. But the Director is a pretty brazen target, unless they were trying to make a statement." He shook his head. "Which is typical."

"I'd like to jump on a plane and go find those bastards."

Harry nodded solemnly.

Ellen tossed her fork onto her plate. "Meanwhile, we've spent —no, wasted—over five hours on this crap and I see nothing whatsoever to pursue. I've checked out fifteen Internet discussion groups and seven local bulletin board systems and they're all the same. Vitriolic, but not criminal. Without a court order . . ." She rubbed her face. "Want to trade places for a while? You work on the PC and I'll go through that stack?"

"Be serious. You know I'm allergic to computers. But what about a court order?"

Ellen shrugged. "If they're doing something subversive, they're not doing it where we can see it."

"So?"

"So most of these bulletin boards have private areas where you need a special password to get in. Maybe they're doing their seditious rap behind closed doors—assuming some nefarious plot is actually going on."

Harry frowned. "I'm sure that Aryan BBS wouldn't willingly give us a password. And if we got a warrant and came pounding on their door, they'd probably just vaporize the evidence, wouldn't they?"

"You've got potential, Harper."

"Which leaves us with two options. We could go 'undercover' on those bulletin boards and try to bluff our way into their hearts, though I wouldn't want to venture that unless we really had probable cause. Or—and this would definitely require a warrant—couldn't we get in there through a back door?"

Ellen's eyes widened. "You want to hack our way into those bulletin boards? Maybe you're not so allergic after all."

"That wasn't exactly what I was thinking, but, yeah, could we do it?"

"Possibly. Depends on what their firewall looks like and whether they're using an encryption program or not. Actually, I'm sure they are; the only question is how long their public-key is and what computing resources we could tap—"

Harry faked a loud sneeze.

"Sorry, I got carried away. I'll try to do this in your language." She took a moment before proceeding. "Okay, there are two parts to it: the structure of the BBS—let's call that the factory—and the messages they send out. With me so far?"

Harry nodded.

"Alright, suppose we go to their factory. They'd probably let us into the reception area, and maybe give us a brief tour, but there would be a big steel door with a huge lock on it that we couldn't get through—unless we had a key. The door is a 'firewall' in computer parlance, and the key is a password. Now, there would probably be a series of doors, or firewalls, and the passwords would likely be different."

"How do we get past them?"

"Depending on their sophistication, we might need only my computer, or we might have to beg the NSA for the use of their supercomputers. It all depends. It's also likely, if they're really into this, that the firewalls rely on more than just passwords alone. Not that they can't be compromised, but—"

Harry started building up for another sneeze.

"Stop that," Ellen said. "Okay, let's just say it's not impossible to get into their secret chamber. Once we're there, however, it turns out they're all speaking a strange language, like Swahili or something. Unless you knew how to translate it, you'd be stuck. Well, that's what encryption does, it converts messages into codes using something called a 'public key.' It gets really complicated from there, but it gives you an idea how they could send things over the Net with some degree of security. These guys are probably not using anything easy, like a 40-bit public key, which an 'unauthorized' person could decode without much trouble. If the key is longer than 128 bits, it would take some serious NSA computing power to crack it. And if the key is like a thousand bits in length, we're screwed. A bank of supercomputers would be cranking away on that for years, while the revolution would have already ended."

Harry was focused on the stack of papers, flipping back and forth between pages.

"What is it?" Ellen said. "You've been through that countless times already."

Harry looked up, a smile slowly spreading across his face.

"Maybe we've got something," he said. "All that talk of secret rooms gave me a flash. I think I missed it before because I was fixated on the words, not the sequence. Look." He turned the stack around to show her.

"This guy suddenly appeared on that Northern California Patriots BBS about three months ago. Calls himself 'SS2.' We'll hold off commenting about his grammar, but you can see how prolific he was."

"And nasty, too." Ellen said.

Harry flipped through several pages in silence. Ellen's eyes scoured the sheets as they passed.

"Wait a minute," she said, "it looks like he's dropped from sight. About a month ago?"

Harry nodded. "I didn't think anything of it until now. And if it wasn't for this little bit—" He flipped to one of the last pages. "—we might assume he'd just fallen off the map."

Ellen read the message. "A town meeting in Sutter Springs. I think that's near Lake Tahoe. Wow, the day after tomorrow."

"Six-thirty in the evening. Want to take a little drive?"

Ellen looked up. "Really?"

"Oh, come on. The guy was Mister BBS for two months or so, and then he disappears without a word. Now he reappears in the public part of that BBS, calling everybody in the area to come show their support at a town meeting in Sutter Springs. You want to tell me he hadn't moved into some private room and learned Swahili?"

"Sacramento is between here and there. Shouldn't we toss it to them?"

"Why do you always want to pass on the good stuff?"

"But you said the other night you wanted to give up undercover work."

"Who said anything about—"

"Harper, be real. Do you think we can show up in suits, shades, and a standard issue vehicle? This place is remote. How obvious would we be?"

"True," Harry said. Then he smiled. "I'll take any excuse not to wear a suit. But get us a truck, not some yuppie four-wheel drive. And make sure it's dusty and a couple years old."

"We could take my Jeep. It's pretty well trashed."

Harry shook his head. "If anyone traced the plates, we could be screwed. And we probably need to leave our cell phones at home. If we get shaken down, we don't want them being able to explore our call histories. Requisition a bag of quarters, okay? They're bound to have pay phones up there."

"Okay, but one other question." Ellen gave him a sly smile. "We can't just walk in as ourselves, right? I mean, if anybody asks us, don't we need some kind of cover? It's a mountain community and people are probably suspicious of strangers."

"What are you getting at?"

"Well, we can't go as a couple. There's twenty years difference in our ages. I think we should go as father and daughter."

Harry groaned. "That's cruel. But you're probably right."

Ellen straightened up. "Thanks, Dad!"

"Don't mention it—please."

Stealth Bomber

Prison was still at the top of Barnett's list of culture shocks, but the scene at the Sutter Springs meeting hall wasn't far behind. If he was going to be fair, he'd have to admit that not all the women had green teeth, and some of the men probably had bathed more than once since Reagan's inauguration.

But why be fair? The log cabin atmosphere was thick with mildew and smoke and enough body odor to choke a rhino. There was more hair than at a barber's convention, exploding in every direction from the faces of the men, and poofed-up high on the heads of the women. Add in the clucking, posturing, and cheap perfume, and this was clearly a high point on the social calendar for Sutter Springs.

Then there was the militia element. Maybe everyone in the hall was armed, beneath all that flannel and gingham, but the contingents in fatigues weren't hiding their habit. The last time Barnett had seen that many guns was when he'd been surrounded by Feds.

And he had staked his future on this group? Maybe the drugs were stronger than he'd realized, 'cause logic didn't explain his presence there. True, he had uncovered some intriguing information about the mysterious "Commander." It was very possible this guy was exactly what Barnett was looking for. But the man couldn't do everything alone, and these heavily-armed hicks were certain to be his foot soldiers.

Sitting next to Barnett was the usually docile Kevin, who had turned into a deranged badger—scurrying to greet the latest flock of camouflage-clad mutants, bleating across the large hall to other factions, then trudging back to Barnett's corner to dispense more insights about the denizens of Sutter Springs and the various militia groups. The last thing Barnett wanted to do was call attention to himself, and here he was next to the local Big-Man-on-Campus.

Kevin had been parked next to him for several minutes now, as the room was nearly full. The commentary had been scintillating.

"Now that lady walking in, she's the baker. A real pain in the butt. Just look at her. Probably pees battery acid, you know? We'll hear something outta her tonight, I'm sure." Kevin chuckled viciously and lowered his voice. "You'd think she learn by now, what with all the little tricks we've played on her. You know, spiking her well, fucking with her car, shit like that. She's pretty sure we're behind it, but there's never been any clues. Besides, the police chief is a good friend of the Commander."

Up at the front of the hall, the town council members were sitting down at a long table, and one of them was tapping on a microphone. The crush of traffic into the hall continued slowly, but steadily, with people now starting to line the walls.

"Hey, look at those two!" Kevin shouted across the hall. "The Mossad is here. Which branch do you think, Walter? FBI? ATF? Secret Service? You're not printing funny money again, are you?" Laughter echoed off the walls.

Barnett turned to look at the door. Standing, quite conspicuously now, were two men who had to be clones. Chiseled faces, serious expressions, both wearing new plaid flannel shirts; the tags were probably still on them somewhere. They had that deer-in-the-headlights look, since most of the people in the room were staring at them. It was a beautiful moment.

Unless . . .

"Aren't you nervous about them being here?" Barnett said.

Kevin laughed. "Nah, somebody's always snooping about, but

they never find anything. A bunch of bozos, really. You can usually spot 'em, though most're not as obvious as those guys. What a hoot!"

The community business got underway, but the procession of people continued at the back of the room. Barnett was watching the door, when he suddenly perked up. He gave Kevin a shove with his elbow.

"Now that's my kind of woman. Can you introduce me?"

He pointed at a woman with blond hair, a black baseball cap, a work-shirt half-tucked into slim, faded jeans, and a pair of sleek sunglasses covering her eyes. She looked about thirty, pretty, and definitely wearing an attitude.

Kevin stared at her for several seconds. "Never seen her, or that older guy. Weird pair. Don't think they live in these parts."

"So why are they here? Your message about this meeting? The guy looks like he might be one of yours, but I doubt she is."

Kevin turned and gave him a big smile. "Want me to go ask?"

"No, just leave it. We'll track her down later. What I want to know is: Where's the Commander? I didn't come up here for my health."

"He'll be here when the time is right. He's like one of those stealth bombers, you know? He just kind of appears, takes care of business fast and clean, and then vanishes." Kevin snickered quietly. "He don't even need to do nothin' most times. He just walks in and . . ." Kevin's hands floated outward as though he was calming the seas.

The meeting progressed boringly enough: bake sale recaps; complaints about noisy kids; and more gibberish which Barnett ignored. Even when they got to the main business, something about permits to carry concealed weapons, it was all orderly and pleasant. Why some exalted "Commander" should show up was a mystery to Barnett.

Then the baker jumped up on her chair and began stomping on the metal seat.

"No! No! No!" her shrill voice cried. "This ain't right. We're livin' off of dirty money and it's gonna come back to haunt us. We've got to stop it right now, while we've got the chance. I don't give a good goddamn how much money we might get from these permits. The State Attorney General is doing us a favor by pulling the plug. This town ain't gonna fold. Let's send a message to the world: we don't need blood money to survive."

"Eloise, it ain't blood—"

"Yes it is, Chief! You've got a goddamned mill here. Drug dealers are coming from hundreds of miles away to get their permits in Sutter Springs. You've seen those cars, folks. And on the streets, everywhere you look, people are carrying guns, serious guns. I feel like I'm living in a war zone, and I'm scared to death that one day some loony is gonna come to Sutter Springs, get his dirty little permit, and take target practice on some kids walking down the road. You issued over 700 permits last year alone, Chief, and we've barely got that many people in this town." She spun around on her chair, eying the crowd. "I know a lot of you folks ain't from this town, so I'm sure you didn't come to hear about our bake sale. How many of you got your permits here, huh? Can we have a show of guns?"

The previously placid crowd erupted. Shouts, pleas, threats, and curses flew from every corner of the hall. Barnett followed the arguments for several minutes, until it got so loud and vehement it dissolved into a mass of noise. This group did not look promising at all. So, where would he go from—

The room suddenly became very still.

The doors at the back of the hall swung slowly open, as if by force of nature. Two young men in denim coats and cowboy hats walked through the opening and stood on either side. Then a man appeared: average height; wiry; with a narrow head and pinched features; age about fifty and dressed like the rest of the crowd.

But there was something distinctive about him, mesmerizing. Even his flattop haircut looked mean—or serious, yeah that was it.

A don't-fuck-with-me haircut. Maybe he never needed to get it trimmed, it was so severely precise; the hairs were probably too intimidated to grow past their appointed length. He had that look. Not in his eyes; those were cold, giving nothing away. But a force crackled around him that seemed to suck all the energy out of the room. A black hole in cowboy boots.

As the man strode into the hall, a path formed in front of him. His gait was neither quick nor abrupt, as might be expected from a man of his size; instead, it was smooth, like a tiger padding slowly along, in total control as it stalked its prey. The murmurs from the crowd were strictly divided, awe or fear, with nothing in between. The only exceptions were Barnett, who was fascinated beyond belief, and the baker.

She was still perched on her chair, glowering. The man looked over at her and said, "Eloise, what are you doing up there? Aerobics?" His voice was calm, but it was impossible to miss the mocking tone.

"George Pilkin," she said, "we don't need you or your thugs here. Contrary to belief, you do not own this town, and I, for one, am tired of being bullied. Get the hell out!"

Barnett wondered if the woman was a plant, because the man put on such a show of being wounded. The militia elements in the crowd ate it up.

"Eloise," the man said, "I'm a citizen of Sutter Springs, just like you. I get one vote, just like you. If I have some influence with others, is that my fault?" He turned and continued toward the front of the hall, his voice raised.

"As for the matter of a vote, is there really anything to vote on? I mean, we can take a symbolic vote if that'll make your heart feel warm. But if you look at what the options are, how can there be any debate? Chief Barring here—" He patted the police chief on the shoulder as he walked by. "—has done more to revive this town than anyone in the past sixty years. And I'm not just talking about money."

As he reached the table, the man with the microphone extended it to him, reverentially. "Here you go, Commander."

The Commander smiled at the man, who backed away, then turned to the crowd. With the microphone held loosely in his hand, he leaned over the table and began to speak, very softly.

"This isn't about money, folks. This is about values. About our community, our precious little town, our very way of life. Our favorite baker here is worried that destruction is gonna rain down on us. But I've gotta tell you, the only way destruction is not going to rain on this town is if we protect it. Protect the town, protect its citizens, protect our rights and freedoms across the board, as set down in the Constitution of these United States and in the commandments of God."

He began to walk with the microphone.

"The Attorney General of California is holding us hostage right now, refusing to process any more permits for a whole rash of cockamamie reasons: 'bad elements;' proliferation of weapons; excess fees; dereliction of responsibility. It's just a sham, folks. The guy's a foot soldier for the U.N. His sole purpose in life right now is to take away as many of your rights as possible, so the Zionist Occupational Government—or ZOG, as we call them—can march in here, masquerading as the U.S. government, and seize your home."

Murmurs rumbled across the hall.

The Commander chuckled crudely. "I can't say the guy is very smart. You'd think he'd try to be devious, to nickel-and-dime us into submission the way most of those Israeli-puppets in Washington are trained to do. Maybe he had too much LSD in his hippie days, 'cause he's going after something so basic: keeping God-fearing Americans from protecting themselves. Well, that ain't gonna happen, not here. And if they're not careful . . ."

The rumbling increased.

"Hold on. I don't want anybody gettin' hurt, at least not in this room. The time for action is coming soon enough, folks, and we shall prevail. It has been ordained by God, and no one—not the Zionists or their bankers or that joke of a yoke we call a government—no one will stop us!"

He paused to study the crowd, brushing his hand across the top of his hair while his words echoed around the hall. Then he smiled.

"For the moment, we're gonna play it their way, okay? That means each one of you has got to write this man. Don't call him a puppet, for God's sake, but flood his damned mailbox. Demand that he leave Sutter Springs alone and stop subverting the Second Amendment to the Constitution."

The sermon went on, as the Commander paced around the hall, building the mood to a fevered pitch. Barnett didn't buy most of the message, but the way the man worked the crowd was amazing.

"I hate to say it, folks, but we could be on the brink right now. Look at that anti-terrorism bill ZOG wants to pass. You think that's not going to launch a police state? And what about that ATF truck someone swiped? It wasn't any militia group, like all the media are making it out to be. Hell, it's a damn plot by the ATF or FBI or somebody, just to give 'em an excuse to confiscate our guns, bill or no bill. Did any of those ATF ninnies get hurt in that raid? No. Why? Because it was an inside job! ZOG is trying to make it look like some patriots did it, so they can have free reign to march in and take over."

He stopped in front of the two "Mossad" clones and picked a piece of lint off one of the new plaid flannel shirts. "You know, some people think it's sad that we gotta live like this. That we've got to have guns and look with suspicion on those we don't know." He turned back to the crowd.

"Well, I don't see it that way!" The Commander's voice suddenly boomed. "God didn't put us here to have someone lick our toes. And He also didn't intend for someone else tell us how to live our lives. Wasn't this country founded on equality?"

"Yes!" several people shouted.

"Do we want some government, some collection of people who've never been to our dinner table or sat in our church telling us what to do?"

"No!" More than half the people joined in.

"Do we want them telling us how to raise our kids or spend our money or work our land?"

"No!" The full crowd roared.

"Do we want them telling us what to think?"

"No!"

"Or what God to believe in?"

"No!!"

"Then don't let them tell you where and how you can carry your gun, a right given to us, not just by the Founding Fathers, but by God Almighty!"

"Yeah!!"

"And don't let them tell us we can't sell those permits here. If you respect yourself at all, if you respect your family and your God, you can't let that happen. Thank you very much."

The people leapt to their feet and cheered wildly. Things were so frenzied that if the Commander had told them to tear down the walls of the hall, it would've happened in a heartbeat. It gave Barnett a new appreciation for mob mentality.

He stood on his chair to try to see the Commander, but the man had already vanished, just as Kevin predicted. Barnett sat back down and smiled.

"Stealth bomber." Nice name for the man who would carry out Barnett's plans.

Mackey's was one of those serious bars; Harry had been in enough of them to know. It was dark to the point of eyestrain, lit mostly by an old juke box, a TV in the corner showing sports, and some neon in the window. The room was nearly empty, except for a few bodies melded to their stools, with faces longer than the bar. The cave-like interior was accented by silent roars from massive bear heads mounted on the wall. Nobody walked into a place like this by accident, at least not more than a few feet. The scowl of the bartender saw to that.

Harry said a quick prayer and walked to the bar. This kind of place had rules, a social order that was strictly enforced. Ellen's bit with the sunglasses had barely survived the town hall; in a place like this, it could be fatal.

Through the perpetual twilight, he scrutinized the bartender, a figure as massive as the bears on the wall. The guy could probably rip the skin off a man with his bare hands. Not a comforting thought, but Harry had faced worse.

"Whaddaya want?" the bartender said.

Harry slid onto one of the stools, taking his time. He put his elbows on the bar and folded his hands together. "Whaddaya think?"

"I think you're in the wrong place."

Harry looked to his left, then to the right. "This is a bar, isn't it. You haven't made it look like this for the ladies' social have you?"

He slapped the top of the stool next to him, an indication for Ellen to join him at the bar. She propped herself up the same way.

The bartender let out a snort and lumbered toward them.

"Who's your little friend?" he said.

Harry locked eyes with the man. "Can we have some respect in here?" He held the gaze until the big man looked away, then nodded at the tap and said, "Two."

The bartender began to draw the beers, but stared at Ellen as he was doing it, trying to peer through her sunglasses. He finally looked back at Harry and said, "So who is she?"

"His daughter, asshole," Ellen replied.

Oh, great . . . Harry counted the steps to the door.

The bartender straightened up. "You let her talk to people that way?"

Harry shrugged. "Got a table we can sit at, so I can teach her some manners?"

The big man jerked his head toward the end of the bar. Past the doorway were a few tables; beyond that, another room with a pool table. There was quite a crowd in the far room, including the man they were tailing.

Harry slid off the stool, grabbed a dish of pretzels, and started toward the tables. "Come on, girl," he said over his shoulder.

Ellen hopped down, gave the stool a shove with her foot, and followed Harry to a table near the doorway. It had sight lines to both the pool room and the bar, but provided enough shadows and seclusion that it seemed safe to talk.

"That was great!" Ellen said quietly. "You handled him perfectly."

"No thanks to you. Between his attitude and your shades, civility was out the window." Harry thought about it a moment, then said, "That may have been a lucky accident."

"What?"

"The way you acted. It might just work in our favor. Usually you want to blend in, particularly in a place like this. But do you see anyone else who looks like you?"

"Just that scrawny guy in there." Ellen nodded toward the pool room. "He's way out of place, but you'd never know it by the way he's standing, holding that beer. Look at that arrogance." Her lips curled. "Something about him is familiar, but I'm not sure what. So, why was that a lucky accident?"

Harry lowered his voice.

"Because we should spend some more time here. I'd like to get to know that head guy a little better, and the only chance I've got is to be as tough as he is. You were right about this daughter bit; being my 'companion' would've been as suspicious as those two robots at the hall. And a guy like that probably has a daughter who's as headstrong and obnoxious as you."

"Thanks for the compliment."

Harry raised his glass. "A+ in Instinct, Ellen."

She started to lean across the table, but Harry waved her back with a finger. "Don't look so chummy or I'll lower your grade."

"So what about those robots? I'm surprised they're not here."

"Maybe the bear up front ate them. I'd love to know who they're with, but there's no way I was going near them. We'll have to find out when we get back. For all we know they could be sitting outside." He started chuckling. "Maybe they'll follow *us*. You're a beacon with that 'WIRED' cap."

"Hey, I'm trolling for computer geeks. Isn't that why we came?"

"With a hat?"

"It's a magazine for the computer world. I figured whoever was posting those messages probably reads *Wired*. Actually, this might be too blatant or lame, but it's worth a shot." She laughed softly. "I ran over it with the truck a couple times today, to make sure it looked well worn."

Harry got to his feet. "Drink up. Just nursing one is way too obvious in a place like this." He disappeared through the door to the bar.

When he returned, Ellen was staring at the ceiling, twirling a pretzel around her finger. "How much longer are we staying?"

Harry glanced toward the pool room, then back at his beer. "Not much is happening, so we'll clear out after this round."

"What are these guys anyway? You rattled off a bunch of names."

"Hmm. Hard to say; there's a lot of overlap. Could be Identity Christians, for all the anti-Semitism and racist rhetoric. In their Bible, violence is virtuous, and we certainly heard bits of that. They're not Aryans or we'd know it by their uniforms. They might be remnants of the old Posse Comitatus, for all that spouting about the Second Amendment and the right to bear arms, but the way that Pilkin guy kept going on about ZOG and—"

"What is that?" Ellen said.

Harry rolled his eyes. "Conspiracy theories. ZOG is an acronym for 'Zionist Occupational Government' and these guys use it as a handle or catch-all for anything relating to the government: Congress; the FBI; IRS; Social Security; and so on. And if it's not a 'cabal' of Jewish bankers that is manipulating things, then some evil core group in the U.N. is scheming to establish a 'New World Order' that will subject us all to a life-sucking 'one world' existence. You also hear things like Trilateral Commission and the Freemasons and the Illuminati and—"

"What?"

Harry shook his head. "The details aren't important. This stuff goes back hundreds of years and across several continents, but it all has the same root: people think government is out to get them. Some suspicions are, or once were, well-founded, but some are out in the stratosphere. I mean, $2000 for a toilet seat? Yeah, something's wrong. But bar codes on the back of highway signs so that an invading army will be able to find their way? Come on."

"Where did they get that 'Posse-something' name? Sounds like guys in funny hats, skinning goats under a full moon?"

Harry laughed. "It actually came from a law Congress passed back in the 1800s, separating powers between the federal and state governments. It's Latin for 'power of the county', which to these guys means that the highest authority they have to obey is the county sheriff. They use it to justify everything from not paying taxes to seizing public land to arming themselves for the coming battle against the government—the same government that passed the Posse Comitatus Act in the first place. But that's another story."

"God, you're a walking textbook."

Harry drained his glass. "Morton was right. I did follow this when I was in Butte. I'm revising my opinion of him."

"Yeah, a big change from the days of Brendan Crowley."

"May he rot in peace."

Ellen waved him off. "Crowley's supposedly cleaning toilets in D.C. He's no threat. Probably still oily and arrogant as Hell, but—"

"Brendan Crowley nearly got me killed. Twice." Harry's eyes were drilling into her. "The less said about him, the better. Okay?"

Ellen nodded. "Sorry. So, these Posse guys. How many are there?"

Harry shrugged. "Who knows? You can probably get stats on how many Klansmen or Aryans there are, but the Posse is underground. Fifty thousand? A hundred? Two? A million? They hit a sympathetic chord with a lot of people in Middle America, particularly in the Farm Belt, so it's impossible to tag exactly. Most are harmless, just angry about their taxes. But the true believers are violent and anarchistic. They'd like nothing better than to wipe out the government. Look at the Oklahoma City bombing."

Ellen glanced at the crowd in the other room. "They seem benign. Deluded perhaps, but otherwise harmless."

"Hey, everybody needs a hobby. That's the thing: most of 'em look like average citizens. Just don't ask to see their arsenal."

"Speaking of which, how about that theory that the ATF heist was an inside job?"

"Didn't surprise me. He could believe it, or he could be bull-shitting everyone." Harry paused. "There's an edge to him that concerns me."

Ellen suddenly took a drink, then held the glass in front of her face, examining it. "We're being watched," she whispered. "Or rather, I am."

Harry grabbed a pretzel, stifling the urge to look. "How can you tell?"

"I'm a woman. We have a sixth sense." She set the glass down. "It's that scraggly-looking guy, the misfit, and one of the—"

She suddenly shoved her glass across the table, and Harry lunged to grab it before it hurtled over the side.

"If you're not going to support me on this, Harry—" Her voice was one notch higher than before. "—then I'll get Mom or Rob or somebody else to bail me out."

It needed no explanation. Harry could hear the footsteps now.

"You're asking me to cross the line, girl," he said, "and I've done that one too many times for you already." He leaned over the table and lowered his voice, knowing the words would be heard anyway. "If I pull any more strings, somebody's gonna come lookin' for *me*, and I can't have that."

A body stalked past them and continued on to the bar.

Ellen nodded. "Where are we going with this?" she whispered.

"Straight to hell." Harry peered past her a moment, then brought his voice back up. "That's where you can go, girl, straight to hell. You may be my—"

He stopped and glared at a stocky young man staring at them from the doorway, holding three glasses of beer. "Yeah?" Harry said, in a less than polite tone.

"Hey, Pops," the young man said, "this is a happy bar. And I'm just bringin' you some good cheer, 'cause I hate to see people fighting. D'ya mind?" He walked briskly to their table.

Without waiting for an invitation, the young man placed the three glasses down and reached over to grab a chair. "My name's Kev and I'm like the Welcome Wagon, only better." He gave them a big smile. "You folks new around here or what?"

Harry took one of the glasses, nodded at the young man, drained the glass in one gulp, pushed it back across the table, then said, "Does it matter?"

The young man was obviously impressed. "You remind me of my old man! So how come we had the honor of your presence at our meeting tonight?"

Ellen grabbed the last beer glass and said, "Do you always ask this many questions?" Then she repeated Harry's feat, only faster.

"Damn, you guys are amazing!" the young man said. "That'd make a hell of a bar trick." He started chuckling. "You in here to hustle us all?"

Ellen looked ready to react, so Harry held up his hand to stop her. "We're here to have a little chat. Got a problem with that?"

"No, God, no," the young man said. "It's just that we don't get a lot of strangers in this town, except maybe for some Feds and stuff."

Harry glared at him. "Your daddy know you talk so loose?"

The young man stiffened. "No, sir." His voice was a hush. "I just, ah—I just wanted to welcome you in here." He swallowed hard. "If there's anything else I can do, just let me know. I'll be right in there." He pointed toward the pool room, and nearly knocked over the chair getting up.

When he was gone, Ellen said, "Talk about A+ in Instinct."

There was some commotion in the pool room as the young man pushed through the crowd. "Watch," Harry said, "we're about to get the once over." A moment later, a sea of faces turned to stare at them, mouthing words that neither Harry nor Ellen could hear. For all the shaking heads, however, the message was clear.

"That's our cue to go," Harry said. "We don't want to try to score the first night; that would be suspicious."

Suddenly, the huge bartender appeared at the door, shouting toward the pool room. "Hey, Commander, you gotta come hear this! Somebody just blew up that #2 guy at the FBI." The man disappeared again.

"Don't move," Harry said under his breath. "Smile slowly, in fact." With great effort, he did the same. "Now, as casually as possible, let's get up and go see. If anything, act like this could be good news."

It wasn't. Two days after the Director of the FBI ended up in the hospital, clinging to life support, the Deputy Director was killed by a car bomb. No way were these random attacks.

Standing under the TV, his heart pounding mercilessly, it took every ounce of Harry's control not to lash out. With a raucous group around him cheering the news, the targets would have been easy. The fact that they were heavily armed was of no concern.

No More Words

Barnett stepped back from the pool table and glanced toward the bar, where the bozos were still whooping it up. Thank God for the break; he'd reached his limit trying to sound like one of the guys. Once this was all over, he'd have to see about having them neutered —a lobotomy would be redundant.

If it wasn't for the Commander, who still hadn't granted him an audience, Barnett would've been out of there an hour ago. The guy had stood there quietly, like Yoda or the Pope, while his fawning troops rattled on about burning down the government, shooting all the politicians, and so forth. The room couldn't be bugged or the Feds would've been there already and hauled them all away. Unless, of course, the Authorities figured these guys were idiots and not worth the trouble, a reasonable assumption if you didn't include the Commander. That man had dangerous eyes.

And Barnett had maybe one chance at the guy. He had come armed with information, so his chances should be pretty good. But something about the man's aura was unnerving.

Barnett leaned back over the pool table to look at his next shot. A tricky combination off the rail, requiring a subtle touch of English to pocket the #3 ball. He took a long breath, then released it slowly. *This man is not a problem. This man is not a problem. This man is not . . .*

The mantra rolled on in his head as he stroked the cue ball. He mis-hit it slightly and the #3 nipped the cushion short of the pocket.

"Bush league," a stern voice said.

Barnett bolted upright. There, in the shadows across from him, was the Commander, his flattop bristling, his expression flat. It took a moment, but Barnett finally found his voice.

"I didn't hear you come in."

"What's the matter with you, kid? You don't give a shit about what happens in this country?"

This was supposed to be the ultimate hack, and he was already on the defensive? So much for this guy being a mere pawn. Barnett had to turn things around fast. No way could he let himself be intimidated.

The room was beginning to fill up again, the boozy war cries even louder. Barnett gave the Commander a big smile. "*They* seem to be enjoying the news. Is this how you look when you're happy?"

"Fuck you. You don't know me and you think you can talk like this?"

"Hey, just trying to loosen you up. We've got something to discuss, and it'd help if your mind was not on killing somebody."

"Maybe I should start with you."

"Might be interesting. But you'll get more out of what we—"

"*We* have nothing to discuss. *You* have two minutes to justify your existence."

Barnett picked up a cube of chalk and smiled. "Okay, screw the subtlety. But could you get rid of this crowd . . . *Jerry?*"

"The name's 'George,' you little shit. No one calls me 'Jerry.'"

Barnett could barely contain himself. "Not even at the bank?"

The Commander stared at him for several seconds, then turned to the others in the room and said, "Everybody out."

Kevin was the last one to leave, giving Barnett a thumbs-up before closing the double doors.

The Commander hadn't moved from the end of the pool table. "Are you wired? I heard you were a felon, but this could still be a set-up."

"After all that crap your boys rattled on about? If I had been wired, ZOG men, or whatever you call them, would've stormed this place already."

"I never opened my mouth. So I repeat: Who are you working for?"

Barnett started chalking the tip of his cue stick. "George, I've been convicted twice; once more and my life is over. What I'm about to say would land me back there in a flash. So I should ask you: Is this room bugged?"

The Commander shook his head.

"Good. Then we can get down to business. Care to shoot a little pool while we chat?" Barnett held out the cue stick to him.

"State your business and get out of here."

Barnett leaned over the table, lined up his shot, and bashed it home.

"My business . . . My business is your business, ultimately. Oh, not the arms trade or the Chinese—"

"What did you say?"

Barnett smiled and moved around the table. "I know a lot about you, George. Much more than you'd expect. Like those mail-order videos. Is your wife into that stuff, too?"

The Commander's face was getting red. Barnett set up and drove another ball into the pocket.

"Hey, that speech you made tonight? That was great. You could've passed a collection plate and I would have contributed. People were about to break out in song, with all that 'We Shall Overcome' business. But I've got to ask you—" Barnett sat on the edge of the pool table and lowered his voice. "—is it real or is it all just hype?"

He tossed his stick on the table.

"Yeah. Like, can you really take on the government? And how would you do it? Tanks? I don't think that would be enough, but what do I know? More fertilizer bombs? Whew, don't want to be around you when you go for that. How about cyanide? Okay, I'm being flip. Forget the cyanide, but how about ricin? Could you really poison a whole town? How about the Pentagon's water supply? That'd be a neat trick!"

Barnett slid off the table.

"Hey, Commodore, you sure talk a great game, but even tonight you bailed out. You know, all that 'we shall prevail' stuff, and then you send these folks off to *write letters?* Maybe I'm wasting my time here. I mean, are you really a man of your convictions, or just a bag of hot air? Who knows, maybe you don't have the—" Barnett couldn't resist; he picked up the cue ball and tossed it in the air. "—the balls to actually do what you say."

The Commander snatched it away on the second toss.

"If you don't show some respect, I'll gut you with a fucking pen knife and leave your carcass for the bears. You better have a beauty of a reason for messing with me, boy—" He held up the cue ball. "—or there won't be this much of you left to piss on." He drove the ball into Barnett's stomach, then dropped it on the table and walked away.

Barnett struggled to find his breath. "Fair enough."

"So where do you come by this 'Jerry' name?"

"I'm a hacker. It wasn't hard."

"Why me? What are you after?"

Barnett leaned against the wall, not fully recovered from the blow. He took a deep breath and forced a smile. "I've got big plans, George. Big, bold, fucking audacious plans, and I need somebody like you to help me."

"If you're talking about muscle, forget it. I'm not in that business."

"Well, why did you decide to meet with me?"

The Commander smirked. "I thought I could use a computer jockey on the team. But you're really just a bunch of worthless, meddling pricks."

"Worthless? Meddling?" Barnett walked back to the pool table, and suddenly smiled. "I'll make this worth your while. Here's $500." He pulled a wad of bills out of his pocket and tossed it on the table. "Pocket any one of those balls and it's yours."

The Commander studied him, then picked up the cue stick. He walked around the table, chose his shot, and started to set up.

"Oh wait, Commodore," Barnett said. "Let's add this to the pile." He tossed a piece of paper in the way, a receipt from an ATM. "Check out that bit of account number it shows."

The Commander stared it, and his face went rigid. He shoved the paper in his pocket and bent over the table. He blew the shot.

"Too bad, Commodore." Barnett said. He started to reach for the money, but the Commander snatched it away. "Oh well, it was your money anyway, though you're not being a good sport."

In a blur of motion, the Commander came around the table, grabbed Barnett, and slammed him against the wall.

"It's 'Commander' you little prick, and I want to know why are you fucking with me."

The pressure on Barnett's throat was so strong, he was afraid he was going to pass out. He strained to say: "Because I need you and you need me."

"Bullshit. For what?" The Commander relaxed his grip.

"What were you talking about tonight?" Barnett broke free. "What is your life supposedly dedicated to? Taking back our freedom? If it's not all hot air, then you must have some kind of plan. What's all the weapons trade for if not to stock up for some coming action? Well, I'm here to put you into action."

"You're a fucking foreigner to me. Why do I need you?"

"You didn't get my little object lesson? How are you planning to finance your revolution, with counterfeit bills? Bogus checks, like those Freeman losers? For starters, I can get you millions that are totally untraceable. I can get them out of the President's own bank account, if that's necessary. But it's not just finances, and I'm not talking about a little guerrilla action. Do you think you can wipe out the government with a fertilizer bomb here, a poisoned water supply there? The IRA has been at it for decades, and their situation is trivial to what we face."

"What are you planning to do?" the Commander sneered. "Fuck up all the computers in the world? I'm sooo scared."

Barnett stared down at the table, shaking his head. "Maybe I'm talking to the wrong guy." He looked up, his eyes drilling the Commander. "Are you or are you not interested in bringing down the government?"

The Commander didn't blink.

"Not just bring it down," Barnett said. "Annihilate it, for all time."

The Commander's eyes narrowed. "Lots of people have tried, lots of people have failed."

"My point exactly! Look at *The Turner Diaries*. If you think you can use it as a model, forget it. We're like a mosquito to the govern-ment, an annoyance, nothing more. Anytime they want, they can flatten us."

"What's your point?"

"We've got to do it fast and we've got to do it big—one chance —and it needs both of us. I shouldn't have to explain why; you know the world runs on computers. I apologize for being a little crude before, but this is serious. The world doesn't need any more blowhards, it needs a few people with true conviction. And if you're really sincere about what you say, we just might have something to talk about."

"What's your angle, son? Or should I say, your beef?"

Barnett shrugged. "I've been fucked over too many times. Set-up, beaten down—"

"I heard it was more like beaten up, and fucked—not fucked over."

Barnett's eyes narrowed. "It's a lot of things. Shall we talk about how you've been screwed? By the banks, by the government, even by the military. Something about being used as bait in 'Nam, right?"

The Commander bristled.

"Why we want this may differ," Barnett said, "but the objective is the same: get the Authorities out of the way. The whole damn government is trying to control what we do, how we live our lives, what we can say, how we make a living—you name it! I've got this world-class encryption program I created. It could make me a fortune, *legally*, and I'll never get a chance to sell it because the Authorities won't let me touch a computer again unless I'm helping some old lady with her e-mail."

He leaned across the table.

"Maybe you don't follow this, but we're being fucked over right now. There's this massive repressive effort going on, by people with no authority, to strip away our civil liberties and control our minds. Cyberspace is the last real frontier, and soon it's gonna be nothing but a sanitized wasteland. This isn't just a bunch of computer weenies whining 'cause they can't get dirty pictures. This is real freedoms being stripped away by so-called governments in the name of decency or safety or whatever ludicrous pretext they can come up with. They are reading our mail, eavesdropping on our conversations, fucking with our finances, subverting our commerce —all done electronically, and illegally. They're doing it because they can, because no one is standing up to them. And if that doesn't scare you, it should, 'cause once they rule cyberspace, they'll do the same thing in every other part of our lives."

"They already are," the Commander said quietly.

Barnett leaned in. "And are you going to continue to let it happen?"

His eyes were burning into the Commander's.

"Let your grandchildren live in oppression because you refused to step forward and save their world?"

His voice dropped to a whisper.

"It's time for action, Commander. No more words."

The militia man pulled his head back slightly, but didn't break the gaze. "Maybe we're not strangers after all."

* * *

And behind Door #1? Harry kept fighting the urge to ask. Their new friend, Kevin, would probably tell them if Harry started probing. The guy had lips like a screen door, flapping madly and holding almost nothing in. The problem was that he would certainly report back on this conversation, and a stranger asking a lot of questions would raise serious suspicions in any intelligent person. After that performance at the hall tonight, the guy Kevin called "the Commander" had to rate pretty high on the intelligence scale. The wariness scale, too.

Meanwhile, Ellen seemed to be having a great time toying with the young hulk.

"So, Kevin, is there anything to do in this town besides hunting rabbits, drinking beer, and whining about the Feds?"

"What more do you want?" the young man replied. He gave her a big wink.

"Forget it. You're not my type."

"Well, what is your type? You ain't got a ring on your left hand. And what's that 'WIRED' shit on your head? What are you, wired for sound?"

"It's computers, moron." Ellen stood up. "Harry, would you occupy this mongrel for a while? I've gotta go to the can."

Kevin watched her walk away. "Whew! She is somethin'. But how come you let her call you 'Harry'?"

"It's a long story."

"I take it it's not her idea to move here?"

Harry shrugged. "Don't know how many choices she's got."

"What do you mean?"

Harry pushed his glass toward the young man. "Why don't you get me another beer, and I'll try to forget that you're getting so personal."

Kevin's face flushed. "Gee, I'm sorry. I didn't mean no disrespect."

"Forget it. It's something I learned in 'Nam."

"Were you in the Special Forces? The Commander was."

The kid was gobbling it up like a crazed dog. He'd probably reveal his blood-type if they hung around long enough.

"So your friends here—" Harry tilted his head toward the rest of the group, still milling about. "—do they have a name?"

"Sierra Sentries! Have you heard of us?"

Harry nodded. It was in many of those BBS postings he'd read.

"How about you, Harry? Are you in the movement?"

Harry narrowed his eyes.

"Wow," Kevin said, his voice a hush. "The Commander does that same thing. You two should meet. He could probably use a guy like you, particularly with your Special Forces background."

Ellen returned, sunglasses still on. She walked behind Harry, tugged on each of his ears, then sat down. She turned to Kevin and said, "Didn't manage to talk them off, did you? You're slipping."

Kevin rocked back in his chair, arms folded. "What's your story, Ellen? How come your father's so decent and you're such a . . . a . . ."

"A gentle flower? A voice of reason? A breath of fresh air in this testosterone-infested swamp?"

"Show some respect, girl. Kevin could end up being our neighbor." Harry turned to the young man and lowered his voice. "She's been a—let's say a 'challenge'—ever since she got out of Chino."

Kevin's eyes widened.

"Sorry, Ellen," Harry said quickly. "That was out of line. Kevin, please forget I said that."

Kevin nodded, a solemn look on his face, and Harry knew the young man was hooked. Nothing like a little "family secret" to form a bond.

Harry lightened his voice and said, "So what did you think about the news, about that FBI guy being blown up tonight?"

Kevin chuckled. "About time, don't you think? As somebody said, the only good Fed is a dead Fed." He raised his glass, and his voice. "Here's to the liberator!"

"Isn't that a little risky?" Ellen said. "I mean, I don't give a shit, but that's a pretty high profile to be targeting. By tomorrow morning, they'll have, like, twelve million Feebs going through everybody's lunch box, trying to find some bastard to string up."

"Hey, maybe this is it! That ATF shipment and the top two guys at the fucking FBI? Maybe it's the start of the Second American Revolution." Kevin raised his glass again. "To the liberators!"

Harry's face grew serious. "The Commander wasn't cheering. Did you notice?" That reaction had been eating at Harry for twenty minutes.

Kevin looked shocked. "Really? No, I didn't see. Christ."

Suddenly, the doors to the pool room swung open. At the back wall was the Commander, looking subdued, perplexed even. At the door was the scrawny young man they had seen before with Kevin, who seemed to be tossing instructions to the Commander. The whole thing didn't fit, and now Harry really wanted to know what had been going on in that room.

The scrawny one turned and started walking toward them, his stride strong and confident.

"Check out this scene!" Barnett said, as he neared the table. "Kevin, you are the man to know."

"Hey, JB, how did it go?"

Barnett smiled. "We'll see." He turned his eyes toward Ellen. "So, Kevin, are you going to introduce me or what?"

"Oh, yeah. Ah, Jeff, this is Harry and Ellen. Guys, this is Jeff." Kevin looked back up at Barnett and added, "They're father and daughter."

"Well, this is definitely my day." Barnett looked at his watch. "But I've got to be going. It's a long drive and I'm wiped already. See you guys around?"

He gave Ellen a wink and said, "Nice hat." Then he walked away, followed closely by Kevin.

Ellen leaned over the table. "I know that guy. I'm not sure

where, but I've seen that face before. I want to go back to the city and do some checks. Something isn't right here."

Harry barely heard her; his mind was elsewhere. The Commander hadn't moved an inch since the doors opened. It was a frightening realization.

Danger!

Barnett was feeling anxious. It was a strange reaction to a TV report, particularly sitting in the Old Farts Home on a Sunday morning, but he was wound up just the same. Some of the guns from that ATF heist had been found on a compound in Montana in the company of a militia group, and the FBI was crowing loudly about how they would soon track down the rest of the shipment. The report droned on about gun control and protecting citizens and . . .

. . . and what if the Commander had a piece of that action? Pretty logical, considering the man had a secret weapons business. What if the Feds knew? Maybe that was why Barnett had heard nothing from the guy in over a week. What if ol' Flattop showed up on TV in an orange jumpsuit, surrounded by federal agents? What would be left for Barnett, to be the next Unabomber? Nah. Couldn't exactly pop down for a cappuccino if you were buried in the wilderness.

It had to be something else. The man really was a walking stealth bomber. And he had been hooked that night, no doubt about it. He would show up eventually, if Barnett hadn't cracked up in the meantime. Staying busy was the only way to handle the wait, and Barnett had been a flurry of activity since returning from the mountains. That was especially true in those gaps when his parole officer wasn't around. She stopped in on Friday, but hadn't been near the place all weekend. For Barnett, Saturdays and Sundays were prime-time.

He wanted to be ready to roll when—if—the Commander called. He had already cataloged the databases he figured he'd need to tap, and was well on his way to securing passwords and entry procedures. Some, like Social Security, were surprisingly easy. Others, like banks, were challenging, but workable.

A few, particularly at the Defense Department, required some serious effort before his fingers could stroll through their databases. The peripheral files like accounting, personnel, and travel schedules were easy targets for anyone. Thousands of people hit those each week. But the critical ones, those which held launch codes and strategic plans, were tough. Seemingly impossible to break into, and just the kind of challenge Barnett loved.

That's where "social engineering" came in. A con game really, coaxing key bits of information out of unsuspecting drones at Defense, the White House, IRS, FBI, and so on, then using those bits to get him past whatever firewall had him stumped. He'd begun a list of names and phone numbers he needed for that angle, and would work it when he had some moments alone with a phone.

Barnett shrugged and went back to what he had been doing, before the interruption about the blithering FBI. He picked up a torque wrench and began tightening screws on the underside of his new laptop, another "present" courtesy of his bald buddy Benny. It hadn't been difficult to install that wireless modem in his new laptop; he just never had enough time alone until today.

What a combo this was going to be: laptops with wireless modems and Barnett's special encryption program. The perfect go–anywhere–say–anything system for a band of revolutionaries. He'd have to write a little program or two to make the workings idiot-proof, but then it would be easy, effective, and totally private —with one or two hidden exceptions.

Barnett smiled. Two more screws to go.

"You're gonna wipe out the government from an old folks home?"

The voice launched Barnett out of his chair. He whirled

around to see the Commander standing behind him, the flattop sitting up as sharp as ever and that same inscrutable, Pope-like grin on the man's face. "Jesus, how do you do that?" Barnett said. "My early-warning system failed."

"Don't underestimate me, kid. It could be fatal."

Barnett smiled. "I half expected to see you in an orange jumpsuit. It's about time I heard from you." He sat back down. "Actually, I'm surprised. Kevin said you never come down from the mountain."

"I figured we needed another face-to-face."

Barnett's eyes widened. "You're ready to do this?"

"Depends on whether I can trust you."

Barnett turned toward the PC and said, "Watch this!"

In the course of thirty minutes, he gave the Commander a tour of Defense Department databases, created a new identity for himself in the Social Security system, and transferred ten thousand dollars, by a circuitous path, from an IRS slush fund to one of the Commander's bank accounts. It was a dizzying rip, and the Commander seemed stunned.

"Christ," he said quietly, "you *are* for real."

"Don't underestimate me, George. It could be—"

Barnett froze. Twenty feet away and churning their direction was the she-devil of the parole corps. On a Sunday? How did she slip in?

Barnett pressed a combination of keys to activate his new restart sequence, then said, out of the corner of his mouth, "Danger!"

A moment later, he popped out of his chair and leaned over the screen. "Officer Gnat, if you keep coming by like this, people will begin to talk. I just know these old ladies would love to see me married off."

Natalie Weston ground to a stop and glared at Barnett. Then she looked over at the Commander. "Who's this?"

"George Jones," said the Commander. "Who are you?"

"His parole officer. And I'd like to know what you're doing here."

"Rehabilitation," Barnett said quickly. "He's heard about all the help I've given his mom. See that lady in the yellow gown over there? And he thought maybe I could advise him about getting started on the Net."

Weston stared at the Commander. "Shall I ask her about it?"

Nobody moved.

"And I suppose that laptop Barnett is holding is yours?"

Barnett looked at the Commander and smiled. "Of course!"

The parole officer shook her head wearily, nudged Barnett out of the way, and spent two minutes going through screens, not bothering to sit down. The whole time, the corner of her eye was on the Commander, as if trying to find an answer, a weakness—something.

Then, she turned and faced the Commander directly. "This man is a convicted felon. He is under orders not to freelance on computers, so if you want some advice, try the Yellow Pages. If I find him with you or anyone else again, I'll have him sent back to Grasslands." She looked at Barnett. "Got it?"

She wheeled on her heels and stormed out.

"You see what I've been dealing with?" Barnett said.

The Commander's eyes narrowed. "That's a problem we've got to take care of. Do you know where she lives?"

"No. But I can find out."

Two minutes and three databases later, Barnett had it.

Harry peered through the leaves at the Federal Building across the street and scowled. Hell of a way to spend a Sunday afternoon. It was one thing to be on guard duty, but like this? Sitting behind a bush, dressed in rags, and smelling like an army of homeless guys had wiped themselves with his shirt? Other agents were posted around the Federal Building in downtown San Francisco, but they got to sit in cars and stuff their faces. Even Ellen at least got to roam the streets on her mountain bike. But Harry was dumped at the corner, stinking of who knew what and wondering who he pissed-off this time. Morton? The Assistant SAC? Some guy in tech services?

And what a great time to be in the FBI! The Director was in a coma, the Deputy Director was dead, and there had been so many threats from copy-cats the past ten days that the new Acting Director, Warren Keller, insisted that armed patrols guard every FBI field office. Adding to the siege mentality was the daily butchering by the press: for lack of leads about the attacks on the two Directors; for lack of progress in finding the rest of the stolen ATF weapons; for fanning hysteria among the citizens; for breathing.

He glanced at the Federal Building. Nothing suspicious. He cleared some rags away from his microphone and said, "Hey, Ellen, how come you never get the shit detail?"

Her answer blared back in his earphone.

"I'm younger, prettier, and have big—teeth!" Her voice cackled in the background.

"It's like my daddy used to say: 'There's no justice in this world.'"

"Guess you didn't believe him, huh? Why else would you be doing such a powerful, or should I say 'pungent,' job?"

"If you ride by here again, I'll make you pay for that. One whiff and you'll be out cold. Where are you, anyway?"

"Coming up Larkin. I'll be able to smell you any second. So, how much longer are we going to continue this foolishness?"

"Until we find a few FBI killers or all get wiped out, I guess."

"Man, nobody's going to hit this building. Why bother?"

Harry saw a blur through the leaves and leaned his head out to see Ellen zoom past. Sweats, sunglasses, and headphones over her ears; she definitely got the better gig today. He watched her hurtle off the curb, hop the bike over a pothole, and dash up the street.

"Show off," he said.

"Just keeping myself amused. I'm going up one extra block this time, Harry. Then I'll swing back along Turk to check the rear of the building."

Harry watched a few cars pass along Golden Gate Avenue, and his mind drifted to Sutter Springs. As it had so often the past ten days, the one lingering image was that closed door meeting between Pilkin and the misfit.

"Hey, Ellen, did you ever figure out who that guy was in Sutter Springs?"

"That guy? You mean the scraggly one? No, not at all. It'll probably hit me in the middle of the night."

"So how's your social life these days?"

"Almost as pathetic as yours. That's the problem with being in the Bureau, you're a social leper. You can't talk about your work and, at least for women, you don't really want to admit you're a Special Agent. Guys either run, 'cause they're afraid you're tougher than they are, or they want someone petit and demure."

Harry chuckled. "Describes you perfectly!"

"Hey, you don't have this problem. What your problem is, I'm not sure, but you don't have to worry about women knowing you're with the FBI."

"Wrong. That was precisely the problem for my ex-wife. It's the same old refrain: not knowing if I'd come home alive; not seeing me for weeks when I was working undercover; not being able to talk about—

Ellen's voice cut him off.

"Harry. I think I'm being followed."

Ellen had no idea how long they'd been tracking her. She might have missed them entirely if she hadn't looked back just as the car turned, slowly, onto Turk. No one drove like that through this area, not on a Sunday, unless maybe they were looking to score some drugs. But the same car had followed her onto Larkin a minute ago, she was almost positive of that.

She crossed Larkin, heading toward the Federal Building, and resisting the urge to pick up her pace. "Harry, I'm going to do a little test, just to be sure. Maybe they're looking for drugs, maybe not. Alert the guys on the street in case I need support, but don't jump yet."

"Where are you?"

"Middle of the block. It's a black car, a—"

"I see it! A Lexus, cruising slowly. Be careful."

She pulled off her headphones. Right now, anything but silence was a distraction. There was an intersection ahead and she swooped into a fast left turn. But she cut back quickly, just as a car was accelerating behind her. The Lexus had to brake hard to keep from hitting her, and Ellen continued on up Turk toward the next cross street.

She took her time now, grooving to internal rhythms, as she paced the traffic signal up ahead; didn't want to get there too soon. The light turned yellow, and she and the Lexus both rolled to a stop. Ellen could feel their eyes on her. She waited until the crossing traffic began to flow, blocking the path of the Lexus, and then whipped her head around.

She had planned to give them a snide little wave, but she was too shocked.

"Harry, it's the Vipers!"

She jumped on her pedals and shot down the cross street, riding against traffic, her heart hammering faster than her feet. There was a screech behind her, and what sounded like a car lurching up onto the sidewalk.

There was an alley just ahead and she jammed her brakes to make the cut. That turn would slow the Lexus down, hopefully long enough for her to make it back to safety.

She was almost out of the alley, when it seemed to explode around her. Bullets just above her head, slamming into the bricks on either side. She dropped to the handlebars, swerved twice, and was suddenly out onto Polk. She cut hard to her right and shot across the street.

"Harry, I'm almost onto Golden Gate! Be ready!"

She heard a car screech around the corner behind her onto Polk—but not from the alley. She started to turn her head, but a flash of gunfire sent her back into a tuck, skidding into the intersection at Golden Gate Avenue.

Ellen flashed around the corner, followed closely by a gray car going sideways and, behind it, the black Lexus. Harry was about to dash into the street, when Ellen suddenly cut behind a parked car and jumped her bike onto the sidewalk where he was.

The first car surged ahead, trying to get even with her, but one of the Bureau cars on detail, charging backwards, rammed it. The sound was like bomb blast. A swarm of FBI agents was pouring out of the Federal Building and racing toward the scene. But no one was covering the black Lexus. It jumped the curb onto the sidewalk and barreled after Ellen, its guns on fire. The only one in its way was Harry.

He didn't have a clear shot. Even if Ellen crouched, she would still be in the way. He needed a different angle. Where?

He hoisted himself onto a parked car, but there were so many rags around his feet that he slipped and fell hard against the hood. His gun popped out of his hand and started sliding away.

With bullets exploding all around him, he dove for the gun, then scrambled to his knees. The Lexus was bearing down on Ellen, maybe twenty yards behind her now. There was no time to set-up properly.

The gun roared in his hand, sending fifteen rounds into the Lexus in a heartbeat. The car swerved to its right, smashing into the side of a building, then lurched sharply to its left, rolling halfway up a parked car and flipping over. It slid several yards on its roof before grinding to a stop.

Harry replaced the clip in his gun, and jumped off the car, but there was no need to cover the Lexus; it had burst into flames. He ran toward Ellen, who had collapsed on the sidewalk, clutching her left arm. A pool of blood was forming.

Her breathing was strained, her body shaking fiercely. Harry put an arm around her and she dissolved against him, sobs pouring out of her. Harry put his hand over the bullet wound, trying to stop the flow of blood, and then carried her to the street, further away from the burning Lexus. Sirens screamed from every direction.

Ellen took several deep breaths, but stayed burrowed in Harry's shoulder. "Oh God, Harry. I thought I—" She coughed suddenly and pulled back from him. "Christ, you *do* smell awful."

He burst out laughing. "Hey, whatever it takes."

An ambulance pulled up and paramedics began working on Ellen. They didn't seem overly concerned about her arm, so Harry turned to check out the other car that had chased her.

Four men were being patted down and cuffed, but their heads kept turning toward Ellen. Being clear of the danger now, Harry had time to let his anger loose. As he began stalking toward the gray car, Ellen's cry of "Vipers!" rang in his ear, and he broke into a run, pulling off rags as he went.

They were clones of Frick and Frack; he saw that from thirty feet, and the language was clearly Vietnamese. When he was ten feet away, all four heads turned toward him. Their voices erupted with rage.

Harry couldn't understand any of what was said, except for two words: "Trong" and "Harry."

The quiet residential street in Oakland was ablaze in flashing lights, a fleet of police cruisers turning midnight into noon around a small house at one end of the block. In the darkness at the other end of the street, amid vehicles locked for the night, was an old truck with two men inside. Watching.

Barnett was awed. Not so much by the force which had descended on his parole officer's house, but by how quickly the Commander had mobilized such an operation. Talk about connections —and stealth.

The police scanner on the dashboard in front of them gave periodic updates: an anonymous tip led to the discovery of a major methamphetamine lab in that house, plus thousands of dollars in cash; the occupant, one Natalie Weston, had not been home at the time of the initial search, but returned an hour ago and was taken into custody; the suspect proclaims her innocence, but could not provide proof of her recent whereabouts or explain why there were ten vials of crack cocaine in her car; she claims she was set up, probably by a former drug dealer she once handled named Fratelli; a spokesman for the Department of Corrections had no comment, pending an investigation, but did advise that the suspect would be suspended from her duties as a parole officer until the matter was resolved.

Barnett couldn't suppress a smile any longer. "That's beautiful. Poetic, too. You guys are fast."

"Thanks," the Commander said. "Think that'll hold her for a while? We can arrange something permanent."

"No, this way she suffers more, being humiliated like that. She deserves it. But I don't think she has to die. I'd love for her to see my face grinning from the tube again; that would kill her."

The Commander started up the truck. "Where to now?"

Barnett pulled an airline ticket out of his pocket and handed it to the Commander. "Ever been to the Washington Monument?"

This Vision

Harry leaned back in his chair and looked around the office of the Special Agent in Charge of the FBI's San Francisco operations. Maybe it was the room. Maybe it was haunted or had a "bad aura," to use one of Ellen's phrases. He'd never had a good moment in the room when Brendan Crowley was the SAC. And while the new SAC, Jim Morton, was a marked improvement, the feeling in the room was still edgy at best. Something about the words: good news/bad news. Even Ellen was fidgeting in her seat.

"Turns out that Trong was running a heroin smuggling ring," Morton said. "We knew about it, but we thought it was run by someone else. Speculation is divided over whether he was doing the chip business to finance his heroin buys or trying to get out of the drug business altogether. Anyway, that was a major coup."

Morton's face tightened. "Of course, your names have shown up on a hit list. We got it from the creeps you nailed Sunday. Your name is at the top, Harry; Ellen, you're right below him."

He leaned across the desk. "They had your names spelled correctly, first and last, which means I've got a leak to plug around here. Don't lose sleep over it, 'cause I'm going to turn up the heat on the Viet gangs, and I'll make sure you're protected when you come back to town. You will need to return to testify. I'll give you as much advance warning as I can. Have you decided how you want to stay in contact?"

Harry nodded at Ellen. This was her province.

"We're going to stay away from e-mail," she said, "just in case these militia guys have someone who can crack codes. Probably the simplest thing is to leave a message on my answering machine. Do you have that number?"

Morton nodded. "Are you going to be okay with that arm? That's a sizable-looking dressing. How long does it stay on?"

Ellen's eyes flashed at Harry. "Three weeks or until I rip it off, whichever comes first. It's not my shooting arm, so that shouldn't be a problem; God save us from having to use those again. But Harry will probably insist on doing the driving."

"The woman's a maniac," Harry said. "Deep cover with her should be an adventure."

"So why haven't I heard of this guy Pilkin before?" Morton said. "Trochmann, Butler, Rumson; those names I know. Is he using an alias?"

"Not exactly," Harry said. "He goes by 'the Commander,' just that alone. It's a common title in most of these groups, but he's the only one recognized like that. I had to go way back in the files to actually find the name 'Pilkin,' back to some early speeches he made on the patriot speakers circuit, before 'Commander' took hold. He dropped from view around the time of Matthews and the Order in '84, and now contributes an occasional article to some patriot publications. Fiery, but cautionary stuff. I also found the name in a few of the informant files from around the country; passing mentions about how he'd been in town to advise the local paramilitary group. The guy seems to have God-like status. You know: 'Inspirational!' 'Awesome!' 'Totally changed our thinking.' Jazz like that. To the outside world, he's in hibernation. But the way he looked the other week, something big is brewing."

"Any estimate how long it'll take?"

Harry shrugged. "Can't rush these things. They're probably twitchy as hell. And if they've got any of that ATF stash . . . How's that coming, anyway?"

Morton groaned. "Frustrating. Slow. And it doesn't help that we're getting very little cooperation from the ATF. Or D.C., I might add. Makes sense, I guess, given the turmoil in the Hoover Building right now. A list of the stolen items is in your packets: rocket launchers; shoulder-mounted SAMs; automatic weapons. Every time I look at that list, I wonder what the ATF was up to."

He handed each of them a large brown envelope. "Here's the other stuff you need: new IDs; new credit cards; new histories in every database we could think of. Someone would have to go to old back-up files to find your real identities, and that requires an operator to load the tapes."

"Military history?" Harry said. "A prison record for Ellen? Debts? DMV? Outstanding warrants? Legal actions?"

"Harry," Morton said, "I put you at risk once. I'm not going to do it again. You want me to assign someone else to this?"

Harry shook his head.

"That's good," Morton continued, "because somebody in D.C. is very interested in the two of you handling this assignment."

That stopped the conversation cold.

"You'd think the people in Washington have enough to worry about," Morton said quietly, "what with FBI killers running loose."

"What's happening with that investigation?" Ellen said.

Morton exploded. "Who knows?! Trying to get an answer on anything is like pulling teeth. Warren Keller, the Acting Director, won't return my phone calls. Everyone I do talk to there is running around like a madman. I know it seems like we're under attack and the focal point is D.C., but Christ! Then I send this routine memo about your plans to investigate Sutter Springs, and it comes back with Keller's initials on it, and says he wants to be personally briefed on your progress."

Harry looked at Ellen, then back to Morton. "Does he know something we don't know?"

Barnett pulled his coat tighter around him, trying to fight off the chill. Only lunatics and tourists would be out in this weather, and there were a fair number of the latter milling nearby at the base of the Washington Monument. The view was panoramic, but the conditions were crazy. The sky was so threatening, and such an unsavory shade of gray, that one of two things was imminent: a 40-year flood or Black Lung Disease. The wind was so loud and strong that flag poles surrounding the monument were ready to snap off. Here it was, April, and Barnett couldn't decide whether to drink his coffee or plunge his hands into it.

And his presence there? Lunacy. It was the only answer. His plan was sheer insanity, but it had rolled through his head every night for more than two years. All that time, festering in his cage at Grasslands Correctional Facility, he saw it, in vibrant shrieks of red and orange and black. A cauldron of color, whirling and whipping him into a frenzy, to where there was no question of possibilities, only fact. It *was* going to happen, somehow.

But now, sitting there, looking across the Mall to the Capitol or past the Ellipse to the White House, plus all that space and all those buildings in between—Justice, FBI, IRS, Treasury, and so on—well, maps didn't quite capture the spread. Conceptually, it was a brilliant plan. In reality? That's what the Commander and his band of merry men were for, wasn't it?

Out of the corner of his eye, he saw a figure stalking toward him, flattop unruffled but otherwise struggling against the wind. Barnett raised his voice. "Hard time finding this place?"

The Commander glared at him. "So what's your big plan?"

"Welcome to you, too, Mr. Commander, sir. Nice flight?"

The Commander's eyes narrowed. "Why are we here?"

"As you guys call it: the Second American Revolution."

"And you're George Washington? Fuck you. I call the shots."

"Wrong."

The Commander grabbed Barnett's coat and yanked him close.

"What qualifies you, you little puke? You haven't earned the right to wipe my ass, much less tell me how this should be run."

Barnett didn't blink. "Then why did you come?"

The Commander shoved him back on the bench. "Follow me."

He stormed off in the direction of the Lincoln Memorial. Barnett trailed slowly at first, until his anger subsided, then trotted along to catch up. Down the path, through the traffic on 17th Street, under the canopy of budding trees beside the Reflecting Pool, the Commander charged onward. Barnett was winded when he finally came alongside.

"So where are we going?" he said. "Pay our respects to Abe?"

The Commander didn't answer, but cut sharply right. They went up over a knoll, and suddenly Barnett understood; they were going to The Wall, the Vietnam Veterans Memorial. The Commander strode ahead of him, down the path toward the center of the monument.

It wasn't anything like Barnett expected. He'd always imagined it was just a slab of granite plunked down on the ground, but this was set into the hillside. Angled, really, or at least the panels were. It was of passing interest at first, the small end panels with a few names on them. But as he got further along, deeper into the piece, the panels towered above him. Thousands and thousands and thousands of names. A blur when he stepped back, and overwhelming when he moved in close. Each one a life reduced to a few inches of letters etched into black marble, a few drops in a flood of names, a flood of lives.

The Commander was a little further on, waiting for him.

"You were just here?" Barnett asked.

The Commander nodded.

"Show me," Barnett said.

The Commander walked to the wall and traced his fingers over several names. He trailed off, shaking his head. Then he walked back to Barnett, his eyes burning.

"This isn't going to happen again," he said.

They walked away, a slow and silent march. They ended up

back at the same bench, at the base of the Washington Monument. Barnett's eyes scanned the landscape.

Finally he spoke, his voice barely audible above the wind. "For two and a half years, I've had this vision. A vision of the D.C. skyline in flames."

The Commander glanced at him, then looked away.

"Huge, fearsome flames torching everything in their path. Dissolving the government as it destroys the edifices. Red. Orange. A sky black with soot. Leveling the White House, the Capitol, all those agencies and bureaus. Like a forest fire, you know? To set things right, sometimes Nature has to burn things down and start over. Too bad about the Smithsonian, but I guess there have to be some casualties."

The Commander chuckled.

Barnett looked at him. "I'm sorry for what you've been through. Really. And I respect your skills, George, I do. But you have to respect mine, too. As a team, we can change history. Individually? Forget it."

"And you think we can change history by burning down the city?"

"Not alone. But if we also get the leaders and vaporize the records, then those who remain will be lost. Right? I mean, if government workers, the military—hell, every goddamned FBI agent—if they can't get their paychecks, 'cause there are no longer any records and no one to sign checks and no office to go to and so on and so on? How long are they going to hang around? There'll be no chain of command, no one for people to turn to but themselves. It'll be absolute anarchy—and it'll be beautiful."

"You got a warped mind, son." The Commander looked at him, then laughed. "But it makes a lot of sense. Of course, it ain't gonna be that simple."

Barnett brightened. "For starters, I think we need a water resource engineer. Do you know any? I figure if we can disrupt the water supply to the city, the sprinkler systems will be useless. Then we torch a few buildings and melt the whole place down. Cool, huh? Maybe we could even pump gasoline into the system, so that the sprinklers really did a job?"

"You're sick."

The Commander got up and walked away, all the way around the Washington Monument. It took several minutes. Finally, he returned to Barnett's spot and sat down. The air around him crackled with energy.

"Our work is cut out for us," he said. "The whole goddamned place looks like a mausoleum, doesn't it? A bunch of stone tombs for ZOG's citadels. How well does marble burn anyway?"

Barnett straightened up. "Got a match?"

The Commander smiled. "I've got more than that. But we might just want to do a test."

He looked at Barnett, his eyes gleaming. "Ever been to New York?"

The Fortress

Harry tuned out the conversation from the front seat and let the rhythm of the towering pines passing his window take him away. He was enjoying the slower pace in Sutter Springs; he had insisted on it, really. The only path to infiltrating the Commander's organization was to act like they weren't planning to do that. They had returned to the area, posing as escapees from a tortured life in L.A., and the only sensible thing in that scenario was to go into near hibernation for a certain period of time. Be seen and not heard, blend into the landscape, become a part of the community. And wait for opportunity to arise. For a group as secretive and paranoid as the Commander's, the opening would have to come from them.

Patience wasn't just a virtue in undercover work, sometimes it was the difference between life and death. Snoop around too soon or too boldly, and you were marked for sure. So in Harry's head, their first two weeks there had not been wasted. If nothing else, no one had tried to kill them.

But Ellen was frustrated by the inactivity, particularly Harry's refusal to try to contact the Commander yet. A new bandage on her arm shared the blame: she'd wiped out riding one-handed on her mountain bike. So, she began hanging out in Mackey's bar, scribbling nihilistic slogans and scenes of destruction on a napkin.

That earned her some snarls from the bear-like bartender, who took a pen that morning and wrote "Get lost!" on her notes. But her presence there also gave them the opening they were waiting for: Kevin.

Whether he sought them out or was just being neighborly, who cared? They needed to work this contact and Kevin seemed to thrive in their company. At the moment, he was driving them around the hills above Sutter Springs, in search of houses to rent, and chattering endlessly.

Suddenly, Ellen barked. "Kevin, stop this piece of shit right now!" She waited until the Jeep ground to a dusty halt. "Okay, look at me and say that with a straight face."

"Satan's spawn."

"You've got to be joking."

"No, they are. Every one of them kinky-haired kikes is de-scended from the devil. It's right there in the Bible." He started driving again. "What people call Jews are actually a bunch of satanic Khazars, the black tribe of Israel. Yahweh—that's 'God' in the Old Testament—He created white Anglo-Saxons as His chosen people, and gave them the Magna Carta, and the Constitution, and the Bill of—"

"That's outrageous," Ellen said. "Where'd you learn that crap? From your—"

"Ellen!" Harry reached forward and grabbed her arm, the one with the cast. He knew that'd get her attention, and Kevin's. "Just because your beliefs are different from his."

"Are you sure she's got any?" Kevin said.

"What if I told you I was a Jew?" Ellen said.

Kevin slammed on the brakes. "You're not. Are you?" He looked at Harry, who was shaking his head.

"What if I said I had converted?"

Kevin's face grew serious. "Don't kid about those things."

Ellen's face broke out in a smile. "Kev-vy, you're such a putz. Oops, that's one of their words. Hey, I believe all that stuff, I do. Yahweh forever!"

Kevin put the Jeep into gear, but he didn't look like he was buying it. "If you really believed, you wouldn't be so—"

"What? Normal? Well-adjusted? Skeptical of bullshit?"

"So ballsy," Kevin replied. "In the Identity faith, women know their place. It's right there in the Scriptures."

"So is Thou Shalt Not Be A Brainless Moron."

"Ellen." Harry said.

"No, come on! Other than not being able to write my name in the dirt when I pee, which I grant you is a significant talent worthy of centuries of domination, I can match you on any scale, bucko. Except stu—"

"Ellen!"

"That's alright, Harry," Kevin said. "Yahweh works in strange ways. So, Wonder Woman, can you shoot?"

"Better than you, I'll bet."

"No way. What about cooking?"

"Grow up."

"Can you work a computer?"

"I can take one apart and put it back together blindfolded. Can you?"

Kevin looked at Harry in the rearview mirror, then back at Ellen. "Well, it's an established fact that some jobs are meant for men. But we do have something we're working on where a computer ace would be real handy. I'd have to clear it with the Commander, of course, and with Bar—"

He stopped the Jeep abruptly and pointed through the trees. "There's the place I was telling you about. Real secluded, but from the upstairs balcony, you can actually see Lake Tahoe." He engaged the four-wheel drive and turned off the road. "If we go up here a little higher, you should even be able to see part of the Commander's compound."

They bounced up a steep grade, tilting around some tall pines, until they broke into a clearing at the crest of the hill. The panoramic view of the Sierra Nevadas was spectacular, and theme songs from old Westerns flooded Harry's head. They got out of the Jeep and walked to a big rock.

"Now over there is the lake," Kevin said, "and if you really squint, you can see some of those ski areas." Then he pointed toward a valley about a mile or so away. "Can you see anything in that direction?"

Trees.

"Well, you'd pretty much have to be inside that valley to see, but there are fifteen buildings there. If you look real close——" Kevin moved his finger a few inches. "——you can see the roof of the main house. Great, huh? It's just perfect for security, 'cause we control the only road into or out of the compound." He leaned toward Harry and lowered his voice. "I'm not supposed to tell people this, but we've got guard towers up on those ridges, too. The place is a goddamned fortress!"

How many people? What kind of weapons? Where are the sentries? So many questions Harry couldn't ask yet. Instead, he nodded solemnly and walked back to the Jeep.

Ellen followed him, but Kevin remained on the rock for a few moments, watching them, then turned his head back toward that valley. Finally, he trotted back to the Jeep and climbed in, a big smile on his face.

"Want to see it?" he asked.

Harry hesitated. "Are you sure about that?"

Kevin gave him an electric smile. "No prob. I've got what you might call 'special privileges' around here."

The path to the compound was even rockier than before, and the Jeep felt like it was launching into space with each big jolt. It didn't seem to bother Kevin, however, who just raised his voice above the din.

"So, Harry, I didn't catch why you're moving here."

"I didn't say."

"But do you have a business or something?"

"What kind of business could survive up here?" Ellen asked.

"I just figured you guys had to have some——"

"Electronics," Harry said. "Import and export. Special goods. And we're tired of the damned city life."

"Speak for yourself," Ellen said.

Kevin was chuckling. "Your daughter's a piece of work, Harry. I'm surprised your hair isn't more gray than it is."

Harry was about to respond, when suddenly a truck shot out of the trees and blocked their path. Kevin slammed on his brakes. As the dust cleared, Harry noticed they were now surrounded by motorcycles. Ominous-looking weapons were leveled at the Jeep, and the riders' blacked-out helmets seemed to heighten the threat.

The door to the truck flew open and a man came stomping out. "Jesus Christ, Kevin! What the hell are you doing coming in this way?" He stopped abruptly when he reached the Jeep. "Who are these people?"

Kevin didn't seemed fazed. "New recruits. Harry and Ellen Chandler. I was just bringing them in to meet the Commander."

"Everybody out!" the man said. He made a sign to another man in the truck, who came over with an electronic scanner in hand.

Kevin slammed his door. "Now hold on a minute!"

"I've got my orders. Search 'em, boys."

A strip search wouldn't have been much more thorough. Harry wondered if it dragged on because Kevin was protesting so much. But the man from the truck finally seemed satisfied and waved the motorcyclists away.

"You better move along, boy," he said to Kevin. "We've got a drill starting at 1400 hours and the Commander will be pissed if you're not in place. I guarantee he ain't got time for no social visits today."

The man started back toward his truck, then pulled a two-way radio from his belt, listening more than talking. He looked back at the Jeep and nodded as he finished his conversation. Then he shouted "Follow me!" to Kevin and drove off.

Ten minutes later, they pulled into the main part of the compound. It really was a fortress, if you looked past the flowers and log cabin appearance of the place. There were ground-level slits, just wide enough for a gun barrel, and cleverly-disguised turrets built into the roof of each building. Harry didn't have a chance to stare, but he thought he saw small video cameras placed under the eaves. The windows were small and probably easily shuttered, and there was a good chance that everything was lined in steel or concrete or maybe Kryptonite. It looked sort of like a fancy summer camp, except for all the men in fatigues carrying assault rifles. And the incredible feeling of tension in the air.

They hadn't even come to a stop when another truck came tearing up. Harry couldn't see who the passenger was, but there was no mistaking the driver. The Commander stormed over to the Jeep, his face burning.

"What the fuck are you up to, boy?! We've got serious business here and you're playing fucking tour guide? Have I got to chain you to this place to keep you in line? Get out of the damned car!"

He practically dragged Kevin across the yard, his curses fierce but not quite audible at that distance. The young man withered at first under the verbal assault, but gradually both men came back to a neutral stance. There were nods from the Commander, and finally both of them returned to the Jeep.

Kevin got there first and stuck his head in the window. "Sorry about that; I fucked up. I have to stay here, but you can take my Jeep back and leave it at Mackey's. Jake—in that truck—he'll lead you out." He forced a smile and stepped back. "So, Commander, this is Harry Chandler and his daughter, Ellen. Guys, this is the Commander."

Harry stuck his hand out the window and said, with reserve, "Nice to meet you." The Commander shook it, then crossed his arms over his chest.

"We're kind of busy here right now," he said, "but Kevin thinks we should sit down and talk some time. Maybe next week."

He gave Kevin a murderous look, then whistled at the man in his truck and nodded toward the main house. The Commander turned and walked off, followed by Kevin and the other man.

Harry got into the driver's seat. They followed the truck out of the compound and down a long dusty road to a large, heavily fortified gate. It was only after they were out of sight that Ellen let off a sigh of relief.

"Suddenly Trong and his buddies seem benign," she said.

Harry nodded. "We've got to call Morton. These guys aren't practicing training maneuvers."

From his second floor window, Barnett watched the procession march toward the house. This obviously wasn't the time for clever comments, judging by how Kevin and the Big Guy looked. The other man, Barnett didn't know. He gathered up his printouts and headed for the stairs. Ol' Flattop would be bellowing his name any second.

He came around the turn in the wide wooden staircase and stopped. Kevin was being crucified for some infraction, and there was no way Barnett was going to get close to that action. Even the other man had melted into a corner of the entry way. The Commander was stabbing his points into Kevin's chest, and the younger man just stood there and took it. Barnett could hear what was being said, but chose to tune it out.

Finally, Kevin slumped off. The Commander turned toward the stairs, and seemed startled to find Barnett standing there.

"Do you believe that shit? The kid keeps pestering me for a chance, then I finally give him one and he's off picking flowers. Goddamned imbecile."

Barnett started down the stairs. "Do you need him? You've got a lot of other guys around here."

The Commander shook his head. "He's thicker than mud, but he's the best shot I've ever seen, me included. He could hit a quarter in a stiff wind from a mile away. It's goddamned remarkable."

"And there's nobody else?"

"Not for this task. Not that I trust enough, provided I can trust

Kevin to get there safely." The Commander's eyes suddenly drilled into Barnett. "Maybe you should go as his second. You could probably keep him in line."

Barnett choked on his tongue.

"Nah," the Commander said, "you'd never pull it off if he went down. We'll stick with the teams we have. So, what have you got?"

"Travel arrangements and the transport schedule. The weather looks good for the next five days, but Friday is the day. Unless this momma collides with a submarine or something, it should dock about 3 P.M. It's been hitting the checkpoints right on time, and nobody's been held up by the harbor master lately. I've downloaded a map of the region for you. Pretty, huh?"

"You're gonna bankrupt me with all this equipment you need."

"I put ten thousand dollars in your account last week, remember?" Barnett wanted to add a snide remark, but after that scorching Kevin received . . .

"That reminds me," the Commander said. "I need you to come up with two million dollars for a little purchase I'm gonna make. Work that out while we're gone. I'll give you the account number it needs to go to."

"Oooh. Buying a small country?"

"No, a big one. Now about those grates, got anything better than a street map?"

Barnett threw up his hands. "It won't print out. Their system was designed by a moron. I marked all the access points on that map. Can't you go from that? I can show you that shit online otherwise."

"Never mind. So what about the travel plans?"

Barnett took a breath. "As we discussed, each team is travelling separately, both out there and back. Kevin and his partner are flying San Jose to Newark, then later Amtrak to Philly and back to Oakland. You and Mackey go Oakland to La Guardia, then take a commuter train from Grand Central to White Plains, pick up a rental car, drive to Boston, and fly to San Jose. The third team will go between San Francisco and Hartford, CT, using a rental car to go to New York and back."

"Won't work, those commuter trains. Think about it."

Barnett ran the scenario through his head and nodded. He expected to have his ears blistered, and was surprised to hear the Commander say quietly, "Just make some other arrangement."

"Sorry," Barnett said. "Everything else is in order: phony names; IDs; etcetera." He smiled. "I just want to know how you're going to get that stuff out there."

The Commander grinned. "FedEx. Going out tomorrow. There isn't much anyway. Except for the—" He turned his head toward a long hallway and shouted, "Bets!"

A moment later, a woman appeared from one of the rooms, brushing strands of long, dark hair off her face with the back of her hand. She'd probably been a beauty queen once, thirty years or so ago. That was obvious despite the simple clothes, lack of make-up, or the lips pursed around a sewing needle. She winked at Barnett as she walked into the foyer, then removed the needle from her mouth—slowly, seductively—and said, "Yes, Master?"

The Commander glared at her. "What's the status?"

She sighed dramatically. "I don't do miracles, I told you that. Thank God there are only six of you, but this reversible crap is a pain to get right."

"Will they be ready by tomorrow?"

"A.M. or P.M.?"

The Commander looked at Barnett.

"Noon?" Barnett said. He was surprised how sheepish he sounded.

Betsy looked at the Commander but tilted her head toward Barnett. "I think I've seen your friend around here, but we haven't been introduced yet. As for this other gentleman . . ."

All eyes turned toward the slightly-built man who had melted into the corner. He stared back at them through formless glasses, but didn't say a word.

"Just get back to work," the Commander said.

Betsy shrugged and spun on her heels, flashing her eyes at Barnett before strolling off. The Commander's mouth tightened, but he said nothing.

Barnett felt compelled to break the mood. "So, George, I'm still not sure about the main target. What if—"

The Commander held up his hand. "I almost forgot. There's a small change in plans." He chuckled lightly. "We need one more ticket."

He motioned for the other man to join them. "This is Willard. He's on loan from Michigan. He's a water resource engineer."

NYC

Harry took a sip of coffee and chuckled to himself. Another beautiful day in paradise! Sunlight streamed through the windows of their rented cabin, birds were chirping outside, and, since Ellen was back in San Francisco getting her arm attended to, things were incredibly peaceful at the moment. Best of all, on this particular morning, he was not in New York.

The all-news radio was carrying the story of yet another big water main break in Manhattan, this time on the east side. It happened during morning rush hour, turning streets into rivers, flooding the Midtown Tunnel, and bringing traffic to a standstill throughout much of the city. Harry had suffered through similar calamities during his years there and knew what a soggy hell things had to be right now. Ah, life in New York.

He took his time getting dressed. It seemed like the whole valley had gone into one long snooze lately. There were a few gun dealers he wanted to check on, then he'd go hang out in town, get his face further known, and see if he could bump into Kevin again. He hadn't felt this relaxed since—what? Fifth grade? Things would revert when Ellen returned that afternoon.

It was approaching 2 P.M. when he finally rolled up Main Street in Sutter Springs and parked in front of Ella's Luncheonette. Usually he got there after 12, but he was still in slow motion. He took a seat at a table near the door. Two minutes later, an older woman in a starched apron approached.

"You're late today, Harry. We're out of the special."

"My loss. Give me a roast beef sandwich instead."

She returned shortly and placed a platter in front of him.

"Hey," she said, "didn't you tell me you used to live in New York? Did you hear what happened?"

Harry chuckled. "Yeah."

"I tell you: the time I went there, you couldn't have paid me to get on one of those subways."

"Subways?"

"Yeah, didn't you hear? God! It's horrible to laugh, but they looked like they were in a horror flick or something. All screaming and bug-eyed and running around like maniacs. It was a fire or something in a tunnel. I don't think anybody was hurt, but it sure looked scary with all that smoke and stuff. Go over to Mackey's; they've got CNN news on the cable."

Harry felt his stomach tighten. Subway fires and electrical shorts weren't uncommon in New York, but he had never gone through that particular hell. He sure could imagine it, though.

"When was this, Ella?"

"An hour ago? Two? Chester dragged me over to see it, 'cause he said they looked so wacko. Crazy New Yorkers."

Just then, the door to the luncheonette flew open.

"Ella! Come quick! You're not gonna believe this!"

Harry bolted out of his seat and followed Ella and the man across the street to Mackey's bar. A big crowd was already there, standing in shocked silence as the TV blared above them.

"*. . . continuing live coverage from New York, here is Dan Charles.*"

"*What seemed an hour ago like a series of unfortunate events for the citizens of New York has evolved into a disaster of unbelievable proportions. Let's take you through the day.*"

The picture switched to a street in Manhattan, where a ruptured water main had caved in the roadway, sending a tremendous geyser of water skyward.

"*At 7:30 this morning, a water main burst under First Avenue near 42nd Street, opening a hole the size of a city bus and flooding the Midtown Tunnel.*

It took repair crews two hours to shut down the flow, and traffic in the area has been bottled up all day. A tough break, but one which New Yorkers have endured before. Then, this afternoon at about 3:30 . . ."

The scene changed to a subway station, thick with smoke. People were lurching in every direction, screaming, trying to find an exit. The camera zoomed into a tunnel, where escaping passengers were silhouetted against a backdrop of fire. Panic shot like lightning bolts off the screen.

"This was the Chambers Street station in Manhattan ninety minutes ago, just as rush hour was starting. The fire began either in the tunnel or on a # 6 train. The MTA hasn't been able to confirm anything yet, because they have been battling similar fires at three other location: Times Square; Grand Central; and 86th & Lex. Area hospitals are treating hundreds of people for smoke inhalation and injuries related to the exodus, but there have been no reported casualties. The same could not be said for traffic, however."

The view jumped to a street, where things were at an absolute standstill. Horns were blaring, people were climbing over cars, and fights had broken out.

"It could not have come at a worse time of day for commuters. All trains have been shut down, including the commuter lines. Gridlock has set in across the city and police speculate it could take hours to get things rolling again. Of course, that was before . . ."

The screen filled with an aerial shot of an oil tanker in full blaze.

"This happened an hour ago in New York harbor. A supertanker of Norwegian registry caught fire, apparently the result of an explosion on board, though we have been unable to confirm any details yet. All available fireboats were dispatched to the scene, as the danger to nearby storage facilities is extreme."

The picture changed to a close-up view of a raging fire, burning out of control. But when the camera pulled slowly back, revealing the scene, it was not the tanker.

Instantly, Harry knew he would remember this moment for the rest of his life.

"You are looking at a live shot of the United Nations building."

The camera panned across the area. The whole complex of buildings was ablaze—huge, savage flames crowned by roiling clouds of thick black smoke. It was a hellish scene.

"We have very little news to go on; things have been happening too fast. Eyewitnesses report a series of explosions striking the tower about thirty minutes ago, but there have been no confirmations whether it was rocket fire or mortars or what. The speed at which the complex was engulfed suggests some kind of accelerant, according to one source. As for the fire department, gridlock has blocked most crews from responding, and the water main break has limited the one nearby fire company to the water in its two tanker trucks. As just mentioned, all fireboats are on the Jersey side of the Hudson, trying to keep that oil tanker from destroying the waterfront there."

The picture switched to a close-up of the reporter, with a raging fire consuming the U.N. behind him.

"There seems to be little doubt that New York has been attacked by a terrorist group. Who? We don't know, though a caller to the U.N., in an Arab accent, gave the operator a one minute warning of the coming attack. That probably saved scores of lives, but the final total won't be known until long after the flames have cooled. Several people reported seeing men in black Ninja suits in the area at the time of the attack, but actual numbers cannot be confirmed. Speculation is that at least twenty commandos were involved."

Harry tuned the rest out. Nothing further would have surprised him and nothing would have consoled him. He found an empty stool and propped himself up on the bar.

A few minutes later, he felt the presence of someone sliding onto the stool next to him. He didn't bother to see who it was. Except for a handful of people, they could all go to hell.

"Man, those Arab terrorists. What will they think of next?"

Harry turned to look at the speaker. It was that misfit they'd seen after the town meeting a few weeks back. The guy didn't seem overly moved by what had just rolled across the screen, and that pissed Harry off all the more.

"Can you believe what's happening lately?" Barnett said.

Harry sighed heavily. "Yes."

"Burning down the U.N.? I mean, that really takes balls."

Harry glared at him. "What's your point?"

"Well, nothing, just . . . Oh, look. Here comes Gordo!"

Harry glanced at the TV screen, where a press conference was underway. "Gordo" was the unfortunate nickname for the President of the United States, but Gordon Carroll seemed to have risen above it all his life. In contrast to the name, he was slim and handsome, the most charismatic president since JFK. At the moment, however, he was raging.

". . . and I assure you that terrorism in any form will not be tolerated. That's why I am asking Congress to redouble their efforts to pass that new anti-terrorism legislation this session. We cannot handcuff ourselves any longer. We need to give our agencies a law with real teeth. This type of threat, whether from outside or within, undermines the basic fabric of our existence. And to strike at the U.N. is a particularly heinous crime. We are a peace-loving people, but I know you will support me in our efforts to bring these villains to justice, through whatever means necessary . . ."

"Through whatever means necessary?" Barnett said. "That's scary. Much as I love the Prez, and while I deplore what just happened, you gotta worry about our civil liberties."

Harry's head snapped around. "Fuck you. Where's your sense of outrage?"

Barnett gave him a half smile. "Sorry if I offended you. Maybe we all just 'process' differently. So how about if we change the subject? My name's Barnett, by the way. I was wondering what became of your daughter."

Harry felt that urge rise up to smash the guy in the face. At certain times, it seemed like that was the only way to get through to people. It was a trait that went back to his childhood. He hadn't actually lashed out since he was a kid, but the feeling still came up occasionally. He stretched his fingers out instead and drummed them on the bar.

"You've got to learn about timing, man," Harry said.

They both fell into silence. The bartender, a different one than usual, came by with a round of beer, but Harry couldn't drink. He just sat there, numb to the world.

Suddenly, the front door swung open and a voice burst into the bar.

"Ah, the highway is my home!" Ellen called out. Her tone changed as she walked into the bar. "Geez, what happened? Did somebody's aunt die?"

Harry pointed at the TV screen. "Look."

He gave her a rundown of the attack on New York, accompanied by the images from the news report. As he finished up, he realized the misfit had vanished. Harry described that exchange as well. When he mentioned the name "Barnett," Ellen's eyes did pinwheels.

"That sounds so familiar," she said. "I know I've heard that name before. Meanwhile, what do you think of my new accessory?"

She waved her left arm in the air. It was free of any bandages. "Windsurfing here I come! And, God, is it nice to have my own set of wheels again. They gave me a brand-new Jeep."

Harry was going to ask her about the supplies he needed, courtesy of electronics whiz Sonia Taylor, but the FBI's emblem suddenly flashed on the TV. A moment later, the face of Warren Keller, Acting Director of the FBI, filled the screen.

"At the instruction of the President, we are instituting new controls to help us prevent any more incidents of terrorist violence. As of this moment, security at all airports will be . . ."

It seemed to go on forever. Keller may have made some significant statements, and civil libertarians were probably horrified at the prospects. But Harry heard none of it. Amid the faces visible behind the Acting Director of the FBI was one that Harry hoped never to see again, especially at such a critical time and place:

Brendan Crowley.

Pay Dirt

The compound was buzzing. Four days had passed since the assault on New York and people were still charging around in a state of near-euphoria. Nobody talked about it openly, but grins and "high fives" were everywhere, even from Barnett. He had never been part of a team before, so this was a new and heady experience. It was as if they'd won the Super Bowl and the World Series on the same day, only no championship ring could match the prize they had claimed.

Even better, the Authorities were out looking for anyone with a dark complexion, certain that some Arab faction was responsible. The bozos seemed undeterred by vehement protests from every known Middle East group, and the media frenzy just fueled public hysteria all the more. Conspiracy theories were rampant, including one posed by several patriot groups that the burning of the U.N. was really the work of Mossad agents from Israel, who were trying to win even more sympathy and support from their puppet, the U.S. government. People in the compound howled every time the news came on.

With one exception: the Commander. Barnett had seen him smile twice in the past three days, otherwise the man just scowled. The FBI and ATF were stepping up surveillance on domestic groups, beyond what had been brewing after the theft of that ATF truck, and the Big Guy was worried that it might spill over onto them as well. He asked Barnett that morning to see if they could monitor internal communications within the FBI, in case an assault on the compound was planned. As if Barnett didn't have enough—

The door flew open and the Commander walked in.

"So much for stealth," Barnett said.

"Your computers are here, plus those other gizmos you ordered. This better be good, 'cause that's a heap of money sitting downstairs."

"Wait a minute. Who is financing this operation, you or me? Have I asked you to kick in even two cents?"

"It's a paper trail. A delivery like that could raise suspicions, and ZOG is probably parked just outside waiting for us to sneeze. We've got to be cleaner than clean." The Commander's tone was that chilling, accusatory one which always made Barnett's stomach tighten.

"We're only talking about a dozen laptops," Barnett said, "plus those special modems."

The Commander shrugged. "I just don't want to call attention to what we're doing. Those phone lines you had put in last week? That's got me real nervous. I thought you said you didn't need a phone for these things."

"Not for the laptops, but I need a line for our BBS to handle inbound calls. I also need one for 'social engineering'; I'm not sharing your house line. Besides, they can't come storming in just because we're online."

"Maybe they want to see what we're up to; they invent all kinds of excuses to do that. Storm in, rough you up, cart off your goods, and later dump the shit back on your doorstep without so much as an apology. And if they find you here—if they find out who you are—you'll go back in the pen and I'll be dragged along as an accomplice. Got the picture?"

Barnett gave him a salute. "Loud and clear."

"What about that two million I need? Got it yet?"

"Like I've been sitting here picking my nose?"

"Just answer the question!" The Commander scowled and tossed a slip of paper at Barnett. "Put it in that account. Today."

They glared at each other, then the Commander went on, his voice modulated. "Are those computers gonna be ready in time? I'm making the calls tonight."

Barnett's eyes widened. "You said a week, and that was two days ago. Will they come on such short notice? How do you know they'll come at all?"

"I've already put them on alert; they'd come right now if I insisted. I have what you might call 'pull' with these guys." He dragged a chair to the window and sat down. "They're all freaking out over ZOG's heavy breathing. Most think there'll be an assault any day now. It's their own damn fault for being so conspicuous."

"And they'll listen to you? They'll accept you—us—as their leader?"

The Commander smiled. "They have no choice. I've got the goods on all of them. I can make 'em or break 'em—" He snapped his fingers. "—like that!"

The man was truly scary sometimes. Barnett rubbed his face to get rid of the momentary jolt. Then he said, "So listen, I'm desperate. Any chance you can get someone to help me set up these laptops? I've got a shit-load of stuff to do online and the last thing I need is to be doing manual labor."

"You've got a short memory. Those background checks you just ran? Well, we'll see tonight." The Commander turned and headed toward the door.

"Hold on," Barnett said. "We've got to talk about the President. I'm afraid we might miss him. It's one guy, easy for a huge contingent of Secret Service to protect, and there's no guarantee that our bait for Congress will draw him in as well. Besides, he's got helicopters, underground bunkers, and who knows what else. We need something foolproof."

"You're asking me? You told me you were the brains in this outfit." The Commander leaned against the door frame and crossed his arms. "What about the Vice President?"

"If I can get the President, the VP should be a snap."

"Then find an opening. It shouldn't be hard for a 'genius' like you."

Harry couldn't stop himself from humming as he drove along the single-lane road to the Commander's compound. The dust kicking up around their truck in the evening's fading glow had a particularly sweet taste: pay dirt! It was funny how often a major case broke open thanks to an unexpected source. Who cared if it took a convicted hacker jumping parole to give them access to the Commander's lair, as long as they got in.

Ellen, sitting next to him, was justifiably jazzed. She was the one who ID'ed Barnett. Now, she wanted to confirm that the misfit really was superhacker Jeff Barnett, not an imposter or a weird twist of fate, before they advised Morton and called in the troops.

They were bumping their way toward an appointment with the Commander and, if Kevin could be believed, Barnett. The young hulk was crowded in on the other side of Ellen, yammering away as usual.

"You're pulling my leg, she-devil," he said. "I waited in Mackey's the whole day yesterday and you never once walked in. If I hadn't seen Harry there last night, we wouldn't be taking this ride right now. So where have you been?"

Ellen poked him in the ribs. "You were gone for three or four days. Or were you just sitting on a rock, baying at the moon?"

Kevin threw his head back and gave a long howl.

Oh, how Harry wanted this to be over. Not just the ride, but the whole case. There were too many mysteries, too many questions which couldn't be answered until they tore the compound apart. Were the ATF weapons there? That was possible, since militia groups often shared their wealth. And Harry had confirmed that Pilkin was indeed a gun dealer, so the man was a likely conduit. Did these guys know anything about the raid on New York? How about the attack on the Director, or the killing of the

Deputy Director?

Answers were there somewhere. All they needed was an airtight pretext to separate the dwellers from their compound, and Harry could comb through the place in painstaking detail. At this point, harboring a fugitive was good enough.

Harry looked in his rearview mirror and realized they had another problem, a big one. A brigade of motorcycles had appeared out of nowhere and was swarming in the dust behind them. As armed as these guys were, and as nervous as they seemed about intruders, it was going to take more than a couple of agents or even a SWAT team to roust them out. The Army's Delta Force was more like it. Otherwise, this might be Waco, Part 2.

The convoy rolled up to the imposing, fortified gate and was ordered to stop. Once again, Harry and Ellen were subjected to a thorough search. And since they arrived in their truck this time, the vehicle got a once-over worthy of the FBI. Expecting this, they had come unarmed and unplugged.

Cleared to go in, they continued on to the main building. Harry drove up to the front steps, while the fleet of motorcycles formed a ring around their truck. Harry got out and looked at the circle of faceless henchmen.

God, don't let us screw up.

They started up the steps, with Kevin in the lead. It was just getting dark out, but every light in the house seemed to be blazing already.

As they walked in the door, the scent of the place hit him: a smell of wood that took Harry back to a cabin he'd known in his youth; lingering whiffs from a fireplace; plus whatever it was that leather exuded. Looking around, the furnishings fit both the smells and the man. For a rancher, it couldn't get any better than this.

It certainly didn't seem like a place where weapons of war might be stashed. But there were fourteen other buildings in the compound, according to Kevin, and there might well be tunnels, subcellars, treetop caches, and so on.

They hadn't advanced past the entry way. Kevin, in fact, seemed to be at attention. A minute later, staccato raps on the wooden floor announced the Commander's arrival. He came around a corner, jerked his head toward the door, and Kevin departed without a word. The Commander extended his hand.

"Ellen, right? And Harry? Nice to meet you. Why don't we sit in here for a minute." He led the way to an expansive living room and settled into a heavy leather chair.

"So I understand you folks want to get involved in our community. Is that correct?"

Harry studied the huge stone fireplace for a moment, then said, "Kevin seemed to think we might have something to talk about."

The Commander nodded. "Said the same thing to me. Gotta wonder what goes on in that boy's head sometimes. Any idea what he meant?"

Harry studied the Commander's face. "I suspect it has to do with what's happening in the world today."

The Commander turned to Ellen. "What about you?"

She shrugged, but didn't answer.

"Well, I guess it's no secret that we're concerned citizens," the Commander said. "You think the guns are a tip-off? And we're trying to fill out our team. I hear you know something about electronics, Chandler."

Harry nodded.

"And you, Miss—" The Commander turned to Ellen. "—are supposed to be a computer nerd. Tell me, is that a coincidence?"

Harry didn't react. Neither did Ellen.

"Cause if I didn't know better, I'd say you were tapping my phones. You wouldn't do something like that, would you?" The Commander's face broke into a smile. "Wouldn't make no difference. We've got a dandy little sweeper to keep the world honest. Hey, you want something to drink?"

He got up and walked to the hall. "Bets! Bring us some beer."

The Commander sat back down. He looked first at Harry, then at Ellen. "As I was saying, we're trying to fill out our team. I've got a guy who can handle electronics, I'm afraid, but a computer nerd might just come in handy. Have you got some qualifications, Miss?"

"You're offering me a job?" Ellen said. "What does it pay?"

That obviously surprised the Commander, because he seemed to struggle for an answer. Finally, Harry spoke up: "Freedom."

The Commander smiled broadly. "Yeah, exactly. Freedom! For us all. And believe me, sweetheart—" He leaned toward her. "—you want to be on this team."

At that moment, a woman appeared. Even with an apron and a few signs of age, she was impressive-looking, like seeing the Mona Lisa with a tray of Bud and beer nuts. What was unsettling was the way her eyes were burning into Harry's. She stopped in the door-way to give him a big smile. Then she glanced at Ellen and the smile faded. She continued into the room and began setting out glasses, not looking at anyone.

"This is my wife, Betsy," the Commander said. "Bets, this is Harry Chandler and his daughter, Ellen."

The woman's focus stayed down on the table, but the smile returned. "You folks new around here or just passing through?"

"We might stay," Harry replied.

She straightened up, stretching her spine slowly, and then started out of the room. "See you around then?" she said. At the doorway, she looked back at Harry and smiled.

"Bets, wait!" the Commander said. "Go get Barnett." The woman spun around and started up the stairs.

"A fine woman," the Commander said, "but I'm not sure ranch life is her real calling. You're either born to it or you're not. So tell me, where are you guys from?"

Harry started into the story of their "life" in New York, giving just enough hints of questionable activities to pique the Commander's curiosity, when Barnett came rattling down the stairs.

The Commander turned to him. "Son, when I ask you to come down here, I expect—"

Barnett blew right by him and went straight toward Ellen. "Good to see you again. You, too, Harry. Are you guys joining the team?"

"Excuse us a minute," the Commander said. He grabbed Barnett's arm and led him out of the room. When they returned, the younger man's enthusiasm was knocked down considerably.

"Yo, Ellen. Let's go upstairs," Barnett said.

"And do what?"

"Nothing funny. Let's just see what your fingers can do." He mimed a rapid-fire assault on a keyboard.

Ellen looked at Harry and growled, "Don't go anywhere." Then she followed Barnett out of the room.

"Man, that daughter of yours is a piece of work," the Commander said. "I'd a throttled her by now if she was mine."

Harry laughed. "It's crossed my mind. Got any kids?"

The Commander's face tightened. "One."

There was an awkward pause, then the Commander grinned.

"So I understand you were in the Special Forces."

Harry's eyes narrowed. "Intelligence. '67 to'69. Where did you hear 'Special Forces'?"

"Kevin." The Commander searched Harry's face. "I'm glad you gave me the correct answer. We ran a background check on you and your daughter." He chuckled. "Even the Secret Service isn't as good."

"That's an invasion of privacy."

"True, but you never would've gotten up here without it."

"Well who said I wanted—"

"Hold on. Didn't mean to piss you off. You passed with flying colors anyway, so what's the harm? You'll have to tell me some day about your electronics 'business.'" A wicked smile crossed his face.

Harry let his apparent anger simmer, so the Commander switched the subject back to Vietnam. And as stories went back and forth, an understanding seemed to develop between them. It wasn't a bond, but Harry knew something of what fueled the man's anger.

He also saw an opening to work the Commander a little. He reached into his pocket to make sure he had a ballpoint pen with him, then leaned forward, frowning.

"Let me ask you about your 'electronics' measures, George. You mentioned phone taps and sweeps and all. Have you been having problems?"

The Commander's eyes narrowed. "Not that I know of. We sweep this place every week. Why?"

"What about other countermeasures? Is this room clean?"

"What's your point?"

"Well, electronic eavesdropping is changing so fast, it's almost impossible to keep up. I'm in the business, and I'm still surprised at what people are cooking up. There's a new radar detector you can buy for your car, not expensive, and with a little work it becomes an audio transmitter, with a range up to a mile, that's impossible to detect using even the best spectrum analyzer."

The Commander shrugged. "I've got more than a mile radius under tight control."

Harry turned to look at a large window on the far wall. "What about optical audio transmissions? Can you protect against infrared laser beams pulling from that window?"

"We put Betsy's vibrator against it. Next?"

"Satellite coverage? Ceramic transmitters? The NSA has got birds all over the sky. They can tell if you're whispering from a thousand miles up."

"Are you trying to sell me something?"

"Yeah, security. It's obvious you've got something brewing, and I'd like to help you make sure it happens. Then maybe you can help me settle a few scores."

The Commander stared at him. "Why are you here? What do you know about me?"

"Only what you've told me just now. Call it luck or fate or—"

Harry chuckled. "—call it 'Kevin.' Anyway, what I want to do in this world, and to this world, I can do alone eventually. But working together, maybe we can both hit our marks faster. Depends, of course, on what you're after." Harry pulled out the ballpoint pen and started clicking it.

"Give me that," the Commander said. It took him ten seconds to disassemble the pen, examine the parts, and put it together again. He handed it back to Harry and said, "So what are you after?"

Harry smiled. "Do you mind if I do a little check first? I'm sure the place is clean, but this is my business, after all."

He got up and started walking slowly around the room, scanning the usual spots—window frames, flower pots, and so on—for listening devices. It was all show; he knew enough to get himself in trouble, that was all.

The coffee table was next, and this was where Harry planned to make his score. He knelt down and began running his hand under the front edge, praying no kid had stuck gum there.

"Those new NSA toys are wild," he said. "They have these ceramic coils that are like neutron bombs. They go through anything and are almost totally undetectable, unless you actually see the coil, or until the Feds come knocking at your door."

He finished his first pass, and was about to go deeper under the table. That would give him time to take apart the pen and remove the coil-like spring inside, just to bait the man. But first, he swept his hand once more in a wide arc.

And he stopped.

There *was* a coil!

He was so stunned he didn't have a chance to cover his reaction. And he knew the Commander was staring at him. He ran his fingers over it again, and there was no mistaking what he discovered. Damn!

He thought he'd been bullshitting the Commander, feeding pieces of jargon he'd read in a memo last month. As best Harry could remember, this stuff wasn't field tested yet, wasn't supposed to be activated until next year.

What was it doing here? And whose was it?

He looked up. The Commander's eyes were as big as Harry's. There was no need to signal for him to be silent. And there was no chance to save the bug. Harry reached under and pried it off. It really was like he had described.

The Commander's face was burning now. He looked at Harry and mouthed the words, "Look around," then stormed out of the room. A moment later his voice bellowed, "Betsy!!"

Harry was still on his knees, lost. Morton had said nothing about other investigations in this region. True, there had been those goons at the town meeting a couple weeks back, but the place had been conspicuously quiet since then. If someone was operating in the area, they were disguised as trees. Another militia group? No, this device was too sophisticated. It was a federal group of some denomination. But who?

One thing was clear: they had to postpone the raid. Something was seriously wrong and he had to alert Morton.

But Harry ran out of time.

One Chance

The room itself was unassuming. Western theme, heavy wooden furniture, throw rug on the floor. But the moment Ellen walked into Barnett's room, she knew they had to change their plans. Not that this wasn't the person they were looking for. How many guys named "Jeff Barnett" just happened to resemble the outlaw hacker in every detail and had a new laptop, surrounded by stacks of printouts? It was those stacks of paper, and the overwhelming air of enterprise in the room, which made her uneasy. Anywhere else, Ellen would pass it off as white collar crime in the making. But in the center of a heavily fortified compound?

She had to kill time anyway, for appearance sake, but her plan to string Barnett along suddenly had new purpose: Why was he there? That question had been lost in all the militia activity they'd seen, but it came roaring back now. The guy had brought his diabolical skills to a deadly new playground.

Ellen scanned the room. "Fabulous digs," she said, "though you don't strike me as the knotty-pine type. Love the filing system for your clothes." She swung her foot out and pushed away one of the piles of discards.

"It's better than my last place." Barnett's voice dropped. "I don't plan to be here long. Then it's Viva Las Vegas!"

Ellen gave him a sour look and walked over to the laptop. "What are you doing with this? Plotting to take over the world?"

Barnett laughed. "Close. Close."

The window caught her eye, and she strolled over to survey

the scene. Barnett's room was on the second floor with a view out to one side. Even from there, through dark shadows, she could see men moving about, each one armed with a serious piece of weaponry. Taking control of this place was not going to be easy.

"Your friends have a thing about guns," she said. "Where's yours?"

Barnett smirked. "I've got a better weapon than that."

She nodded at the laptop. "If this is your weapon, I think I'd take one of theirs in a close fight."

"The trick is to not be anywhere near when the guns go off."

She gestured toward the stack of laptops against the wall. "One is not enough? Oh, I get it, you're supposed to be these guys' computer tutor." She gave him a nasty laugh. "Nice gig."

"Okay, Hot Shit. Your rap sheet says you did time for—"

"What do you know about me?" she said.

"Chapter and verse. Want to quiz me? Breaking and entering, real and electronic; theft of phone company manuals; cellular fraud. Small time, but impressive."

"Oh, like you're big-time or something?"

Barnett grinned. "Or something. So what do you know?"

"What don't I know?"

"Can you change boards?"

"Check."

"Write code?"

"Check."

"Phreak? Crack?"

Bingo!

Ellen smiled slowly. "What did you have in mind?"

Barnett smiled back. "Easy or hard?"

"Whatever."

"Can you run a tap? On, say, the FBI's phones?"

Ellen's eyes widened. "Adventurous. For real?"

Barnett gave her a coy little shrug. "What about info tracking? On people, specifically: credit histories; bank records; travel schedules; etcetera."

"Why?"

"Amusement. Wouldn't you love to be the first to know that, say, the President was secretly a cross-dresser or something? Like maybe he puts on one of the First Lady's nighties before heading off to the Oval Office?"

Are they targeting the President?

Ellen shook her head, as much to clear it as anything else. "You're a scream," she said. "So why am I really here?"

"I need help. You got something better to do? You don't strike me as the cowgirl type, though I've been wrong twice in my life. Don't make it three."

"What's it worth?"

Barnett smiled slowly. "Whatever you want. $5000 a week?"

"Ten."

"God, ask for a hundred! Money pales compared to the chance to work with me."

Ellen looked at him warily. "So I've got to audition for you?"

"Just show me something. Be creative."

She walked over to the table and sat down, taking her time as she tried to figure out what to do. "Okay," she said finally, "but go sit over there. I don't want you looking over my shoulder."

"Come on, there's nothing you could teach me. Don't you know who I am? The name 'Barnett' doesn't mean anything to you?"

"Oh, yeah. I thought you were in jail. Well, stay back anyway. I don't want your hot breath on me."

She tapped the keys lightly, as if warming up her fingers. And then it hit her. Talk about audacious! It was risky showing this to Barnett, but since he would be back in prison soon, what was the harm? She looked up from the screen and gave Barnett a huge smile. Then she started bashing away on the keys.

Her fascination with computers was mild. Beasts more vicious than the Barnetts of the world demanded her professional attention, but she had a core of friends outside of work who were real tech-heads, and she had become buddies with several of the system operators inside the Bureau, bugging them for favors and special access when she could.

And if the sysops found out what she was doing now, they'd yank her special privileges so fast. She wasn't going to change anything, but she needed to move around freely, to make it look like she had actually hacked her way into the FBI's personnel files.

She whistled merrily as she dialed in and worked her way through the various Bureau databases. Some of what she did was just filler; she wanted Barnett to think it was taking her longer than it actually was. That gave her an opening.

"So why do you want to know about the President?" she said. "The guy's the most squeaky-clean person on the planet. He almost makes politicians seem respectable."

"That's the point. Nobody can be that wholesome. Just imagine what the tabloids would pay for some dirt on him."

"Hey, did anybody come up with something negative about him in the last election? No, and they sure would've used it if they had." She looked up again and said, "One more minute." She couldn't believe she was doing this. Then she waved Barnett over and said, "Voila!"

Barnett smiled slowly, broadly. "Very nice. Care to share that?"

Ellen returned the smile. "You keep your secrets, I'll keep mine. But watch this."

She brought up a new screen and started filling in information, chuckling as she did so. "I've created an identity for myself in their database: 'Special Agent Ellen King.' Like it? Right here, I'm ordering new credentials and a new badge. 'Reason'? Oh, let's say they got lost in a gun battle." She cruised through the rest of the form and specified that the items should be shipped to a special address, the cabin she and Harry had just rented nearby. "Think that might come in handy?"

Barnett smiled. "What rock did you crawl out from under?"

"The same one as you, Jeffy-boy. The same one as you."

Ellen exited quickly from the FBI files, before Barnett could push for further explorations. And since she seemed to be in control at the moment, she decided to take things a little further.

Without asking, and without really thinking about a warrant to do this, she began trolling through Barnett's computer. There had to be directories or files which would explain the connection between hacker and militia. Ellen's fingers were going so fast, with windows flashing on and off the screen, that Barnett was either mesmerized or didn't care what she found.

Then she hit a directory labeled "NYC," and Barnett suddenly snapped down the screen of the laptop. He gave her a thin smile.

"Like you said, you keep your secrets and I'll keep mine."

She wanted that machine; right now! If she walked away without it, whatever was lurking there would be vaporized an instant later. Forget about other incriminating evidence on it; Barnett's skipping parole was enough to put him away again. But that directory had to hold the link to the militia.

NYC? No, it couldn't be.

Suddenly, there were shouts from below. A moment later, the lights went out, plunging the whole compound into darkness. An eerie silence settled in, for all of about ten seconds, and then it seemed like the world exploded.

There was a huge flash of light outside and a tremendous bang. Automatic weapons fire erupted from every direction. A helicopter—two? more?—roared in, hovering just overhead, the battering pulse of the blades threatening to crush them by sound alone. It was like being in the middle of a war zone.

Ellen started toward the window, but wheeled around when she heard steps pounding on the stairs outside Barnett's room. She lunged for the door, but it flew open in front of her, and the Commander burst into the room.

"Grab your gear and follow me!" He rushed over to the stack

of laptops, lifted most of them, and lumbered out.

Barnett yanked the cables to his laptop out of their sockets and began jamming papers in a bag. He turned and shouted, "Ellen, get those other laptops, plus that box next to them!"

Ellen's heart was pounding. Should she blow her cover and grab Barnett's laptop? It would never hold up in court. But what was going on?! Who was out there? She was momentarily paralyzed.

Then she grabbed the laptops, plus Barnett's box, and carried the lot out of the room. She didn't know what was going on outside, but it didn't matter. The house could disintegrate around her, but she was not letting Barnett's laptop out of her sight.

The Commander was crouched down at the end of a long hallway. "There's a secret door here." He rapped on the baseboard, and a small door swung open. "Slide those things in first, then go down after them."

"What's going on?" Ellen said.

"We're under attack. It's ZOG! I've gotta get back downstairs. Make sure Barnett gets in here. We'll collect you later."

The Commander ran down the hall and disappeared. Ellen shoved the laptops and the box down the chute, then turned to get Barnett.

He was just coming out of the room, his arms loaded, when a window halfway between them shattered. A man in full body armor came flying into the hall. Barnett screamed and the man spun toward him.

Ellen didn't hesitate. She dove for the man's knees and knocked him to the floor. She was grabbing at his belt, trying to find a weapon, but he rotated sharply and slammed her into the wall. She managed to keep a grip on his belt and finally yanked something free—a large flashlight.

The man leapt at her, and Ellen barely had time to bring her knees up in front of her. That created just enough of a delay to allow her to drive the flashlight into the man's face. It connected with something solid. Night-vision goggles!

She reached up and grabbed the goggles, then kicked out with both feet to knock the man backwards. The goggles came off in her hand. She jumped to her feet, fumbling with a switch on the flashlight—where was the 'Normal' beam?—and then leveled it in the man's eyes from six inches away.

The attacker screamed and rolled onto his stomach, clutching at his eyes. This was it, Ellen's one chance to get Barnett away safely. She took a deep breath—*You have to do this, El!*—and clubbed the man with the flashlight. His body went limp.

"Come on!" she shouted at Barnett. Together, they dragged the man to the window, hoisted him up, and pushed him out. She said a silent prayer that the guy would survive a two-story fall—and somehow dodge the hail of bullets still raging outside.

Barnett was shaking, frozen in place. Ellen grabbed his arm and pulled him to the pile of equipment and papers he had dropped.

"Gather this shit, fast! We've got to hide."

She picked up Barnett's laptop and ran down the hall.

Harry pulled back from the window, just before a barrage of weapons fire strafed the darkened room. Who was it? It had to be "family" out there, but which agency? And why? And why the fuck didn't anybody tell him this was coming? If he hadn't been so scared, he would have been furious.

He had just found a second ceramic coil in the Commander's study when the lights went out. Moments later, a huge explosion went off, and the force of it blew out the windows in the room. The only thing that saved him from being shredded by glass was that he had been on his hands and knees, wedged between a couch and a chair. Then, the air filled with weapons fire and choppers like he hadn't heard since Nam.

Going to the window was suicidal, but Harry had a mission:

get rid of the ceramic coils. Something this new and exotic was probably important to whoever planted it—and who launched this fucking raid without warning him or Ellen. So if the assholes wanted their toys back, they'd have some explaining to do first. The coils were Harry's one bit of leverage and he was in no mood to be charitable, even if Morton himself came looking for them. He waited until there seemed to be a lull in the shooting, then tossed the coils out the window. No one would expect to find them there.

He made it back along the wall, staying low, until he reached the living room. He got about six feet into the room, and something leveled him from behind.

When Harry came to, he was sprawled out in the living room. All the lights were on and the gunfire had stopped. He was hand-cuffed, and a vicious-looking young man in riot gear stood over him, face streaked in black. The guy was patting Harry down, carefully, so it wasn't a gun the guy was looking for.

"What's up, buttercup? Have a nice snooze?" The man chuck-led crudely and poked Harry's side with the toe of his boot. "Hey, Jimmy, come over here. Is this the one?"

Another storm trooper walked over and looked down at Harry. "Yeah, that's the one. Greetings, Gramps, from an old friend of yours."

Harry said the name in sync with the man: "Brendan Crowley." It figured. He didn't know how, but it figured.

He got up and dropped on the couch, shaking pieces of glass off his shirt. He hadn't checked to see if he was actually bleeding; he was too wired to care. This was a critical moment: to step across the line and join the other Feds, or try to hold his cover? He didn't really have a choice; he had to maintain the cover. Ellen's life could be in danger, and he wouldn't risk that. Besides, he had no faith that these goons had accomplished anything here, except to make the Commander even more wary than before.

Of course, it was academic if the goons blew his cover for him. They nearly did a moment ago, but the only other person in the room who wasn't from the invading force was Betsy, the Commander's wife. She was across the room, balled up in a chair and shooting daggers at the agent named "Jimmy."

It was strange: she was glaring just at him, with an intensity that pricked at Harry's follicles even from across the room.

Four other goons milled about, dressed in black, with probably dozens more outside. It was bizarre, and unsettling, to be on the other side for once.

Voices came from the stairs, and then the Commander appeared, followed by three more goons. His face was granite—solid, gray, and unmovable. "I'm telling you, that's all the people I've got. Get a thermal scanner if you like. It's just me and Bets and Harry here in the house."

Jimmy-the-goon swaggered over to the Commander. "I thought you guys always said: 'When they come to get my guns, they'll have to pry my cold dead fingers off the trigger.' What happened? Chickened out at the crucial moment? Your guys just stood there."

The Commander glared at him. "Why were you firing?"

"Well, somebody was firing at us. You want to explain that?"

"Unmanned turrets, firing blanks."

The goon gave him a big smile. "Well, ours were just warning rounds, to make sure nobody tried anything. Don't worry, none of your boys are dead." He looked at the other goons and snickered. "Of course, a few of them are going to have some mean headaches for a while, and a bunch of those guys on motorcycles aren't gonna feel much like talking, but mostly they'll all just need a change of underwear. It's not too pretty."

The rest of the goons broke out laughing. The Commander looked over at Harry and shook his head. Just then, several more black-garbed aliens burst through the front door.

"Where's Pilkin?" the one in front asked. He was pointed toward the Commander. "Special Agent Murdow," he said, flashing his badge. "Would you like to show us where your other weapons are stashed or shall we search for them ourselves? I can't vouch for the tidiness of my boys."

"The only weapons we have are the ones in our hands," the Commander replied. "All legal, all registered with ZOG."

"Suit yourself," Murdow said. "Do you want to stay here or come along?" He walked out, trailed by his crew. The Commander waited a moment, then followed behind, looking stronger and more fierce than ever.

Harry closed his eyes, trying to make the bullshit go away. He heard people walking out, others talking low, but nothing was really worth listening to. He didn't know what had become of Ellen or Barnett, but at this point he had to hope for the best.

That calm moment didn't last. The first goon, who so cheerfully greeted his recovery, kicked him. Not hard, just enough to piss Harry off. He bolted up, but the man pushed him back on the couch. Harry noticed that they were alone.

"What's going on?" Harry said. "You guys could've killed us."

The goon sneered at him. "We're professionals, Grandpa. You weren't at risk. And now if you'd tell me where the coil is."

Harry stared at him. "The what?"

"You heard me."

"A coil?" He raised his brows in mock surprise. "What's that?"

The goon leaned in close, his breath hot. "You can help me, or you can sink yourself all the more. Your choice."

When Harry didn't answer, the man shouted, "Jimmy, I'll check the study, you look in here."

A moment later, Jimmy-the-goon came tromping into the living room whistling something inane. He looked at Harry and smiled. "So, the old guy doesn't want to help the good guys, huh? Fine by me, and Mister C."

He got down on his knees, searching for the ceramic coil, whistling again. Harry felt like kicking a table at the guy. The only consolation was that the goon was being painstakingly thorough in his search, and Harry knew he'd never find it.

There was a movement, very small, at the entrance to the living room. Harry glanced up to see Betsy, her head peeking around the corner and her finger over her mouth. This did not read right, but Harry was spellbound.

She crept forward slowly, silently, her hands behind her and her eyes riveted on Jimmy's back. When she got close, she brought her right hand forward, raising a long carving knife above her head.

"Bastard!" she shouted, and lunged for the goon.

Harry dove across the coffee table, intending to intercept the knife despite his cuffed hands. But the goon was turning around with a gun. Harry pitched onto his side, rolled into the goon, and knocked the man's aim away from the woman. They barely got out of the path of the blade.

Betsy raised the knife again, shouting "Bastard!" with even greater fury. Her arm started down—and was kicked back by Harry's foot. The knife went flying across the room.

"Bastard," Betsy moaned, and collapsed on the floor. Harry helped her up, with what vestiges of energy he had left, and led her to the couch. She dissolved in tears.

The goon picked up his gun and started toward her, but Harry stopped him. "Get out of here," he said.

The man glared at him, then looked over at Betsy. He smirked and blew her a kiss, collected the carving knife, and walked out of the room.

Betsy glanced up at Harry, her eyes desperate, her voice barely audible. "Don't tell the Commander," she said. "Please don't tell him."

Harry nodded and lowered himself into a chair. He had nothing left.

Five hours later, it was all over. The cuffs were removed, a few guns were confiscated, and five guys were taken away on outstanding felony warrants. But from the fuming looks of the departing force, the goons never found what they were looking for. So, except for damage to the buildings, and a lot of frayed nerves, it was almost as if nothing had happened.

It was after 4 A.M. when the Commander saw the last of his men off at the door. He walked slowly into the living room and dropped into the chair next to Harry. Slowly, the granite facade began to ease.

"I saw your truck," he said. "It's got some new ventilation."

Harry laughed. "Thanks, I needed that."

There was a long silence. Finally, Harry looked over and said, "Why did you do it, George? Why did you call off the guns?"

"Because . . ." The Commander tilted his head back and closed his eyes. "Because this wasn't our fight. I didn't want to jeopardize what's coming up. That's why no one breathes a word of this to the media either." He opened his eyes and looked at Harry. "But when it's over, I want to get those guys. Are you in?"

Harry forced a smile.

The Commander suddenly jumped to his feet. "Oh, shit! I just remembered." He dashed out of the room.

A minute later, he returned, followed by Ellen and Barnett, who was clutching his laptop like it was a security blanket. Ellen looked rattled, but Barnett was off the charts.

"You should've seen her. She was amazing! The way she nailed that guy, blinded him, *and then threw him out the fucking window!* It was awesome! You should call her 'Rambo' from now on."

The Commander turned around and looked at her. "Is that true? Where did you learn to fight like that?"

Ellen shrugged. "I'm a military brat. Ask him." She tilted her head toward Harry.

"'Rambo,'" the militia leader said. He turned to Harry. "And I should call you 'Sweep.' Well, you're both welcome to join us if you want. We could use you."

Harry nodded at Ellen. No turning back now.

* * *

It was nearly dawn when they finally pulled up in front of the cabin. Neither had spoken the whole way. The A-frame structure loomed large, an ominous black shape silhouetted against the first hints of light. The stand of tall pines around the cabin looked more like huge steel bars than trees.

Harry unlocked the door and held it open. Ellen stumbled past, started to reach for the light switch, but then stopped. "Let's leave 'em off, okay? I can't make it further than the couch."

Harry bolted the door behind him and headed in the direction of the kitchen. It was habit more than anything else. There had to be something in there to—

He froze. Someone was coming toward him in the dark. It was impossible to see who. Harry's gun was somewhere in the cabin, but it wasn't on his body. Twice in one night he needed it and he was unarmed.

"Don't move," a man's voice said. It was low and threatening. Somewhere behind Harry, Ellen let out a small scream.

A flashlight clicked on, ten feet away. It surveyed Harry first, then Ellen, then went off again. "Are you guys alone?" the man asked.

Harry found his voice and said, "Yes."

"Were you followed?"

Ellen groaned. "Who knows? Who cares? And who the hell are you?"

The flashlight briefly illuminated the man's face.

It was Morton!

"Sorry about that," he said, "but I'm not taking any chances. Find a seat, Harry. We'll leave the lights off."

"What's going on?" Ellen asked.

"I thought you guys could answer that," Morton replied. "All I've got are questions, and you're not going to like them. For starters: Did you guys have anything to do with that raid?"

"What?!" Harry and Ellen said it in unison.

"Who was it?" Morton said. "The Hostage Rescue Team?

What were they after? How—"

"Hold on!" Harry said. "We're the ones with the goddamned bruises. That was HRT? It figures."

"What do you mean?"

Harry exhaled sharply. "One of the goons knew it was me lying on the floor. He brought greetings from Brendan Crowley."

"Crowley? HRT?" Ellen said. "What is going on?"

Morton cleared his throat. "We may be screwed. I hope not, but I don't know what to believe now. Are you guys okay?"

"Yeah, fine. What are you talking about?" Harry said.

Morton got up from his chair. It was getting a little easier to see now, and the man looked almost as wretched as Harry felt.

"I was called to Washington earlier this week," Morton said. "An emergency meeting for all the SACs. Your friend Crowley was there, Harry, plus Keller and maybe three other guys."

His voice darkened. "I don't know if you heard, but the Director died last night. He never made it off of life support. Anyway, we were all summoned to a special meeting with Keller. You wouldn't believe the tension inside the Hoover Building. If somebody sneezes, there are four guns in his face. People on the streets of D.C. seem edgy enough right now, but inside it's impossible."

"I don't like your set-up," Harry said.

"Got that right. Keller has effectively instituted martial law within the Bureau. No one speaks to the press but him, anywhere in the country. No one spends more than a thousand dollars on anything without his approval. SACs have to provide detailed analyses of every program under investigation, and anything related to terrorism or militias or weapons must be put through to him personally and immediately."

"God, it sounds like we're under attack," Ellen said.

"Those were his words exactly. The assaults on the Director and the Deputy Director, the theft of that ATF shipment, the terrorist action in New York, and a host of other rumblings from around the country. He says we're in danger of losing control, and if that happens we'll be overrun. He's extremely concerned about the media stirring up the public, so information flow is one way. It's like this damn raid tonight. I should have been alerted days ago; you guys should have been warned at the very least."

Morton shook his head. "This isn't the way the Bureau is supposed to operate. Keller says it's short-term, until we get the most serious elements under control, but I . . ."

He looked at Harry, then at Ellen. "Want to know how I found out about this raid? I get a call, in the goddamned airplane coming back, from Simmons, the SAC in Denver. He wants to know why his SWAT team has been called to an action in Northern California, and why didn't I tell him about it in the first place? I start checking around. Sacramento knows nothing. Reno, Vegas, Phoenix: nothing. But Atlanta has boys on the way, and HRT was sent out from Quantico two days ago! You getting the picture? I run off the plane, jump in my car, and start heading east. By this time, I've got a rough idea where to go, since Keller seemed to have such a big interest in what you guys were working on."

"What happened?" Ellen said. "Why didn't you show up?"

"I did, but they wouldn't let me past their cordon. They said 'the Director' had to approve it, and I couldn't get through to him. So I tracked down this place and hoped you guys would return."

"I'm glad you didn't walk in," Harry said. "At this point, our cover is still clean. If anything, the raid gave us credibility."

"What were they looking for?"

"Weapons. The ATF shipment, I guess, unless they are launching similar strikes against groups all over the country."

"No way," said Ellen. "This was major. The Commander was targeted specifically, which means someone else has been working this case a while. So what were we, bait?"

"Maybe just another angle," Morton said, "but to put you guys at risk is inexcusable."

"Want to hear something wild?" Harry said. "The Commander ordered his men not to fire. He told me later that he didn't want to jeopardize something that was coming up. Apparently that was a standing order he issued only in the last day or so, which makes me think he knew something."

"No chance," Ellen said. "The look on his face when he came to get Barnett and me? Nobody's that good an actor. He may have suspected, or was getting really paranoid because—get this—he asked Barnett to try to tap the FBI's phones."

Ellen suddenly frowned. "That's not the worst of it. There's a directory on Barnett's computer. I didn't get a chance to look inside it, but the name of the directory was 'NYC.' Maybe it's nothing, and maybe it is."

"You think they staged the attack on New York?" Harry said.

"Who knows? I'm desperate to check into it, but Barnett wants me back as soon as possible to start prepping a stack of laptops. Can we get some people to help us, sir?"

Morton shook his head. "At this point, I'd like to keep the circle as tight as possible. Isn't Sonia Taylor a friend of yours? Maybe we can include her, but the fewer people we involve the better. I'm going to have enough of a challenge shielding you guys from whatever it is Keller has got going."

"Maybe these will help," Harry said. He reached in his pocket and pulled out the two ceramic coils. "I'm going to try to find out how they got into the Commander's house in the first place, but you might want to see who they belong to. A couple of the goons were desperate to find them, which makes me think that the taps weren't legal. It doesn't surprise me, knowing that Brendan Crowley is associated with this."

He turned to Ellen. "What was that about prepping computers?"

"Twelve of them. He says he's under a tight deadline."

Harry looked out at the rising dawn. "Then so are we."

Justice: None.

Harry drove past the fortified gate in his newly-ventilated truck, unescorted this time. It was almost one o'clock in the afternoon, but he hadn't really slept. Between visions of Armageddon and the fangs of Brendan Crowley, the few hours he tried to rest had been worse than fitful. Ellen's and Morton's nightmares were probably different, but the result was the same. It seemed like the whole cabin was tossing and turning.

Then came the banging on the door at 9:30 A.M. It was Kevin, seriously amped up, coming to drag Ellen out. "Work to do!" he'd said, with too much cheeriness. "Come by when you're ready, Harry," he added, on his way out. "Maybe noon?"

Fortunately, Morton had been stashed away upstairs, and the SAC's car was hidden in back, so Kevin never noticed that they had company. After Ellen left, Harry and Morton talked about how to proceed. Much of the detail was going to fall on the SAC's shoulders, since it looked like Harry would be spending most of his time at the Commander's compound.

So Morton drove off in search of recent eavesdropping warrants, plus any other news which could explain what was going on at the Hoover Building. And Harry headed back toward the compound, with too many questions to even bother thinking about. Today, he was just going to cruise.

As he reached the main yard, he slowed the truck to a crawl. The scene was amazing. Men were scurrying everywhere, picking up glass, repairing damaged buildings, photographing the "crime" scene. At one corner of the main building, some of the troops were staging a reenactment of the attack for a video camera. It seemed like everyone was going full force, and this was barely ten hours after the agents had left. Didn't these people sleep?

Harry parked the truck so it would be out of the way, but it wasn't far enough. A horde of guys with cameras rushed over, wanting to document this latest piece of damage. It might have been amusing, but a chilling thought ripped through Harry's head: *I can't be seen!*

He turned and made a wide circle toward the house. The raiders really had made a mess of things, but the people cleaning up seemed buoyed by it. Either they were thick with visions of conquering the beast using only their courage, or they were delirious from lack of sleep.

Harry was almost to the house when he noticed the Commander on the porch, in the midst of a heated discussion with the bear-like bartender, Mackey. Actually, the Commander looked calm, but the other man was raging. Pretty strange to see a tantrum in such a terrifying frame.

The man stormed off the porch. His head swiveled in Harry's direction, and he stopped. The eyes, overwhelmed by the heavy brows and broad forehead, seemed to disappear as the man stared at Harry. The lips curled amidst the thick beard, and then the man stomped off. A trail of dust followed him around the corner of a shed.

"He can be a little emotional."

Harry jumped at the voice behind him. He turned his head to see the Commander standing nearby.

"If there was another bar around, I'd suggest you do your drinking elsewhere for a while," the Commander said. "But I'll keep Mackey in line. He's never actually poisoned anyone, least that we know of."

"What's his problem?"

"A change of command. He blames you."

"Me?"

"Well, you found those ceramic coils, he didn't. And he *had* been my chief of security." The Commander folded his arms across his chest, and his gaze narrowed. "But I gotta ask you, Chandler. How is it that you just happen to appear, and you find these mysterious new listening devices, and two seconds later, all Hell breaks loose. Doesn't that strike you as the least bit suspicious?"

Harry didn't break the gaze. "I didn't ask to meet with you; I was summoned. You didn't even want my help, only Ellen's. You were the one who brought up surveillance, not me." He was picking up steam. "How the hell do I know that you didn't plant those coils yourself? You were the one doing background checks. Maybe this whole thing was staged to set *me* up!"

"What?! Take a look around! See what's been done to my property and then tell me again that I set this up."

"Hey, you're the one with the conspiracy theories. Maybe once I drive off, the Feds are going to waltz in with the Corps of Engineers and repaint the place pink! Tell me something: how is it that nobody got shot last night? And how is it that you had time to warn your men? If anyone knew something in advance, I'd say it was you."

The Commander stared at him hard for several more seconds. Then his body relaxed. "I'd never paint this place pink, you asshole."

They exchanged grudging smiles and started to laugh.

"That was a hell of a night," Harry said. "Bastards!"

The Commander nodded, and then motioned for Harry to follow him. They passed a few of the buildings in silence and headed into the woods.

"I've gotta thank you for what you did," the Commander said. "The way you rescued Betsy and all. She told me about it this morning, how that white trash attacked her and you stepped in, pulled that guy's knife out and ran him off. I'm sorry I missed it, except I would've killed the guy."

The Commander turned to Harry. "If you see that animal again, you let me know. I want his head."

They started walking again. "Sorry about that little scene back there," the Commander said. "I had to ask, you know?"

Five minutes later, they stopped in a section of the forest. It seemed like any other place there—trees towering overhead, dirt and shrubs and pine needles scattered across the ground, with shafts of light creating pools of illumination. The Commander motioned for Harry to stay where he was, then made a slow circle, surveying things in the distance. He pulled out a two-way radio and whispered something into it, listened with the device at his ear for a moment, then put it away. He walked back to Harry and smiled.

"I'd like to show you something," the Commander said.

He reached under a nearby bush, cleared away some pine needles, and then lifted the end of a rope. With a yank, he pulled open a thick wooden door, the size of a manhole cover. He motioned Harry over. It was pitch black inside.

"Go on down those steps," the Commander said. "You'll hit bottom at about twelve feet. Step off to your left, then I'll get the lights."

Harry started down, wondering if this was another test. Was the Commander going to seal him in here? He'd gone maybe halfway, unable to see anything more than the ladder and the wooden wall in front of him, when the trap door slammed down with a thud. It was suddenly utterly black.

"Keep moving or I'll step on your head," the Commander said.

Harry found his way to the bottom and stepped to the side, trying not to give in to claustrophobia. A moment later, the lights went on.

The room was about fifteen feet square, lined on every wall with cabinets. It was obviously their provisions room, from the labels on the cabinets. Through a passage was another room that looked to be a duplicate of this one.

"Enough food for a year?" Harry said.

"Two years, for fifty people. Come on."

The Commander lifted another trap door in the center of the floor and started down. This series of rooms had to be what the raiding party was looking for: an amazing array of assault weapons, in racks that ran floor-to-ceiling, plus mortars, rocket launchers, grenades, and so on. It was staggering. Harry had never seen such an assortment outside an army base. It was warm in the room, but he was suddenly very cold.

He peeked into the adjoining room, which was a duplicate both in size and armament. There was also a small door in one wall.

"Tunnel system?" Harry asked.

"All the way," the Commander replied. "It was just easier to come through the woods, since we weren't under attack. One more level."

They went down again. This series of rooms seemed to be sleeping quarters, but there was a small door going off in a different direction. The Commander opened the door and led Harry down a narrow hallway, maybe twenty feet long. There was a door at the end, a more substantial door than any Harry had seen at the compound. It was instantly clear why.

Inside was a bomb factory, an active one. No one was in the room at the moment, but projects were clearly underway. Harry thought about going in, but decided not to seem nosy—until he spotted the trap door in the floor of the room. It, too, was heavily plated, with a huge lock on it.

"Where does that one go?" he asked.

"Service entrance," the Commander replied, grinning. He closed the door to the bomb room and led Harry back out.

When they were standing under the trees again, the Commander said, "So what do you think?"

"Impressive," Harry said. "How've you avoided detection?"

The Commander smiled. "Kind of like those ceramic coils. Some special sheets which reflect or shield or something, so that scanners and detectors and all that electronic shit is totally worthless to find it. That's why our rooms go down, not across, so we need less of that stuff to line the key walls. It's expensive, but it's worth it. A couple of guys in the movement developed it. A pity it'll never win the Nobel Prize."

"George, I've gotta ask: Why show me this?"

The Commander started walking. "There's a job I'd like you to do. Everybody's gonna say I'm crazy, but I'm a good judge of character, and right now I need somebody I can totally rely on. I'd like you to be my special advisor, on security and such."

"What?"

"I can't make you chief of security, 'cause there's no time and I've got enough hard feelings to deal with already. Mackey's going to continue to handle the day-to-day, but I want you to make sure we're protected; you know, 'big picture' stuff. That'll be really critical as we move east."

Harry cleared his throat. "And where are we going?"

The Commander laughed. "You wouldn't want me to spoil the surprise, would you?"

They were a study in contrasts. There was Ellen, a stew of darkness on the floor of Barnett's room, surrounded by mountains of computer gear. Energy: low. Mood: black. Pace: glacial. Conversation: almost none. She was making conversions to the laptops—installing boards, adding new software, configuring modems—but she was not setting any speed records.

Barnett, meanwhile, was in constant motion and babbling away. Drugs might have been the cause, except he was getting more energized as the day wore on. He had become one endless, piercing screech on the blackboard. Ellen would have told him to chill out, but the part of her that was awake was dying to know: What was

Barnett getting worked up about?

He wasn't writing code. All those "Yeah"s and "Um-Hmm"s and "Okay!"s; he was definitely hacking into someone's system. Was he setting up taps on the FBI while she sat six feet away? That'd look good in her file.

But what could she do? No warrant, no dice. Besides, too much was going on outside, not to mention these laptops, to pull the plug just now. So she snailed along with the conversions and endured Barnett's chatter.

"I mean, have you met even one person here with a brain?" Barnett said. "Present company excluded, plus Ol' Flattop. Otherwise they're all a bunch of idiots. At least Kevin is good for comic relief."

"You're so charitable."

"Yeah, maybe I should be grateful. If one of them had known anything about computers, we probably wouldn't be having this chat. Don't get carried away, but you're the first—Oh, shit! I didn't even think about that."

"Hmm?"

Barnett groaned, got up from his chair, and began pacing in what little space was left in the room. "Jesus, if they're as dense as the rest of them, it'll be fucking Nightmare City."

Ellen looked up. "What are you babbling about?"

"These computers!" Barnett said. "We've got twelve bozos coming in today—*today* for God's sakes, not four days from now like I was told. So we're busting our ass to get these things ready, *and they may not know what the hell to do with them!*" He suddenly became very still.

"Ahem."

Barnett sat down again. "Sorry. I just saw my life pass before my eyes."

"And?"

"And I need your help to teach them how to use these."

"Huh?"

Barnett nodded at the laptops Ellen was working on. "There are twelve big-time militia leaders coming here today, and we're going to give each of them a laptop. I'm setting up a private BBS and—"

"You don't need a special laptop to do that."

"Of course not. But these have my encryption program and it's guaranteed bullet-proof. And I'm sure they don't have one of these wireless modems."

"Are they all dense? Maybe they're like the Commander."

Barnett's eyes brightened. "He doesn't know everything."

"So you want me to teach them where the space bar is? No thanks."

"Come on. This is just going to take a few weeks."

"What's it worth to you?"

"A new Porsche?"

Ellen snarled and went back to work on the conversions. She had three more to go and she definitely needed a break.

Barnett went back to his task as well, whatever the hell it was. He was quiet for the first fifteen minutes or so, but quickly became even more animated than before: bouncing on his chair; humming madly; and grinning wider and wider. Finally, he jumped up from his chair and shouted, "Yes! Yes! Yes!"

Then he turned on the printer, stabbed briefly at the keys, and pounded out a quick drum riff on the table. Again, he attacked the keys and then did another drum solo. The process was repeated six or seven more times; Ellen lost count. When the printer finished rolling out pages, Barnett snatched them from the tray and bounded out of the room.

That was too much for Ellen to ignore. She went to Barnett's laptop and looked at the screen. A series of documents were displayed, which had to be what Barnett just printed out. They were layered one over the other, probably a progression. If Ellen clicked on each window in order, and did it quickly, she could run through the sequence and Barnett would never realize she had seen it.

The window in front was someone's travel history. Behind that were IRS records, a county assessor's report, DMV, bank statements, something about "Global Charities Foundation," and more IRS forms. It meant nothing so far, except that Barnett had seriously flaunted the law. Despite the risk of being discovered, Ellen decided to start over.

1) Recent travel records for a Merilee Alton, from the database of ExecuTravel in Tysons Corner, Virginia.

2) Income statements for Merilee Alton. $170K the past two years, less than $20K the two previous years. Barnett had obviously copied segments out of the woman's tax forms and pasted them onto a single page.

3) County assessor's record for a property in Reston, Virginia. Owner: Global Charities Foundation. Value: $300,000.

4) Virginia Driver's License for Merilee Alton. Age: 25. Address: same as the property listed in the county assessor's record. Picture: stunning. Ellen never remembered looking that good even when she'd tried her hardest, and this was a DMV photo! Justice: none.

5) Bank statements for Merilee Alton. Direct deposits from Global Charities Foundation: over $14,000 a month. Check amounts: varied, but nothing regular or substantial like rent or a mortgage payment.

6) Bank statements for Global Charities Foundation. Mortgage payments for the property in Reston, coded WiHab. Payroll for Merilee Alton, coded WiHab. Miscellaneous, including ExecuTravel, coded WiHab. Few other listings with that code.

7) Background information on Global Charities Foundation, an umbrella organization funding a variety of charities and trusts. Among the charities: Wildlife Habitats, based at that same address in Reston. Contribution to Wildlife Habitats: $170,000 a year.

More IRS forms pasted together, detailing substantial gifts to charity by someone in each of the past four years. For all the details, the list varied little from year to year, either in recipients or amounts donated. With one exception: the amount given to Global Charities Foundation was increased two years ago by $170,000.

Ellen moved the view up to the top of this document. Sure enough, Barnett had left the tax filer's name on the first form. And it was now so clear. The names at the top read: "Gordon and Catherine Carroll."

The President of the United States. Husband to CC, one of the most charismatic televangelists on TV. Mr. Family Values. And, it would appear, keeper of a drop-dead gorgeous mistress in Reston, Virginia.

On another day, in another place and time, it would have been a sunset to savor, particularly with a cold beer in hand. But Ellen had a massive headache, and neither the Bud nor the vista from the far end of the porch helped.

Activity around the compound had slowed, but it still felt like these guys were on alert. Not fearful, though—expectant. Well, Barnett had said something about a group of militia heavyweights coming in. Ellen might have gone back to the cabin, but Harry's truck had been temporarily confiscated by the evil bartender. So here she sat, waiting to play chauffeur.

The door to the house swung open, and Harry walked out with the Commander. They were talking softly, with the Commander pointing at various places around the yard. They didn't notice her, forty feet away, either because of the deepening shadows or because of the seriousness of their conversation. Ellen closed her eyes and tried to empty her mind.

The sound of boots approaching on the wooden porch brought her back. She opened her eyes just as Harry was sitting down next to her.

"They said I'd find you here," he said quietly. "Tough day?"

"I've had worse," she whispered, "but not by much. I'd like to crucify Crowley or whoever it was that planned that raid. We could use one right now, and there's no chance of it happening."

Harry chuckled wearily. "Is this one-upmanship? Like who's got the most damning evidence? I'd bet mine against yours."

Ellen sank further in her chair. "Yeah?"

"I got a full tour. Fortifications, communications facilities, tunnels, arsenal rooms, and . . . a bomb factory. Plus, there's a locked vault below the bomb room that he wouldn't show me. Can you top that?"

"Wow. I don't know. You probably heard that a group of militia leaders are coming in tonight, but did you know they're going to have a secret computer network? What does that suggest? *And,* Barnett discovered something really big: the President has a mistress."

"What?!"

"Keep your voice down. He didn't tell me directly, but I saw the results of his efforts when he went dashing out of the room."

Harry's eyes widened. "Was that two hours ago? Barnett came racing out and dragged the Commander off. Five minutes later, they returned, grinning like a couple of idiots."

Ellen nodded. "That was it. God, what are they planning? Barnett mentioned something about the tabloids yesterday, but that seems too tame. With all the laws he violated just to get that information, I can't see him needing to exploit it for the money. He can get cash in other ways."

"Did you have a chance to find out anything more about that 'NYC'—"

The door swung open just then and Barnett walked out. He spotted Ellen and Harry, and began walking toward them.

"Hey, Harry, how's it going?" Barnett said. He pulled himself onto the porch rail opposite Ellen. "I've got some news, but I'm not sure you're going to like it. I was about to transfer some money into your checking account, feeling magnanimous as I was, and I discovered something strange: your bank accounts were frozen today."

"You're joking!" Ellen said.

Harry grimaced, then shook his head. "FBI, I'm sure."

"Want me to change that?" Barnett said. Then he jumped down. "Got to go see His Highness. Catch ya later."

Ellen waited until Barnett was off the porch, then whispered, "How long before we can nail these guys? I don't want to be sitting here watching another disaster on the news."

"Well, tonight's too soon. Besides, we need to find out what this big meeting is all about. Maybe you can sneak out and call Morton, alert him to what we've discovered today. I've got to stay for the festivities. Get this: I've been made the Commander's special advisor."

"Nice. Does it carry a pension plan?"

Harry laughed. "I'm not sure I want to know."

There was a flash of light on the buildings, and the yard erupted with noise and dust and headlights and people. The first militia dignitary had arrived, accompanied by an escort of motorcycles, a scene that would be repeated long into the night. Ellen and Harry stayed in the shadows, observing the early arrivals. Harry said he'd probably recognize some of the names later, but so far the faces were strangers.

Then Harry's truck pulled up in a cloud of dust. The passenger door flew open and a man stepped out. He was no more than six feet tall, but he was built like a mountain: craggy; sharp angles; imposing stone face; rough movements. In a word, intimidating.

The man greeted the Commander, curtly, and walked toward the house. As he reached the door, the light spilling through illuminated his face.

Harry turned away, quietly but quickly. When he spoke, the words were barely audible.

"I know that guy, and he may know me."

A Little Test

The ground was still moist with morning dew when the Commander began the tour of the compound. Sunlight filtered through the tall pines in a patchwork pattern, illuminating the remaining shards of glass and shell casings strewn about. In the quiet of a new day, it wasn't a scene from Hell, but it was sobering to the twelve visiting militia leaders. They followed the Commander quietly, nodding their heads, occasionally grunting or cursing. The longer they were silent, however, the more enraged they appeared to become. Harry trailed the group, trying to blend in.

It was unnerving in such a pastoral setting to be surrounded by so much turbulent energy. They were all wearing guns, though none of them needed to. Savage power and cold calculation flashed in every glance. They weren't all poured from the same mold. Some were large and menacing like Eugene Rumson, the man from Montana whom Harry was trying desperately to avoid. Others were smaller, more wiry, the type to surgically rip you apart.

As the tour went on, Harry tried to ease the threat he felt. Maybe these guys smiled sometimes. Maybe they had hobbies that didn't involve guns. Maybe they petted kittens or played with puppies on the floor. And maybe Harry would win the lottery tomorrow. This was one time when he missed having a gun. Not that it would do him any good against all the weapons around him, but having it would still make him feel a little less naked.

On their home turf, each of these guys probably strutted around like a king. But there was a deference paid to the Commander that went beyond his status as host or as recent victim. It was obvious in the way some of them paused, waiting for the Commander to move, or hesitated when it seemed like he would speak. There were little side conferences between some of the men, mostly variations on: "If it could happen here, it could happen anywhere." The only one who exuded any sense of challenge was Rumson.

They were coming back toward the yard, having finished the tour, when Rumson turned on the Commander. "What?! You told your men to lay down and not return fire? That's disgraceful! You call yourself a leader? What the hell are we doing here, men?"

Suddenly, there were similar rumblings from the rest of the group, as if the floodgates of opportunity had been thrown open. All that throttled angst came pouring out, jacking up the tension.

But the Commander didn't seem ruffled in the least. He looked at Rumson and shook his head, then put his palms up to quiet the crowd.

"Five minutes, gentlemen!" He said that loudly, then dropped back to a normal tone. "In five minutes, I'll explain the whole deal, and you'll see two things: one, I had no choice, unless I wanted a bunch of martyrs on my hands; two, it was the only way to make sure that ZOG wouldn't bother us again."

The rumbling resumed, and he had to raise his voice again. "Hold on! In five minutes, you'll understand how brilliant a decision that was."

"Why not now?" one of the group said.

"Look, you came all this way. Have a little patience."

"And nothing in the media?" another one said. "What's got into you, Commander? I'd a milked that for all it's—"

"And that'd just turn up the heat all the more." The Commander shook his head. "Typical."

"You know what fries me?" one said. "You had a perfect chance to lay some hurt on the Feds and you let 'em off without a nosebleed."

The Commander chuckled. "Well, we got one. Harry here—"

He pointed behind the group, and every head turned. "—his daughter beat one guy with a flashlight and threw him out a second floor window. That was priceless."

Harry got nods from most of the men, and a disturbing stare from the stone-faced man from Montana.

"Follow me," the Commander said. He led the group toward a large barn across the yard.

Harry hung back. He intended to stay with the group, but his survival alarm was clanging relentlessly. Eugene Rumson, the most powerful militia leader in Montana, maybe the whole Northwest, had stopped to wait for him.

Harry had dealt with a lot of rough people in his twenty-seven years in the Bureau, but few as harsh as Rumson. Malicious, ruthless, evil; the guy had been called it all. He had a fanatic following and ruled the other militia groups in the state by force of will alone. No one dared cross Eugene Rumson.

And during Harry's two-year stint in Butte, he did just that.

Rumson had devised a "cleansing" campaign to drive all the Jews and blacks and other "undesirables" out of the state, according to an informer. The town of Jeremiah, Montana was Rumson's test case.

The actual crimes committed were minor—slashed tires, poisoned wells, broken windows, gunfire, obscene graffiti—and there was no clear pattern of abuse. Rumson obviously knew how far he could push things without drawing official FBI interest. But it caught Harry's eye.

His options were limited, of course, so he called a few reporters in New York, suggested they check out what was going on in Jeremiah, and left them to their task. Within ten days, the cleansing campaign stopped. Harry's plan worked better and faster than anything he could have done directly, and without risking a confrontation between the FBI and Rumson's militia.

Through it all, Harry's name and picture were kept out of the papers. Rumson was scrambling to find and punish the source, and the FBI was a logical target. Somewhere, he might have gotten a lead on Harry. Fortunately for Harry, he was transferred to San Francisco and quickly forgot about Rumson.

Now the man was waiting for him, ten feet away. They had never met, so Harry decided to take a direct approach. He looked at Rumson and nodded.

"I know you," Rumson said. His voice was raspy and low.

"Really?" Harry didn't break his stride. "From where?"

Rumson fell in step beside him. "You ain't from Montana?"

Harry shook his head.

"Well, I know you, mister. I don't know exactly where. Seems to me a few years back, but I know your face. What's your name?"

"Chandler."

The man squinted at Harry, repeated the name "Chandler," and then stalked ahead of him.

Walking into the barn was like stepping into his past. The cows, the feed, the oil on the equipment, the dust from the hay; the smells, heavy and musty, dragged him back to Missouri.

At the far end of the barn was a wooden ladder going straight up, and standing guard at the bottom was Mackey, the human bear. Rumson started up, then Mackey swung suddenly in front of Harry and lumbered up. The guy practically growled at him. If only Trong's cousins had been there, Harry would've had a veritable fan club.

At the top of the ladder was a hay loft, but a small passageway had been opened between the bales. On the other side was a space that looked more like a board room than a barn. There was a chalk board on one side, a couple pictures elsewhere, an American flag, and a large oval table with water pitchers and glasses on it.

It was crowded, both with bodies and energy. There were no windows, and it felt like a hundred degrees in the room. This was a gathering of dangerous men, and only the Commander looked at ease.

Kevin was moving around the table, setting little name cards in front of each seat: Alabama; Arizona; Arkansas; Georgia; Kansas; Michigan; Montana; Ohio; Oregon; Tennessee; Texas; West Virginia. Putting state names to faces, Harry figured he knew five of these guys, counting Rumson; the rest were strangers. He sat on a bale of hay and tried to fix the states in his head.

The Commander was in the far corner, listening to Rumson's fevered whispers. Then he nodded and moved to the head of the table, motioning for the others to take their seats. Kevin dropped onto a bale across from Harry.

"We've done this alphabetically," the Commander said, "so that no one feels snubbed. And maybe we'll just keep this by state names anyway; a lot cleaner, you know?"

Michigan looked around the table. "Where's the Northeast?"

"You want them pansies here?" Alabama replied.

"Hey, I heard they got a militia in New York City," West Virginia said. "Can you picture it? Doin' drills in pin-striped suits, carrying martinis?"

"Fuckin' A-rabs shoulda torched them too," Georgia said.

"So what's the agenda?" Michigan said. "I think we should prepare a declaration of defense or a manifesto of resistance, something like that. We don't want ZOG to be able to get away with this type of attack again."

"Yeah," said Kansas, "but no leaks to the press like with 'Project Worst Nightmare.' We got to have plans, but they got to stay secret."

"Wait a minute!" Texas said. "The whole point of a declaration is that everyone knows about it—that's the deterrent! It's like the Cold War. Nobody used any nukes, 'cause they knew a nuke would be comin' back at 'em."

"Who's talking about—"

"Gentlemen, please!" the Commander said. "We need a little order here. We could spend all week talking about—"

Rumson stood up. "Hey, your men just rolled over and let the Feds piss on 'em. I've got fifteen men in jail right now, 'cause somebody set 'em up. I want revenge, gentlemen."

Oregon burst out laughing. "Hey, Rumson, didn't you know that was a set-up? The Feds—ATF, FBI, somebody—dangled that truck out there waiting for someone to snatch it. Only trouble is: we double-crossed 'em! I heard you didn't ask too many questions about where those guns came from. Maybe you should have."

"I guess Yahweh didn't protect his property so well," said Texas.

"Montana's the biggest fucking showboat around," Georgia said. "You shoulda never brought him here, Commander."

"Hey, cracker!" Rumson said. "When you're through wipin' your ass with that white sheet of yours—"

"Gentlemen!" The Commander slammed his hand on the table. "Let's keep personalities out of this. I know some of us have had our difficulties in the past, but the only way we're going to meet ZOG's threat is with a united front."

"The Feds are coming from everywhere lately," said Kansas. "Gun raids, tax harassment, and now all these 'disasters' they're staging to give them more excuses to bash us. They've got to be stopped, once and for all."

"They're the ones behind that new anti-terror bill in Congress," Alabama said. "Couldn't get one passed after Oklahoma City, not one with teeth anyway. Ditto after that TWA bomb and the one at the Olympics. But it sure looks like they're gonna get it done now. And you know who it's aimed at, don't you?"

West Virginia got up from his seat. "Any of you been visited about this FBI killer? I was, maybe just 'cause I'm closer than the rest of you. Fuckin' Feebs said it was a social call, and they damn near ripped my place apart! It's been a month since those two guys were killed, and I'm sure they know who it was. They're just hushing up so they've got an excuse to rough us up."

"Well, somebody's got to blow the lid off of that ATF heist," Rumson said. "It's a plot, no doubt, and the world's got to know it."

"What about New York City?" Arizona said. "The press says

the FBI is still sniffing out Arabs, but that had to be the Mossad—or the Feds themselves, just like in Oklahoma City. That attack had ZOG's fingerprints all over it."

For the next five minutes, theories about what happened in New York were batted back and forth. Everyone applauded the burning of the U.N., but that's where the agreement ended. As the discussion went on, the voices got louder and the theories became more absurd.

The Commander hadn't said a thing. He merely watched, a bemused look on his face. The others were oblivious to him, but not Harry. The man was practically levitating, drawing strength from the ruckus around him. Harry did not like what he was seeing.

Then the Commander nodded at Kevin, who threw back a tarp and picked up two small rocket launchers. Kevin set them on the table, and the weapons were quickly passed from one man to the next. These were exotic pieces, and the militia leaders' curiosity finally brought the conversation to a close. A smile creased the Commander's lips.

"You wouldn't classify these as defensive weapons," he said, "but sometimes a bargain comes along that you just can't pass up. By the way, they are from that ATF haul; got a few other choice items, as well."

He started walking slowly around the table. "There's something else about these pieces that's special. Can you guess?"

The militia leaders passed the weapons around again, their faces a study in concentration and confusion. The Commander returned to the head of the table, his face beaming.

"Here's a clue: New York wasn't the work of Arabs or the Mossad. Not even the FBI." He chuckled. "And it didn't take fifty commandos."

The air was hot and thick and ready to ignite. Harry's heart was pounding. The others seemed pinned to their chairs, awaiting the news.

The Commander picked up one of the rocket launchers. "You

see why I didn't want to provoke ZOG? They did a shit job of looking around the first time, but we might not be so lucky the next. By the way, your fingerprints are all now on these weapons."

Several of the men groaned in unison. Anger started building on some of the faces, fear on others. On a few, wry smiles appeared. But no one had the energy to respond. The critical words had yet to be spoken.

"It may be occurring to you," the Commander said, "that I didn't invite you here to talk about defensive measures." He took his time, looking from one face to the next. "In the past twelve hours, and for Lord knows how many years before, I've heard each of you go on about how the government has to be stopped, how it's illegal and so on, 'til you're blue in the face. 'Our victory is ordained!' you'd say. Or 'Every last one of the bastards has to die before we can be free!'"

He put his hands on the table and leaned forward. "The time for words is through, gentlemen. Each one of you has preached to the world about the Founding Fathers." His voice dropped to a whisper. "Now it's time to be one."

Ellen rolled the Jeep slowly down Main Street and parked in front of Ella's Luncheonette. That wasn't how she normally drove through town, but she was scanning the area as she went. If there were "eyes" out there, she didn't see them, but then there had been Bureau forces in the area before the raid that neither she nor Harry had been aware of. Behind her dark sunglasses and attitude, she was now constantly on alert.

She hopped out of the Jeep, back in character, and burst into the luncheonette. "Hey, Ella!" she called out. "What's happenin'?"

"Your uncle is outside," the woman said. She jerked her thumb past the kitchen. "He looks kinda upset."

"Morose" was the better word. Jim Morton was back in the woods, pacing slowly between the trees, a mass of dark, brooding energy. He looked up as Ellen approached, then continued pacing. Ellen stopped nearby and waited. It was almost a minute before he spoke.

"In all my years in the Bureau, through all the bullshit that's come and gone, I've never experienced something like this." He stopped pacing. "I found no warrant anywhere for electronic surveillance on Pilkin's place. The other stuff, yeah, but not that. Maybe somebody's hiding it, or maybe there wasn't one to begin with. Either way: highly illegal and totally unethical."

"Did you find out anything about the raid itself?"

Morton scowled. "I talked to Warren Keller himself, finally, and he was full of answers." He began counting the points on his fingers. "1) They had intel that some stolen ATF weapons were at Pilkin's place. 2) They used HRT and 'non-locals' so that Pilkin wouldn't be tipped off. Why? Because, 3) Keller believes someone in a California field office told the militia about that shipment in the first place. He hadn't ordered polygraphs yet because he didn't want to alert the militia. 4) He got all this from an informant in Oregon. The guy apparently was pissed off at the meager cut he got following the heist and is ready to trade information for money and a new identity."

"So why weren't we informed of the raid in advance?"

"Five: they had no way to reach you without blowing your cover."

"Bullshit! That one guy brought greetings from Brendan Crowley. How do you explain that?"

"I can't. And I didn't mention it."

"So do you buy this crap?"

Morton reached into his pocket and pulled out the two ceramic coils. "Six: Keller said Harper was hallucinating about eavesdropping; said it was probably a recurrence of battle fatigue."

He rolled the coils around in his hand. "These might as well have 'FBI' stamped on them; we're the only agency that has them. Which means either Keller is lying or there's some rogue element in the FBI which he doesn't know about. I'd put Brendan Crowley at the top of that list."

"Did you say that to him?"

"Of course not. That'd get me nowhere. The one time Crowley's name came up, Keller said the man had been terribly maligned in his career and he, Keller, was honored to have him as a lieutenant."

Morton began pacing again. "If this was just internal bullshit, an annoyance factor, I could let it slide for now. But you guys could've been killed the other night. And if things really are brewing at Pilkin's compound . . ."

"They are. I couldn't tell you this over the phone, but twelve big-time militia leaders are sitting there right now, and I'm sure they're not talking about baseball. And Harry is in there with them, if you can believe that."

Morton shook his head. "We can't go to D.C. with this, not when there's a rogue loose."

"You know what? We don't need to. We can hit it ourselves, the sooner the better."

Morton started to protest, but Ellen cut him off. "Listen, Harry is in a room with these guys as we speak. He's not wired, but he has to have some ammunition by now. And Pilkin and Barnett have sunk themselves already. Yesterday, Pilkin showed Harry a secret complex complete with weapons, a bomb factory, and a mysterious locked vault. And Barnett has violated so many databases I've lost count of how many times he's broken the law. Get us warrants for Barnett and Pilkin, and we'll take them into custody in private. We should be able to do it without any shots being fired."

"It can't be that simple."

"Come on. They wouldn't expect it so soon, especially not from Harry and me. We could do it tonight!"

"No, I'd want back-up, and no way am I going to call D.C. I'll have to bring agents out from the city. Can it wait 'til next week?"

Ellen's face suddenly soured. "Here's another reason why we

need to move fast. I'm loathe to say it, but I'm afraid Barnett is going to let this out." She took a breath. "The President has a mistress."

"Jesus! Really? Are you sure?"

Ellen explained the evidence she had seen.

Morton shook his head. "Poor CC. If she finds out, it'll kill her. All that publicity? So much for her days as a preacher." Then a dark laugh came out of him. "God, I'm more worried about the man's wife than I am about the impact on the country."

He looked at the coils, still in his hand, then put them in his pocket.

"What are we going to do about those?" Ellen asked.

"I haven't worked that out yet."

"Do you think the goons are still in the area?"

"Some of them. You don't put in that kind of effort and then just walk away. I'm sure these coils weren't their only source. At the very least, they've got to be running phone taps, and probably without a warrant."

"So they may know about the visiting militia leaders."

Morton shrugged. "Crowley's boys wouldn't remobilize so soon, not after being embarrassed that way. This could just be a logical gathering in the wake of an attack like that, not a war conference."

"Like hell."

"You know what scares me?" Morton said. "If we've got a rogue at headquarters, there could be abuses all over the country. Who knows how many investigations might be compromised? These militia guys could be plotting to blow up the world, we could have them dead-to-rights, but if someone in the Bureau violates the law, the criminals walk."

"So on top of everything else, we need to make sure our own guys don't screw us up?"

"Something like that."

Suddenly, Ellen smiled. "Hey, can I have one of those coils?"

"What for?"

"Bait. I think it's time to go fishing for goons."

Silence followed the Commander's announcement, but things were not quiet. Not inside Harry's head, at least, and there had to be a similar uproar in the heads of the militia leaders. Was the Commander crazy? Was he serious? Could they do it? Would they try?

A new sense of mission gripped the room. It was obvious in the eyes, blazing with possibilities. It was clear in buoyant postures and in the giddy way this circle of rough, combative figures began to look at each other. They began to laugh—nervously, excitedly, and ultimately raucously, even viciously. After years of fervent proclamations about commitment and action and revolution, it must have been staggering to be suddenly face-to-face with one's words and ideals. It also had to be liberating.

Then the questions and comments began. Tentatively at first, but it quickly became a whirlwind, comments shooting back and forth, louder and louder, one on top of the other, as if they had to hurry before the dream disintegrated.

"We've got to hit FEMA! In an emergency, they've got more power than the President."

"What about the military? You think they won't react?"

"What's going to happen to farm supports? Or the mail?"

"Wait a minute! Are we talkin' mass murder here?"

"Whoo-whee! It's gonna be the Day of the Rope!"

"If you'd would give me a moment," the Commander said.

"What about foreigners? They won't just sit back and watch."

"Are we talking only the federal government, or do you want to wipe out all the state governments as well?"

The Commander pounded on the table. "Gentlemen! We're gonna get nowhere if we keep this up. Be quiet a minute." He walked over to the chalk board and began writing. "Let's see: Feds; States; Foreigners; Programs; Military; Media." He brushed off his hands and stepped back.

"We'll start with those. I've purposely left off issues like blacks and the larger Zionist conspiracy, 'cause we'll just get sidetracked again. When the time comes, you can do whatever you damn well please in your own neighborhood, but let's not waste time squabbling like a bunch of politicians."

The Commander paused, but no one interrupted him this time.

"Good. Now first: we're not talking mega-casualties. Why? Cause this ain't guerrilla warfare. We're gonna do it in one clean sweep. At most, I see a couple thousand deaths. Fifty thousand, max. Anybody got a problem with that?" Every head swung side-to-side. "Hell, unless somebody goes wacko, the only people who will get it are the ones who deserve it anyway."

"Like the Jews and niggers and—"

"Rumson!" The Commander glared at him, then continued. "As far as states go, again that's up to you. The question is: Once the federal government has been wiped off the face of the earth, will the states try to re-create it? I don't think so, certainly not in its current form. And if they do . . ."

West Virginia raised his hand. "What about the threat from other countries. Won't we be sitting there, just waiting to be raped?"

The Commander shook his head. "This is ZOG's stronghold. Once that's decimated, they won't be able to muster enough forces to do any good. Somebody like NATO might try to 'save' America, but who would they attack? If we're quiet about this, they'll have no target to aim for. Besides, it'll take too long to get organized. And if somebody did attack—Russia? China?—where would they hit? The cities! Anyone here care if all our big cities are leveled?"

Georgia laughed. "Ya got balls, man! Where do I sign?"

Arizona chimed in. "What's this about being quiet? Don't we want to let the world know who's behind this movement? I say we take over the media installations first and—"

"Hey, you want exposure or independence?" the Commander said. "I'm not sure you can have both." He looked around the table again. "We've tried preaching at people for years, hoping to win a convert here or there. We've pestered the government with liens and lawsuits and who knows what else, and it hasn't done a damn bit of good. The Freemen, the Davidians, those Republic of Texas guys; they've all failed. Why? Because ZOG is still around, still flashing its big teeth and immoral laws. The only way to change this is to eliminate the thing completely." He leaned over the table. "And the only way to do that is to wipe it out in one swift, total move. Fast and complete." He smiled. "And we're not gonna need a huge army. When you—"

"Talk, talk, talk!" Rumson said. "Do you do anything but talk?"

"Hey, I've kept my men out of jail, which is more than you've done!" The Commander took a moment to calm himself. "There was also a certain little bonfire at the U.N."

Rumson sneered at him. "How do we know you're responsible?"

The Commander picked up one of the rocket launchers and tossed it at him. "Here! Take that to the FBI and have them run a ballistics test on it."

Silence raged between the two men.

Then, Michigan spoke up, smiling. "It was him. We sent out one of our boys, and that water main break had to be his handiwork. Nice going, Commander."

"Thanks."

The Commander walked back to the chalk board. He picked up the eraser, stared at the labels he'd written, and then wiped them off with long, harsh strokes. He turned back to the table, his eyes narrow, his mouth set.

"We could talk until eternity about this program or that situation or whatever. We can analyze until we're blue in the face. But at some point we've just got to do it. We won't have all the answers, but neither did the Founding Fathers. They took a leap of faith and so must we."

He leaned against the chalk board, studying the faces at the table. "This probably came as a bit of a shock to some of you, maybe all of you. I imagine you'd like to go home and think about it a little."

"At least sleep on it," Ohio said.

A few nervous chuckles joined in.

"Well, we don't have time to sleep! The enemy swept through here two days ago and they'll be on your doorstep any minute. Every second we spend yapping away is one more second they've got to try to stop us. The time is here, the time is now. You're either in or you're out."

He took a long breath, relaxing his face, but the rest of the group was like stone. The Commander began to speak again, his voice quiet.

"I can't impress on you strongly enough how critical this mission is. We only get one chance at this, but together we can make it work. But I've got to know now. I can't be handing out assignments and then find that a couple of you guys aren't up to the task. If you're not 100% into this, leave now. There'll be no hard feelings, and I'm sure you'll protect our need for silence. Anyone?"

No one moved.

The Commander started walking around the table, his face no longer challenging, but inciting. "This will take a commitment like you've never known. A fanatic's conviction. It doesn't matter what your specific beliefs are. In this arena, we all share the same goal."

He reached his hand toward the center of the table. "It needs to be a blood oath, because we'll all be butchered if anyone breaks the chain. You've gotta have absolute trust, absolute conviction, and you've absolutely got to deliver—even if it means your life."

There was absolute silence.

The Commander straightened up slowly. "Well, I think we

should do a little test, just to make sure everyone is in." He chuckled wickedly. "You may even enjoy this." He pulled a revolver out of his holster and spun the cylinder, looking from face to face.

"You see, we got ZOG scum in our midst. FBI, to be exact."

There was a loud, collective gasp. Silent accusations shot across the table and around the room. Harry tried to be inconspicuous, but he was caught in the glare as well. From Rumson, it was a steady stare. All the while, the Commander continued to spin the cylinder of his gun.

"Now, we just can't have that," he said. "So I'd like one of you, as proof of your commitment, to take this gun and shoot the traitor. Sound fair?"

"Who is it?" said Arizona.

The Commander looked around the table, then raised his eyes and pointed his finger. "There."

Every head turned to look at Kevin.

The young man shrieked and stumbled away from the bale of hay, but Mackey was blocking the exit. Kevin backed up against the wall, his face white, his mouth moving, but silent.

"It's tragic," the Commander said, "but this type of betrayal cannot be tolerated." He looked around the faces again, put the gun on the table, and slid it across to the man from Oregon.

"Do it," the Commander said.

Oregon stared at the gun, but didn't pick it up. He looked at Kevin, then back to the Commander. Then he pushed the gun back across the table.

"This ain't a sideshow," the man said. He stalked out.

The Commander watched the man go. His eyes were piercing, but he said nothing. After a moment, he gave a small nod to Mackey, who followed Oregon out. The tension in the room soared.

"I kind of expected that," the Commander said quietly. "I think he would have been a liability."

Georgia cleared his throat. "Then why was he here at all?"

"I needed to confirm it, which I did last night."

"What about the Fed?" Rumson said. He glared at Harry.

"He's right," the Commander said. "We can't let one man's failure deter us from our course." He picked up the gun and began circling the table, dangling the revolver from one finger as he searched each face in succession. Twice he paused, about to hand the gun to one of the men, then continued circling again. Every heart in the room seemed to pound in unison.

Then the Commander walked away from the table—and went straight to Harry. He held the gun out at arm's length.

"Do it."

Harry froze. Every impulse screamed at him to turn away. But in those milliseconds, without raising his eyes, Harry knew the entire room was zeroed in on him.

There was no choice. He couldn't kill Kevin, but he also couldn't walk away. There had been something ominous in that nod to Mackey.

He reached out and took the gun. The Commander stepped back.

Harry turned toward Kevin. The young man was whimpering, trying to melt into the woodwork ten feet away. His face was red and contorted, and a dark stain was spreading across his pants.

Harry looked down at the gun, his heart pounding. He was a good shot and had used a weapon in tense situations before—but never anything like this. He could feel his palm getting wet. Maybe he could pull the shot to the left, aim past Kevin's ear, and hope the gun didn't slip or his aim wasn't twisted by the panic he felt.

He was taking too long. Maybe it was only seconds, but these guys were waiting, demanding action. Harry cocked the hammer, raised his arm, and said a quick prayer. A moment later, he squeezed the trigger.

The gun thundered in his hand, and Kevin crumpled to the floor.

No one moved. No one breathed.

Harry held out the gun. The Commander took it and turned

to the others. "That's commitment." He put the gun back in his holster and walked over to Kevin. "Come on, boy, get up."

A gasp echoed around the room, and everyone's eyes went to the wall. There was no blood, no bullet hole—the shell had been a blank! But the cowering, shattered heap on the floor made it clear that this hadn't been staged. With great effort, the Commander helped Kevin to his feet and began to drag him toward the exit.

As they passed Harry, the Commander whispered, "That was your final test."

The others in the room were still in shock. There was no hint of bravado anywhere. After more than a minute, a few of them started to move.

Then a huge explosion rocked the barn.

Free

It was a frantic dash to get out. The militia leaders raced from the barn, guns drawn, shouting "ZOG!" and "Fucking Commander!" Harry followed, his head reeling. *Crowley's goons again?* He charged toward the light, expecting Armageddon, and was jolted by the relative calm in the compound. No SWAT team, no gunfire, no helicopters, and no hysteria from people walking around. Normal, not chaos. It was totally disorienting.

The militia leaders struggled with it, too, like a stampede suddenly forced to a halt. But these horses had heavy weapons ready to fire and most of them were still twitching, looking for a target.

Fifty yards away was the Commander, talking with two of his men. A half-mile or so beyond, easily visible through the trees, was a furious blaze. It wasn't wide, like a forest fire, but narrow with long, shrieking flames. Harry squinted and saw a few people around it, merely watching, not tending or dousing it. As the flames danced in and out, he realized the source of the fire was a car.

The men around him saw it, too. Guns were put away and every head turned toward the Commander, who was now approaching.

The Commander walked up, shaking his head. He stopped in front of the group, scanned the faces, and gave a shrug of resignation. "Bad choice."

"What?!" said several of the men.

The Commander crossed his arms. "One of the boys was

installing a new transportation 'device'—a car bomb. Hadn't planned to set it off, in fact he had left it for a few minutes to get a dummy charge for testing. Everybody here knew what he was working on, so he figured it was safe to leave it." He took a deep breath. "It seems our friend from Oregon came storming out and decided to hop the nearest vehicle. Looks like he chose the wrong one."

The chill was instant. No one moved his head, but Harry could see the eyes of the militia leaders flicking to one another, searching for something. Several shifted uneasily.

Then Georgia folded his arms and said, "Such a shame." It was almost light-hearted, and it broke the paralysis of only a few.

Kansas cleared his throat. "Was this another test? Are we going to see Oregon walk out of that barn?"

The Commander pointed at the blaze, still raging in the distance. "Go see for yourself, though there's not much left."

Ohio looked at the men around him, his face grim. "I'm going to ask this, because somebody needs to. Are you planning to hold us hostage?"

The Commander exploded. "For what?! You're no good to me sitting here. An hour ago I admitted to something that'd get me sent to the chair. What leverage is your ass gonna provide? If you want to go, get the hell out of here!"

"Like that?" said Tennessee, tilting his head toward the fire.

"Any goddamned way you want! Pick any vehicle here; I promise they're not rigged. But if you go, you'd better be damn well sure you keep your mouth shut or you *will* have to watch what you drive."

The Commander stomped off toward the house. He went about thirty feet before he wheeled around and glared at the group.

"I'm going inside to continue this planning. If you're with me, come along. If not . . ." His shaking head completed the sentence.

No one followed at first. A few spoke quietly with others. Then a solemn march began, shuffling through the dirt, up the wide wooden steps, and into the house. Harry was in the middle of the group, and stopped in a far corner of the living room where the Commander waited. Eventually, all eleven of the militia leaders collected in the room.

Barnett was there as well, sitting near the big stone fireplace where the Commander stood. Barnett had cleaned himself up, but there was no way, in his black shirt and black jeans, that he fit in with the others. He was getting suspicious looks from most of the visitors.

"Let's have a moment of silence for our brother Hendricks from Oregon," the Commander said. He barely paused before continuing.

"First, this here is Jeff Barnett. We'll get into his specialty in a few minutes." The Commander chuckled. "Don't be put off by his looks. The guy is a goddamned genius, and we definitely need his help."

"Thanks, Big Guy."

"Easy. Okay, let's talk about strategy and tactics. Harry, could you pull down that screen over there? And Barnett, if you'd hit the light switch." The Commander flipped on a projector sitting on the coffee table.

The militia leaders turned toward the screen. The air was still ripped with tension, but also layered now with apprehension. A few had recaptured that earlier eagerness, but not all.

"We're going to concentrate most of our energies on Washington," the Commander said, "so we'll start with the field of engagement. This map shows the center part of D.C. We've got individual packets to give you later that have this same map, marked up. How many of you guys have been there before?"

Six raised their hands, plus Harry. The Commander walked over to the screen.

"The major targets are circled in red: the Capitol Building; the White House; FBI; Justice and FEMA; IRS; ATF; Treasury; and so on. Notice anything particular?"

"Yeah, they're all clumped together," Texas said.

"Exactly. Now, these blue dots? Those are firehouses. The city is so broke that some are about to be closed, but to be safe, we'll target them all—all the ones within this area, that is." He ran his hand in an arc over the top part of the map.

"What we need to isolate is really a small part of the city, maybe a two mile radius at best. It's bounded on one side by water, with only a few bridges to contend with. And around our target area are all these traffic circles, plus a couple of squares. If you've been there, you know how messed up traffic gets when one of these things is blocked. Are you starting to see a pattern here?"

Georgia started laughing. "That's beautiful. Blow up the traffic circles—How many? Seven of them? Eight?—and you cut off the center from the rest of the city. Roll some gas trucks onto the bridges, torch 'em, and nobody gets in or out. You'd have the place surrounded by flames. Brilliant!"

"But why only firehouses?" West Virginia said. "Why not police stations or federal installations? That town is crawling with guns."

The Commander looked around the room, gauging each face and letting the suspense build. It seemed to go on forever. Harry knew this had to be the punch line, the reason these men were gathered here.

The Commander smiled.

"Because we're going to burn the place down."

The place erupted. They were shouting, cheering, condemning the Commander, and deifying him. It took several minutes to settle things down. Then the Commander began again.

"We're going to do this by stealth, not numbers. That's why we're not worried about the cops or Feds or whatever. Look, we did that whole thing in New York with just seven guys. It's all about timing and having the right tools."

"How did you set fires in the subways and then get over to the U.N. in time?" Arkansas said. "The streets were jammed."

"Timing devices?" Texas said.

The Commander nodded. "It was so easy it was scary. Makes you wonder why it hadn't happened before."

"Then why don't you torch D.C. yourself?" Ohio said.

"Too many targets that need to be hit at the same time. Besides, we've got things going on outside D.C. as well."

"The Pentagon, I'm sure," said Arizona. "Can't wait to hear that plan. And you'll want to take out Langely, Quantico—"

"You're talking buildings!" Rumson said. "We're being fucked by people, not buildings."

"It's all related," the Commander said. "The blood-suckers, their lair, the money, the databases. We need to wipe out all those things to be able to eliminate the government."

Barnett chimed in. "If there are no leaders and no data and no offices for people to go to . . ."

"What about the military?" said Texas.

"We'll scramble their databases and take out the top guys," Barnett said, "so there's no clear chain of command. And who are they going to attack, anyway? We'll be so underground they won't know who hit them."

"I can feel the media question coming on," the Commander said "but let's hold off on that. Continuing with Rumson's question about people—"

"Yeah, what about the President?"

The Commander smiled. "Barnett's going to tell you about that later. Let's just say, we don't expect the man to be a problem."

"That reminds me," Barnett said. He took a folded sheet of paper out of his pocket and handed it to the Commander.

"What about Congress?" West Virginia said. "They've got a chain of command and they can meet anywhere."

"We've got three weeks, gentlemen" the Commander said. "That's how much longer Congress is in session. After that, it'd be near impossible to get them all together again until the Fall. But with all the press that ridiculous anti-terrorism bill is getting, everybody's sure to be around to vote on it."

"You're out of your mind!" Rumson said. "First off, the place will be crawling with Feds. They've got so many disaster contingency plans, you won't be able to spit without hitting some kind of ZOG slime—FBI, ATF, military, Secret Service, District police."

"You're right," the Commander said. "They'll be on the rooftops, in the Metro, on the bridges, in the skies. But only afterwards, after the whole place is up in flames and all the snakes are smoked. There'll be too many targets for them to concentrate on and too much hysteria and confusion for them to be able to manage. They've got defense plans and contingency ops for all kinds of scenarios: attacks on the White House; Congress; the bridges. But none of them are any good until the shit hits the fan. That's our advantage. We get in, we get out, the place ignites—and there'll be so many of them running around looking for an enemy that they'll probably be shooting at each other. You'll see how it plays out when you get your individual assignments. It's all about timing and tools, gentlemen." He gave them a sly smile. "Including one special little item you won't believe."

He shut off the projector, then turned on the lights.

"Now, I think it's in everybody's best interest to not know all the details of what's going on. That way, if any cell is compromised, the plan still has a good chance of success."

"Hold on!" Rumson said. "Who elected you as grand wizard? Every man here should know exactly what's going on. Otherwise, how do we know you won't just hand us over to the Feds?"

"Hey, my fingerprints are all over those rocket launchers from New York. You think anybody'd cut a deal with me? Look, I just want to get this done. And for all the talk over the years, for all the hair-brained attempts, no one has been successful."

He pointed at Barnett. "He and I know how it needs to be done. Quick, clean, and complete. We're your buffer. We're the only ones that everyone can point to as being involved. Hell, we're shielding you."

"This is a side of you I ain't seen before," Georgia said.

The Commander smiled. "I've been waiting years for the right battle. And, boys, this is it."

He picked up a stack of envelopes and began passing them out, each marked for a specific person.

"We're going to take a lunch break here in a second. Sorry it's so late. These packets have your specific assignments, plus information about the other cells which will be tying in with yours. We expect you'll each need no more than ten people for the tasks you'll have in D.C., plus some side targets. Barnett's going to tell you after lunch about our special communications system, and I'm free to talk with each of you about your 'equipment' needs."

He finished passing out the envelopes and returned to the fireplace, passion blazing in his eyes.

"Gentlemen, we have a tremendous task ahead of us. Barnett and I are your guides, that's all. Within a month, when this is over, you will be free from ZOG's shackles. Free to run your community the way you want. Free to run your lives the way you want. Free to include or exclude whoever you want. Free. Free. Free."

Harry's brain was reeling. These guys were dangerous in their own right. But banded together? He needed fresh air and a chance to think. He folded up the projection screen and headed for the door.

He was reaching for the knob when someone grabbed his arm and spun him around. It was Rumson, a barely-throttled inferno.

"I know you, Chandler—'cept that's not your real name."

Harry had to yank to pull his arm free. "I got no beef with you."

"Well, I do with you." Rumson leaned closer, his breath hot. "I'd bet everything I own that you spent time in Montana, around a town called Jeremiah. Ain't it so?"

Harry just looked at him.

"I'd even bet you're not one of us. In fact, I'm sure you're

ZOG scum. Who are you with? FBI, ATF, something like that?"

Harry fought the urge to swallow. That was the one question he couldn't deny, not according to the law. But to answer now, to answer it properly, would mean his death. The only option would be to lie, and then try to stop these guys by himself, working outside the law, violating every principle he had sworn to uphold. But there really wasn't a choice, not if thousands of lives or the fate of the nation hung in the balance.

It took milliseconds for these thoughts to rip through his brain, and Harry never broke Rumson's gaze. That would have been fatal. He took a breath—and was pushed aside by the Commander.

"Some questions shouldn't be dignified with an answer," the Commander said, his eyes drilling into Rumson. The two men stared at each other for several seconds. Then the Commander grabbed Harry's arm and pulled him toward the door. "Come on, we've got work to do."

In all Harry's years, in all the tight jams in the military and through twenty-seven years in the FBI, he had never been rescued so fast or so dramatically. He wanted to say "thanks," but that was not the right line. The last thing he wanted to do was open the question again.

Before he could reply, the Commander spoke.

"That asshole has been pestering me about you since last night, since he saw you pass through the house. Said he had a bad feeling about you."

They cleared the porch and the milling crowd and were headed out of the yard, but the Commander lowered his voice anyway. "I'll say this, it gave me a beauty of an opening for that little test back in the barn." He glanced at Harry. "It also let me check you out under pressure."

Harry fought to restrain his anger. "What if I had failed? Would you have sent me off like that guy from Oregon?"

"Hendricks?" The Commander glanced at him. "Yeah, probably. But you didn't fail. Didn't even hesitate. That's why I've got this little task I need you and Kevin to handle."

Kevin? Oh, God! With all the horrible discoveries of the past hour, Harry had forgotten about Kevin. Forgotten about the look on his face and the wrenching despair Harry had felt for the young man.

The Commander led him past the outlying buildings, toward a large garden. At the far end were two figures sitting on the ground, huddled in conversation. As Harry got closer, he realized who it was, and his heart sank.

Kevin turned as they approached. His body jerked and his face went white, a mix of fear and anger. Behind him was Betsy, cold fury in her eyes, casting accusing blasts, first at the Commander, then at Harry.

"Okay, den mother, get lost," the Commander said. Betsy didn't move. "Beat it, woman!" he said, and took a step toward her.

Betsy got up slowly, never taking her eyes off the Commander. She patted Kevin lightly on the shoulder before walking away, and gave Harry a withering glance as she passed.

"Get up, boy," the Commander said, prompting, not ordering. "I'm not going to apologize again, so you'll just have to get over it. I've got a job for you and Harry. It needs both your skills."

Kevin stood and snapped to attention, his hands sharp at his side and his face set grimly forward.

"That's better," the Commander said. He took out a folded sheet of paper, opened it, and handed it to Kevin. "This is the address for a cabin near King's Canyon. You shouldn't have any trouble finding it. You guys need to leave before nightfall. It's about five hours south of here, Harry."

"What's going on?" Harry asked.

The Commander smiled. "We're going to do a little surveillance. You'll need to get Mackey's kit—maybe you should do that, Kevin—plus those micro video cameras from the cabinet." He turned to Harry. "You've probably got better equipment, but unless it's at your cabin, there isn't time to collect it."

Kevin spoke up, in crisp tones. "What is our objective, sir?"

"A young woman. Barnett put her picture onto that sheet of paper. We want to record her activities with a certain visitor."

"And that visitor is?"

The Commander grinned. "The President of the United States."

Harry blanched. "You're joking." The Commander shook his head. "How do you know that?" Harry said.

"Barnett discovered it, through a long, winding paper trail. He's been checking her travel history the past few days, and she made a reservation for this cabin yesterday. She's arrives tomorrow for a two night stay."

"So?"

"So the President flies to Yosemite today for a four-day conference of tree huggers. Yosemite is maybe half-an-hour from this cabin. You want to tell me that's a coincidence?"

Harry tried to act excited. "That's heavy ammunition."

The Commander laughed. "The best, and not a shot fired."

"But what about Secret Service? Won't they be covering the place?"

"Come on. This is Gordo, Mr. Lily-white. Do you think he's going to let anyone near him while he's stuffing some broad? Maybe they'll sweep the place in the morning, but I'd bet the ranch there'll be no one within miles when the sun goes down. That cabin has got to be really remote."

"Excuse me, sir!" Kevin said. "If we don't have to be there until tomorrow night, why do we need to leave today?"

The Commander shook his head. "You want to answer that, Harry?"

"Recon. Contingencies. Things like that," Harry replied. "We don't want to be rushing into it at the last minute."

"Yes, sir! And, sir? Shouldn't we take a few scouts with us?"

"Good point," the Commander said. "Take Bix and Mike. It's

1420 hours right now; try to get under way by—"

There was a loud, grating sound in the yard, accompanied by a giant cloud of dust. Then a vehicle door slammed and Ellen burst out of the cloud, charging toward the house. "Doesn't she know how to drive like a normal person?" the Commander said. He started laughing, and Harry joined in.

"Well, I gotta get back," the Commander said. "Barnett is about to do his bit. Good luck, men, and get me that tape. No screw-ups!"

Harry waited until the Commander was out of sight, then turned to the young man. "Look, Kevin, I'm sorry about—"

"Fuck you!" Kevin said, and stormed off.

Harry watched him go, then began walking slowly toward the yard. Talk about days you wanted to start over.

He was just passing one of the sheds, when the door opened. In the shadows, Harry could see Betsy's face. She was motioning him inside. He had a bad feeling about this, but he went in anyway. As he crossed the threshold, the door slammed shut and Betsy shoved him against the wall.

"Listen you!" Her voice was controlled, barely. "You lay a finger on that boy again or point a pistol in his direction, blanks or no, and I'll kill you. That's a promise."

"Hold on," Harry said, not pushing her away. "I had no choice. Somebody was going to shoot him, and I was just as glad it was me. I aimed past his ear, and got lucky that the shell was a blank." He paused. "It was a 'test', Betsy. Unfortunately, Kevin was the chosen victim. If you want to strike back at anyone . . ."

Betsy burst into tears and collapsed against Harry's chest. Raw, heaving sobs shook her body, and the meaning was clear.

"He's your son, isn't he?"

Betsy's sobs increased.

"And the Commander's?"

She pulled her head back and looked at him, fighting back tears. She tried to speak, but all that came out was: "Bastard!"

She dissolved in a heap. Harry knelt and put an arm around her, saying nothing.

As the moment dragged on, the prospect of a larger tragedy filled his head. Within hours, eleven men would leave the compound, armed with plans. Individually, they couldn't do a lot. But together, they held the potential for destroying the nation. It was an absurd idea.

How could they stop this? He and Ellen were screwed if it was just up to them. But help from the Bureau looked—well, there was no help to be had, not with the resurgence of Brendan Crowley.

Harry suddenly flashed on that scene the other night, when Betsy appeared with a knife and attacked one of the goons. It hadn't been a random act. The way she tore across the room, she wanted revenge. Which meant she knew something, even if she didn't realize it. The question was how to get it out of her.

She was drying her eyes with her sleeve, leaning back against the wall of the shed. She glanced at Harry, then looked away. "Sorry about that," she said. She shook her head, then her face tightened again. "Someday . . ."

Harry cleared his throat. "Betsy, this is a bad time to ask, but there'll probably never be a good time." He took a breath. "The other night, when those agents stormed in and you attacked one of them. What was that about?"

Her eyes widened.

Harry put up his hands. "I'm not going to say anything, I promise. I'm furious with George, too. But there are other things going on here, big things, and I'm worried about those men coming back. You don't need to give me details, but I suspect some of those goons were here before. Is that true?"

Her eyes were on the floor. Slowly, she nodded.

"And maybe one of them kept you occupied while the other . . ."

"They came to install a new phone line," she said. "Three of them, but I guess only one was with the phone company." She turned away, her face bitter. "I spent some time with one of them, the one I tried to kill."

She looked up. "Do you know where he is?"

"No," Harry said. "But we might be able to find out. And maybe we can find out what's going on, so nobody else gets hurt."

Betsy shook her head. "Right now, I want to hurt somebody, bad."

Barnett stood with his back to the stone fireplace, trying not to sweat. Well, he was sweating already, but he prayed it wouldn't show; the hostile crowd in front of him would pounce on that. It hadn't been ten minutes since he started his presentation, and he was already in danger of losing control. This was not how he had expected things to go.

Maybe it was all those little whispered conferences these guys had during the break. Maybe they had a thing against computers. Maybe they were just getting back at the Commander by whipping him. Whatever, it was clear from their personal attacks that lunch hadn't slowed them down, despite how much some of those monsters put away.

"Now just supposing this pipsqueak is right," Alabama said, "and the President is having an affair. And he's going to meet up with her tomorrow. And the Commander's boys can somehow get it on tape. Right there, you gotta lot of leaps, sonny. But anyway, suppose you get the tape in hand. Well, how the hell are you gonna get the President to look at it, much less get him to wipe your ass on command?"

"Yeah!" Michigan said. "Gordo's got so many layers of fat around him that CC probably needs official clearance before she can crawl into bed with him. And if he is gonna be porking some broad in the forest, you can bet the place will be crawling with Secret Service."

"Not necessarily," the Commander said. "Look at the problem

with leaks he's already suffered through. You think he's going to let more than three or four guys know what he's up to? Anyway, leave that task to me."

"How many men are you sending?" Rumson asked.

"Four."

There was a chorus of shouts.

"Hold on," the Commander said. "If I had told you that I was going to turn New York upside down with seven men, you would have said that was impossible, too. Timing and tools, gentlemen. That's our approach."

"The runt here still hasn't answered my question," Alabama said. "Just how do you plan to get to the President, supposing you do get the goods on him? Are you gonna walk up to the White House and knock on the door?"

"I'm going to get him to call me," Barnett said. "From the fucking pay phone of my choice."

"Oh, right," Arkansas said. "Can't you hear it? 'CC, I'm gonna pop down to the corner for a sec. Got a quarter I can borrow?' Give me a break."

"Seriously," Georgia said, "how would you do it?"

Barnett smiled. "Get into their e-mail system and plant messages. Not in the President's mailbox; I'm sure he's got someone monitoring it for him, someone not high enough to make a difference. I thought I'd go through the chief of staff, give him some incriminating bits from that progression I showed you earlier, with threats about tax fraud and a little video clip from the tape we're going to make. You know, enough tweaks to get the Presidents ear."

"Well, I know something about computers," Tennessee said, "and it seems to me that, even if you do get the President's attention, they could track you to wherever he sends his response."

"Nope. I'll get my responses from Gordo's own account. He'll send an e-mail to himself, and I'll pick it up from there. I've already been into their system to check things out. It took me a while, but I finally got in."

"But what if they attach a virus to the e-mail?"

Barnett turned his eyes to the doorway, where Ellen was standing. "Hey, babe, we've got a winner!" He looked back at the man. "This is my business, okay? I think I know enough not to get fucked-up by some White House geeks."

"Which is why you've been in prison *twice*, Mr. Bar-Net?" said Arkansas. "Say, how do you spell that anyway? Sounds like a Jew name to me."

The Commander spoke up, wearily. "B–A–R–N–E–T–T. And I wouldn't piss him off, especially you." He looked at Barnett and grinned. "You want to show him? He's the one from Arkansas."

Barnett chuckled wickedly and reached for a file folder he had set on the coffee table. He leafed through it, pulled out a particular sheet, and set the file folder back on the table. He did a Groucho imitation with his eyebrows, then folded the paper and handed it to the militia leader from Arkansas.

The man looked at the page, and his face turned white. One of the men next to him tried to read over his shoulder, but Arkansas quickly crumpled the paper and shoved it in his pocket. He looked at Barnett, his face still ashen, but his eyes beginning to rage.

"How did you get this?"

"Fuck that!" Rumson said, and he lunged for the file folder.

Barnett grabbed it first and handed it to the Commander.

"Have you got stuff on all of us?" Texas said.

Barnett looked at the Commander and they shared a smile.

"Just call it our insurance policy," the Commander said. "Insurance that everyone will carry through on their assignments. We can't have anybody doing double duty for ZOG."

"Like you?" Rumson said. "What about that girl over there?" He cocked his head toward Ellen.

"Rumson, I'm not gonna tell you again. Shut the fuck up! And the rest of you, let's be a little civil here. Okay? Barnett, carry on."

For the next thirty minutes, Barnett went through a description of the secret bulletin board system he had set up, the special laptops and wireless modems he had configured for each man, plus the procedures they would follow in communicating back and forth. The laptops were passed out and questions were raised, ranging from absurdly basic to advanced.

"No," Barnett said, "we've got two levels of passwords, to ensure the security of the system. You'll be asked for the first one when you turn on the machine and the second one when you click on that BBS icon. Let's set those now. Click on the box that says 'Set Passwords' and choose two different ones, but don't use something like 'sex.'"

"How about 'porno'?" Georgia said. That got a few laughs.

Texas looked up. "Will the Commander have his own laptop?"

"Of course he will."

"Will you be able to see what we write?" Arkansas said.

"Only if you send me a message. Otherwise, it's private."

Arkansas grinned. "So I could send Texas here an e-mail that says 'Let's kill the pipsqueak!' and you'd never know it?"

Barnett sighed and nodded his head. This clown had just jumped to the top of his get–this–guy–once–it's–all–over list. Pipsqueak, my ass!

"This is ridiculous," Tennessee said. "I've got my own computer, my own Web site, and there are hundreds of BBSes already out there. Why are we wasting time with this bullshit?"

"Does the Chinese Remainder Theorem mean anything to you? Ever worked with asymmetrical cryptographic algorithms? You guys are amateurs. Those Web sites and BBSes are probably so thick with Feds, it's like maggots. To latch onto an existing system would be a fucking invitation to our party. As for your equipment, I'm sure you don't have a modem like this. Even if you did, you don't have the configs for our BBS or my encryption program, and we don't have time to screw around with different machines. Use your old PC for other tasks if you like, but all communications regarding Torch Day must be through these laptops. You couldn't get in otherwise, thanks to my encryption program. It scrambles everything, going in and coming out. It is totally, totally secure."

The man from West Virginia slammed down the screen of his laptop. "I'd rather pick up the damn phone. These things give me a headache."

"Come on," Tennessee said. "If the Feds are watching and see lots of calls between us, they'll know something's up."

"Didn't you listen?" Barnett said. "These have wireless modems. You can use them anywhere. They couldn't find you if they tried. And I've got the number you're connecting to routed through Venezuela, so they won't pick us up here at the compound, either."

"This thing is crucial," the Commander said. "Once you leave today, the only way we'll be meeting is over this network. It'll be even more important as we converge on D.C. We all have to move together, and this network will help us do that."

Barnett nodded. "It's idiot-proof."

"Watch your language," West Virginia said.

"Hey, why should we get involved at all?" Ohio said. "If you're so brilliant, Barnett, why not just redirect all our missiles to fire on Washington?"

"It's one thing to fuck-up their launch codes," Barnett said, "and quite another to reprogram them to a specific target. That's a level of artistry I could probably pull off, given time, but you don't want to be sitting in a Defense Department database picking your nose. They'll nail you eventually."

"Well, what's the rush?" Kansas said. "You think we can do this in three weeks? Christ, it takes me that long to take a dump."

"The longer we wait, the greater the risk," the Commander said. "You were the one moaning about pressure from the Feds. How much longer do you want to remain under their yoke?"

Georgia burst out laughing. "Hey, if this kid could make us all billionaires, I might be content."

Barnett smiled. "You'll all be rewarded, substantially, once this is over. In the meantime, check your bank balances when you get home. I've given you a little advance from the government's coffers. A cool one million dollars each, done in a way so as not to attract attention from the Authorities."

Nobody leapt to their feet this time, but the group was in upheaval anyway. The comments were quiet, the reactions varied, yet every one of the militia leaders went through the same progression: excitement at the sudden windfall; fury at the intrusion to their privacy; and, finally, nervousness about what else the hacker might do. Barnett could barely contain himself as he watched the faces reach that conclusion.

Score one for the pipsqueak.

The Jeep crept along the back roads toward their cabin, moving so slowly they weren't even kicking up dust. Ellen was behind the wheel, but Harry would not have driven any faster. He was trying to make sense of a day that defied description. He'd delayed the departure with Kevin for an hour, claiming he had to get some equipment, when what he really needed was time alone with Ellen.

There was hope, but things were happening so fast, so fiercely that the assault on the compound was a vague memory, and that happened less than 48 hours before.

"It's not going to be enough, just taking in the Commander and Barnett," Harry said. "And I'm not convinced it'll be as easy as you think. But even if it is, we've got eleven more guys to contend with, all heavily armed fanatics."

Ellen exhaled sharply. "Yeah, Zealots On Parade, sharpening their spears while Barnett and the Commander gloated nearby. I couldn't believe how blasé they were about expected casualties. Thousands of deaths and it's nothing to them? Gleeful even? It knocked the wind out of me. And then Rumson started charging toward me after the meeting. He would've ripped out my jugular if I hadn't dashed off."

"He nearly did nail me. Stopped me at the door and asked if I was a Fed. You'll never guess who rescued me."

"Santa Claus?"

"The Commander."

"No way!" She broke out laughing. "You'll have to send him a thank-you bouquet, once he's in jail."

Then her face tightened. "Too bad about Kevin. Can you imagine growing up with a father like that?"

Harry shook his head.

Ellen pressed down on the accelerator, just enough to change the mood. "Hey, whatever happened to the twelfth guy? I only saw eleven there."

"It's wild. He was given the gun first, but refused to do it and walked out. A few minutes later, we hear this huge explosion. They blew him up with a car bomb."

"Jesus! Nice way to treat your friends. Where was he from?"

"Oregon. Supposedly, this guy had been double-dipping, and the Commander only brought him in to confirm his suspicions. Apparently Hendricks was deeply involved in the ATF heist and was the conduit, or a conduit, for the weapons. It sounds like the Commander was a recipient, not an instigator in the heist, but he was beaming about something. More than once, he said he had acquired a special little tool."

Harry's mind suddenly raced back to that first meeting with Morton. Something nagged at him then, and it came back to him now. "I don't think we got a full accounting of what was really in that truck. Remember I asked about it, and Morton just stared at me? We've got to press him on it."

"Won't that be moot once we take the Commander in?"

"Maybe, unless he passes it along to one of the others."

"Which is unlikely," she said, "since he's such a control freak. I'm just worried about how we're going to get the rest of these lunatics without a bloodbath. How many of these guys do you know?"

"Five. I've memorized the states where the rest are from, but we'll need help from other offices." He held up a hand. "I know, we've got a problem."

"Well, with Barnett, too. A mind like that, who knows what disasters he could be launching. The sooner we take him out the better, though I'm going to try to pry as much as I can out of him in the meantime. Which reminds me—" She pulled a ceramic coil out of her pocket.

Harry smiled. "Great minds think alike. I got some background from Betsy about those goons the other night. Apparently two of them accompanied a telephone repairman to the compound last week. The telephone guy was there to put in a new phone line."

"Probably several, for Barnett."

"Anyway, these two goons came along, one to distract Betsy, one to plant the bugs. And from the way she attacked that guy the other night, it must have been quite a distraction."

Ellen chuckled. "She's a trip."

"Yeah. So can you follow up on that tomorrow? I don't think I'll be back from Kings Canyon for at least . . ."

Harry's voice trailed off. They were half a mile from their cabin and something caught his eye. He glanced over at the speedometer: 20 mph; barely above a crawl. He stared at the mirror on his side: very little dust from the wheels. He looked out the windshield again: dust hanging in the air; not clouds of it, but enough.

"Are there other houses up this stretch?" he said. "Or county facilities?"

"What is it?" Ellen said. "You're making me nervous."

"Keep your pace steady, but look at the air. See the dust? Someone has been on this road recently. Maybe I'm just spooked by everything else, but this is the first time I've seen any signs of life up this way."

"Maybe it's Kevin."

"He's not due for thirty minutes, and he wouldn't be early."

"Morton? No, he told me he was heading back to the city." She turned into the driveway. "Hey, it was probably a fisherman or some hikers looking for new territory."

But they were both on alert as they got out of the Jeep—silent and serious, scanning the area—a tense, tenuous moment made all the worse because neither of them was armed.

"Meet me around the back," Harry whispered.

They went opposite directions, checking the corners, gauging the landscape for signs of trouble. When Harry came around the last corner and saw Ellen standing by the back door, he let out a sigh of relief.

Then he looked at her face—grim, stony—and his heart went into overdrive. Her hand was on the doorknob, and she slowly mouthed the words: "Did you lock this?"

Harry nodded.

Then Ellen turned the knob and pushed the door open.

"Sloppy," Harry whispered. He motioned for her to follow him away from the house. When they were thirty yards out, he stopped.

"It's probably not booby-trapped," he said, "or they would have primed the back door as well."

"Unless they ran out of time, or only expected us to come through the front. What are the chances someone is waiting inside? We've been surprised once already."

Harry shrugged. "I think somebody might have been looking for something. Maybe Rumson dashed over here to get the goods on us, except he would have had to pass us on the road. Mackey's taken over my truck, and that's nowhere in sight. God, could Trong's buddies have found us up here?" He turned to look at the cabin.

"Oh, shit." he said. "I think I know." He put his finger to his lips and walked back to the house.

It took him all of ten minutes to find the first coil. It was under the coffee table. Ellen found a second one five minutes later in the back bedroom. They left things undisturbed and went back outside.

"We're not going to accomplish anything by ripping them out," Harry said, "so we'll just have to watch what we say."

The next thought hit them simultaneously. It didn't need words; the wicked grins said it all. They bolted around to the front door.

Harry threw the door open. "God, what a day!" He fought the urge to raise his voice.

Ellen was right behind him. "These guys are frightening."

Harry headed for the kitchen; had to maintain that routine. Over his shoulder he said, "You know what I can't figure out? Why would Rumson insist on having the meeting down here?"

Leverage

Harry would've killed for some earplugs. Whatever it was that Kevin had blaring on the radio, it was drilling into Harry's head. Equally as painful was the numbing series of state highways they trudged along as they made their way south toward Kings Canyon. Kevin kept the rattling pickup dead on the speed limit, while all manner of vehicles raced past. There could only be one explanation: "Don't screw up!"

Darkness settled in and time dragged on, void of any conversation. The first hour, Kevin had kept his eyes straight ahead. The next hour, his eyes glanced at Harry, then quickly retreated. It got so Harry felt them coming. By the third hour, Harry couldn't take it any longer.

"What?"

Kevin looked at him, then shut off the radio. After a long pause, he said, "I'm trying to figure you out. Betsy told me what you said, about what happened."

Harry nodded. "I feel awful about it, Kevin. Really. There was no way I was going to shoot you, you have to know that. I pulled the shot to the left, and we both were lucky those shells were blanks. If not, I'd probably have met the same fate as Hendricks. But I would not have hurt you."

Kevin didn't look at him, but the corners of his mouth turned up hesitantly. Then he took a deep breath and relaxed his body.

"Do you ever have doubts, Harry? About what you're doing, even when you believe it with all your heart?"

Harry laughed. "Too often, kid. Why?"

"I don't know. Maybe it's all just happening so fast and I'm too stupid to catch on. That's what the Commander says."

Harry snapped. "Why does he treat you that way?"

Kevin shrugged hesitantly, his focus far away. "Disappointed, I guess." He swallowed hard. "Some things happened when I was a kid that he got, well, angry—embarrassed—about." His voice got softer. "I can't really talk about it."

"Sorry for asking," Harry said. He waited a moment, then added: "You've got to have faith in yourself, Kevin. You're not a bad kid."

The reply was barely audible. "Thanks."

Then the young man's face lightened. "You know, when things get really bad, I just pray to Yahweh and He sees me through. What about you?"

Harry wanted to say: "A bottle of Jack Daniels." Or: "Nothing beats the charms of a woman." Anything to keep from getting deeper. But being flip now would only trash the kid's fragile grip, so Harry just nodded.

Then he said, "How did you get into the teachings of Yahweh? I haven't heard the Commander mention the name."

Kevin smiled. "I've been doing some reading, trying to better myself. Growing up, it was kind of all around you, though you're right about the Commander and Yahweh. He believes, though, in his own way."

"Where did your—Where did the Commander grow up?"

"Iowa. Son of a preacher. Man, you should've heard *him* talk! They moved on to Illinois, had a farm 'til it was stolen by the bank, and moved out here in '62. Actually, not far from where we're going."

"Where did he meet your mom?"

"Betsy? Down in San Diego. He was at Camp Pendleton before being shipped out to 'Nam. She waited for him for four years." Kevin's face tightened. "Sometimes I wonder why."

He looked over at Harry, his face growing serious, even severe. "Why are you doing this? Why have you joined us?"

Harry was silent for quite a while, then simply said, "Justice."

A smile spread slowly across Kevin's face. "Yeah, justice. That's it!"

Kevin looked away suddenly, fighting a quirky grin. He glanced back at Harry, obviously weighing something in his mind. Then he said, "You don't think I'm stupid, do you?"

Harry shook his head.

"Well, see, there's something I've been dying to try, but I haven't had anybody I trust. I'd never try it in front of the Commander, at least not until I was sure it really worked."

"What are you talking about?"

"The Arm Test. Ever heard of it? You know, you ask Yahweh a question—Yes or No—and then pull down on someone's arm. If the arm stays up, it's 'Yes;' if it falls, that's a 'No.' They say it's the surest way to tell if someone is a true believer."

Harry's brain was racing; he had heard of it somewhere. Wasn't there was a trick to it? Then an image popped into his head, something about some guys sodomizing a goat. A moment later, the full story blossomed and a wave of nausea passed over him.

On an obscure compound in the Midwest, back in the 80's, some self-made prophet had used the Arm Test to hoodwink a band of disciples. Others employed it, too, but this guy took it to extremes, using it for everything from testing people's will to choosing which cereal to have for breakfast. He convinced his followers that the women could only be infused with his seed, but that the men were welcome—in fact, required!—to fornicate with the goat.

There was more to the story, but it was too repugnant and vile to repeat, even to himself. He could only hope Kevin wouldn't end up with a group like that someday. The kid was such an innocent.

Harry shook his head. "Maybe later? I'm too tired right now."

Kevin looked at him and smiled. "I don't know what you're complaining about. I'm the one doing all the driving."

They continued in silence, being passed by the occasional truck on this back route. Lights were few, and Harry was starting to drift off. Starting to let the horrors of the day fade into . . .

The buzz of something snapped him to attention.

Harry opened his eyes to darkness, a vast, consuming void. His vision slowly adjusted, but it didn't help his comprehension. They were in a forest, dwarfed by massive sequoias. He checked his watch: 4 A.M.

The other door swung open and Kevin leaned in. He chuckled softly. "You are one sound sleeper. Don't tell me my beeper woke you up?"

"Where are we? Kings Canyon?"

"Near there. Actually, between that and Yosemite. This is gonna be perfect!"

That was not what Harry wanted to hear. "What do you mean?"

"First off, the cabin she rented is at the end of a box canyon—you know, sort of horseshoe-shaped?—so they won't expect someone to come over the canyon walls. I checked it out already; there are two paths we can take. Next, they did some aerial surveillance, and that sucker found nothing."

"Where were we? Wouldn't they be using heat-seeking scanners?"

Kevin grinned. "The Commander warned me about that; told me to park outside the old family cabin if it was far enough away."

"Your old family cabin?"

"Yeah, it's about five miles from this lady's place. The surveillance plane went straight over us, but what's suspicious about a truck outside a cabin? I waited an hour, then went off-road to get to here. I'm surprised you didn't wake up, the way we were bouncing along."

Harry would've sworn this was a nightmare if he hadn't felt a pounding in his head. "So what's going on now? What was with that beeper?"

"Skytel! From Bix and Mike, remember? They're down in the valley, posted near the entrance to this little canyon. Like you said: recon. And it looks like we're getting more company, so get your sleepy butt out of the truck."

It wouldn't have been an easy hike in the best of conditions. In heavy darkness, after being wrenched out a deep sleep? Harry lurched side-to-side as he tried to follow Kevin. For someone so solid, the kid was surprisingly nimble.

When Harry got to the rim of the canyon, Kevin was flat on his stomach, hanging over the edge, peering through a pair of binoculars. Harry got down in the dirt as well.

They were maybe half a mile from the cabin. Even without binoculars, Harry saw a rush of activity. Several cars were parked in front, headlights on, motors running. Men were scurrying about, obviously sweeping the place for bugs or bombs. It was a scene of frenetic activity, which meant one thing: the President was going to be there later. There was no doubt.

The sweep took less than an hour, enough for such a small cabin. Then every car except one roared out of the canyon, stirring up eddies of dust that lingered long after the cars had gone.

Kevin's eyes were still glued to the binoculars. "It looks like they're all out of the house. We'll go around the ridge in a minute for another vantage point, but I think it's just two guys snoozing in their car."

He looked up at Harry. "We gotta find a way to get you inside there. The Commander wants a video tape and I'm gonna bring him one."

"Be serious! Those are Secret Service. They'll be on rotating shifts. Do you plan to knock on their window and ask to use the toilet?"

Kevin shook his head. "I don't care what it takes. I'll kill 'em if I have to. But no way am I going to fail the Commander."

* * *

It was long past noon and Ellen felt like she'd been in Mackey's Bar forever. She rattled the ice in her glass, both to distract herself and to annoy the bartender, Mackey. Waiting was not something she did gladly or gracefully. But it was critical that she talk to Jim Morton, and this place had the only telephone in town with an enclosed booth. It sucked that she couldn't just use a cell phone.

She'd done a quick check for bugs before placing the call, praying there wasn't a tap on the phone. All she got was Morton's voice-mail. She made a quick call to Barnett's parole officer, who was amazed to learn where Barnett had disappeared to and asked to be around when Barnett was arrested.

Ellen came back out of the booth and told Mackey she might be there a while, waiting for an important call from her mother, and asked him not to hog the phone. Then she sat and waited. And sat. And waited. And went through a string of club sodas. Finally, out of boredom, she decided to engage Mackey in conversation.

"Are we ever going to get our truck back?" she asked.

"You got other wheels."

"So what? It's ours and it's been five days."

Mackey crossed his thick arms. "Tell your pa to come get it."

Ellen didn't try to continue. She considered making an obscene gesture at the human bear, but she didn't want to risk being thrown out. She needed to be there for Morton's call. Thirty minutes later, it came.

She had so much to tell him—about the plans to burn down D.C, wipe out key databases, and kill off all the politicians. About the Commander's admission regarding the attack on New York, and about harboring some "secret weapon" from the ATF heist. She also told him about Barnett's special network and how each of the eleven other fanatics had separate, sealed orders.

"I thought there were twelve of them," Morton said.

"There were, but they killed one of the guys. Blew him up with a car bomb. A guy named Hendricks from Oregon."

"Damn! I wanted to talk to him. I'm flying up to Portland

tonight to talk to that associate of his, the informant Keller mentioned."

"Not trusting it to someone up there?"

"Not at the moment," Morton replied. "The heist took place on my turf. Also, two of my agents could have been innocent victims in a raid I knew nothing about. Think I got a case? Besides, I'm going to be meeting with SACs from Portland, Seattle, and Sacramento. There's a lot of discontent out in the field."

Suddenly, the urgency and dread which Ellen had been throttling burst forth. "We're going to need help, sir. These guys have gone home to start preparing for an all-out attack on the Capitol. If you had seen the blood-lust in their eyes. Even once we capture Barnett and Pilkin, the others may go ahead with their plans. If they're even just partially successful, the whole country could be up for grabs. You know how copy-cats are. People will come out of the woodwork to start shooting at their favorite targets. They might launch an anarchy without lighting a single match in D.C."

"Hang on," Morton said softly. "We've got to keep our heads."

"Wait! You're gonna love this! Someone bugged our cabin."

There was a brief silence. "Ceramic coils?"

Ellen filled him in on their discovery, and how they began feeding false information to whoever it was with the tape machine.

"So if we can get Crowley or whoever is leading this chase to go after these other guys, we might get assistance without having to ask directly. That's why we made such a strong pitch about Rumson being the leader. If we're lucky, maybe the goons will be waiting for him when he returns." Her voice darkened. "He nearly exposed us. The guy is really dangerous."

"How about the other ones?"

"Evil. Harry knows four of them besides Rumson; the rest I could pick out from pictures or mug shots. We just don't have much time."

Just then a huge hand pounded on the booth. Through the thick glass, Ellen could hear Mackey bellow: "Get off the phone!"

She opened the door a crack. "I'm talking to my mother, asshole!" Then she closed it and said, "Sorry. That was the local Neanderthal."

"I've got to run in a second," Morton said. "The warrants for Pilkin and Barnett are being processed, but don't jump yet."

"We can't anyway. Harry is out of town for a day or two. Get this: he's been sent to catch the President and his mistress on videotape." Ellen heard a low whistle through the receiver. "Also, Pilkin has gone off somewhere. I'm sure he'll be back soon."

"Okay. Let's shoot for Wednesday or Thursday next week; I'll be up north over the weekend. And Harry has to be in San Jose to testify before the grand jury in that Trong case. He needs to be there Monday, possibly Tuesday, as well. Be sure to tell him."

Ellen hung up and went back to the bar, under the glare of Mackey the bear. She wouldn't have stayed, but her schedule there wasn't complete.

Ten minutes later, Betsy walked in the door. She had a scarf over her head and large, dark sunglasses over her eyes. Her movements were short, her mouth was tight. She walked up to Ellen. "You wanted to see me?"

"Yeah, thanks for coming. You want a beer or something?"

Betsy looked at Mackey and said, "Gin and tonic."

Ellen put a $20 bill on the bar and said, "Coors." Then she led Betsy to a small table in the back.

"Harry told me about your conversation yesterday," Ellen said, "about the storm troopers Tuesday night and the one you attacked. We'd like to talk to him. We think we might be able to turn him into an informant for our cause."

"Your cause . . ."

Ellen waited a moment, and softened her voice. "Harry also told me about what happened with Kevin. I'm really sorry, Betsy." She leaned across the table. "That's all the more reason to get these guys, so nothing bad happens to Kevin. And others. These guys are on the loose, Betsy, and we can—"

She stopped short. Mackey was approaching with their drinks. He set the glasses down hard, glaring at Ellen with acid eyes. In response, she gave him a beaming smile. "Thanks, sweetie!" she said. "And don't keep the change."

Both the women waited until Mackey disappeared, then Betsy picked up her glass and drained half of it. She set it back down and looked at Ellen. "So what do you need my help for?"

"You know these guys. Harry knows them, too, but he's out of town. They'd recognize him anyway and figure something was up. But they didn't see me." She leaned across the table.

"I've set things in motion already. I tracked down the telephone guy who came out to install those lines. I told him his 'friends' had left something behind, something really valuable, and the lady of the house wanted to return it. I told him to tell his friends to meet you here tomorrow night—" Ellen chuckled. "—and said you'd leave your knives at home."

Betsy picked up her glass and drained the rest of her drink. "Harry sure told you a lot. Fucking men."

Ellen nodded. "Most of 'em, most of 'em. Harry's not usually so crass, but he figured it was necessary." She took another sip of beer. "Whatever happened is your business, Betsy."

Betsy's eyes were fixed on her glass. "So what do you want me to do?"

"Just make contact. It's going to be Saturday night, so this place'll be jammed. All I need you to do is go up and start chatting with him, or them." She chuckled again. "Maybe mime like you're stabbing the one guy in the back. I just need to be sure who they are. Then I'll come over and take it from there."

"What are you going to do?"

"I've got some of Harry's electronic equipment and I'll wire myself for sound. Then I'll coax whatever I can out of him, enough to hang him, and let Harry take it from there." Ellen paused. "You might do me one other favor. Actually two, since we're about the same size."

She stood up. "Let's get out of here. I hate this place."

Ellen took off for the door, with Betsy's footsteps not far behind her. She passed the long bar, whistling merrily, and was just about to reach for the door handle, when suddenly Betsy shouted: "Ellen, look out!"

She started to turn, but was caught midway by Mackey's massive arms. He slammed her against the wall, knocking the wind out of her. He clamped one hand over her mouth and the other over her throat, and Ellen's brain was on the verge of blacking out. The only thing that kept her sharp was his breath, hot and putrid.

"I'm tired of seeing your face," he said. "You and that pa of yours. You've been nothin' but trouble for me since you first slithered in here. I want you guys out of here, out of Sutter Springs." He pulled her head back and then slammed it against the wall again. "Is that clear?"

Ellen jerked her knee upwards with all her strength. She hit the target with a sickening thud. Mackey screamed and doubled over, grabbing for his crotch. Ellen brought her knee up again, hard. This time, she flattened the big man's nose, a crunching sound echoing off the barroom walls. As his hands went to his face, she shoved him back into a stack of chairs. He fell to the floor in a pile of splintered wood.

Ellen's throat was gripped with pain, but she managed to croak "Fuck off!" in Mackey's direction. Then she grabbed the door and stalked out.

Harry covered the gap between the sheltering redwoods and the back porch of the cabin in eight silent strides. It had taken him forty-five minutes to travel maybe 200 yards. Not because the vegetation was thick, but because it wasn't. A hundred feet up, the branches blocked the sky; at ground level, there was little growth between the massive stands. And thus, there was no protection other than the width of the huge trees.

By the time he made it to the porch, Harry was drenched with sweat. It wasn't from exertion, it was from all that time waiting, then scurrying to the next tree. Then waiting, then scurrying. Like a child's game, but with deadly consequences. Two Secret Service agents in a cruiser out front were taking turns making rounds of the cabin: walk to the back; scan the forest; check the doors; return to the car. The process took less than four minutes and was repeated every fifteen minutes like clockwork. Harry made his move to the porch ninety seconds after the last round. Barring any problems, he should be out in five minutes.

He heard whistling off to the right. Between the trees, he could see Kevin strolling casually along. The kid had changed into shorts, a dirty T-shirt, a bandanna, and had a backpack on his shoulders. He was headed toward the Secret Service agents.

Harry had argued against it, insisting he could get in and out unseen. But Kevin said he was taking no chances. If he didn't see Harry get into and out of that cabin, he was going to kill the Secret Service agents and do the job himself. He wasn't worried about how well-trained these men might be; he said his skills were better.

That removed Harry's last thoughts of subterfuge. At this point, he just needed to get the damn thing over with. He reached into his pocket and pulled out the lock-picking tools Kevin supplied. It had been ages since he'd done this, but the lock was a simple one and popped open with little effort.

He pushed the door slightly, waiting for an alarm; there was none. He advanced through the small cabin in a crouch, slinking up to the front door and the small inset window. He could see Kevin on the other side of the big sedan, in the midst of a lively discussion with the agents. They were relaxed, totally at ease with the situation.

Harry surveyed the layout. He had two micro video units to plant, each the size of a wine cork, and four options: a bedroom; a bathroom; a living room; and a kitchen. The units were wireless, so he didn't need cables, but he had to remember to stick the jump box somewhere outside the house, so the feed would make it up to the canyon rim.

The big challenge was where to put the units. He had two cameras and four rooms, so where was the President most likely to do it? The bedroom? The bathtub? On the kitchen table? In front of the fire?

Sweat was pouring out of him. He did not want to be doing this. He thought he had come to terms with this, convincing himself it was just another job and somebody was going to do it. But now that he held the video units in his hands, the thing that most came to mind was stomping them into the floor.

Bad option, of course. Too much else was at stake. If they didn't return with the video, the Commander would find some other way to get Gordo. He was probably planning to torch the man anyway, and was just using this as leverage to make sure the President was in the wrong place at the wrong time. But if they returned empty-handed, Kevin would likely be thrown in a dungeon and Harry would "Hendricks-ed"—maybe Ellen, too.

So he returned to the unsavory task of deciding where and in what positions the President would be most "photogenic" as he betrayed his wife, CC. Where would Harry get the most damaging shots, the fuel which would be used to help compromise the nation? It made him ill.

Just then, there was a soft buzzing in his backpack. It threw him for a moment, until he remembered that Kevin had stuck his pager inside, "Just in case." Harry shoved his hand in the pack, searching for the little device. He yanked it out and looked at it.

It read '122,' the code from their scouts that someone was coming up the road. Shit! There was no more time for thinking. Screw the President.

Harry flipped a little switch on the back of each video unit, turning them on. He placed one of the units above the front door, pointing toward the thick couch and the fireplace. They would miss someone entering the cabin, but pick them up once the person moved into the room. Harry put the other unit over the door in the bedroom, aimed at the bed. They would lose the doorway, but probably pick up the traffic in and out of the bathroom. It would have to do; there was no time to check the feeds.

He picked up the pack and slinked to the back door, checking for anyone coming past the house. It seemed clear. He snuck outside and started away, but suddenly remembered the jump box and dashed back. He placed it under the eaves with adhesive putty.

A car was coming up the road. Harry couldn't see it, but he could hear it. He said a silent prayer that the agents were not making further rounds and dashed for the nearest redwood. He threw his back against the tree and waited, listening. There were no shouts, no shots; he had made it.

An hour later, he was back up on the canyon rim. He had not turned around after he was clear of the cabin. He didn't want to think about it.

But Kevin was there, back in his jeans and hunched over the small monitor they had brought. He looked up and gave Harry a lecherous grin.

"She's here!" Kevin practically sang the words. "Check out this honey. No wonder Gordo is so hot for the babe."

Harry's breath stopped. The woman was stunning, even though clothed head-to-toe. Kevin was manipulating the controller, switching between the two cameras and trying to follow the young woman as she moved around the cabin, settling in.

"Hey, Harry, we should hop down and get some of that action after Gordo is through. It's only fair, don't you think? He's gotta be balling her on taxpayers' money."

Harry groaned. This was going to be a long night. A long couple of days, in fact, unless the President didn't show up. That would be worth the wait. But the chances of that were the same as for achieving world peace: none. Not the way this woman was shuffling around, preparing her love nest. Candles were set out, food strategically placed, a lacy nightgown draped across the bed, just as the Commander had said they'd see.

The sky was warming and darkening toward night. The young woman had spent nearly an hour in the bathroom, emerging finally with a towel around her hair and, to Kevin's dismay, another around her body. She looked at her watch, then picked up a small case from a side table and swept the nightgown off the bed. It had be close to show time. That was obvious from Kevin's breathing, and Harry's heart rate.

Fifteen minutes later, the pager buzzed and Kevin dove for it. "122!" he sang out. Two minutes after that, headlights appeared far down the road to the cabin. Inside, oblivious to signal, the young woman walked around lighting candles. Was this such a routine that she knew precisely when Gordo would arrive? Maybe he climaxed on schedule, too.

The car ground to a halt in front of the house. Harry couldn't see it from their vantage point, but the sounds made it to the rim, and the dust cloud wasn't far behind. A car door slammed. The young woman peeked out the window, then headed out of the bedroom, turning off the light as she went.

If there hadn't been all those candles, the rooms would have been too dark to film, at least right now. But as the woman made a last pass through the living room, with a sea of candles behind her, the camera gave a tantalizing view of her figure through the filmy material of her gown. This was going to work.

Then the woman disappeared below the view of the living room lens. She had to be greeting Gordo at the door. Kevin flipped rapidly back and forth between the two cameras, trying to catch the action. He reached out and punched the record buttons on the video decks. This was it.

The young woman suddenly appeared, coming in beneath the lens in the bedroom. She was backing up slowly, seductively. Her hands went to her shoulders. She gave a coy smile, and then slid the straps of her nightgown down her arms, one after the other. Harry's breathing stopped.

She went further, pushing the nightgown all the way to the floor and then stepping out of it. She reached out one hand and dragged her lover into the room, into a swooning embrace.

They broke the kiss—and both Harry and Kevin shrieked.

It was CC!

The Big Reveal

Ellen stuck her arm out the window of the Jeep and waved at the guys in the guardhouse, then jammed the accelerator and roared up to the compound. Back into the jaws of the beast.

She almost welcomed it, after the fitful lull of the past few days. Harry still wasn't back. Barnett didn't need her. And those agency goons she'd hoped to trap on Saturday night were stringing her along. The meeting was postponed for just one day, but only after a flurry of messages back and forth.

She ground the Jeep to a stop in her usual way, then hopped out and walked toward the house. Betsy was going to help her prepare for the evening's event, and it promised to be a bizarre experience. Ellen was just about to the porch when she heard a voice shouting from above.

"Hey! Where the hell have you been? Get your ass up here!"

Barnett was hanging out the window, borderline catatonic. It was comical, but it also demanded an explanation. Betsy would have to wait.

Barnett gripped the door, waiting for her as she reached the top of the stairs. He was even more harried at close range, slamming the door behind her. The room looked like a tornado had just passed through.

Ellen snickered. "New trends in interior design, I see."

"Fuck off. Why did you abandon me? You, the Commander, Harry and dork-boy—everybody! I'm stuck in this sinkhole while you're off partying."

"Slow down. You said on Friday you didn't need me."

"That was Friday, this is Sunday. The world is collapsing."

"Never one to go for hyperbole."

"Hey, you try keeping these militia geeks in line. So much for this being idiot-proof. Here I am, trying to get real work done, and I have to play wet-nurse to a bunch of lunatics. If they're not crashing their laptops, they're bogging down the network with—" He stopped and took a deep breath.

"I hear it coming," Ellen said.

"Please?! I've talked with that guy Keener from Georgia four times in just two days. He gives 'stupid' new dimensions. The others aren't much better. Tennessee keeps running different routines, seeing if he can crash the system. I'm about two minutes from frying his computer with an electromagnetic pulse."

"The Commander would love that."

"If he shows up again. He disappeared two days ago and nobody's saying shit about it. The guy is so mysterious it's spooky. And if Harry and dufus don't come back with the goods, we're all fucked."

Ellen cleared a spot on the bed and sat down. "Patience, boy."

"There's no time for patience! Torch Day is less than three weeks away and I've got so many databases to hit it's absurd. There's no way I can get everything done if I've got to baby-sit these morons. Name your price: Ten million? A hundred million? Help me with these jerks and it's yours."

"And you're going to be doing?"

"Logic bombs, pulses, shit like that. Sorry, but I have to keep the good stuff for myself. I don't have time to teach you right now."

Christ, if Barnett had already planted logic bombs!

They wouldn't actually blow up a computer, but logic bombs could scramble a computer's operating instructions, and the result would be just as dramatic. By wiping out the information on a system—there were numerous ways to do it—he could render that computer useless. The bombs would probably all be set to go off on a specific day and time, thus multiplying havoc and hysteria. What did he call it? Torch Day?

If Barnett located the back-up sites as well, he could effectively erase all trace of Social Security numbers or IRS records or a bank's holdings or . . .

That was probably where these militia guys fit in. For all that talk of burning down D.C., some of them had to be going after back-up sites and disaster recovery facilities. A little gasoline, a few firebombs in concert with Barnett's electronic attacks, and the country would be on a course to disaster.

It was outrageous, but this bizarre alliance really could erase the country that way. And though buildings and cities were defensible, short of pulling apart Barnett's brain, Ellen might never find all his targets or how he was going to hit them until it was too late.

"Come on, what do you say? Don't play hard-to-get."

Ellen sighed. "Those guys give me the creeps. Thanks, but—"

"You can't refuse me! What will it take?"

It was a double-edged sword. If she refused, Barnett would be distracted by the militia leaders, but she would lose her access to him and complicate the takedown tremendously. If she agreed to help, the takedown should be easy, but he would have a couple more days of freedom to concentrate on electronically bombing the world.

Then it hit her, and she smiled. "Can I look over your shoulder when I'm not playing sysop or doing telephone support?"

"You can look in my pants. Anything!"

She shrugged. "Okay. But not tonight."

"Why not?"

Ellen smiled. "Girls' night out."

Suddenly, there was a chorus of horns in the yard below. Barnett vaulted past her to get to the window. Ellen stepped up in time to see Harry and Kevin getting out of an old pickup truck. Kevin was waving a small video box around and grinning like some conquering hero.

"Yes!" Barnett shouted, and dashed out of the room.

Ellen followed at a slower pace and found Harry on the porch. She dragged him toward her Jeep.

"You don't look as cheery as Kevin does," she whispered.

"It's worse than you think. Right family, wrong adulterer."

Ellen gasped. "And you got it all on tape?"

Harry nodded.

Ellen motioned for Harry to get in the Jeep, behind the wheel. She got in on the other side. "You'll need to take this to San Jose, since Mackey still has your truck. You have to be there in the morning—maybe Tuesday, too—to testify before Trong's grand jury. Any problem getting away for a few days?"

Harry shrugged. "I'll just go and work it out later."

"What about the tape? The earliest we can grab these guys is Wednesday. Jesus, CC is the adulterer? With a woman?"

"Isn't that a kicker? The woman is stunning, too." Harry shook his head. "They want it for some kind of leverage, so we should be okay. They were talking three weeks before things would explode."

Ellen groaned. "Speaking of 'explode', watch out for Mackey. He slammed me against the wall the other day and threatened me. My response probably didn't help." She jerked her knee upwards.

"Ouch! Warning taken. What about the rogues?"

Ellen briefed him on the sting planned for that night.

"They're doing a little gamesmanship," she said.

"So why did they agree to come?"

Ellen laughed. "I found a copy machine and ran a print of the coil, then added a note: 'Who gets this? CNN or you?' I left it for them at the pharmacy. I kept changing locations for my drops, to keep them guessing."

"But what about Mackey's bar. If he sees you in there . . ."

She smiled. "He won't recognize me. And there's nowhere else."

"I don't like this," Harry said. "Can't it wait?"

Ellen shook her head. "Those other militia guys are back home now, wherever that might be, and we can't cover them alone. We need help, and Morton is concerned about being sabotaged or ignored."

"I just don't like you soloing on this."

She put her hand on his arm. "I'm a big girl, Dad."

The first time through the videotape, Barnett was silent, his pulse quickening as the action moved toward the big surprise. He, too, shrieked at the discovery about CC. Then he went silent again, feeling a different kind of tension as Kevin skimmed through highlights from the video. It had been way too long since he'd gotten sloppy with a woman. He was going to have to work on Ellen; she was probably a wildcat in bed!

The Commander arrived back at the compound as Kevin rewound the tape. He joined them in the library and they played the video again, this time with running commentary from Barnett.

When it was over, Barnett got up from the sofa and turned to Kevin. "Outstanding! Absolutely outstanding! The only way it could have been better is if Gordo had joined them for a three-way." He pounded Kevin on the shoulder. "Great work, buddy-boy. You really surprised me."

Kevin blushed and cast his eyes toward the Commander. The older man looked at him and slowly grinned, nodding his head. "Nice work, son. Very nice work."

Kevin shrugged, holding back a smile. "Well, I can't take all the credit. Harry got in and set those cameras." The smile burst forth. "But I was the one who pushed it, who made sure we came home with the goods. You shoulda seen it when I walked up to those Secret Service agents!"

"Nice work," the Commander said again. Then he turned and started out of the room. "Come on, Barnett," he said over his shoulder.

Barnett gave Kevin another pat on the shoulder, then hurried after the Commander. Ol' Flattop was headed upstairs, toward Barnett's room.

The Commander was at the door when Barnett got to his room. "Look at this mess. Don't you have any personal pride?"

"No time," Barnett said. "I could make my bed or I could work on databases. Which would you prefer?"

The Commander pointed at Barnett's computer. "Get on that and take back that two million dollars, the payment you sent to Oregon this week. And make sure it can't be traced."

Barnett sat down and started tapping at the keys. Once he had the process under way, he looked over and said, "What's up?"

The Commander shrugged. "The man won't need it any longer. Transfer it to that 'Jerry' account of mine and I'll figure out what to do with it later. Don't clean out his account, just that two million."

"Shall I ask why?"

"Do you need to?"

The tone was vaguely threatening, so Barnett dropped it. Whatever this bozo did on his own time was of no concern, as long as it didn't come back at him. But Barnett resolved then to start working up some protective measures, just in case he needed leverage, something even guns would be powerless against.

"So how are the boys doing with their computers?"

Barnett groaned. "Disastrous. They're either brain-dead or trying to sabotage the system. But that's not—"

"I thought you said this was idiot-proof."

"That's not the worst of it. Most are having second thoughts, either about their particular assignments, or about you as their leader, or even carrying through with this in the first place! Seems the magic of your presence has worn off."

The Commander's eyes drilled into him. "They told you this?"

"Of course not. They're unanimous in wanting to lynch me."

"Then how would you know?"

"You think I can't watch everything that's going on from their laptops? This is Barnett you're talking to. I'm sure the messages slamming me are just a test to see if I'm looking in. It's really putrid stuff, but I refuse to react."

He almost added: *I'll get my revenge later.*

"So the natives are restless?" the Commander said.

"Not all of them. Texas, Georgia, and Alabama are with us all the way. West Virginia, Arizona, and, ah, Michigan are just not happy being second fiddle. Arkansas wants me dead and that asshole from Tennessee is determined to crash the system. He thinks what he's got is superior, though I suspect he has some other agenda. And Kansas and Ohio are blitzing everyone else's mailbox, trying to talk the others out of it."

The Commander snorted. "I half suspected it. Once they got home, it was bound to come up. A bunch of women."

"So, time to bring in the heavy weapons? You said you had 'the goods' on these guys."

"All I'm worried about is someone running to the Feds."

"Wait a minute! What if they start dropping out? A mutiny is brewing and you don't care? Christ, what about the plan?"

"It's not a problem," the Commander said quietly.

"Not a problem? Not a problem?! How the hell are we—"

The Commander held up his hand. "It's not a problem. Things have changed. We don't need them now, not in D.C."

"What are you talking about?"

The Commander smiled. "I have a new weapon. That's what that two million dollars was for."

Barnett exhaled slowly. Something about the Commander's tone gave him short, cold pangs of dread. He almost didn't want to ask, but the words came out anyway.

"What is it?"

The Commander waited, gauging Barnett's eyes, letting the suspense build. Then he smiled.

"It's a nuclear bomb."

"What?!" Barnett's head jerked involuntarily. "A nuke? That's outrageous! Where did you—"

"Keep your voice down. No one knows this but you and me. Got that? This baby will flatten a couple square miles, I'm told, enough to wipe out our entire target zone, so we don't need those other guys in D.C. We probably don't even want them nearby, if it risks alerting the authorities."

"Why didn't you tell me? Why did we go through all that B.S. with those dirt farmers? I've wasted so much time on—"

"We're going to need them anyway, and I wasn't sure I would get it. I only picked it up yesterday."

"Is it here? Where?"

"In the car. In a suitcase."

"Really?!" Barnett's eyes nearly blew out. "God, is it safe? What if it goes off?"

The Commander shook his head. "Unless somebody shoots at it or we get in a car wreck on the way to D.C., it's safe. It won't detonate without an auxiliary charge."

"Do you have experience with nukes? How do you fire it?"

"Easy. I'll use a trigger charge. Just wrap some plastic explosive around it, detonate that, and a large part of Washington goes with it. The casualty toll will be higher than we expected, but this is D.C. we're talking about, so who cares if it's a couple million. Besides, freedom has its price."

"A nuclear bomb. That's awesome! Where did you get it?"

"It was in that ATF truck. Hendricks and his crew did the job, but this one guy grabbed the nuke before anybody realized what it was. He and Hendricks were already on the skids, so he called me to see if I was interested."

The Commander sighed. "I had to kill him. He was working both sides. I found out he planned to give me the bomb, then turn me in to the Feds."

Barnett's breath caught. "Maybe they followed you here."

"No way. He didn't give up my name. He was jerking ZOG

around for a bigger payoff. Greedy bastard, like Hendricks."

Barnett's brain was spinning. A nuclear bomb? Outrageous! That changed everything. Or did it?

He exhaled sharply. "We can't forget about your friends. We've got so many other targets—my targets. Plus things like the Pentagon and such."

The Commander nodded. "We also need them to take out people at the state level, remember? We don't want a conference of governors setting up an interim government afterwards. These guys need to help discourage that. We don't have to kill all fifty; ten or so should prime the pump for the rest of the country. This movement is just waiting for a spark."

The enormity of it all flashed in Barnett's brain, and his stomach fluttered. Nerves? Fear? Excitement? Probably all three. But for all his anxiety about a possible mutiny, he was feeling energized now.

"So we need to change their orders?" Barnett said.

"We've got time. We don't want people to get itchy trigger fingers. But I want to know what *that* is doing here." The Commander pointed to a FedEx box on the top of Barnett's bed.

Before Barnett could answer, the phone by his laptop rang. His body sank. He let it ring, shaking his head. Finally, he turned to the Commander. "Can you answer that? Don't say 'hello.' Just say: 'Press the Escape key, Roy.'" He picked up the cordless phone and tossed it.

The Commander caught the phone and gave Barnett a wary look. Then he raised the phone and said, "Press the Escape key, Roy." His eyes flicked to Barnett. A moment later, he said, "Glad to help. Goodbye."

He tossed the phone back. "What's with Keener?"

"The guy's a moron. I'm pushed back on other tasks because of calls like that, plus the rest of the crap from these guys."

"Well, where's Ellen? I thought she was gonna help you."

"She is, now."

"So why the FedEx box? I thought I said no more shipments."

Barnett exploded. "Do you think this shit happens by magic? Do you think I can just shove that videotape in this little slot on my laptop and instantly send pictures through cyberspace? I have to convert it, George, and that requires extra equipment. Tools, man, I need 'em, too."

The Commander nodded. "I'm just leery of people coming up here. So, what did you get?"

"An external hard drive to hold the video conversions, plus some new software and the appropriate cables. I figured sending Gordo stills from the video might not be enough. You can fake a lot of things in a static computer image, but it's a lot harder in a 30-second video clip."

The Commander frowned. "What if it isn't clear? What if he thinks it's an actress. What if he wants to see the whole thing?"

"Good point. I hadn't considered that. How would we get it into his hands?" Barnett's mind went into overdrive, testing routings and timing and logistics in a dozen different permutations.

"We would have to get a copy out there," he said. "Somewhere near enough to the President that he could go out by himself to look at it."

"Our man in West Virginia could do it," the Commander said.

"Not if we want to do something technical with it. He's almost as bad as that fool Keener in Georgia."

"Why do you need to do something technical?"

"Control. If I have the President online, I own him. I can follow or even direct everything he sees. If he's out in the boonies . . ."

Barnett's mind raced away again. After a moment, a smile began to spread across his face.

"I've got it. It'll require some more equipment, and I'll have to talk Ellen into jumping on a plane, but—" That low, maniacal laugh erupted. "—this'll be classic!"

The Commander gave him a puzzled look, then shrugged. "You know, I didn't hear you mention Rumson. Is he leading the mutiny?"

"Not on the BBS. I haven't seen a word from him. I figured that was a good sign."

The Commander shook his head. "It's not."

Ellen took a deep breath and pulled open the door to the bar. If anyone recognized her in this get-up, she was dead—from humiliation. Long eyelashes, rouge, a bow in her hair, and a push-up bra? Sacrilege! A complete repudiation of her San Diego surfing past. And this was of her own doing, for the first and last time in her life. It was a good thing Harry was on his way to San Jose or he would be rolling on the floor.

Mackey's was crowded for a Sunday night, but that was probably just as well. Ellen spotted Betsy sitting at the end of the long bar, her back to the wall, deep in conversation with another woman and working her way nervously through a cigarette. Betsy was wearing a plaid shirt tucked into jeans, with her hair pulled back and tied up with a ribbon. It looked natural on her, as did the make-up. On Ellen, the white blouse with appliquéd flowers and the "war paint" on her face was off the scale. And the small tape recorder hidden under the short jeans skirt was starting to chafe.

She moved slowly through the crowd, ignoring the stares she was getting. Were they laughing inside or was she, as Betsy had put it, a slab of fresh meat? Ellen tuned into the stares; yeah, fresh meat. Typical.

She wasn't rushing it, but Betsy finally made eye-contact and gave a subtle shake of her head. No, the goons weren't there yet. Then Betsy flashed a smile and straightened her back, and Ellen slowly did the same. Slouching was out of character with the bow.

She had gone as far as the middle of the bar and stopped. Might as well get the big test over with. She cleared her throat, rehearsed the words in her head, and then found an opening at the bar. She propped her arms up, pushed her garment-aided chest forward slightly, and gave Mackey a warm smile.

"Hi, there," she said, in a soft Southern accent. "Could I please have a gin and tonic?" She batted her eyelashes once and prayed madly.

The gruff, menacing bear looked at her quizzically, nodded slowly, and turned to fix the drink. That baffled look was still there when he set the glass in front her. "$4.50," he said.

Ellen reached into the too-cute purse Betsy had lent her and pulled out six dollars. She slid the bills across the bar and said, "Thanks, hon. Keep the change." She picked up the drink, flashed another quick smile at the man who tried to choke her two days before, and walked away.

Yes! It worked! The scam was on. No one would—

There was a hand on her shoulder, and someone's breath in her ear.

"Is this what you do for fun?" Barnett said. "I don't know whether to laugh or puke."

Ellen cast a glance at the bear—he wasn't watching—and grabbed Barnett's arm, dragging him toward the next room and away from the crowd. She nodded at Betsy as she passed and pushed Barnett to a table in the corner, taking the chair with a sight line to the bar.

"What are you doing, following me?" she said.

"Hey, I get to crawl out of the cave once in a while. How many other places are there, anyway? I was just standing there, enjoying a brew, and I see this mutant walking by." He looked down at her chest. "A rather ripe mutant."

"Give it a rest. I'm trying to set up one of those goons from the other night. In two minutes, you've got to scram."

"Whoo, Commando woman! Pretty cutsie disguise." He stuck his finger in his throat.

Ellen glanced toward Betsy, then leaned over the table.

"Listen, this is serious. Don't push me, Barnett. If you want me to help you, you've got to help me, and that means vanishing. Okay?"

Barnett sat back and smiled. "Okay, here's the condition. I need you to take a little trip."

"Out of the question."

"Hear me out. It's either you or Harry. We need to set-up Netcams in a couple remote locations. You know, like little TV cameras to send pictures over the Net? I also need to get a video-tape to the D.C. area as soon as possible. And, if you're really helpful, you could do a little on-site computer support of that Keener bozo in Georgia. What do you say?"

There was no time for this. The sting was going to roll any second. And the takedown of the Commander and Barnett was coming up in a matter of days; she couldn't run off now. That thought looped back in her brain several times, but it didn't reach a resolution. Something else was tweaking her.

Working with the guy in Georgia. Getting past the password protection of Barnett's BBS. Making a personal contact with one, maybe two of these militia leaders. Those were opportunities she wasn't sure she could pass up.

She looked up. "When? Where? Why?"

Barnett smiled. "Tuesday. I'd send you now, but I'm not get-ting new equipment until late tomorrow. Where? Atlanta first, then D.C. The guy from West Virginia will pick up you there. The sooner you get all this done the better, from my standpoint, but I can't imagine you'd want to spend a lot of time with these guys anyway."

"I absolutely have to be back by Thursday. It's personal."

Barnett leaned across the table. "Don't you want to get per-sonal with me? I'd even take you in costume."

God, how Ellen hated that wormy way guys tried to insinuate themselves. In less than a week, she'd be able to really tell him what she thought. But not yet. "Maybe when I return. For now, beat it."

Barnett sat back, drained his beer, and got to his feet. He gave her a wink and disappeared into the crowd.

Ellen looked at her watch. The goons were late, as expected. The big Q was when they would show up, and how many there'd be. She wasn't worried, she just didn't want to waste all night. She was too pumped already.

But she had the ace—the coil—and only one of them. The goons would be looking for two, and until they got both, they'd probably submit to anything.

She was swirling her finger around in her drink when she saw Betsy stiffen. Not abruptly, but clearly enough. The goons? Betsy didn't look over, but she made a little stabbing motion on the bar. That was the signal; the goons were definitely here.

Ellen's pulse jumped several notches. Until now, this exercise had been academic, played out on paper and in her mind. Suddenly, a surprising emotion washed over her: anger. At the arrogance, at the invasion of privacy, at the illegal bullshit they were trying to get away with, and, most of all, for risking her life and Harry's without warning or apology. In a flash, merely trapping and exposing the goons wasn't enough; they had to suffer.

She slipped her fingers inside her blouse to double-check the position of the small microphone she had pinned to her bra. Then she stood up, straightened her skirt, plastered on a smile, and headed for the bar.

Betsy had moved down ahead of her. As Ellen worked her way through the crowd, she saw Betsy step between two men—young, tall, definitely HRT types—and put an arm around each one's shoulders. That had to be tough, given how Harry described the last encounter. As Ellen got closer, she could see the strain in Betsy's face, forcing her way through small talk. It was definitely time to rescue her.

Then Betsy did something surprising. She raised her left arm and pointed at that man's back. She didn't make contact, so neither man noticed, but it gave Ellen the direction she needed. If she was going to nail one of these goons, that was the one.

Ellen slid around behind the trio and snuggled in against the man on the left. She heard the name "Jimmy" tossed his direction. She leaned around him toward Betsy.

"Hey, girl," Ellen said, in her fake Southern accent. "You gonna be selfish here or share the wealth?" She smiled up at Jimmy.

He looked her over. "We're talking business here."

"This is a bar," Ellen said. "Ain't no place for business."

Jimmy chuckled. "I like forward women, just not right now."

Ellen frowned. "I'm so disappointed. Here I got all dressed up, even brought along my best new broach. Want to see it?"

The two men looked at each other and rolled their eyes.

"Yeah, I got it right here." Ellen dug into her pocket. "See!"

They looked like they had been electrocuted. It was a better reaction than Ellen expected to the little ceramic coil she was holding up. She giggled and stuffed the coil in her bra.

Jimmy grabbed for it, but she slapped his hand away.

"Have some manners. We're in a family place, and they won't take kindly to your pawing at me that way."

He stepped close, his eyes menacing. "Give me that thing."

Ellen looked around him to Betsy. "Has he always been this rude?" She leaned in close to the man, dropping her accent and matching his glare. "You want this back? Then you'll give me some respect, and you'll answer my questions. Got it?"

The man stared at her. "What do you want?"

Ellen snapped back into the accent. "Well, not here. Why don't you send your little friend away for a while, and we'll go in the back and talk." She looked over at Betsy. "Thanks for the introduction, Bets, and if I'm not home at a reasonable hour, you know what to do." Ellen looked over at the other man and whispered loudly: "CNN."

She laughed wickedly and looped her arm through Jimmy's, leading him toward the back room. As they worked their way through the crowd, she looked up at the man.

"You're an impressive specimen, Jimmy. Big. Strapping. But

I've found that size doesn't always correlate when you get down to the nitty-gritty. Is that true for you?"

"Keep it up."

Ellen led him to the back room. Two men were at the pool table, but they were talking more than shooting. Ellen walked over, pulled a $20 bill out of her purse, and set it on the table. "Could I treat you boys to some drinks? My friend and I would like to play."

"Sure thing," one said. He picked up the $20 and they left.

"Alright, hand it over," Jimmy said.

Ellen pushed herself up and sat on the pool table. "It's not a one-way street, chum. You've got to give before you can get."

"Who are you?" Then he shook his head. "You're King, aren't you?"

"Isn't that irrelevant? Certainly was the other night. The question is: Who are you working for?"

Jimmy exhaled. "You *are* King. You and your flea-bag partner. I'm surprised you got through Quantico looking like this."

"Fooled you, asshole, though I suspect that isn't hard to do."

He moved towards her, his hand out. "Give me the coils."

Ellen leaned back, shaking her head. "I told you, you've got to give before you can get."

"What the fuck do you want?"

"For starters, why were there no warrants for eavesdropping? Not exactly legal, is it?"

"This is not a game, King. Give me those coils. There's gonna be hell to pay if you jerk me around."

"Is that a threat? Authorized by whom? Brendan Crowley? Warren Keller? The Attorney General? Yourself? Why did you raid Pilkin's place?"

"Don't be stupid about this."

Ellen reached inside her blouse and pulled out the coil. "*This* is not stupid. *This* is illegal. *This* is going to be awfully embarrassing for the Attorney General to see in the New York Times. You want that on your record?" She shoved the coil back in her bra. "What's your name, anyway? Tell me now or this meeting is over."

The man pulled his credentials out of his pocket and flashed them, fury building in his face. He snapped the wallet back and shoved it in his pocket.

"Okay, James Rodriguez. You're assigned where?"

"Quantico. On special detail to Brendan Crowley. And you're wasting your time."

Ellen shook her head. "How long have you been out here, and what exactly was the purpose of this surveillance?"

Jimmy sighed. "Three weeks. Looking for illegal weapons, stolen from that ATF shipment."

"And why here?"

"I follow orders. Something you seem to be incapable of."

"I'll say it again: Why Sutter Springs? Why George Pilkin? Why the illegal surveillance?"

"Because the guy was involved in that ATF heist."

Ellen smiled. "Say what?"

"I just *told* you: the—"

His face suddenly paled. His eyes closed as the realization sunk in. "You're wired, aren't you? Do *you* have a warrant?"

Ellen grinned. "Would I do somethin' like that? That's your M.O. Jimmy, not mine." She undid a button on her blouse and opened it enough to reveal the microphone. "Oops, I *am* wired!"

Suddenly, he lunged at her, his hands on her shoulders, pushing her back. Ellen crashed onto the felt and over several of the balls. She landed with such force that it felt like her ribs were going to crack. Jimmy was on top of her immediately, his massive frame pinning her in place, countering every attempt she made to break free. The weight of his body threatened to suffocate her.

Then he raised himself up and slapped her hard across the face, wrenching her out of the fear and pain, and shooting her into a rage. Her left hand was free and she swung at his head. He caught her wrist and slammed it back to the table. It felt like he had broken it.

She jerked her knee toward his crotch with all her might, but he turned his body sideways, deflecting the blow. Then he clamped his left hand on her throat and pressed with all his strength, choking off her breath.

She could only get little gasps in. The act of breathing took all her focus. It was impossible to fight him, impossible to think.

He shifted his weight, and Ellen suddenly got more air. But it wasn't a gift; he was changing his position for something. He reached down and yanked at her blouse. It took two tries to rip it open. He snatched the microphone off her bra and hurled it across the room. Ellen knew what was next.

She bucked her body upwards as best she could, but he crushed her against the table and the pool balls again. He reared up and slapped her even harder this time, and it sent her consciousness hurtling toward the edge.

But then his hand was in her bra, and her mind snapped back. *Go with the force, not against it!*

The pressure on her right side was minimal now, so she hooked her legs against the pool table and rolled that direction. She slid off the table, feet first, flowing out from under him as he fished around for the coil.

She landed on her hands and knees, and he was instantly on top of her, flattening her against the floor. It knocked the wind out of her, leaving her powerless to fight. Jimmy got up, spun her around, then reached down and tore her bra away with one ferocious yank. The coil went rolling across the floor.

He snagged it and shoved it in a pocket, then went back to Ellen. "Where's the recorder?" he demanded.

He looked at her, splayed across the floor, and grinned. "Only one place it could be. Or is it *really* hidden?" He chuckled nastily and reached for her skirt.

Suddenly, there was a blur of motion behind her, above her. It came so fast that all Ellen could see was a pool cue streaking through air. The stick slammed into the base of Jimmy's skull with brutal force, his body lurching forward involuntarily. Someone stepped up and swung the cue stick again, and again, and again until the stick finally splintered. By now, Crowley's goon was lying still on the floor.

Ellen pulled her blouse over her breasts and raised her eyes.

It was Barnett!

She closed her eyes and took several deep breaths, hurting everywhere; if nothing was broken, it would be a miracle. She opened her eyes again. It really was Barnett standing there. Talk about miracles! She was speechless.

He looked down at her, a pained smile on his face.

"Just returning the favor. And I had to protect my investment."

A Concerned Citizen

Harry wasn't, by nature, a morning person. Being in the office at 7:00 A.M. was usually torture, even with three cups of coffee to fortify him. But today, it was a breeze; a pleasure, even, to be able to walk through those doors again, as if life was back to normal. He'd spent two nights in his own bed, read the junk mail just because it had his name on it, and walked through San Francisco without worrying that someone was out to get him.

Well, his guard had been up a little. After spending all of Monday in front of the grand jury in that chip-theft case, he couldn't totally forget about Trong's buddies. His name had been on their hit list. But he'd had a phalanx of Special Agents around him at the courthouse in San Jose and a support team trailed him when he wandered out last night. Not a Viet Viper in sight.

For such an early hour, there was already a crush of activity in the office, but it was actually comforting. Harry dodged some of the agents hurrying past, deposited his briefcase in his cubicle, and headed for Jim Morton's office. It had been seven days since he'd seen the SAC, a lifetime in Pilkin-years.

Morton glanced up as Harry entered. "You look relaxed," he said. "I'm envious."

Harry chuckled. "It's fake, chief. I don't need more work."

"I wasn't suggesting—"

"I know. I'm just relieved with this Sutter Springs biz wrapping up. I couldn't take another week like the last one. Are we still on for tomorrow?"

Morton nodded. Harry noticed that he looked unusually tense.

"The takedown will be at midnight," Morton said. "Fifty agents will leave here in the morning. Ellen's friend, Sonia Taylor, will be handling the communications; I'll be there by 9 P.M. I trust you and Ellen still have access to Pilkin and Barnett. Any problem with you coming down here?"

"None that I know of. This should go down smooth and easy."

Morton took a long breath. "We have a new problem. I'm not sure how to say this." He paused, then looked up at Harry. "There was a nuclear bomb on that ATF truck."

"What?! That's impossible! Why did ATF have a nuke?"

"How should I know? You think anybody is going to admit to a loss like that? Not the Defense Department, nor anybody else for that matter. Hell, I barely got the ATF to admit they'd had it, let alone how they got it."

Harry dropped into a chair. "I knew something was up. Why didn't you tell us this sooner?"

"I only found out myself the other day, up in Portland. Apparently the informant had the nuke until the other day, but he sold it to some militia guy."

"Who? Where? When?"

Morton shook his head. "The guy is dead. The SAC in Portland talked to him Friday night, but he never showed up for our meeting Saturday. His body was found yesterday in a river in eastern Oregon, dead a couple of days."

"Executed?"

Morton nodded.

Harry's eyes burned through him. "Are you sure about this? The nuke, I mean. How reliable could this informant be? Maybe he was setting you up."

"It's been confirmed, both by ATF and Keller in D.C."

"Then what are they waiting for?!" Harry shot to his feet. "What about the Nuclear Emergency Search Team? Or the military? God, if that makes it to Washington, it could level the city. Park it in the middle of the Mall and you could wipe out the entire government, not to mention a million or so people."

Morton raised his palms. "I'm told this is under control, straight from Warren Keller's mouth. He said NEST had already been notified and we should stick to the business in front of us."

Harry sat back down. "Fucking bureaucrats."

Morton leaned forward. "I really wasn't stringing you along. I was told there was something significant on that truck, but that was all. I raised holy hell after I found out what. If I had any goodwill with Keller before, it's shot now."

"So now we've got to deal with a nuke as well? That'll complicate the takedown if Pilkin has it."

"Could there be anyone else?"

"Rumson. He's the only one I know vicious enough to use it." Harry frowned. "Though it was Pilkin making sly comments about his special little tool at that meeting last week. God, a nuke?"

Morton nodded. "Here's what we're looking for: a large, black suitcase; weighs about a hundred pounds. It's supposedly stable." He exhaled sharply. "It has a blast radius of more than three miles. Outside that: burns, blindness, radiation sickness, and cancer for decades. The devastation could go way beyond D.C."

Harry groaned, his eyes withered shut. "We need help for this takedown, sir, rogues be damned. That's dangerous stuff to be dealing with and, personally, I'd rather not see it at close range. They have experts for that kind of thing."

"I'm working on it," Morton said. "What about the other eleven guys? Any chance they know about this?"

Harry shrugged. "Pilkin was pretty circumspect, but anything's possible. I imagine he would keep it to himself, though. But we've still got to take these others seriously; they redefine 'fanatic.' Any chance of getting help from the other SACs?"

"We're working on it, since we're getting no feedback from D.C. Everyone is concerned about the rogues ignoring the law."

"Forgive me," Harry said, "but after several days with these guys, choking on their fervor, I'd want to make damn sure the country was safe first, and then worry about justice—particularly if they've got a nuke. They'll use it, sir; don't underestimate them."

Morton nodded. "I just hope it doesn't come to that."

They were silent for quite a while. Finally, Harry said, "Anything new on the investigation into the deaths of the Director and the Deputy Director?"

"Who knows? Information continues to go one way. Every SAC I've talked to has been told the same thing: 'If we need your help, we'll ask. Until then, worry about your own cases.' Even Hoover wasn't that tight-lipped. An old friend, Abe Potter, is the SAC at the Washington Metropolitan field office. He's going to check around quietly to see who's assigned to that investigation. But he's right under Keller's nose, so there's a limit to what he can do."

"How long is this going to go on?"

"Got me. We just have to take it a day at a time, gather resources as we can, and pray the President doesn't permanently install Warren Keller as Director."

There was a knock and the door to Morton's office flew open. Ellen surged in, tossed a micro-cassette tape at Harry, and dropped into a chair.

"Sorry to bust in," she said, "but I've got ten minutes before I have to leave for the airport. Did you get my message, Harry?"

He didn't answer. He was stunned by the bruises on the side of her face. "What happened? Your message said you were okay, but this—"

"Forget how I look; nothing is broken. I got a confession from one of those goons, the one that Betsy tried to attack. It's on that tape. I'm off to the East Coast, so you guys have to run with it."

"Slow down," Morton said. "You've lost me already."

Ellen took a long breath, then launched into the story of the sting on Sunday night, of the goon's attack, and how Barnett came to her rescue.

"It was absolutely remarkable," she said.

"There's a problem," Harry said. "Excuse the pun, but you exposed us. They know we've got incriminating information now; they're not going to ignore that. I'm surprised they didn't come after you."

"I spent Sunday night at the compound and they weren't about to storm in there. Betsy and Barnett insisted I go back with them, and I was in no shape to refuse."

"Weren't they suspicious?"

"Didn't seem to be. I told them I was trying to turn the guy into an informant, since we discovered that coil. They thought I was trying to help the cause."

"Have you been back to the cabin?"

Ellen shook her head. "I spent last night in my own apartment, and the only person who came knocking at my door was Barnett's parole officer."

"What?" Harry and Morton said it together.

"Yeah, I've been in contact with her. Her name is Natalie Weston and she's dying to get her hands on Barnett again. By the way, we have to wait until Thursday now for the takedown."

"Why?" Harry said. "What's going on?"

Ellen reached in her handbag and pulled out a videotape. "Look familiar? This is a copy, which I'm taking to D.C. for Barnett. I'm also going to be setting up some Netcams and doing computer support for one of the militia leaders."

"You're losing me," Morton said. "The videotape?"

"You don't want to know," Harry replied.

"Netcams?"

Ellen reached into her bag and pulled out a small cube with a lens on one side. "These hook up to a laptop with a wireless modem. It sends a live image over the Internet, like having a TV camera hooked to your laptop, except the image is not as sharp and jumps around. Barnett plans some type of surveillance, but why he wants one in Georgia and one in the D.C. area is beyond me."

"And the computer support?" Morton asked.

"The guy in Georgia; his name is Roy Keener, if that rings a bell. He's so dense when it comes to computers that it's becoming a problem, and this computer network is critical to their plans. I agreed to go because it may be our only chance to look at the system in use. It should also give me an opening with this guy if we need it later."

Harry frowned. "I feel like I should go with you, but I'm stuck in San Jose today."

"It can't wait," Ellen said. "And we can't fry this tape either. I've got to carry through with Barnett's instructions or I won't be able to get near him for the takedown. This tape is just a set-up. Their target date is weeks away and they'll be iced long before that. It won't spare the President, but . . ."

"We've got some other news for you," Harry said.

Ellen's face went white as Harry explained.

"A nuke?" The words barely made it out of her mouth. She took a long breath. "These guys would use it, too."

"That's why we've got to wrap this up as soon as possible," Morton said. "When will you be back?"

"Tomorrow night, unless something else comes up. I should be back in Sutter Springs Thursday morning at the latest, so we can do the takedown at midnight Thursday."

"I was going back tonight," Harry said. "Want me to wait?"

"No. Barnett's parole officer is going to give me a ride. She wants to be around when we capture him."

Barnett was in the zone, a sort of hacker heaven where ideas poured through his fingers before they even hit his consciousness. Nothing existed outside of the screen in front of him and the challenges that lurked on the other side of cyberspace. It was a hyper-reality, tossing commands into the ether and seeing the equivalent of a bank vault fly open with a silent bang. It didn't happen every time, of course; not every network or database was open to him. But like Thomas Edison, he just kept going, absolutely certain that he would succeed. And when things were flowing, when he was advancing despite formidable obstacles, getting closer to the grail–du–jour, that was the zone.

It was a rarified state, one where time didn't exist, sleep didn't matter, and food was irrelevant. Anything that kept him away from the machine was a distraction, and could be a point of advantage for his opponents. Speed was key when you were deep into something like the White House computer network, and all these government lackeys were scurrying to stick their fat fingers in the dike. But they were outmatched, no matter how good they were. They were facing off against Jeff Barnett.

They didn't know that, of course. He slipped into the White House network unseen at 1 A.M. Monday morning. He hadn't planned to start so early, but he'd been too wired after rescuing Ellen to go to sleep. It was now Tuesday afternoon and he had barely slept.

He had started with the playing field: how the network was set up; access points; encryption and authentication procedures; user status levels. Then he went into the e-mail system, studying usage patterns, message content, and so on. He needed to find someone who read their own mail, who didn't rely on an assistant to do their computer work for them, as the President did. What Barnett had to say might be lost on a low-level twit.

And his hunch was right: Bernard Jessop, the President's chief of staff and a renowned tech head, sat at the computer and read his own e-mail. There were lots of clues, but the key was how soon a response was sent once a message was read. Secretaries didn't fire off replies so quickly.

But Barnett wasn't ready at that point. He needed to steep himself in the communications between Jessop and the President: how messages were titled; writing styles; depth of content; etc. He needed to know his prey.

Finally, at noon on Monday, he sent his first e-mail to Jessop. Barnett tweaked the code so it looked like the message came from the President. He titled it: HAVE YOU HEARD THIS ONE? The text read:

· There once lived a man in the White House,
· With a wife discontent as the First Spouse.
· To Yosemite she came,
· Will the press say: "Fair game!"
· Since her lover wears skirts and a blouse?
· …A concerned citizen…

Barnett followed that with one titled: FOR YOUR EYES ONLY.

· Sorry about the limerick, but this is serious. Gordon's career is in jeopardy (and yours too, of course). Ask him what CC was doing while he was in meetings at Yosemite. She was climbing, but not through any *granite* fissures.
· …A concerned citizen…

He sent one more message after that, titled: YOSEMITE.

· Don't dismiss this: I have video to prove it. No offense, but Gordon should be the one to see it. I've attached a snapshot from that video to show you. You'll recognize the suit she's wearing, or was. When you're ready to proceed, send an e-mail message to yourself, titled: OK.
· …A concerned citizen…

As Barnett expected, there was a furious amount of activity on the White House computer network after Jessop retrieved those messages a few hours later. The sysops even took the system down, turning off all their computers at once. It was an extraordinary step, but Barnett expected it. Welcomed it, actually, since it forced him to take a break. He used the time to configure and test the equipment he was sending off with Ellen.

After that, he ate and collapsed on a pile of clothes. At 10 P.M., he went back to the White House system. He knew the entry routines would be changed. He knew people would be watching for marauders. It only made the challenge that much more exciting.

It took several hours, routing finally through a CIA computer, but he got back in. He knew the White House sysops wouldn't be able to completely change the firewalls, not in just a few hours. They had to be scrambling, trying to figure out how and where they had been breached.

Barnett's one disappointment, sitting in front of his screen, was that he couldn't see the panic on the other end—the flurry of phone calls, the shouts and accusations, curses and despair, even the terror of the unknown. All from a few well-placed keystrokes. It had to be a beautiful thing to witness.

Now it was time for Round Two. Barnett had been patient, doing other database work on a second laptop while he left his first one connected to the White House network. He noticed that Jessop had been on the system several times that morning, but had not left the "OK" message. So at noon, Barnett sent a brief reminder, with the title: OK TO SEND TO CNN?

A response from Jessop showed up two minutes later, titled: NO!!! 'OK'??? The message was short:

· *What do you want?*

From there, they went into "chat" mode, and their electronic conversation fired back and forth in rapid succession:

· I want to talk to the President.
· *Impossible.*
· Does he know?

- *That's classified.*
- Should this go up on the Net?
- *No!!!*
- Does he know?
- *Perhaps.*

And on it went. Jessop was stalling. Barnett knew the connection couldn't be traced, but he was tired of Jessop's game. He sent this message:

  · Put the President in front of this computer in thirty minutes or the video goes up on the Net and a copy of the tape goes out to the media. Got it?

Thirty minutes later, the President was there. Barnett was sure on two counts. First, the words were typed in halting fashion, not rattled off as Jessop had done. Second, the word choices were not archly careful as Jessop had been. It was like talking to a real person; angry, but real.

- *Who are you? Why are you attacking my wife?*
- I'm concerned about the example she sets. Do you KNOW what she really is?
- *That's my business, not yours.*
- Wrong. You set the standard for the nation. If your life is a lie, why should people trust you?
- *What do you want?*
- Justice.
- *Too vague. What do you really want?*
- Influence.
- *Who are you?*
- Sorry. Let's just leave it as "a concerned citizen".
- *You're a criminal. I don't bow to threats.*
- Spoken like a true politician, one whose place in history will

be marked with derision from his sham of a marriage, as his wife shamelessly flaunted her lesbian lover by night and preached to the masses by day. All your good work as President will be forgotten. Great legacy for your kids, Gordon.

There was a long silence from the other end. Finally, a message came back from the President.

· *Can you prove what you say?*
· I can arrange for a showing tomorrow afternoon.
· *What do you want from me?*
· Influence. My request will surprise you, but let's wait 'til you see the tape before proceeding. Be back at Jessop's computer tomorrow at 4 P.M. your time, then be ready to take a drive. Okay?

There was another long pause.

· *Okay.*

He had followed the man for two days, cataloging practically every step. He knew where the man lived, what the man ate, how the man combed his hair, and most of all, he knew the man's name, the man's real name.

All that time, his anger hadn't abated, it had intensified. By now it was a knife, hot and sharp, burning through his stomach. Several times over the past two days, he had thought about purging his anger, pulling out his gun and killing the man. For all the humiliations, and worse, this man deserved to die.

But it had to be in a more painful way than a hail of bullets on the street. The man needed to know it was coming, needed to weep with fear and beg hopelessly for his life. He needed to suffer.

Harry Harper would meet that fate when the Commander

learned the news. The evidence couldn't be denied.

He had pictures of Harper going in and out of the Federal Building in San Francisco, in and out of a courthouse in San Jose, in and out of his apartment, in and out of a bar. He had a picture of a receipt with Harper's name on it and another of the name on the apartment listing. He had also seen, but couldn't photograph, Harper flashing his FBI shield at the courthouse. Pilkin would love that part. So much for the Commander's golden boy.

He finished his notes, gathered the pictures, and put it all in a large brown envelope. He drove to the FedEx office in downtown San Jose and mailed the evidence to Sutter Springs. He regretted not being around when the Commander received it, but he had a plane to catch.

Moon Over Georgia

Harry turned off the highway onto the dirt road leading to their rented cabin. The sun was high over the trees now, dappling the forest floor with shadows, but it didn't feel bucolic this time. Somewhere in the vicinity lurked a weapon of dark, hideous powers. That had kept Harry up all night. He got an early start on his return to Sutter Springs, just to be in motion.

He wasn't going to push the issue of the nuke. If the Commander really had it, he was probably jumpy as hell. Any questions would just tweak his paranoia. And Harry didn't need the distraction anyway; the takedown would demand all his concentration. He couldn't afford thoughts of mushroom clouds billowing across the sky, reverberating through the landscape.

He had to forget about it. That was something for the nuke squad to worry over. Unless the Commander had the thing booby-trapped. Or hadn't brought it to the compound. Or it was Rumson with the bomb! That was the scariest scenario of all. Rumson had no discipline whatsoever. He might launch it at someone who sideswiped his car.

As Harry got further up the road, something crept into his senses. Not dust in the air as he'd noticed before, after the goons had bugged their cabin. This was different. This was . . . smoke?

He slowed down. Yeah, smoke. Not overpowering, probably from a distant forest fire and some brainless day-hiker who tossed a match. But it was the smell only, not actual wisps of smoke. Maybe something from a few days—

He stopped the Jeep, his heart pounding furiously. He should have been able to see their cabin from here, but what he saw was chillingly different. A shell—no, not even that much was left of the cabin. The charred fragments which remained of the two-story structure barely hinted at its former shape. Surrounding it, where once stood lodge pole pines, were rows of tall, blackened spikes, ghastly testaments to a hellish scene.

He drove the last quarter mile in shock, his horror mounting the closer he got. The ground was scorched two hundred yards out from the house. The trees that far away were only brushed by flames, but it was clear that somehow a major forest fire had been averted, a fire whose epicenter was his cabin.

He didn't have long to ponder how or even why. As he neared the burned-out shell, he noticed something not far from the front of the cabin. It was his truck, the one which had been "ventilated" by the goons. The one which Mackey had taken the week before. There wasn't much left of it, but it was clearly his truck. As he walked over to it, a lingering smell of gasoline stormed his senses.

This was meant for him.

He started toward the ruins of the cabin. There had to be a clue somewhere, something to turn the crime around on its author. But he barely reached the steps. The silence was shattered by motorcycles charging out of the woods. It was the Commander's cavalry, and they weren't there to protect him. The circle of weapons confirmed that.

Harry was searched, twice. No one asked him any questions and no one responded to his. Finally, he was ordered to get in his Jeep and proceed to the compound. The motorcycle brigade trailed him the whole way.

He got out of the Jeep in front of the main house, raging on two accounts: the attack on his cabin, and the attack just now by the motorcycle menaces. Plus one conflicting, terrifying thought: he'd been found out.

He brushed off the handlers who tried to escort him into the house. He had spent enough time around the Commander to know where the man was likely to be. Harry walked into the study and slammed the door behind him.

"What's the meaning of this?" he said.

"I'll ask you the same thing," the Commander replied.

"Your house is standing, mine is not. Then I'm all but strip-searched? You tell me what's wrong with that picture."

The Commander lowered his voice. "You tell me why your house was booby-trapped. Why you've been missing for three days, while your place goes up in flames. Got an answer?"

"Yeah! Your friend, Mackey, torched the place. He's been on a short fuse since my first day here. Have you been up there? Smelled the gasoline? It's obvious what he did. He's gotta be furious that I wasn't there to burn as well."

"He's dead," the Commander said. "At your cabin. Explain that."

Harry took a breath. It wasn't what he expected. For all the murderous thoughts he'd had before, they were suddenly tempered.

"Who knows?" he said. "Maybe Mackey created a spark at the wrong time. Maybe he wasn't paying attention. But that fire was no accident. He attacked Ellen a few days ago at the bar and told her we'd better get out of town. He's been holding onto my truck for a week, refusing to return it, and now it's sitting up there a burned-out hulk. If he died doing that, it was his own fault."

"It wasn't, not initially."

"What do you mean?"

The Commander shrugged. "He may have been planning to torch your place; those gas cans in the back of that truck certainly goosed the fire. But that's not what started it."

"What was it?" Harry said. A thin blade of dread carved through him.

"A bomb, with nails and other bits of metal wrapped around it. We know, because the doctor pulled all kinds of crap out of Mackey's corpse."

Harry's face tightened. "When did this happen?"

"Night before last. The only way we knew about it was the explosion. Actually, there were two; one at each door, we figure. The first one sent us running—at eleven o'clock at night—and the second went off as we got close. Probably set off by the fire in the cabin. We were too late to save Mackey, but at least we kept the valley from going up in flames. As dry as things are, it could've been disastrous if we hadn't caught it in time."

"How can you be sure it wasn't Mackey?"

"The guy refused to go near anything with a fuse. I know that for a fact." The Commander's eyes burned into Harry's. "So the answer lies with you. Either someone is after you or you were trying to stage some kind of scene. Which is it?"

"Fuck you! My place is burned to the ground and now I get this inquisition? I'm the one who's screwed, George. The doctor was supposed to be pulling shrapnel out of me!"

"Why?"

"That's my business."

The Commander slammed his hand on the desk. "Right now, it's my business. Too much is at stake for anyone around here to be keeping secrets. We can't be compromised by an attack from an unknown enemy. Got it? Don't make me have to ask you twice, Harry. I've given you the benefit of the doubt so far, but it's not gonna last. I won't tolerate a double-cross."

"A double-cross?"

"Answer the question! Where were you?"

Harry wasn't prepared to answer. He hadn't expected to face this kind of probe, or maybe he hadn't thought about it all. But he needed an answer that was credible, and he needed it now. The only thing that came to mind was the truth, or a variation on it.

He matched the Commander's gaze. "I was in court, in San Jose. The victim of a double-cross myself. ZOG got to him before I could, but I'll get my revenge in time. For now, I was only too happy to trade my testimony for a clean bill on some other matters.

Ever heard of a guy named Trong?"

The Commander's eyes narrowed. "What was it about?"

"Gray market computer chips. The Vietnamese own most of that racket, but they tried to muscle me as well. I wouldn't budge, so Trong put out a contract on me."

"We've seen no gooks up here. Are you saying they did that torch job?"

Harry shook his head. "You've been in the woods too long. They could buy anybody. From what you said, it sounds like it was a professional hit. That's just like them."

Then another candidate popped into Harry's brain, a real one, and his anger flared anew. "Or it could've been Rumson. You saw how he came after me; Ellen, too."

The Commander nodded, his face grim. "It occurred to me. The thing is, we're not going to get a chance to ask him."

"Why not? Send him a message on that computer network."

The Commander shook his head. "You obviously haven't heard. Rumson was captured by the FBI this morning when he got back to his ranch in Montana. They had already rounded up his men and were just waiting for him to show. There haven't been many details, but the Feebs are crowing about how they've broken up a major militia ring. The fuckers have probably been following that asshole around. Makes me nervous about this place. I'm not sure how much longer I want to sit here."

Harry's heart was racing. God bless the rogues! But this wasn't time to relax, not with an apocalypse lurking in a suitcase nearby. At least it gave him an opening.

"So what does that do to the plan?" he asked.

"Nothing."

"What? What about all those envelopes?"

An odd smile spread across the Commander's face. "It's no threat. I didn't expect much from Rumson anyway, but I had to include him. As much as everyone hates him, he's the symbol of rebellion. Nobody would've taken these meetings seriously if

Rumson hadn't been there. But his assignments were only for regional action; I wasn't going to let him near D.C. He had to know about it, though, so he could spearhead disruptions in the North-west."

"You don't sound too sorry."

"He had it coming," the Commander said. "The only risk for us is that he might expose the plan in exchange for a lighter sen-tence. It depends on who he hates more, me or ZOG. My guess is he'll stay quiet for a few more weeks, expecting to be set free by his men. After that, we'll have to watch our backs."

"You got some great friends, George."

The Commander nodded. "Ain't it the truth. I'll be glad when this thing is over. Real glad. I've been so busy lately I've barely had time to blink."

He got to his feet. "In the meantime, you and Ellen are gonna need a place to stay. I've got an extra room upstairs, next to Bar-nett's, if you can stand the music and zombie laughs all night long."

"I appreciate it," Harry said.

The Commander walked over and thrust out his hand. "Sorry about the treatment. Just can't take any chances. But we're gonna do it, Harry." A smile oozed across his face. "By God, we're gonna do it."

Harry went back out to the Jeep, his mind gone. The fire, Mackey, Rumson, the rogues, nearly being pinned on his where-abouts, and the closest thing to an admission about the nuke as he was likely to get. He climbed into the Jeep and headed back to the cabin, unescorted this time. He wanted to sift through the rubble to see if he could find an answer or two. It was kind of an aimless exercise, something to keep himself busy; it would all be a charred memory once the Commander and Barnett were locked away.

As he drove up to the fire scene, however, flickers of rage came back to him. Those ashes were meant to include his.

He got out and walked to the rubble of the cabin. As he stood at the spot where the front door had been, he could make out the blast pattern of the incendiary device. It must have done a nasty job on Mackey. So that was one suspect off the list.

He walked into the remains of the living room, burned down to the base of most of the furniture. The stone fireplace had survived the blaze, standing naked against the open air, a clearer sign of devastation than the fragments of walls standing here or there. The only thing not totally wasted was the back bedroom, but it wasn't worth salvaging.

Harry kicked over the brittle skeleton of the coffee table and the legs crumbled from the jolt. He shuffled through the ashes toward the kitchen, trying to figure out how and when Rumson could have done this. The timing was right, if he'd just returned to Montana this morning. But how had he gotten the materials for two bombs in such short time?

Harry's mind took a sharp turn, back to the coffee table. He tried to quiet his heart as he picked his way through the ashes, being careful now about his steps. He knelt down next to the table and ran his fingers over the bottom.

The coil the goons had planted there was gone.

He sifted his fingers through the ashes where the table had stood, on the chance that the coil had fallen off during the fire. It was ceramic, so it wouldn't have burned, but perhaps the adhesive or whatever had been used to fasten it had melted. Harry spent fifteen minutes in painstaking search, but all he came up with was a growing fear.

Then he remembered the second coil—they'd put it in the back bedroom. If that was gone . . .

He rose slowly, hoping and dreading at the same time. He walked through the rubble to the back bedroom, feeling like his chest was going to implode. He went to the dresser, took a breath, and reached behind the mirror. He ran his fingers lightly over the frame.

The coil was gone.

So Rumson didn't plant those bombs.

And the goons weren't just overzealous.

Which meant his life was still in danger. And Ellen's. Morton's, too?

His body stiffened.

FBI killers? Professional hits? Secret investigations? What was lurking at HQ? If someone was desperate enough, and confident enough, to try to kill him, where did it end? What wasn't possible or likely in the rogues' minds? Did they kill the Director? The Deputy Director? The prospects were staggering.

Harry charged through the remains of the cabin, down the steps, and into the Jeep. He had to get to town, had to alert Morton. There was no time to waste, on anything! The takedown had to be moved up to that night. They couldn't wait and hope the goons wouldn't kill them first. With or without Ellen, Morton had to get agents up to Sutter Springs by midnight.

And then they all had to go underground.

Barnett could barely contain himself. If there was ever a hacker Hall of Fame someday, the events of the next two hours should be the lead exhibit. No one could touch this, not on technical merit or creativity or sheer, fucking audacity. He was about to make the most powerful man in the world sit up and beg.

There had been no new defensive measures on the White House network in the past twenty-four hours. The President had obviously taken the threat seriously. Barnett had slipped into the system a few hours earlier, from the same CIA route, but he suspected he could have walked in with a neon sign this time. Jessop's computer was also engaged.

It was nearly time for the call. Barnett's heart was racing, not from nerves but excitement. He flexed his fingers, then punched a few keys, bringing up the "chat" mode. He typed: IS GORDON READY TO ROLL?

The reply—terse, but affirmative—came seconds later. Barnett gave the President a phone number and told him to call in exactly twenty minutes from a secure line. He could have demanded that the President call right away, from any old phone, but he needed to give his quarry time to jump. It wouldn't have the same impact otherwise.

Barnett cut off his connection to the White House computer. It took him two minutes to make the next connection, saying a silent prayer over his pounding heart until the video link appeared in a frame on his laptop. When the image finally burst onto the screen, he shouted "Yes!" He was looking at a live shot of a pay phone.

There was an Out-of-Order sign on it. The few people who passed by barely gave it a glance. And no one in the campground at Stone Mountain had noticed the laptop stuck up in the trees fifty feet away, or the small camera lens trained on the pay phone. Ellen had done her job well.

Barnett watched the video link and waited, chuckling to himself. Stone Mountain was less than twenty miles from Atlanta and there should be some activity at the scene very soon. The only question was who would hit first, the gendarmes or the President.

The phone next to him rang. The gendarmes lost the race.

Barnett let it ring a few times. He knew they'd be trying to trace the call. But thanks to the wonders of modern technology— from a Georgia pay phone to a switching center in Venezuela to an out of service number in Albuquerque to the phone beside him— he knew he was safe for several minutes. His message to the President would be brief, but he wanted to have some fun with the lackeys, and convince Gordo of who was in control.

He picked it up on the fourth ring.

"Hello, Mr. President! How are you today?"

"Let's get this over with," the President said. "Who are you and what do you want? No games."

"Oh, life is a game, sir. One big, fucking—"

"Don't talk to me like that!"

Barnett bristled. "I'll talk to you anyway I want. I'm the one with the trump card, Gordo, not you. Understand?"

There was silence on the other end.

"Understand?"

"What is this influence you want?"

Barnett paused. "You've got to promise not to laugh."

"What?!"

"You have to make sure that anti-terrorism bill gets passed. Let's be dramatic; have them do it in a joint session of Congress. And pull whatever strings you need to, but make sure it has real teeth. Finally, it's got to be voted on exactly two weeks from today."

The President's voice dropped to a growl. "What is this about?"

"Wait, I'm not done. Once it's passed, I want you to sic the FBI on a particular militia group that's given me problems. I'll give you details later about what I want you to do to them."

"Who are you? Wait, I know: a concerned citizen. And a coward."

Barnett's voice was harsh and low. "Watch what you call me, Gordo, or people will be calling you much worse. What I'm asking is not illegal, maybe just a little outside the bounds. But you and your wife: talk about—"

"Leave her out of this!"

A moment later, the President continued, his voice controlled. "Why the joint session? Why the specific date? What do you have planned?"

"A demonstration of my powers to these morons; call it an object lesson if you like. Then you can let the FBI lower the boom. Anyway, the timing is my business, the execution is yours."

There was a long silence. Barnett didn't know if the President was thinking or stalling, probably both. But at that moment, in the video window on his laptop, he saw the cavalry streak into view.

There were four cars in the picture, and likely more he couldn't see. Men flew out of the vehicles with guns drawn, sweeping the area for some heinous villain that—hah, hah—wasn't there. It took mere seconds before the men's intensity dropped, replaced by confusion.

Barnett started laughing. "Hey, Mr. President, you still there? I wish you could see this! There's got to be twenty guys, all walking around this phone booth in Georgia, all looking like chickens with their heads cut off. I figured you'd send some people out, but I had no idea it would be so many. Are you still there?"

The voice was low, angry. "How do you know this?"

"I see all, know all. But I'm going to reveal my secret, because I don't want your guys roughing up the campers. Now, there's a guy near the phone booth in a striped shirt. He's holding a gun in his left hand. Take a second and confirm that with your aides. Once you've got that agent's attention, have him wave the gun over his head."

He rattled off a command on his keyboard and put the video link into "capture" mode. Fifteen seconds later, the man on the screen waved his gun back and forth over his head. A maniacal laugh rippled out of Barnett.

"Okay, now I want you to have him do something else. You're the President, Gordon, so he'll have to obey. Ready? Have the guy get up on that black car and drop his pants. I want him to moon the campground."

"What?! Don't be absurd!"

"Hey, Gordo! Piss me off and I'll ship a copy of this tape to the networks. They'd love to see CC's sex techniques."

"How do I know you won't do that anyway?"

"You'll just have to trust me. Look, if you don't do everything I ask, and I'm not asking that much, then I guarantee this tape will hit the evening news. If you do comply, there's a strong chance that you and Hot Stuff will be left to work things out in peace. Now, have that guy drop his pants."

It was a priceless moment. The FBI agent's face went white when he got the command. Then, fuming, he climbed onto the car, unbuckled his belt, and pulled his jeans down to his knees. It crossed Barnett's mind to have the President repeat this himself later, but there were limits.

"That was great, Mr. President. I'll send you a tape. Meanwhile, here's your next task."

Barnett gave him a different phone number and directions to a park in Virginia, admonishing the President to leave the dogs home this time. Gordo could have an army outside the area if he wanted, but there were to be no more than three others around him when he got to the campground.

"Is it really worth all this?" the President said.

"You'll see in thirty minutes," Barnett said.

He hung up and checked his watch. He'd almost gone too long. Got a little carried away there, but it was a golden chance to tweak the Authorities. What he wouldn't give to make his parole officer moon the world!

He had time to kill, so he wandered down to the kitchen to get some food. He found Ol' Flattop there, staring out the window.

"Man, you missed it!" Barnett said. "One of the finest Barnettisms ever, to be surpassed only by the next phone call." He raised his hands and kissed each of his fingers in succession.

"Too bad you don't have an ego, son."

"You had to see it. And the best is yet to come. Gordo is eating out of my hand. This hand right here. You may kiss it if you like." He held it out.

The Commander laughed. "You are one twisted son-of-a-bitch. So he's buying it?"

"Lock, stock, and barrel. Hook, line, and sinker. Choose a cliché. When he sees that tape in a short while, he will be ours."

Barnett went back through the call and the President's responses, then gave a gloating recount of the moon over Georgia.

"I got the idea last night when Ellen and I were testing out the video link. I tried to get her to flash the camera, but she refused."

The Commander studied him. "You getting cozy with her?"

Barnett raised his eyebrows. "Not yet, but we'll see. She'll be back tonight and she's promised to have dinner with me."

"And she got everything squared away with Keener?"

"As far as I know. I talked to her this morning when we ran the test on the set-up in Virginia. She said she had to write down every step on a piece of paper and Keener taped that next to his laptop. Let's just hope he doesn't forget it when we start moving on D.C. Is he dependable?"

The Commander shrugged. Then a puzzled look crossed his face.

"What was that business with her the other night, anyway? I just heard something about it from Betsy."

"She and Harry were apparently going after those agents who'd stormed this place last week. Trying to trap them or something; make sure they didn't come back again, I think. She was pretty secretive about it."

The Commander's eyes narrowed. "Really? Isn't that interesting. Maybe those were the ones that torched Harry's cabin." His face soured. "I don't like this. Things are getting too warm around here. We've got to be out soon. I don't want to be caught with my thumb up my ass again."

"You're so colorful," Barnett said. "Come on, let's go have fun with the President."

At precisely 2:00 P.M. Pacific time, the phone next to Barnett's laptop rang. This time, he picked it up on the first ring.

"Hello, Gordon. Are you in the park? Good. Follow the main road around until you find a green tent with a peace symbol on it. Go inside the tent and you'll find further instructions there. Have one of your bloodhounds check it out first if you like, but I promise you it's not a set-up. That would do me no good."

Barnett hung up the phone and attacked his keyboard. With the video link to this new camera completed, he and the Commander waited. The Netcam was pointed toward the entrance to a small tent. Barnett explained that the lens was on top of a battery-operated TV/VCR player. He was practically hopping on his chair as he waited.

Six minutes later, the video link showed the flap of the tent opening. A man with dark sunglasses peered around, waved some device through the air, then backed out again. A minute later, the face of the President appeared. Barnett's heart jumped.

The President looked around nervously, then crawled into the tent. He nearly filled it as he got into a sitting position. He reached forward and snatched at something below the level of the camera. He brought his hand back and held up a sheet of paper. A moment later, his face set in grim furrows, he reached forward again.

"He's going to run it now," Barnett said, his heart at a fevered pitch. "This should be great!"

Expressions flashed across Gordon Carroll's face: pain; anger; revulsion; and, ultimately, sadness. Devastating sadness. He was so totally absorbed in the video that he seemed to forget where he was.

Then his eyes rose, and with them a terrible fury, burning through the little lens into Barnett's laptop. The President reached up a hand—

—and the screen went blank.

"Shit! What did he do that for?" Barnett said. He spun out of his seat, not believing what had just happened. "Is he crazy? Christ, how could he do that to me?"

The Commander smirked. "I'd probably have blasted the thing if you'd done it to me."

"Are you siding with him?"

"Of course not. I understand, that's all." The Commander shook his head, a wry smile on his face. "You're a scary one, Barnett."

Just then, the phone rang.

Barnett looked at the Commander, his eyes wide. He let it ring several times before picking it up.

"Hello?" he said slowly.

As Barnett listened, a grin spread across his face.

Control

The sky to the west was shimmering gold when Harry turned off the interstate, two exits before the one to Sutter Springs. He'd been on the move all day, roaming aimlessly to avoid possible confrontations. At this point, he just wanted the damn thing to be over.

He drove through the underpass and guided the Jeep toward the lone gas station. He pulled up to a pump, gave the attendant a $20, and began filling the tank. As he stood there, his eyes jumped around. He wasn't worried, he was waiting. But there was no sign yet. Where was she?

The pump stopped and Harry returned the nozzle to its cradle. He was just climbing into the Jeep when he saw a flicker of light from the darkened woods. He shook his head and drove around behind the station.

He hadn't even come to a stop when the passenger door opened and Ellen hopped in. Harry pressed on the accelerator and headed back for the highway.

"Weren't you a little premature with that signal?" he said.

Ellen groaned. "Slack please. I'm running on fumes."

"Sorry. I'm just so anxious to be done with this."

"I know what you mean. Morton told me about the cabin."

"That's the thing. It's not over yet. We've got a nuke to worry about and ten more guys to—ahh, I can't even think about it any longer!"

Ellen patted him on the arm. "Soon enough, Harry."

He glanced at her and smiled. "How did things go back east?"

"Too well. From the way Barnett was crowing on the phone a few hours ago, he's probably got the President locked up." She shook her head. "The only positive thing is that I'm in good with this guy in Georgia. He's such a sleaze. I endeared myself to him by showing him how to get porn over the Internet. If we're lucky, he'll get so caught up with that he'll forget all about the revolution. It's a contact I can work later if needed. That alone was worth the loss of sleep."

Ellen smiled. "The other benefit is that Barnett thinks I walk on water. He was only too anxious to meet me for dinner tonight, so it'll make this part of the takedown a snap. Natalie and I should have him wrapped up by 10:00, giving me two hours to get to the compound to help you out."

"What if Barnett notices his parole officer first?"

"He won't. She dropped me off an hour ago, so the chances of them running into each other are slim. And she said she had changed her looks enough so he wouldn't recognize her even if they bumped into each other."

Harry took the turnoff for Sutter Springs. They had another ten miles to go and rode in silence most of the way. As they reached the outskirts of town, he slowed the Jeep.

"I think I'd like to wait and make sure this goes okay."

"Harry, if we can't take this mongrel without your help, we should be sent back to class. A couple pairs of agents should be here already, Natalie and I will be inside, and an army of support is on its way up. By midnight, the area will be crawling with agents. Besides, you need to be in place well in advance, just in case, God forbid, something does go wrong."

"That's my point. The Commander is really jumpy now. He's likely to have armed guards patrolling the streets. If they get a whiff of something."

"That's *my* point, Harry. You have to take him early if there's any sign of a problem. The SWAT team is primed for midnight, but—" She forced a smile. "But it'll all go smoothly."

"Provided the goons don't start shooting both directions."

She put her hand on his shoulder. "Like you tell me: sometimes you've just got to go on faith."

Harry nodded and pulled up to the restaurant, a cozy-looking place glowing warmly against the dark sky. He turned and studied her. "So, how will you get up to the compound?"

"I'll take Natalie's car. See that old Dodge over there? Tell the guys at the guardhouse to expect me in that, otherwise I may get hassled coming in."

She got out of the Jeep and gave him a wink. "Give 'em hell, partner!" Then she closed the door and headed for the restaurant.

Harry watched her go, then put the Jeep in reverse and backed out of the parking space. As he put it in drive, he saw a brief flicker of light, a signal, from a car nearby. Okay, maybe everything was in control.

Ellen paused just inside the door to the restaurant, letting her eyes adjust to the light. Gingham everywhere. Booths along one wall, with high seat backs to provide privacy. Large tables in the middle of the floor; tables for two along the other wall, below a series of windows. In the far corner, with her back to the door, was Natalie Weston. Ellen knew it by the coat she wore; otherwise, the woman was featureless. The rest of the squad was outside, surrounding the restaurant; too many strangers inside would be suspicious.

In the back were doors leading to the kitchen. The lighting was atmospheric, coming from sconces on the wall and glass globes over candles on each table. The checkered tablecloths were almost too clichéd, but this was Sutter Springs, not San Francisco.

Defining the scene like this was a habit for Ellen, nothing more; she didn't expect any problems with Barnett. The quieter this takedown went, the better, since Harry would be at the compound. If there was a big show of force here, the news would certainly get back to the Commander.

Barnett wouldn't require a major effort anyway; his weapons were his mind and his computer. Ellen could probably do it alone, but she accepted Morton's plan to have three teams of agents on hand. The rest of the crew coming up from San Francisco would be deployed at the compound.

Ellen slid into a booth near the front, with her back to the door. That way, it would be easier to signal Natalie. Ten minutes later, the door swung open and Barnett strutted in. Ellen had seen him gloating before, but never quite like this.

"Hey, Wonder Woman!" Barnett slid in across from her. "God, you're a sight. You looked better as a cheerleader the other night."

She ran her hands through her hair. "It's your fault, Barnett. I've been all over creation and back in the past forty-eight hours."

It would have been easy enough to take him right then, to coax him outside and read him his rights. But the situation would change dramatically once she did that. At the moment, Barnett was friendly and frisky and probably primed to talk. As soon as she flashed her badge, he would become granite.

She didn't need to string him along to get more evidence. Her concern was what damage Barnett planned to inflict, and what he might have initiated already. This could be her only chance to find out.

Over the next hour and three rounds of beer, she had learned enough to terrify her, but not prevent anything. Computer systems and databases all over the country had been targeted—government, military, financial, and on and on. Some things he planned to wipe out entirely, with the aid of the militia groups; others were targeted for electronic scrambling. Along the way, he was going to siphon off billions of dollars to new accounts he had set up in a Swiss bank. He was talking so fast and in such broad strokes that she was having trouble remembering everything. The problem was compounded by her exhaustion and the effect of the beer.

Barnett was picking up steam, leaving the euphoria behind in his race to repaint the world. Politics, society, ethics—subjects and summations poured out of him, the floodgates of some mighty damn thrown open. He became increasingly animated, gesturing sharply, rising to his own bait.

If she didn't break the mood, he was likely to burst into flames. And she needed details, not diatribe. She pushed the glass globe aside and leaned across the table, staring at him until he suddenly noticed and stopped talking.

"Why, Jeff? Why are you doing this?" she said quietly.

His whole focus zoomed inward and far away. Then his face began to tighten, harden. His lips pinched, his eyes narrowed. He looked at her and opened his mouth to speak. Then he shook his head and turned away.

"Come on, Barnett. What—"

Ellen froze in mid-sentence. Walking toward them was Barnett's parole officer, a look of agitation on her face. Jesus, what was going on? Had she given the signal inadvertently or was this woman taking things in her own hands? Damn it!

She had about five seconds before Natalie reached the table. There was no time to say anything more. She gave Barnett a shrug and reached for her purse. She pulled out her shield underneath the table and waited. It crossed her mind to reach for her gun, but this weenie wasn't dangerous without a laptop.

Natalie slid in next to Barnett, moving up tight against him, a vicious smile on her face. He looked over, uncomprehending at first. Then suddenly his eyes went wide, a silent scream of recognition. His head jerked toward Ellen.

Slowly, she raised her shield and held it up in front of him. His face drained of color, his lips twitching. He looked up at her, and through her.

"Hi, asshole!" Natalie said. "Welcome back to reality." She was swinging a pair of handcuffs from one finger.

Barnett didn't seem to hear. All his focus was on Ellen.

"You bitch," he said, barely audible. "You betrayed me."

His voice suddenly roared. "You *betrayed* me!"

"It's over," Ellen said calmly.

Barnett's hand shot out and grabbed the glass globe. Before Ellen could stop him, he smashed it against the edge of the table, shattering the end of the globe into a dozen jagged points. He whipped around and put it to his parole officer's throat, pressing the dagger-like shards against her skin.

"Sit back down," he said to Ellen. "If you move, if you scream, she dies. That fast. I'll do it, Weston, won't I?"

The woman's frantic eyes blinked "Yes." She was trembling, drawing beads of blood in spite of herself.

"I'm leaving with her," Barnett said, "and if anyone comes near, she's your corpse. Got it?"

Ellen nodded, unable to speak.

"Now, very slowly, put your purse on the table."

Ellen complied, and Barnett grabbed it.

"Have you got a gun somewhere?"

Ellen didn't move. Barnett pressed the shards into Natalie's throat and she yelped in pain. Blood oozed from several points.

"Stop it!" Ellen whispered. She reached inside her jacket, slowly, and pulled out her gun. She set it on the table in front of Barnett.

He picked it up, glaring at her. "I'm not through with you, whoever you are. I'll hunt you down, count on it. You'll wish you were Weston here by the time I'm through with you. Nobody fucks with Jeff Barnett like this."

He put the gun to his parole officer's head, then pulled the broken globe away and hurled it against the wall. It shattered into a thousand slivers that skittered across the floor. Barnett nudged Natalie out of the booth and toward the door. A moment later, they disappeared into the darkness.

Ellen sat there, paralyzed. Then she heard shouts and bolted for the door. Barnett was getting into Natalie's car, the parole officer already behind the wheel. Three pairs of agents were standing nearby, their guns held aloft, in the grip of a hostage situation no one had anticipated. Within seconds, Natalie's car roared off.

The situation was melting down in front of Ellen's eyes.

Harry took another sip of coffee. It was strange hanging out alone in someone else's kitchen, particularly when you were about to cart that person off to jail. But he had to be patient. It wasn't just him against Pilkin. The Commander's men would be quite happy to kill a federal agent. Fanaticism incited people that way. Kevin would lead the charge, seeing it as the ultimate way to gain his father's approval. He had the zeal, and Harry had heard the kid was a phenomenal shot.

So, Harry stared out the window and waited. It was almost 10 P.M. Ellen would be there shortly, and the rest of the troops should be setting up just outside the perimeter. As for the compound, it was quiet. That should make the takedown easier, but it also suggested that their work there was about through. Did that mean the nuke was already on its way to Washington?

He felt, more than heard, someone walking up behind him.

"You don't need to move," Betsy said.

Her voice was low, almost purring. She stepped up close, not quite against him, but near enough that he could feel the heat radiating from her body. He swallowed, a reflex action.

She put one hand lightly on his arm, then reached around him with the other and picked up a coffee mug. Her body was touching him now and he was suddenly mesmerized by her movements: stretching for the coffee pot, pouring the liquid, then drawing the mug back out of view. She tilted her head around and smiled at him. "Thanks," she said softly, and moved away.

Harry took a moment, and a long breath, then turned to face her. She was leaning against the kitchen table, studying him. Her eyes were dancing.

"I was going to stay angry at you for a while," she said. "But how could I? Just look at you."

Harry groaned silently and tried to smile. Wouldn't that be perfect: the Commander walks in while his wife is flirting shamelessly and shoots Harry before he has a chance to yell "Freeze!" A fitting end to a checkered career?

"Betsy, you know I'm fond of you," he said, "but this isn't a good idea. First off, you're the Commander's wife. And so much is going on right now."

She scowled at him. "All this planning crap. All this toy soldier shit. When's it gonna end? Where's it gonna end? Do you know what it's like to sit around while you boys play your little games? Why do you think I—"

A harsh voice cut her off. "They're not games are they, Harper?"

By reflex, Harry's body responded, turning toward the sound. It was a subtle movement, but the reaction was obvious. If he'd known it was coming, he could have stifled the impulse; out of the blue, he reacted as he had for more than fifty years. In the next heartbeat, he became very still, hoping that would deny the first response, but he knew deep inside it was hopeless.

At least the charade was hopeless. "Harper" wasn't a name that the Commander would have plucked out of the air. But Harry had been found out before and managed to survive. He couldn't remember *how* at the moment, but there was always hope. Harry raised his eyes, confirmed that a gun was now pointed at him, and shrugged.

"How did you find out?"

The Commander threw a large envelope at his feet and pictures scattered across the kitchen floor.

Harry glanced at the record of his two days back home and a chill shot through him. Was this the FBI rogues? They knew about his connection to the Commander. What better way to kill him off than expose him like this. Harry exhaled sharply and met the Commander's stare.

"Who was it?" he asked.

"Rumson. The one time I should have listened to him."

Harry shook his head. It wasn't comforting news.

"What's going on?" Betsy asked.

"He's with ZOG," the Commander said. "Fucking FBI."

Betsy gasped. "Ellen, too? What about Barnett?"

"I'm sure he's not," the Commander said.

"No, Barnett is having dinner with her right now," Betsy said.

"What?!" The Commander looked at Betsy, then at Harry. Then he turned his head toward the stairs. "Kevin! Kevin, get down here now!"

Nobody in the kitchen moved. Moments later, there was a tremendous pounding on the wooden stairs, and Kevin burst into the room. His eyes were wild and there was a gun in his hand. "What? What is it?" he said. He seemed confused at the calm after such loud shouts.

"Where's Barnett?" the Commander said.

"He's out with Ellen. Why—" Kevin stopped, noticing the gun pointed at Harry. His face hardened. "What's wrong?"

"Our 'friends' Harry and Ellen are FBI agents," the Commander said.

"No." Kevin's face flushed with rage. "No!!!"

He lunged at Harry, his hands going for Harry's throat. A moment later, the young man was hurtling toward the floor, his legs cut out from under him, crashing at Harry's feet. The Commander stepped forward and took away Kevin's gun.

"Sorry, son, but we can't kill him just yet. He might be an insurance policy for us later. If you want to rough him up a bit—"

The phone rang, startling everyone.

The Commander snatched the receiver off the hook. His expression went from anger to alarm to rage, all in the space of twenty seconds. He slammed down the receiver, his body shaking.

"ZOG is coming." His voice was quiet and harsh, his eyes burning into Harry's. "They nearly got Barnett, and they'll be on their way here. I want to be gone in two minutes, understand? Betsy: grab some clothes and bring the van around. Kevin: go get Barnett's computer and any disks you see. Don't piss around, either of you. Meet out front in two minutes. Got it?"

"What about Barnett?" Kevin asked.

"We'll pick him up on the way. Now go!"

Kevin and Betsy dashed off. The Commander walked up, keeping the gun pointed at Harry's face. "Give me your gun," he said.

Harry removed it. He couldn't overpower the Commander, not yet anyway. He had to continue as instructed and trust that Ellen and the others would be able to rescue him. Or that there would be enough of a lapse, somewhere in the hysteria of trying to leave the compound, for him to make a move. He held out his gun.

"I trusted you," the Commander said. The condemnation in his voice seemed pointed as much at himself as at Harry.

Then he said, "Turn around."

Harry complied, trying to keep his mind clear. He had been in this position before, but it never got easier.

Then pain cracked across his skull and everything went black.

Ellen raced through the house, barely pausing at each room. There were no signs of struggle anywhere, which was a mixed blessing. It increased the chances that Harry was still alive, and almost guaranteed that he had been taken hostage. Their Jeep was parked in the yard, now riddled with holes after a brief, ferocious gun battle with the Commander's remaining troops, so Harry had definitely been there, and was definitely gone.

She checked the secret room where she and Barnett had hid only a week before. Nothing. She found the door to the tunnel system, but it was bolted and locked. She kicked at it and listened; no sound. It figured. For all the chaos in the yard when she and Morton's crew arrived, it was certain the Commander left quickly.

So, the chance of Harry being behind that door was slim. She made a mental note to ask Morton to have someone check it anyway.

She dragged herself back outside, feeling the weight of disaster bearing down on her. Maybe if she hadn't been so cavalier? Maybe if she'd heeded Harry's concerns and let him sit in the dark while she baited Barnett? Yeah, he would still be with her if she had. Barnett might have gotten away, and the Commander too, but at least Harry would be safe. She stopped in the middle of the yard, tears rolling down her face.

She heard footsteps behind her, but she didn't move. Couldn't move. Then someone put his hands on her shoulders and squeezed, tight and warm.

"We'll find him," Morton said quietly. "I promise you that."

Ellen turned around, searching his face for a sign of conviction. It seemed to be there, or he was a hell of an actor. She brushed away her tears and nodded.

"We've got people out on the roads," he said, "and we know where they're headed eventually."

"But Harry might not be with them." Desperation clung to her words.

"We'll just have to hope that he is."

She shook her head. "I didn't think it would happen like this. I'm so sorry. They've probably got the nuke with them."

Morton shrugged. "I expect you're right, but we'll tear this place apart just to be sure. Meanwhile, we need your services elsewhere. I hate to say it, but we've got to put you on an airplane again."

"Georgia?"

He nodded. "You have to try to get inside their computer network. It may be our only chance to track these guys."

"I hope you've got friends there," she said. "I can't do this alone. I need warrants and back up when I go see Keener."

"The Atlanta SAC, Brett Rodgers, is an old buddy of mine."

Morton forced a smile. "We'll do what we can."

Ellen shook her head. "That sounds so fatalistic."

Morton nodded.

If they didn't get there soon, Barnett was going to explode. It was pitch-black out, thick brush hid him from the road, and huge trees blocked any light from the sky. But he felt vulnerable anyway. There was nothing to protect him but Ellen's pistol and that wretched Weston, whimpering nearby. He had slapped her several times to get her to shut up, but it hadn't done any good.

Her car was ditched further into the woods. He knew from the start that the Authorities would be searching for it. It had taken him almost fifteen minutes of driving just to find a pay phone to call the Commander, and he hadn't wanted to stay on the road much after that.

But that was two hours ago! How long did it take to get from the compound to this God-forsaken spot? Unless they'd been captured.

Those thoughts looped through his brain in an endless, ragged stream. He couldn't even concentrate on what to do about Gnat, he was so desperate just to be gone. Few vehicles had passed by, but even though they were hidden by bushes, he still felt exposed.

This shouldn't have happened at all. Fucking Commander! Letting two FBI agents slip into their organization was beyond impossible. It was a criminal breach of intelligence, and further evidence that the world was populated by morons. Make that three types of people: himself; morons; and vermin like Ellen and this maggot next to him.

He heard a sound just then and quieted the raging voices inside. It was a car—not far away, not going fast, but there were no lights on the road. Barnett dropped to the ground and crawled forward a few feet through the brush. His heart was hammering against his chest.

A few seconds later, he saw it: a dark panel van. He couldn't see the occupants at first, but as it passed in front of him, he saw Kevin leaning out the window, searching the brush.

Barnett popped to his feet and shouted "Hey! Over here!" He fought his way through the thicket to the road, where the van had rolled to a stop. The side door slid open.

"Where've you been?" Barnett said. "I thought the Feds—"

He noticed Harry slumped in the back of the van, blindfolded.

"What's he doing here?"

"Insurance," the Commander said. "Get in. We're wasting time."

Barnett stared at Harry and his anger flared out of control.

"Just a minute," he said. "I've got to do something."

He turned and charged into the brush. That witch of a parole officer had run, but it didn't take long to find her. The frenzied moans, as low as they were, made a perfect beacon.

A moment later, a gunshot shattered the stillness of the forest.

Harry awakened to blackness, a blindfold pinching his face. His hands were behind him, cuffed. He was in the back of a van, from the rattle of equipment and the ping of voices, but he had no other sensation than movement and no way to steady himself as the van lurched and careened along a winding road. It was so disorienting that he felt nauseous almost immediately. Adding to the bedlam in his brain was the argument raging on.

"You're the one who fucked up, Georgie," Barnett said. "You and this idiot, Kevin. How could you give credence to such a moron?"

"What about those background checks you did?" the Commander said. "They would never have been allowed into the compound if you hadn't been duped so badly."

"Duped? Duped?! You redefine 'duped,' your exalted majesty.

You were practically licking this agent's butt here."

"What about you and Ellen? You wanted to jump in her pants. So much for Barnett-the-great. My biggest fuck-up was listening to you. The question now is how badly you're going to screw up when things really get tight. You're just a goddamned con man. Totally worthless."

"Then stop this crate and shoot me, Commodore." Barnett laughed derisively. "You haven't got the balls. This plan is worthless without me. I've got the President, the networks and databases; I'm the only one who can deliver. The one thing you and dork boy are good for is muscle, plus this little suitcase. Hell, if it wasn't for me, Harry here would've had your ass behind bars right now. If anyone is worthless, Commodore, it's you."

The van screeched to a halt and Harry tumbled forward, crashing into someone. A foot kicked him back.

"Listen, you," the Commander said, his voice low and ragged. "I'm not gonna tolerate much more of this. We both fucked up, okay? We're gonna get nowhere by continuing like this."

There was a sharp click, a bullet popping into the chamber of a pistol.

"I have no qualms about using this," the Commander said, "so settle down. Understand?"

Barnett grunted a reply.

The van surged forward suddenly and Harry slammed into the back door. Between that and the horrible sense deprivation, his brain was reeling. He didn't know how much more he could take, as waves of nausea rose faster and faster.

The Commander spoke again, his voice a touch louder. "Hey, Harper. This is a nice little piece Barnett recovered from your friend. Comfortable, good weight, probably nice action. Ever faced it from the other end? Up close and personal like? We'll have to see what you think." He chuckled crudely.

Nothing else was said for a long time. The van just lurched and jerked and rattled horribly as it made its way to somewhere.

Harry couldn't hear any other vehicles go by, so they had to be taking back roads. Twisting back roads. Which made the ride all the worse, which made his nausea all the worse, which finally led to . . .

He couldn't see it, but apparently his lunch scored a direct hit on a pile of automatic weapons. The van skidded to a halt, spreading the mess forward and over who knew what. The curses and exclamations that ensued were worth the previous agony, and the rough handling he got when the men scrambled to clear out some of the stench.

The other benefit was that he got to ride for an hour or so with the blindfold off. He couldn't see anything significant, but it gave him a chance to assess the arsenal. It was small, it was deadly, and it was sticky at the moment. And the nuke they had been so desperate to find was sitting two feet away from him. He couldn't take his eyes off it.

It didn't look ominous—just a large, black suitcase—but inside lurked instantaneous death. A cruel, ugly, blistering death. Something that only the most wretched people would wish on their worst enemies, and he was sitting maybe 24 inches away from it. He felt only slightly comforted by the fact that there was no unearthly green glow filling the van, but that was fiction anyway. Sitting next to it, this seemingly benign suitcase, was like sitting next to a caged cobra. You couldn't relax, and you couldn't ignore what would happen once it was let out of its cage.

The sky was just starting to turn light when the Commander pulled off the road. He came around to the back and put the blindfold over Harry's eyes again, looser than before, and admonished Harry to advise him of any new, pending explosions.

That was a wise move. Half way into a rough, bouncing ride up a mountain road, his nose thick with dust, Harry had to call for a timeout. After that, there was nothing more to give. He was drained in every way possible.

They stopped somewhere up high. The air was cool and brisk.

When he snorted out the dust and offensive smells of before, Harry got a strong whiff of pines. He could hear them, too, as the wind brushed through in an easy, rolling flow. It was probably a beautiful place, if he ever got a chance to see it. But he felt so battered, physically and emotionally, that he didn't really care. If they were going to kill him soon, they would've done it already.

A hand, softer than the previous ones but no more friendly, took Harry's arm and pulled him along. "Step up," Betsy said, but Harry tripped on the step anyway. The floor boards creaked loudly on the porch, and only slightly softer in what had to be a cabin. It would be impossible to sneak around in this place.

She gave him a push and Harry fell against a large chair. "Sit," she said, as if he needed the command. It was difficult to get comfortable with his hands cuffed behind him, but the thick leather chair lessened the burden.

For the next several minutes, footsteps tromped in and out of the cabin, obviously unloading the van. From the movements in and out, there seemed to be a couple bedrooms off the main room; it sounded like the living room and kitchen shared the same space. That was typical of an older cabin, as were the creaks, as was the road outside. Harry didn't know how far they were from civilization, but "too far" was apt enough.

Suddenly, frantic footsteps pounded across the porch and into the cabin. "Look at this!" Barnett's voice wailed. "He nailed my laptop as well. I'm going to have to strip it down and clean it out."

"Can Kevin do it?" the Commander said.

"Be serious. At this point, I wouldn't trust him to hold my dick." His voice moved. "If you hadn't left that other equipment behind . . ."

"I said I was sorry," Kevin answered.

"Sorry? 'Sorry' is worthless, you cretin! Do you think the revolution can wait while you try to cover for your mistakes. That was fuck-up #2, bested only by your bringing these goddamned Feds into our lives."

"Hey, Barnett," the Commander said. "I'd a probably done the same thing. We were racing to get out of there."

"Don't defend him!" Barnett said. "He's a flake, a first-class fuck-up. You told me yourself the guy's a moron."

There were three quick footsteps across the floor, and then Harry heard a ferocious slap. Barnett yelped in pain. Betsy's voice followed, as fearsome as her fist: "Leave him alone."

Footsteps stormed out, leaving a heavy silence. Finally, the Commander said, "How long 'til you're in operation again?"

Barnett let out a long breath. "Since there's puke all over my laptop, it'll take an hour to get it cleaned and dried. And since the village idiot left my server behind, I'll have to try to reconstruct the network from memory."

"Which means what?"

"Which means it'll be a couple of hours, maybe even a day, before I can have the system running again. I've got to find a university computer somewhere to park us on. Anyway, until then nothing goes in or out to your friends in the field."

"What about the computers we left behind? Can the Feds get anything out of those?"

"Not in our lifetimes."

"You're sure?"

"George."

There were footsteps heading out the door.

"Where are you going?" Barnett said.

"Business," the Commander said. "I'll be back before dark."

"What about this piece of shit?"

"Harry?" the Commander said. "Let him rot."

Stay Calm

Ellen wedged herself out of the cramped seat. She looked wretched, felt wretched, and after two days on the go, probably smelled that way, too. The most she'd slept recently was three hours on the floor of the San Francisco airport, waiting for this flight to Atlanta. The rest was a miserable half-sleep populated by leering Barnetts and images of Harry that never quite focused.

The one benefit was that no one jostled her as she dragged herself off the plane. No "Hey, babe" glances, either. With her dark sunglasses, leather jacket, matted hair, and burning scowl, furtive eyes didn't linger long.

It would probably work with Roy Keener, too, since that's how he expected her to look. He had given her all kinds of grief two days before about her "punk" look. Of course, that hadn't stopped him from sleazing all over her. The guy was one raging, red-neck hormone.

She wasn't going to waste time with Keener like she had with Barnett. Her plan was: get him online; read him his rights; head for the airport. It didn't allow for problems, they had no time for that. Hopefully, Morton had lined up help from the Atlanta field office, but she'd do it alone if it necessary.

The trek from the plane to the rental car counter was one long slog. No one had shown up to get her, or else Ellen hadn't noticed. Once she'd picked up the car, she would call the office and head to Keener's place.

Someone tapped her on the arm. It was a woman, a few years

younger, who could have been Ellen's clone except for the brown hair. The clean brown hair. And the rested look. The fresh clothes. And the big grin. She'd probably had a decent meal, too.

"Ellen?" the woman said, her voice annoyingly chirpy.

In that moment, Ellen finally understood the term "pup," the dismissive label for rookie agents. This woman was panting and fidgeting like a beagle. It gave Ellen a new perspective on Harry, and on their first meeting. It was a wonder he hadn't smacked her.

"First office?" Ellen said.

The woman's eyes widened. "Yeah, how did you know?"

"How long?"

"I graduated three months ago. Look, I've got a car outside."

On the way out of town, Special Agent Hailey Adams was a talking machine. She started with a review of the plans to take Keener and company: Ellen gets inside; takes Keener in private; signals the team; a hundred-plus agents swoop in. All approved by S.F. SAC James Morton.

With business out of the way, Hailey alternated between pumping Ellen for information and dispensing her own pups-eye view of the world.

"That's the trouble with the system today," Hailey said. "We're being manacled by the courts. Either them or these obnoxious, overpriced defense lawyers. We've got witnesses that don't want to get involved. Juries focused on movie deals, not justice. And on and on. There's no sense of order anymore, no respect. The criminals are laughing at us, strutting around with their millions, thumbing their noses, while we work for pittance and have the courts dump on us. And if it's not the career criminals, it's these militia weirdos spouting the word of God as they gunned down the Director of the FBI."

"Do you know that for a fact?" Ellen said.

"Come on. Why are you here in Georgia? They've got some big plot going and that has to tie in. Look at the weapons used— taken from that ATF heist, right? Fortunately, we got their leader, that guy in Montana." She grinned at Ellen. "So how many more are there after this Keener yokel?"

This was going way too fast for Ellen's brain at the moment. "Forgive me, Hailey, but I need to concentrate on just this one action. Okay? I'll fill you in once we get Keener under wraps."

Hailey gave her a half-smile. "Has this been a tough one?"

Ellen said "Yeah," but it was barely audible.

"So what happened? How did we come up empty-handed?"

"What in the world are you talking about?" Ellen said.

"That raid in Sutter Springs. Some of the guys from this office were involved in it. I thought you knew. So how is it possible they got nothing?"

Ellen blanched. Some of these guys were part of the rogues' raid in Sutter Springs? These guys backing her up now, whose buddy she had baited? Whose friends had set a deadly trap for her and Harry?

Her throat was gripped by an invisible iron hand. She reached up to check the gun Morton had given her, suddenly uncertain of who she might have to defend herself against.

"I didn't realize that was such a tough question," Hailey said.

Ellen took a breath to try to calm herself. "Forget it. Like you said, this has been a tough one."

"So, listen," Hailey said. "I really think you should wear a wire. There's no telling what Keener might do. That way we can jump in early if it seems like you're in trouble."

"Which is exactly what I don't want. If people storm in early, I'm dead. Guaranteed. These guys are paranoid, even more since Rumson was captured, and they'll probably do everything but strip search me. I'm sure they'll do a scan, and they'd pick up the wire instantly."

"What about your gun? Or your shield? What about—"

"Does someone have a laptop and tools for me? Morton should have asked for that."

"Yeah, they're in the back."

"Okay, so I yank the board out and put my shield and the warrant in there. I'm not going to try to hide my gun. I was just here two days ago, so they should accept me with a weapon, and certainly with a laptop. Nobody's going to question that, not at this place. I need one more thing: a cell phone, so I can call you guys when it's time."

They pulled off the road behind two other cars, one of which was for Ellen to drive to the compound, according to Hailey. A trim man came over, introduced himself as Brett Rodgers, the SAC from Atlanta, and took Ellen aside to discuss final preparations. He said there was no formal staging site, so as not to alert Keener's scouts in the area. Support troops were positioned at points around the map, linked by secure communications lines. Once Ellen went in, they would proceed slowly until they got her signal.

He wanted to wait until dark, another two hours or so, but Ellen insisted on leaving immediately. Barnett was out there somewhere, probably with a laptop now, so every second was precious. If he or the Commander got to Keener first, there would be Roast Ellen on the menu that night. Rodgers, the Atlanta SAC, did not overrule her.

So Ellen took off for the final ten miles to Keener's compound. It wasn't as strategically placed as the Commander's, and thus not as easily defensible. Keener himself had told her that, pointing out his sentries as he drove her in two nights before. But he had said it with bravado, claiming his boys were a lot smarter than the Commander's, and no way would they roll over if an army of Feds marched in on them. That thought went around in her brain as she drove the last couple of miles. It seemed like a flip statement at the time; now, it was about to be put to the test.

She was near the turnoff for Keener's compound, when an old pickup darted out of the woods. Ellen cut her speed as it approached. She knew she'd be checked out before she got near Keener's place, but she was counting on the impression she had made on this group two days before. The sassy blond "punk" from

California, sent by the almighty Commander, had been intriguing enough. But when they heard she could help them get "porno from cyberspace" . . . Well, everybody was grinning at her.

As the truck pulled even with her, she waved at the two green-teeths inside. It took a second, but suddenly one's eyes went wide. He smiled broadly and poked his friend; they both waved back. Then they tailed off, spun the truck around, and headed back down the road. No one stopped her the rest of the way, but a lot of guys waved as she went past. Word traveled fast.

Keener was waiting at the door, a formless hulk of a man. His face drooped like a bloodhound, but his eyes were always moving and his mouth was plastered into a perpetual grin. He was chuckling at the moment and shaking his head, which was a good sign. Ellen grabbed the gutted laptop and walked over.

"Just couldn't stay away, could you?" Keener said. "What is it? My charm? My hospitality?"

"Your computer. Barnett wants me to change something in the config file so the Feds can't crack the code. You heard about Rumson, right?"

"Asshole. Is that gonna mess with our plans? I haven't gotten any new mail on my computer in a day or so; I was starting to get itchy. I miss those little beeps that thing makes when a new message comes in."

"That's why I'm here," Ellen said. "Let's get moving."

One of Keener's assistants gave her the once-over with a wand. They didn't even comment about the gun. Maybe this was going to be easier than she thought.

They went into Keener's rec room, where the laptop was perched on the bar. Ellen walked up and ran her hand over the keys. They were warm, a sign that it had been used recently, and for more than two minutes. Probably wallowing in the smut again. She looked at him and chuckled.

"Should I ask what you've been up to?"

He shook his head. "I've been a good boy, teacher. Except for those dirty pictures. You gonna show me some more? The boys love this thing."

"Let's take care of business first. You bring up the BBS screen and I'll pull the board I need to swap out of my machine. You do remember your passwords, don't you?"

"Of course, 'porno' and 'XXX'. You think I'd forget that?"

She probably could have worked those out eventually, given Keener's single-minded focus, but knowing them would save her a lot of time. This laptop was going to be critical in their race to stop the Commander's forces. Could there be something on the BBS about the nuke?

That thought energized her, vaporizing the exhaustion. Her mind and body were racing now, anxious to get through this quickly and safely, then get back to California. She pulled a torque wrench out of her jacket and began loosening the case on the gutted laptop, as the modem on Keener's PC hissed its way into cyberspace. She slid the cover of her machine back an inch, then waited until Keener's eyes were glued to the screen.

Suddenly there was a beep from Keener's laptop.

"Hey, I got a message!" he said.

Ellen's heart caught in her throat. Barnett?

She yanked off the cover of the gutted laptop and pulled out her shield. Then she stepped behind Keener and removed her gun.

He was hunched over, reading. Then he bolted upright.

"Holy shit! We've been infiltrated by Feds! Goddamned Rumson brought them in, it says, and we're supposed to watch for—"

His body stiffened.

"Don't move," Ellen said. She clicked off the safety on her gun and tossed her shield on the bar next to Keener's laptop.

Keener looked at it and shook his head. "Fuck. I bought it all the way. Is Barnett in on it, too? And the Commander?"

"Nope. They're just a couple of criminals. You might want to distance yourself from them. The charges against you will be a lot more lenient if you cooperate."

"Cooperate? Fuck you, little girl!" He spun around. "You're not walking out of here in the first place. Are you wearing a wire?" He grabbed at her shirt.

Ellen took a step back and leveled the gun at his eyes.

"Back off, Roy. I'll shoot if I have to."

His eyes ground into hers. "You don't know who you're messing with. I eat chicks like you for lunch. You ain't got shit on me."

"How about sedition? Conspiracy? Weapons violations? We don't have you for murder yet, and I'd rather not add that. Now, I'm going to make a call to my guys, then you're going to alert your guys, and hopefully everyone will be intelligent about this. I've been assured by the Special Agent in Charge that this will be peaceful if everyone stays calm."

Keener spit in her face.

Ellen wiped it off with her sleeve, fighting her primal instinct. "Don't fuck with me, Keener. The safety is off, the gun is too close to miss, and I'm pretty tired and twitchy at the moment."

She kept the gun at his face as she made the call to Rodgers, the SAC. Keener was ready to boil over. Ellen just smiled and said, "Your turn."

He didn't move.

"Look, your men could be slaughtered otherwise. They'll do your movement no good as corpses. You can bullshit their families about them being martyrs, but you're not going to win any converts."

"What do you know about our movement?"

"Enough to know that piling on deaths is a waste. You've got the power, Roy. You can save your men or send them to die."

Keener still didn't budge.

"Your men are not the ones we want. You're not even the main one we want, Keener. You're a conduit, you and this computer. If you get all righteous, you're condemning them to death. It'll be a useless, bloody disaster."

There was a long silence. Keener's eyes raced back and forth across Ellen's face, his lips grim and twitching almost as fast. Finally, he turned his head toward the door. "Buford! Get in here!"

A large man came rumbling in, and slid to a stop when he saw Ellen's gun. His started to reach for his gun.

"Don't or Roy's a dead man," Ellen said. "I'm with the FBI. A force of Special Agents is on its way here. Tell your buddies to stand down. Right, Roy?"

There was no answer.

"Isn't that right, Roy?"

Slowly, he nodded.

"A little louder, please."

Keener looked at his associate. "Stand down, Buford. Spread the word fast. I don't want anyone hurt."

The large man's face went white. He looked at Ellen, then back at Keener. He stumbled out of the room, muttering.

"Very good," Ellen said. "Now, if you'd step aside a little bit."

"Can I see that warrant you've got?"

She handed it to Keener, then moved to the laptop to scan the rest of the Commander's message; once Keener was secured she could read it in detail. There was something about Rumson, something about the network—and a mention of Harry! They had him in custody and planned to . . .

Her heart jumped. He was alive!

Suddenly, there was movement to her left. Ellen turned as Keener swung a whiskey bottle at her head. She ducked just in time and the bottle crashed against the bar, showering her with whiskey and slivers of glass.

Ellen surged forward, pushing Keener back against a counter and into a row of glassware. He tried to wrap his arms around her, but she slammed the gun so hard into his chin, it sounded like she had cracked his jaw. Keener went reeling to the floor, hitting it with a sickening thud. His body went limp, splayed out on his back.

She kept him there until reinforcements arrived. It wasn't a long wait, but the deathly silence made it seem that way. The whole time, she expected to hear an orgy of gunfire. There was none. It was an incredible relief to see those first agents sweep into the rec room.

Keener was taken outside, and the house became a swarm of activity. Ellen needed to check the files on Keener's laptop, but she was in no rush. The next flight to San Francisco wasn't for two hours, so she sat at the bar absorbing the scene. It was nice to let her mind drift for once.

Hailey was in and out every few minutes, giving Ellen a big smile each time she entered the rec room. Someone else kept looking at Ellen, too. Tall, jet black hair, very handsome face; odd time to be grooving that way, but he had a smoldering quality that tweaked her brain. His glances were anything but cheery, however, and his slight limp added an edge that made Ellen uneasy. What a juxtaposition of reactions.

Hailey the beagle popped in again, so Ellen waved her over. "There's a guy from your squad, walks with a limp. Who is he?"

"A limp? Oh, Jack Townsend. Why?"

"He's been staring at me."

"Hey, you're the star of the evening."

"That's not it. What's with the limp?"

"He got banged up in that raid last week; thrown out of a window."

Ellen's breath caught. This was the guy she had bashed with the flashlight! This was one of the rogues!

For all the activity around her, Ellen felt alone. If they were going to get her, there was probably no better place than this. The only questions were how and when.

God, what if they wanted this computer? If the rogues didn't know about Barnett's BBS before, they sure had to now, once she requested a warrant to look at Keener's laptop. Would they attempt to beat the passwords out of her?

She tried to appear calm as she walked over to the laptop. She was going to absorb as much as she could now, in the few minutes she had before heading to the airport. But she couldn't let them have this machine, no matter what. It was her only link to Harry, her only hope of being able to rescue him.

She started with the message still on the screen. There wasn't more about Harry than she had first seen, but it was so nice to read those lines again, threat and all.

Going backwards were messages from the other militia leaders, arguing the wisdom of carrying through with the Commander's plan. Some of the guys were for it, like Keener. Some were strongly opposed, but would join in if things seemed to have a chance for success. As she raced through the collection, she saw names and other identifying bits of information. This thing was a gold mine!

It crossed her mind to pitch herself as Keener, to go online and try to bend the course of the plans. She didn't hold out a lot of hope for that, but it might be worth a try.

The machine beeped just then, startling her. It was a message from the Commander. She held her breath as she brought it up. It read:

· ALERT! ALERT! Schedule is moved up ONE WEEK. All forces should ship out ASAP. Be ready to switch to—

The screen of the laptop slammed down suddenly. Ellen barely got her fingers out of the way, and then the laptop was pulled away from her.

"Hey, wait a minute! I was in the middle of—"

She froze. There in front of her was the agent with the limp. The man she had thrown out the window. His hands were gripping Keener's computer, his eyes cold. If Ellen wasn't so furious, she might have been scared.

"We need this," he said.

"Hold on!" Ellen said. "You've just fucked me over royally."

"Like you did to me in Sutter Springs? It was you, wasn't it?"

"Listen—it's Townsend, right?—well, I was sent out here to get that machine and you're not going to walk off with it. You'll have to shoot me first. Where the fuck did you learn manners, anyway?"

Townsend was about to answer, when Hailey appeared between them. "Come on, guys. We're on the same team."

Ellen and Townsend both glared at her, then back at each other.

"Suit yourself," Hailey said. "Ellen, do you need this other laptop any longer, the gutted one? If not, I'll take it out."

Ellen waved her off and waited until the beagle had left the room. When she spoke, her voice was low.

"Listen, Townsend. This country is in huge, fucking danger. If we have any hope of stopping that threat, I need to have that computer." Her voice caught. "And it may provide the only chance I have of saving my partner's life."

Her voice rose, bitter. "Screw that. You and your buddies tried to kill us anyway. But if you have any concern for your country at all, forget about your own little plans—you and Keller and Crowley and whoever else—and let me out of here with that laptop. You can get back to your agenda later."

Townsend's eyes were wide. His head snapped around to survey the room; they were alone. "What do you know about plans? Keller and Crowley and others?"

"I don't know exactly what you're up to, but—"

"Keep your voice down," he said. "I'm not in on any 'plan,' but I know something is going on. I heard talk during the raid that's got me nervous."

"But you were in on it."

"Just following orders, King. You must've done that once or twice. But we're wasting time. Are you going back to San Francisco?"

"Yeah, in just over an hour. I've got to split now, in fact. Hailey said I could leave that car at the airport."

"Forget it. I'll give you a ride and we can talk. Come on."

He took off ahead of her, at a surprisingly brisk pace despite the limp. When they got outside, there was still a lot of activity going on.

"Hold on a second," Ellen said. "I've got to get my bag out of the other car." She went to the vehicle she had driven into the compound and grabbed her shoulder bag off the front seat. She noticed the gutted laptop on the floor, but didn't think anything about it.

She was just getting into Townsend's car, when Hailey ran up.

"Hey, are you guys taking Keener's machine? I was supposed to guard it."

"You'll get it, Adams," Townsend said. "King here needs it a while. Just log it with the rest of Keener's things and make a note that it was checked out to Special Agent Ellen King from San Francisco. Easy enough?"

Hailey looked flustered. "Oh, okay. Um, shit." She looked at Townsend with beagle eyes. "Could you do me a favor? Could you take this other laptop with you back to the office. It'd save me a trip tonight. That is, if you don't mind."

She didn't wait for a reply, but darted to the car Ellen had driven and grabbed the laptop. She was back a moment later, holding it out to Ellen.

Something didn't quite fit, but Ellen took the laptop anyway and got into Townsend's car. Hailey waved merrily and disappeared.

Townsend swung his car through the maze of FBI vehicles and out onto the road. He stomped on the accelerator and the car leapt forward.

"That was strange," Ellen said.

"I was thinking the same thing," Townsend replied. "She seemed anxious, which isn't like her. Usually she struts around the office like she's queen of the hill. Who knows, maybe she was cowed in your presence. You do make an impression on people, hopefully not with a flashlight most times."

Ellen gave him a sheepish smile. "I'm really sorry about that. Someday maybe we can have a beer and I'll tell you the whole sordid tale."

He smiled back. "I'd like that."

"Meanwhile, what do I do with this piece of junk?" She hoisted the laptop Hailey had given her. "I stripped the board out of it, so unless someone wants to—"

She stopped and raised the laptop again, testing its weight.

It was heavier than it should be—much heavier!

She was so nervous, she could barely talk. "Pull the car over now," she said quietly. "I think this thing is rigged. I don't want to risk throwing it out the window."

Townsend jammed on the brakes and skidded off the road.

"Go! Go!" she said.

They burst out the car doors, hit the ground, and started rolling.

Five seconds later, the car exploded, sending a fireball a hundred feet in the air. Ellen covered her head as flaming debris rained down on her.

She raised her eyes and stared at the burning heap. Somewhere in the blaze was Keener's computer—and her hope of saving Harry.

A Huge Spike

Barnett squinted at the crack between the floorboards; something was moving around down there. He scanned the room. Was there any place it could get in? At least at Grasslands, he only had to watch his back. Plus the caliber of felons was more engaging. Here, he met a stony silence whenever he left his room. Just Betsy and Harry-the-rat were around, but that was two people too many. The one thing keeping Barnett sane was counting the days.

And he only had five more to endure. Five days until the country, in one blinding flash, entered a new realm. God bless that nuke. Things would be jarring, there would be chaos, but ultimately everyone would be happier for it. Maybe grudgingly at first, but people always resisted change.

Barnett smiled. This was going to be fun to watch.

The one thing he would miss was the capture of the cretins, George and Kevin. That had consumed his brain lately. Just wiping out the government wasn't enough; he wanted to make sure Ol' Flattop couldn't come after him once this was all over.

He probably had a cushion of time, since the two bozos were due to leave for Washington the next morning. But Barnett wanted to ensure that a week from now, or a year from now, he wouldn't be ambushed by a group of smelly thugs. They deserved it anyway, for their incompetence and the way they had treated him lately. The only bright spot was that they had both been gone for a day, and within twenty-four hours they would be out of his life.

Barnett was back inside the White House network again,

watching the activity on Chief of Staff Jessop's account. At exactly 9 A.M., a message appeared, with the title: HE'S HERE.

Barnett went into the "chat" mode.

· Greetings, Gordon. Thanks for coming.
· *What do you want?*
· A schedule change. I need you to get the vote moved up on that anti-terrorism bill. It's got to be next Wednesday, not the week after. Got that? NEXT WEDNESDAY.
· *Not a chance. This is Congress you're talking about.*
· Hey, you're the Prez. Call in markers, make deals, promise them the moon, but make sure everybody is there to vote on it next Wednesday and make sure it's TOUGH.

There was a pause before the President responded.

· *What's the hurry?*
· Things are heating up. If we wait too long, they may get me and the videotape. You're popular, but not with these guys.
· *Why don't we just take care of this quietly?*
· AND BREAK THE LAW??? No, you have to get these guys legally. I want them to be humiliated in public before being cast away for the rest of their lives. So, let's stick with my plan.
· *When do I get the videotape?*
· I'll give it to you before the voting begins, as a sign of good-faith. You'll probably want to be in chambers anyway. Get the VP to join you and the heads of the various investigative branches.

There was another pause.

· *And the follow-up "action" you mentioned before?*
· I'll be back to you next week about that.
· *How do you know I'll carry through?*
· Well, you know how easy it is to duplicate a videotape . . .

There were several sharp raps on Barnett's door just then.

"He's gotta go!" said Betsy's muffled voice.

"I'm busy," Barnett shouted. "He can do it himself."

"Not this. You know the Commander's instructions."

"I'm online with the President, for God's sake! Help him yourself."

Barnett turned his attention back to the screen. Here he was, chatting with the most powerful man in the world, trying to set up the destruction of the government—and he had to be bathroom monitor? There was no sense of perspective in this world.

He shook his head. Five more days.

Harry was getting weaker. He had been given little more than water and bread to eat since they had arrived. Judging by the movement in the cabin and the taunting smells from Betsy's cooking, this had to be the second day there. Is that Friday? He wasn't sure. The permanent darkness that the blindfold imposed had affected more than his eyes. His hearing had become incredibly acute, but the rest of him was numb.

He wasn't feeling fatalistic, not yet anyway. They needed a warm body as their "insurance," which meant they probably wouldn't kill him for another three to five days. Which gave Ellen and Morton and the rest a little time to work things out. Harry suspected his location was the family cabin near Kings Canyon, but he couldn't be sure even if the blindfold was off. He'd been asleep when Kevin drove there last week.

And if no one found him? If they didn't stop this monstrous plot? He would be dead, of course; there was no sympathy from anyone in this group. As for the bigger equation, it was too harrowing to even consider. Somewhere in this room lurked a suitcase with the potential to rewrite history.

Betsy's footsteps came up.

"He's not going to take you," she said.

"What does that mean? Am I supposed to make a mess of myself here or stumble blindly outside and soil my clothes under the pines? Unless you've got some clean ones in my size, it'll be pretty nasty around me."

Betsy groaned. "Come on. No funny stuff; I've got a gun."

She got him to his feet and led him outside. He didn't trip stepping off the porch; by now, he had the cabin and the porch mapped out in his brain.

The sound of the wind in the trees, a few birds singing far away, even the crunch of their feet on the dirt; they were a tonic to his brain. He turned his head in Betsy's direction.

"Could a condemned man make a request?"

"What are you talking about?"

"They're going to kill me, right? We both know it. So I was just wondering if I could have a last request?"

"What do you want?"

"Could you remove the blindfold? I'd like to see again."

Betsy didn't respond, but led him along in silence.

"I suppose it can't do any harm," she said. "But it's got to be on before the Commander is back." She stepped behind him and untied the blindfold.

A moment later, the world burst into view. The sky was so bright, he had to shield his eyes until they adjusted. Once they did, it was a moment of pure joy—fleeting, but wonderful even so.

He looked at Betsy and smiled. "Thanks."

She snarled at him. "Let's get this over with."

She stalked off toward a stand of trees, but Harry followed more slowly. He looked around at the towering sequoias, the stark granite cliffs, the puffs of clouds high in the sky. It was heaven.

"Beautiful place," he said. "Are you guys going to stay up here once this is all over? I don't imagine you can go back to the compound."

She glared at him. "We have you to thank for that, don't we?"

"I didn't mean it that way."

"Regardless. The fact is that you've fucked up my life. Robbed me of my possessions, put my family at risk, and sentenced me to this dump for who knows how long. If you'd raped me, you couldn't have violated me more."

"Hold on, Betsy."

"No, you hold on!" She shoved him against a tree. "The only difference between you and that other goon is that he got laid and you didn't. How does that make you feel? All this work and you didn't even get fucked. I'd say you're the bigger loser."

She backed up and stared at him. She chuckled crudely.

"Couldn't even make the right request as a dying man. Well, maybe I should help you out. What do you think?"

Harry's heart was pounding.

Betsy walked up close, but held her gun between them. Then she reached forward and started stroking him through his pants.

"How about it, dying man? Want a last piece of ass? It's the best you'd ever have. Come on, I want to hear you beg for it."

Harry struggled to breathe. "Betsy, please don't do this."

Her stroking became more insistent, more probing, and Harry's body began to respond. Despite all his efforts to resist, his body was responding.

"Oooh, that's better," she said. She dropped to her knees, put the gun against one side of his penis and nuzzled the other side with her mouth.

She looked up at him with half-closed eyes. Her voice was soft, purring. "Don't you want this, Harry? Come on, beg for it. Beg me for the greatest fuck of your life."

She sat back on her heels and, with one hand, began unbuttoning her blouse. She pulled it out of her jeans, spread the blouse open, and then unhooked the front clasp of her bra. Her breasts tumbled out. She reached her free hand up to her mouth, ran a finger over her tongue, and began circling a nipple.

"This would be kind of fitting for a man in your profession," she whispered. "Sex with a gun at your head. Kinky, huh? Maybe you've had dreams about it."

She leaned forward and ran her hand over the bulge in his pants. "Oh, that's got to hurt by now, doesn't it? I think we should remedy that."

Harry's body was screaming. His mind was fighting a losing battle to maintain control. Weakly, he said, "Betsy, please don't."

"Yes, Harry." Her voice was hard, vicious. "You fucked me, now I'm going to fuck you."

She grabbed the zipper on his pants and drew it down slowly. She pulled his pants part way down, then reached up and did the same with his underwear. His penis leapt out of his shorts.

"Oh, my," she said. "Too bad this will be retired soon."

She reached out and began stroking him.

"You shouldn't have fucked with me and my family, Harry. Really."

She moved her hand to his balls, cradled them for a moment —and then squeezed them with all her strength. "You shouldn't have fucked with me!"

A primordial shriek burst from Harry's lungs. Bolts of pain shot through his body. He lurched upwards, but she yanked him back. The pain was off the charts.

He collapsed on top of her and she lost her grip, but she began pummeling him with her fists. "Bastard! Bastard! Bastard!"

Harry's hands, still cuffed, were somewhere in between them. He felt the brush of metal and grabbed at it. It didn't matter if the safety was off or not; they planned to kill him anyway.

He felt the gun again and surged upwards with the cuffs. He wrapped his hands around the gun and yanked down, then cocked his wrists sharply. Betsy yelped in pain and Harry rolled onto his side. He had the gun!

She lunged at him, trying to pin him, but a new jolt of energy flooded Harry's veins. He rolled onto his stomach, with Betsy still on top of him, then drew his legs under him and vaulted upwards.

She fell to the ground at his feet.

Harry turned the gun toward her, then retreated a few steps. It was tough with his hands cuffed, but he managed to pull his clothes back together. Betsy glared at him as she did the same.

"I *will* kill you," she said.

Harry took a breath. "Betsy, I was just doing my job. It was nothing personal. I actually like you and your son."

"Bullshit."

"It's true." He leaned against a tree. "That's made all this harder. In another time and place . . ."

"Bastard!"

"No, that would be your husband. I don't know if he confides in you, but he's planning to wipe out the government. He and Barnett and a few others. Kevin is participating, though I suspect it's because he doesn't know any better."

"You leave my son alone!"

Harry nodded. "I wish we could. But if he goes off to D.C., he's in it. Did you see that heavy suitcase George has been carrying around? Do you know what's in it? A nuclear bomb."

Betsy's face tightened.

"Do you know how many thousands, even millions of people that could kill? How many sons just like Kevin will die innocently? Sons and daughters whose only crime is to be in the wrong place at the wrong time?"

Her eyes were boring into his.

"My life is over," Harry said, "but Kevin's doesn't have to be. And neither do thousands, maybe millions of others."

Betsy's focus dropped, to somewhere far away.

"You've got to talk to him," Harry said. "You've got to make him see. You're the only one who can do it, who can get him to stop this madness. It may be the only chance to save all those lives."

She glared up at him. "This is just another trick, right?"

"How? George has me locked up. Even this gun won't help. Here." He tossed it in the dirt. "It would do me no good to take you hostage. Kevin would shoot me in a heartbeat, while your loving husband would probably say 'Sorry, babe, but the cause is bigger than both of us.' True?"

Betsy grabbed the gun and pointed it at Harry, her hand trembling.

"What do you know about my marriage?"

Harry shrugged. "If you're passing out favors to the phone man, there's a problem somewhere. And from the looks of things, I'll bet you're the one making most of the sacrifices."

Betsy's eyes reddened. Her trembling increased.

"Marriage isn't easy," Harry said softly. "But how far does loyalty go? 'Til death do us part? Even if millions of others die? What justifies that? Who has the right to decide? How loyal has George been to his son?"

Betsy stared at him, searching his face, her eyes wavering between fury and despair. It seemed he had gotten through to her, until she raised the gun.

"Turn around and get down on your knees."

Harry closed his eyes. He couldn't believe his life would end this way. He turned and dropped to his knees. He was too much in shock to be nervous. He raised his face to the tree tops and waited.

Betsy stepped up close behind him.

"There's a photo on my bedside table of a man I once loved without reservation," she said quietly. "A man who rescued me from a miserable existence, who was loyal to me when nobody else was. Somehow the little things, the daily things, as bad as they've been, have not wiped out that image."

A moment later, the blindfold went back over his eyes. Harry's heart jumped into the stratosphere. Betsy pulled the blindfold tight and stepped away.

"Find your own way back," she said.

Her footsteps faded in the wind.

* * *

Ellen sat in the small, windowless room, with a telephone and a cup of coffee in front of her. She was staring at nothing, thinking about nothing. Just waiting. For once, it was a welcome state. Too much had been happening too fast.

She was at the Atlanta field office, snuck in through a back door with Jack Townsend early that morning, both in disguise. To the rest of the world, they were dead, obliterated in a car fire the night before. It wasn't in the news, pending an investigation, but people in the Bureau heard about the tragedy. Only Jim Morton and Brett Rodgers, the Atlanta SAC, knew the real story: there was a killer loose in the Atlanta field office.

Ellen and Jack had spent the night at a motel in Marietta, in separate rooms, though that was worth reconsidering later on. If this had been a movie, they would have made mad, passionate love in a desperate release from a near-death experience. Instead, they had Super Value meals and scoured Wal-Mart for a change of clothes, but it beat the last four dates she'd had by miles. Add in a long shower and a decent night's sleep, and she was feeling okay.

Now, she was waiting. Waiting to talk to Morton, waiting for the nod from his friend, Rodgers. Jack was in another room, making calls.

The phone rang. Ellen picked it up immediately. "Hello?"

"Ellen?"

"Hi, chief! I'll bet you're surprised to hear my voice."

"Relieved. Thrilled. I heard from Brett last night, but it is nice to hear your voice," Morton said. "That must have been awful."

"It was close. Way too close."

"Well, I almost met the same fate."

"No! You were targeted? When? How?"

"Last night. Same deal: plastic explosive in my laptop. It obviously runs in the family. I walked in on the guy as he was rigging it. He's a pup, one of those Doberman types big on swagger but not always thorough. He didn't bother to make sure I was really gone last night."

"Do I know him?"

"I don't think so. He's nine months out of Quantico, but he's been on different assignments than you. I questioned him last night with his lawyer present and he refused to answer anything."

"Damn!"

"Hold on," Morton said. "He didn't answer verbally, but I hit him with a surprise question and got a real spike. It couldn't have been any clearer if he had been hooked to a polygraph machine."

"What was it?"

"Remember when you were attacked by those associates of Trong? I think you called them Vietnamese Vipers? If you recall, we learned later that your name and Harry's were on a hit list, spelled correctly."

Ellen's breath caught. "You said you had a leak to plug."

"That's right. Out of the blue, I asked him about Trong, and there was the briefest flare in his eyes. His lawyer saw it, too, and changed the subject, but you could take that flash of panic to the bank."

"What about the suggestion that someone in a California field office alerted the militias to the ATF shipment?"

"It's crossed my mind," Morton said, "though I heard it from Warren Keller. If he's the head rogue, would he have fingered one of his boys?"

"Good point. So if this guy was responsible for that tip, it might let us wipe Keller's name off the rogues' list."

"I'm going to work that angle shortly. You may be right about Keller. I had a call from him an hour ago, unprompted. News travels so fast through the Bureau, it's scary. Anyway, he said he's devastated by your death and pledged every resource to try to find Harry. He apologized for being tied up with other things and promised to give this his highest priority. He said he had just been on the phone with the Nuclear Emergency Search Team—"

"Why didn't he call NEST a month ago?"

"Ellen, at this point, with militias ready to move on D.C.—"

"They already are, sir. I saw part of an alert from Pilkin, and they're moving up the schedule one week, whatever that means. Everyone was told to leave ASAP, so there's a force of undermined size now advancing on D.C. Including, we have to assume, a weapon of mass destruction. I figure that gives us three days to a week before 'Torch Day,' as Barnett calls it."

Morton exhaled. "Then we really need Keller's cooperation."

"Probably so. At least we know most of their targets, and we've got a rough idea of where they'd put the nuke. But we still don't know their strike date and if we throw a dragnet around the city, they'll just back off and come back once the heat has died down. Can you imagine the hysteria if news of this leaks out? This has to be quieter than quiet."

Morton cleared his throat. "What about the computer targets?"

"To be honest, I haven't had time to think about those, sir. Between dodging bombs, worrying about that nuke, thinking about Harry—"

She stopped, her voice heavy. "Are there any leads?"

"Not so far. That's a big country out there and a lot of distance between California and Washington, D.C."

"What about Kings Canyon? Has anyone searched that?"

"Good point, though from what I've seen on a map, it's a tough place to cover without a major effort. The thing is, we both expect Harry and the nuke to be together, right?"

Ellen swallowed. "Yes."

"So maybe NEST can do some fly-bys of Kings Canyon, but our focus needs to be on D.C. We're trying to get portable devices from the military that we can station at checkpoints outside the city. They bombard suspect vehicles with radioactive particles, like x-ray machines for trucks. They're not foolproof, but if Pilkin doesn't know they're out there, he won't take counter measures. We'll set them up at each of the bridges, plus as many of the land routes from Maryland as we can cover with what we're given. We might even co-opt their plan for the traffic circles and put the devices there."

"Didn't you say this is in a suitcase or something? They might bring it in on a train or the Metro, you know."

"You're right," Morton said. "So, we'll put people by the rails and stop anyone with a suitcase or carton big enough to hold it. We're going to need pictures of these guys, too."

"Barnett's will be easy to get, though I doubt he'll go to D.C. I don't know if Pilkin has a criminal record, but we should be able to find a picture from his military files. As for the other guys, I got a quick look at their names. If we can't locate pictures of them, I can reconstruct their faces with a sketch artist."

"So where are you going now? No sense in returning here."

"I thought I'd go to D.C. once we're done with the interrogation, since that's where the action is going to be. I'd love to be able to dive into files at the Hoover Building, but I'm leery about walking in the front door."

"Understandable," Morton said. "And since everyone thinks you're dead, I'm not sure we should relinquish that advantage. If nothing else, it might keep the bombers away—the rogue ones, anyway." He chuckled. "I didn't even let on to Keller. But I'll tell Abe Potter. He's the SAC for the D.C. field office and an old buddy of mine. He can help you out until I get to town, which should be Sunday at the latest."

They hung up. And all the pressure Ellen had held down overnight came crashing back: Harry; the nuke; the rogues; Barnett's insidious computer bombs. She had forgotten all about that particular problem, and those could be as catastrophic as the nuke.

It felt like the walls were closing in on her. There was no place that felt safe at the moment, not even this room. Rodgers could be one of the rogues, for all she knew. Maybe that was why it was taking so long. Maybe they had locked her in, planning to kill her later. Of course, they could have done it last night, and why would they have brought her in, and . . .

She got up from the chair. If she stayed in this room any longer, she would go berserk.

The door opened quietly and Jack Townsend stuck his head in, smiling at her. "Gone crazy yet?"

"Definitely."

"They're ready for us. Let's go."

He led her down a series of narrow hallways, then into a small, dark room. It was an observation booth, blocked from peering eyes in the adjoining interview room by one-way glass that ran the length of one wall. On the other side of the tinted glass was the SAC, Brett Rodgers.

Jack gestured toward a chair and Ellen sat down. He dropped into the seat next to her. "This has been going on for two hours now," he said. "None of the interviews have lasted more than ten minutes. Rodgers has been low-key about this, with no polygraphs, so everyone assumes it's a routine interview in the wake of yesterday's tragedy."

The door to the interview room opened and Hailey Adams walked in. She looked relaxed, even cocky, just as Jack had described her usual persona.

Pleasantries were exchanged, then Rodgers began asking about her experiences in Atlanta and with the FBI so far. After ten minutes it sounded like a routine personnel chat, not a search for a sinister rogue.

Then Rodgers, leaned back and stretched out his arms. "I need to ask you a question or two, Adams, about that incident in the field yesterday. We're talking to everyone, trying to piece together the scene."

Hailey's face paled. "That was awful. I feel so bad about Jack Townsend and that woman from California."

"That 'woman'?!" Ellen said, her words safe behind the glass. "She practically knew my blood type by the time we got to Keener's." Her pulse kicked up several notches.

"Do you have any idea what happened?" Rodgers said.

Hailey shook her head. "I barely saw them. I gave her a ride to meet you; that's it. I heard later about an explosion."

Rodgers nodded. "Any idea what happened?"

She shrugged. "I'd look to Keener. Didn't that agent come to get his laptop? Maybe it had a self-destruct mechanism in there, with C-4 or something."

Ellen snarled. "Bullshit. I prepped that machine myself."

"Of course it's crap," Jack replied. "Did you expect better?"

Rodgers frowned. "Would it still work with plastique in it? And how would it detonate if Keener was in custody?"

"It might have been rigged to blow if the user didn't give a certain command before shutting it off."

"It was off already, wasn't it?"

"Who knows?" Hailey said. "It never came back from Keener's, and the two people who had it . . ."

Rodgers leaned forward. "You may be on to something. Can we explore this a little further."

Hailey smiled. "Yeah, sure."

Rodgers pressed a button on the phone next to him and said, "Bring it in, please." He looked at Hailey. "This'll be painless."

When she saw the polygraph equipment being rolled in, there was a brief crack in her facade. The SAC was looking away, maybe by design, but Ellen and Jack saw it in minute detail. Then Hailey forced a smile.

"Why are we doing this?" she asked.

"Are you unwilling to take a polygraph?" Rodgers said.

"No, I've got nothing to hide. I just don't think it's necessary."

Jack leaned over to Ellen. "She's trapped and she knows it."

Once the equipment was hooked up, the technician ran through a series of basic questions—What is your name? How old are you? etc.—to create a baseline for comparison later when key questions were asked.

Ellen couldn't see the chart, but she could follow the swing of the needles. After Morton's mention of visual clues, she was particularly focused on Hailey's demeanor.

There was an edginess to Hailey's responses during the baseline questions, but that wasn't unusual in a polygraph exam. For the most part, the needles swung in smooth, regular arcs. The first part continued for several minutes, led by the technician.

Then Rodgers said, "Okay, regarding this theory of yours about the exploding laptop: Did you know that someone tried to blow up the SAC in San Francisco last night, using this very same technique?"

The needles carved a huge spike. "I hadn't heard," Hailey said.

"An FBI Special Agent was caught installing it. Could there be a connection to the bomb here?"

The needles twitched along with Hailey's face. "Maybe."

"And to the blast that killed the Deputy Director?"

The needles traced jagged peaks as Hailey tried to shrug. "How could I know that?" Her voice was getting weaker.

"Good question. Would Brendan Crowley know the answer?"

The needles jumped. "What is this about, sir?"

"Attacks on FBI officials. That attempt on a SAC last night. The exploding laptop you gave Special Agent King yesterday."

"You don't know what you're talking about."

"She told me so."

The needles flattened out. "She's dead."

Rodgers turned to the glass. "Really?"

Jack nudged Ellen. "That's our cue."

When they walked into the interview room, the needles began to slash wildly. The color drained from Hailey's face.

Rodgers looked at Ellen and Jack, and smiled. "Who would like to read Special Agent Adams her rights?"

"This isn't possible," Hailey said, her voice hushed, her eyes riveted to Ellen's. "How could you have gotten away?"

"Who is behind this?" Ellen said. "You're not working alone."

"This isn't possible! You were dead!"

"I'd advise you not to say anything without a lawyer present," Rodgers said. "And then I suggest you cooperate fully. The charges against you are very serious."

"Cooperate? With what? A pathetic swipe at justice? I'd advise *you* to get out of the way and let us do what we were sworn to do."

"And that is?" Ellen said.

"Crush criminals. Punish the wicked. Make the world safe."

"By killing off dissenters? What about due process?"

"The Constitution is outmoded, King. We're being shackled by a document drawn up over two hundred years ago by some ignorant farmers. It's time for a new Constitution."

"And you're going to write it?" Jack said.

"If necessary."

"Who is leading you?" Ellen said.

Hailey shook her head.

"Brendan Crowley?"

Ellen glanced at the needles. They were sweeping back and forth in steady arcs, meaning there was no tension in Hailey's defiant silence. Thus, she hadn't been surprised by the question. Could that be read as a "Yes"?

"Warren Keller?" Rodgers said.

The needles continued their steady sweep.

Stay of Execution

Barnett flipped down the screen of his laptop in disgust. The whole fucking thing was unraveling. He should have expected it, really, but he'd been carried away with visions of a lasting peace, Barnett-style. Something about that image of Washington in flames had been too overpowering for him to think clearly.

That was the trouble with humans, you couldn't hack them. Machines were dependable, predictable creatures. Ask them a simple question, get a straight answer. "Can I go through this door?" *"What's the password?"* "Blurp." *"Come right in."* With people, it was always: *Why? Maybe. Later. What's it to you?* or *Make it worth my while.* Even machines programmed to be devious were predictable when you got to their core. It made for an ordered universe where logic, intelligence, and creativity could flourish.

But people . . . The only two he could count on were the President and the Commander, and those because he had them by the balls. One knew that; the other probably feared it, or should.

As for the militia morons, they were striking out on their own, flashing e-mail messages back and forth as they tore down the original plan and rebuilt it to their liking. They were indeed moving on D.C., but only to take advantage of the Commander's timing. Otherwise, thanks to news of the infiltrators, Georgie-boy had lost all credibility.

According to the e-mails, the morons were not switching to secondary targets, as instructed, but were moving directly on the Capitol—in much larger numbers than planned. Armageddon would not be in the wheat fields but on the streets of ZOG's satanic palace. They had waited too long to let a megalomaniac deny them their God-given victory, or so the drivel went.

Barnett raised his middle finger in the air. Screw 'em all! He wasn't going to Washington, so who cared? If the mutineers made life difficult for the Commander, so much the better. As long as that bomb got through. And if it didn't, Barnett would still wreak his revenge on the world and then retire to the South Seas somewhere.

Of course, Ol' Flattop would be livid when he found out about his buddies, if he ever returned to this dump. It was now Saturday, four days to Torch Day, and the guy was still missing, along with the idiot savant. At this point, all Barnett needed them for was a ride off this godforsaken mountain.

Once he was down, he would disappear. But not before he made life Hell for a certain Ellen King. Late last night, rooting around FBI databases, he had confirmed that name, along with her address in San Francisco. He was too tired after the "seek" phase to start the "destroy" part of the process, but that could wait a day or so. As for her rat partner, Harry was already scheduled for execution at the hands of the Commander.

More pressing for Barnett was the demise of Georgie-boy. The best scenario had him melting along with Harry and the politicos as the bomb went boom. If Barnett could time things right with the President, it just might work. If not, there was always the complete liquidation of all financial records, deeds of property, credit cards, and so on. There was something poetic in eviscerating the man without drawing a drop of blood.

Tires crunched to a halt on the gravel outside. Finally! Barnett took his time heading out of his room—and was nearly run over by Kevin, carrying a load of boxes to the other bedroom. Barnett passed Harry-the-rat, blindfolded and sitting glumly in a chair, and said, "What are you looking at?" He chuckled and continued outside to the porch, where the Commander was talking in hushed tones with Betsy.

"Did you get lost buying party favors?" Barnett asked.

"You've got ten minutes to get ready," the Commander said. "Don't waste it yapping, it's going to be a long trip."

"To Sacramento? A couple of hours."

"To Washington, stupid. You're coming along."

"What? Hold on, this was not in our agreement."

"Neither was letting those two ZOG scum in. We're short on drivers, so you've got to go with us."

"What about Betsy? Or your clan at the compound?"

"They're either captured or scattered. And this is men's work; I wouldn't put Betsy at risk."

Barnett stormed off the porch. "No way, George! No way in Hell! This was not in the plan."

The Commander glared at him. "Sonny, if this plan has a prayer, you're going to have to come along."

"It doesn't have a prayer. Kansas and Ohio are staying home, and the rest are taking things in their own hands. You've lost control."

"What are you talking about?"

"Your buddies have been burning up the wires, plotting to burn down Washington in their own little way. They're headed there now, expecting to capitalize on whatever you've got planned."

The Commander exploded. "All of them?!"

"Just about. Texas and Alabama don't hate you, but they joined the mutiny because they figure it has a better chance to succeed. Kansas and Ohio will initiate local action if and when the opportunity arises. The rest—Arizona, Arkansas, Michigan, Tennessee, and West Virginia—are rolling out their entire squads to make sure this succeeds. Hundreds, maybe thousands, of guys are headed to D.C. right now. Between forging new plans, anger at you and your Fed friends, plus debate over who gets to slice me up, the network has been getting quite a workout. Arkansas really wants me to have an ugly death."

"What about Keener?"

"Not a word out of him for two days."

The Commander groaned. "Nice going, Barnett. Your 'girl-friend' probably got to him."

"Hey, that bitch is going to get sliced in ways you can't even imagine."

Kevin passed, headed to the dark blue van, and the Commander followed him. "Your fucking network has screwed us," he called out. "What are you going to do about it?"

Barnett stormed after him. "My network? It's your 'friends' who are out of control, Commander! What are you going to do about that?"

The Commander wheeled around.

"Pull the plug. Shut down that goddamned network."

"And lose a chance to follow their movements? Be serious."

"Fuck 'em! You said they were on the move already, so if we cut off their communications, they'll be isolated. That'll cut their resolve. The last thing we need is guns going off when we're trying to get to town."

Barnett shook his head. "If you read those e-mails, it's like they're on a holy crusade. These guys have no minds anymore. I say we let them proceed. They'll be a diversion if they're caught and, as you say, 'insurance' if they're not."

"And if they're caught," the Commander said, "my name will be the first thing off their lips. So pull the plug—Now!—and get ready to roll. Don't make me have to force you."

The action between their eyes was fierce.

Finally, Barnett snarled and headed toward the house. "But I'm not going to Washington!" he said, over his shoulder.

He stalked through the cabin, giving Harry's chair a kick as he passed. Fucking Fed. Fucking Commander! Barnett stormed into his room, fuming. He wasn't going to wait to throttle this guy, he was going to do it now.

It took him only a moment to shut down the BBS, setting the loose cannons adrift. Then he went for the first of the Commander's seven bank accounts. Thirty seconds later, his heart froze.

It was closed yesterday!

He went through the rest of the accounts. Each one had been closed, either cleaned out or transferred to a bank in Switzerland. The man didn't exist in the System any more. What was going on?

Barnett burst out of his room and started for the front door. Then he spun on his heels and headed for the other bedroom. There was a stack of large boxes piled against the wall, the growing collection Kevin had been ferrying. Barnett grabbed a box and dropped it on the floor. It landed with a clank. He ripped off the sealing tape, and the Commander's plans were suddenly clear.

Gold gleamed back at him—coins and bars. If the rest of the boxes held similar stashes, much of the Commander's fortune was probably sitting right here. No wonder he and dirt boy had been gone so long.

There was a click behind him. Barnett whirled around, into the glare of a monstrous looking pistol. "Step away from the box," the Commander said. "What's in there doesn't concern you."

"Like hell it doesn't! You're cashing out, aren't you? You have no plans to go to Washington."

"Oh, I'm going. I've waited much too long for this opportunity. I just don't want anyone messing with my property while I'm gone."

The Commander held up a large envelope. BARNETT was written on it. "This isn't for you," he said, "it's about you. It catalogs your recent offenses, including the murder of your parole officer, plus a recent picture. If I'm not back within seven days, Betsy is going to take this to the authorities. Then you won't be looking at more time, you'll be looking at death row."

Barnett was shaking, a mixture of panic and rage.

"Why are you doing this?" he said.

"Insurance. I want to make sure our trip goes smoothly. If you fulfill your part of the bargain, once we get back here, the envelope is yours."

"How do I know you won't kill me first?"

A wicked grin answered back. "You'll just have to trust me."

Ellen gave up on pacing and went to the window. To the right was the Washington Monument, silhouetted against the fading sunset; to the left was the Capitol Building, an alabaster sentry in the dark. Between them, popping up above the rooftops of central D.C., was the FBI's Hoover Building, ablaze with lights on a Saturday night. Ellen stared at it for the longest time, trying to summon X-ray vision. What had happened to the D.C. SAC?

"Do you think they might have found out about Potter?" she said. "Maybe my phone calls tipped them off."

Jack didn't even look up from his newspaper. "I think you asked me that four or five hours ago."

"Well, what's taking him? We've been in this damn hotel room for over a day. I can't bear another room service meal."

Jack lowered the paper. "You must great on stakeouts."

"Jack, a nuclear bomb is headed this way, not to mention an army of fanatics bent on wiping out this city. We'll have ringside seats for the meltdown unless Potter gets here soon. We can't just sit around. I can't. I'm going out."

She pushed away from the window and started for the door. But Jack stuck his leg out to block her path.

"Don't mess with me," she said. "I beat you up once before."

"It wasn't a fair fight. And you're going to accomplish nothing out there. We need Potter. He's the only local we can count on, according to your boss. If he's delayed, there's probably a good reason."

"Twenty-four hours?"

"Look, it must be crazy inside the Hoover Building. Potter is the SAC of the D.C. field office; he probably gets yanked into HQ matters all the time. And I'm sure he's got to be careful about getting out to see us. The rogues are probably watching him. So, be patient, bucko."

"Fuck you," Ellen said, and turned back to the window.

"Well, that would certainly pass the time."

She snarled and reached for the TV remote, throwing herself on the bed to channel surf yet again. An hour later, as she was trying to decide why truck-and-tractor-pull competitions were getting air-time, there was a quiet knock at the door.

Ellen bolted upright. She walked quickly to the door, with Jack just behind, his gun drawn. She looked through the peephole in the door and saw a middle-aged woman, fashionably dressed, holding what looked like two shopping bags. Ellen opened the door as far as the chain allowed.

"This is from Potter," the woman whispered. By the time Ellen had the chain off and the door open, the woman was gone.

The bags were from Saks, with tissue paper over the top of the contents. Jack stepped forward and nudged each bag with his shoe. Nothing moved or rattled or ticked. He used his gun to lift up the tissue paper on one of the bags. It revealed several large binders, plus envelopes and folders. The second one held a similar collection.

Ellen started to reach for one of the bags, but Jack stopped her, his eyes fierce. "Let me handle these," he said. "If they're rigged or laced with something, it's better that I be the one, not you. Your knowledge is more valuable than mine right now."

Her breath caught. This *could* be a set-up, if the rogues knew she was here. She hadn't even thought about it, but she hadn't expected anything like this either. Her heart started hammering wildly. She couldn't let him do this, to take a risk that was solely hers, but she also couldn't deny his logic; what she knew had to be protected. She looked at him, not sure what to do. Her mouth was too dry to speak.

"Wait down the hall," he said. "I'll call you when it's clear."

Several agonizing minutes later, he signaled for her to return. Ellen dragged herself back to the room.

"This is taking a toll on me," she said, not meeting his eyes as she passed. She sat on the bed, then looked up at him. "Thanks, Jack. I'm really glad you're here."

He nodded, then smiled and gestured toward the items strewn across the floor. "Do you like the mess I made?"

"Beautiful. Thanks. And I apologize for my conduct before."

He smiled and handed her a note. "It's from Potter. Big apologies. He'll be here later and you should go through these in the meantime. Looks like a hell of a lot of fun." He rolled his eyes. "You sure I can't call room service?"

"Order the whole menu. It's going to be a long night."

In two hours, Ellen got through the entire collection. Out of the whole mess, she found only three militia leaders: Arizona, Ohio, and Texas. That left six more faces to reconstruct with a sketch artist, a daunting prospect in the best of times. She closed her eyes and tried to sleep.

The phone rang suddenly, and Ellen lurched out of bed. As she scrambled for the phone, her eyes caught the clock: 3 A.M. How long had she been asleep? She picked up the receiver, listened a moment, then set it down.

Jack appeared as groggy as she was, though he still looked handsome, proving there was no justice in this world. Ellen brushed the hair off her face and tried to straighten her clothes.

"That was Potter," she said. "He'll be here in five minutes. He said to pack everything up; he's taking us to another site."

Three minutes later, there was a quiet knock at the door. Ellen looked through the peephole and picked up the man's nervousness, despite distortion in the lens. She opened the door quickly.

"Abe Potter," the man said. "Let's go."

He took off down the hallway at a brisk pace, headed for the stairs. Ellen had to trot to keep up with him, a Saks bag heavy in her hand. It sounded like Jack was having a tough time behind her.

Potter looked like a badger from behind, thick and round, with stubby legs. Ellen got a better glimpse of his face as he turned into the stairway. Round face, narrow eyes, taut expression, strands of hair plastered over a balding pate. A worrier, or was it just the moment? Maybe both.

Ellen turned back to Jack and grabbed the other Saks bag out of his hand. "Come on, gimp. I owe you." They had fourteen flights to go.

She was exhausted by the time she got to the bottom. Potter put a finger to his lips and led them outside. As they moved toward the street, a car rolled forward, its lights off. Potter grabbed the passenger door while the car was still in motion. Ellen opened the rear door and threw the bags on the backseat, then jumped in. Jack hobbled in behind her.

Potter turned around, dabbing his face with a handkerchief. "Sorry about the delay. It's been a nightmare lately. I'm sure you understand."

"What's going on?" Ellen said.

He shook his head. "You were right not to come to the Hoover Building. It could have been dangerous if you'd been seen. We got a lot of suspicious looks when we were gathering those pictures for you. Things have been spinning out of control, just when we need a tight organization. The only thing that's going to save us against the militias is this network of SACs."

"Have you seen any signs of them?" Jack asked.

"Nothing conclusive. Agents are watching key facilities outside the city—power stations, comms facilities, government offices—and have witnessed a little suspicious activity, but nothing overt yet. I understand you may know something about that, Agent King. About the timing, I mean."

"It could be tomorrow," she said, "or any time in the next six days. It's linked somehow to this session of Congress. They've been talking about a 'Torch Day,' but they moved up the schedule by a week, probably in the wake of our actions in California, so I'm not sure of anything now."

The car pulled into the garage at L'Enfant Plaza and wound

its way past rows of cars to a stairwell.

"What are we doing here?" Ellen said.

"There's a hotel up above, one that's safer to get you in and out of. I've got a sketch man waiting upstairs; I'm sure you didn't get everything you needed from what I sent over."

Over the next ten hours, Ellen worked with the artist to develop sketches of the six remaining militia leaders. It was grueling work, and she did her best not to get testy with the man wielding the pencil. She wanted to get these images right, but she was losing her grip on sanity.

"No, Tennessee's face is more gaunt than Michigan's," she said. "Cut down the cheeks and concentrate on the eyes. Tennessee has this lazy right eye that draws all your focus. Yeah, that's better. It's really deep set. You can't miss this face. The teeth are anybody's guess, since I never saw him smile."

She got up from the desk and stretched, feeling like she'd been whacked with a board. She walked to the window, staring out at the afternoon sky, and sighed.

"We still have a couple more we should do. Pilkin's son is sure to be along, plus maybe Pilkin's wife. And we need to get Harry's picture out of the Bureau files. I think—I hope—he'll be with them."

"I'm sure that's enough," Potter said. He was sitting in a stuffed chair near the bed, where Jack was propped up. Potter stood and gave her a round of applause. "Hell of a job, King. We couldn't have done this without you. The sketches will go out to the field tonight. Between that and all the background you gave us on their plans, we'll stop these bastards."

Ellen groaned. "That's only half of it. We haven't gotten into all the computer assaults Barnett, the hacker, is setting up."

There was a voice from the doorway.

"Interesting timing, King."

It hit her like a sledgehammer. Ellen didn't even look up. She knew the voice too well.

"Brendan Crowley," she said. "What a surprise."

She raised her eyes to a trim, broad-shouldered figure in a perfect blue suit. The dark hair was slicked back and the face was more tan, and more unctuous, than before; his ego looked to be in orbit. He was an irritating sight when she worked for him years ago. Now, here, his appearance was wrenching.

"You may have just earned yourself a—well, not a reprieve," he said, "but certainly a stay of execution. I guess we didn't appreciate what this guy Barnett was up to."

"That's typical of you, Brendan."

He waved his hand dismissively. "You're wasting your breath. You always did."

Bitterness crashed over her. "Nice how you set this up. Especially your use of the baby sitter." She threw a disgusted look at Jack. "You all strung me along really well."

"It wasn't hard," Crowley said.

"Christ, who wasn't in on this? Rodgers, too?"

Jack nodded, his face serious.

"And Morton?"

Crowley snorted. "If he was, would we have tried to kill him?"

"And you killed the Director, and the Deputy Director?"

Crowley glanced at Potter, then back at Ellen, a thin smile on his lips. "Dangerous words. They could get a person killed. Of course—" He shrugged. "—you're going to die anyway."

"Who is leading this charade?" Ellen said. "You? Keller? Were the militia guys right? Is this the Zionist Occupational Government in action, or are you just a bunch of murderous thugs?"

"You've been hanging out with the wrong crowd. We're just trying to make this a decent place to live again." He turned toward the door. "I'm wasting my time here. Thanks for the info, King. We'll be back later to drag the rest out of you. Meanwhile, see if you can figure out when these guys are going to strike. At least do that much for your country."

"Jesus Christ! There's a nuke on its way here. That's the real threat, Crowley! And you barely have a clue of what's going on. If you kill me, you're killing your best chance at saving this nation."

Crowley pulled back in mock surprise. "Well, aren't we important all of a sudden? It just so happens we know where the bomb is. We've known it for days. It's in a blue Dodge van, California plates, last seen on Interstate 70, heading this—"

"What?! Why haven't you intercepted it?"

A maddening grin spread across Crowley's face. "We're going to let them get close, then do a dramatic seizure just outside the city with lots of press around. It'll be our crowning moment. People will never trash the FBI again."

"You're playing with fucking fire, Crowley! How can you put this city, these people at risk?"

"There is no risk. None at all. NEST gave us the target— thanks to you, actually, for the suggestion of where to look. We're monitoring their progress, and we'll have teams around them for the last hundred miles. We've got the perimeter nailed down tight."

Ellen was burning. "Keller is involved, isn't he?"

Crowley laughed. "It was his idea in the first place! The team, the 'reorg'—everything. I'm just a happy #2. Actually, I have you and Harry to thank for me being here in the first place."

Pain ripped through Ellen's heart. She tried not to let it show, but she knew her voice was going to betray her.

"You said you've been following the van."

"At points along the way. We don't need to watch it full-time."

Ellen took a deep breath. "Harry is likely to be with them."

A crude smile creased Crowley's lips. "Harry is dead."

Day became night became day became night, trapped the whole time in a hot, rattling metal cage. The buzz of the tires was just annoying enough to deny Harry sleep, while the cramped conditions in the back of the van made any hope of comfort impossible. Trash and scraps of food were piling up around him, pitched back by the ones up front and starting to smell badly. With handcuffs cutting grooves in his wrists, there was little he could do to improve his situation.

And worse was the constant reminder of what lurked inches away. If they had a blowout at high speed and careened into a ditch, the nuke could go off.

Considering what they planned to do to Washington, however, that might be the better option—sacrifice a rural locale, keep the body count down and the government intact. Still, if there was any chance to resolve this safely, to keep the nuke from detonating, then they had to make it to D.C. That was where Ellen and Morton would expect to find it.

How they would find it, and him, was another matter. So far, there had been no opportunity to pass word along. But Harry had dropped the idea of trying to subvert the trip itself; they had to arrive, bomb and all.

Doubt was increasingly filling Harry's head, however. Not about whether he would survive; he couldn't allow himself that thought. What worried him was the Commander. The man was now completely unbalanced.

The first signs of that arose in the hectic exit from the cabin. Shrieking at Kevin, cursing at Barnett, barking orders at Betsy. There was a waver in his voice that hadn't been there during the attack on the compound. The way he blistered Kevin for the young man's lingering goodbye with Betsy was painful.

Since then, it had been push, push, push. As the hours wore on, the Commander's intensity twisted tighter and tighter. At some point it was going to explode; the question was *when* not *if*. The challenge was how to delay that moment. Kevin obviously realized it, too. But Barnett snapped back at the Commander on every occasion. It made for an ulcerous trip.

They were on a dark, desolate stretch of highway between Kansas City and St. Louis at the moment, with the dashboard clock moving toward 11 P.M. Harry had been freed from his blindfold to avoid any eruptions, which allowed him to follow the course of the trip in flashes of road signs and billboards.

Kevin was behind the wheel, the Commander was snoring on the floor, and Barnett was limp in the passenger seat. Harry was half awake, watching the pattern of headlights across the sides of the van, as cars passed in the barren darkness.

Faintly, he heard an "Uh–oh." He looked up to see Kevin clutching the steering wheel. The young man's eyes were glued to the rearview mirror. Kevin cleared his throat, but the sound barely came out.

"Commander?" he said.

Suddenly, Harry saw red and blue lights flashing in the van. They were coming from behind, not too close but near enough.

"Commander," Kevin said, more loudly.

The lights were getting closer.

"Commander, wake up!"

The Commander sat upright and looked around. His eyes caught the flashing lights. "God damn it, Kevin! What the fuck did you do now?"

"Nothing, sir, I swear! I've been right on the speed limit!"

The flashes were lighting up the inside of the van, getting brighter by the second. Harry's pulse accelerated along with the lights. This could be his ticket out, or a bloodbath. The handcuffs felt tighter than ever.

"If you're lying to me, boy . . ."

"Honest! I didn't fuck up! I don't know why he's there. Maybe he's just passing us."

The Commander raised up to look out the back windows. "He's tracking us. Shit!"

He dropped back down and leaned toward Harry, his eyes blazing. "If you say anything, if you do anything, he'll be dead and so will you."

"You're going to kill me anyway," Harry said.

"But this man won't die unless you cause it."

"Commander?" Kevin said. "What do I do?"

"What do you think? Pull over, stupid! Try to act calm, if that's possible. And don't go for your gun; I'll shoot you before he does. Barnett, hand me Harry's wallet."

The patrol car was right behind them now. Kevin slowed the van and eased it off the road. He reached up with a sleeve and wiped sweat off his face. The van was awash in frantic energy.

"Here he comes!" Kevin said.

The van was silent as footsteps crunched on the gravel outside. Then a beam from a flashlight raked the front of the van.

"Driver's license and registration," the trooper said.

As Kevin scrambled to gather these items, the man stepped to the front of the van and shone his light inside. It paused on the Commander's face, then Harry's, then over the collection of boxes and tarps. What was actually a nuclear weapon looked like a suitcase to the guy.

"Here you go, officer," Kevin said. "What seems to be the trouble?"

"You've got a taillight out on the left side."

"What?" the Commander said.

"Plus you were driving the speed limit, which is highly unusual in this area at this time of night. And you've got California plates and your van is riding low. That's a combination that's mighty suspicious in these parts."

The Commander moved forward, into the trooper's view. "What in the world are you talking about?"

"Who are you, his interpreter? We've got gangs coming here all the time from L.A., loaded down with drugs. The way you passed, I figured that's what was up. But after looking at your bumper sticker, I know that's not the case. Open up the back of the van please."

Kevin's body went rigid. Barnett choked.

"I can't do that for you," the Commander said. He flashed Harry's badge. "FBI. We're on special assignment."

"May I see that please?" the trooper said.

The Commander paused, then handed it through the window.

The trooper scrutinized the credentials, then shone his light on the Commander's face. "This isn't you." The trooper reached for his gun, and Harry heard a safety clicking off inside the van.

The trooper pointed his gun at the Commander. "Step out of the van please, all of you, including the man in the back."

The air was hot, thick, and impossible to breathe. Harry saw both the Commander and Kevin slowly raising their weapons, still out of sight of the trooper. Whoever moved first wouldn't lose, they would die.

"Hold on!" Harry shouted. "I'm Special Agent Harper. We're on a training exercise. Lower your weapon please, trooper."

The man wavered, then shifted his light into the back of the van, illuminating Harry's face. After several seconds the light snapped off. As Harry's eyes adjusted to the darkness again, he heard the safeties clicking back on.

"Would you step outside please, Special Agent Harper?"

"You'll have to come around the back," Harry shouted. Then he whispered to the Commander. "And take these damn cuffs off."

It crossed his mind to counterattack once he was freed, but he looked up to see Kevin watching him. This wasn't the moment.

The Commander got him out of the cuffs quickly, then unlocked the back doors and swung them open. Harry hopped out, stiffly, and nodded at the trooper. The man took several seconds to scrutinize the photo and the badge, then handed them to Harry.

"What was he doing with your creds?" the trooper asked.

"I'm not at liberty to say."

"What are you doing way out here?"

"Sorry."

"You gonna let me look inside your van?"

Harry shook his head.

"Well, tell me one goddamned thing. What's *that* doing on an FBI vehicle?" He pointed to a bumper sticker. It had a red circle with a slash through it. Beneath the slash were the letters "ZOG."

Harry started chuckling. Behind him, he heard the Commander clearing his throat. "Camouflage?" Harry said.

The trooper shook his head and started to go.

"Just a minute," the Commander said. "We need your name and badge number. We have to ask you not to report this meeting. If word gets back to us, you'll have Hell to pay."

The trooper glared at him, then at Harry, who nodded slowly. The trooper frowned and scratched out something on his pad, tore it off, and handed it to Harry. Then he walked back to his cruiser, turned off the flashing lights, swung his car across the median, and roared away into the night.

Harry watched him go, praying like hell the trooper was not intimidated by a federal agent. Some were, many weren't. This guy seemed to be his own man. He had to report this, and it had to filter through to somebody who could make a difference.

"Good work," the Commander said. "You can die knowing you saved an innocent man's life. Now get back inside."

Sixty seconds later, they were off. The bumper sticker was gone, but the handcuffs once again bit into Harry's wrists. Except for a screaming level of tension in the van, it was almost as if nothing had happened.

The Commander slapped Kevin's head, hard. "What the fuck was that bumper sticker doing there? I told you to take it off. What are you trying to do, advertise our presence? You could have fucked up the whole mission."

Kevin cowered in the driver's seat. "I'm sorry. It was so crazy when we were trying to leave the cabin. I don't know, I just missed it. I'm really sorry, sir."

"You *are* sorry, you and your fucking mother. If you'd paid attention like I ordered, instead of getting all gooey with her."

"Wait!" Barnett said. "Betsy is your mother?" He looked at the Commander. "Does that mean he's your son?"

"Unfortunately."

"Christ! It all fits now! No wonder you've coddled this loser. We're in deep shit because you've got a mongoloid for a son."

The Commander's hand slashed across Barnett's face. "Don't say another word."

Barnett opened the passenger door. The sound of the road rushing by filled the van. "You want me to jump? It'd be a pleasure. I'm sick of your abuse. Treat me with respect or I'm out of here. And you can shove your little dossier; it's nothing compared to what I've got on you."

The door hung open as they raced down the highway, the standoff raging between them. Finally, the Commander scowled and turned away.

"Close the door. You're slowing us down."

Barnett slammed it shut and nothing more was said for the next hour. They were virtually alone on the highway, but every car they passed was scrutinized by the Commander. In between cars, he studied the terrain, looking for something.

Finally, he spoke up. "We've got to unload this van. I don't trust that trooper. Keep your eyes peeled for roadside rests or cars parked nearby. I don't want to steal one if we can avoid it. We'll buy one in Indianapolis, if we make it by daybreak. But we'll do what we have to. There's no way we're driving this thing into D.C."

Harry's tiny bit of hope evaporated.

A Goddamned Guarantee

Beyond the haze of fractured sleep, Ellen heard voices, low and casual. She opened her eyes a crack. Still in the hotel room, lights dim, clock radio glowing 2:01 A.M. It had to be the changing of the guard; the death squad would've been louder, more intense. She closed her eyes again.

She didn't have a plan. With a guard in the room, another outside the door, an untold number behind the mirror on the wall, and no weapon to combat such a force, all she could do was wait. She held out the slightest hope that an opportunity would arise, but these were the rogues she was up against.

There was a thump near the foot of the bed, loud enough to startle her.

"Give me a break," she said, without looking up.

"Nobody sleeps on my watch," the man said.

It was Jack.

Ellen's brain ignited. She reached her hand under the pillow until it found the clock radio, then in one motion she snapped into a sitting position, yanked the radio out of the wall, and hurled it at him. It barely missed his head and smashed into the wall.

Ellen was on her knees a second later and leapt at him, pure fury in her attack. Jack caught her wrists and hauled her off the bed, dragging her around and pinning her against the wall.

He smiled at her. "We've got to stop meeting like this."

"Fuck you."

"You keep saying that."

Ellen tried to bring up her knee, but Jack countered it and spun her around, bending her over.

"I know your moves by now," he said, smiling. "Brains beats brute force every time. Had enough?"

Ellen struggled to break free, but the more she fought, the more he bent her over, until she was almost doubled in half, her arms high in the air.

He gave her another little shove, until her face was almost touching the newspaper he'd dropped on the floor. "Had enough?" he repeated.

And then she saw it, three inches from her nose. A note was taped to the newspaper. It read: *Room bugged. Cameras, too. Read first section, page 7. Sit with your back to the wall.*

"Enough?" he said again.

"Yes!" Ellen tried to keep loathing, not surprise, in her voice.

He let her go and she stood up slowly, rolling her shoulders to shake off the pain. She turned around and looked at him, wanting desperately to speak the words in her head. But he spun on his heels and headed for the bathroom.

"Don't cross me again," he said over his shoulder.

Ellen fell backwards on the bed, her eyes searching the ceiling for an answer. Was this another set up? If they were trying to disorient her, to disable her brain, they were doing a hell of a job.

But why the secrecy? Knowing Crowley, they could be trooping in with drugs at any minute to turn her mind inside out. And why the reminder about surveillance, unless Jack really was trying to hide something from the other handlers? Ellen was totally thrown.

The answer had to be in the newspaper. She rolled up to a sitting position, looked at that first note again and then shifted through the stack of papers with her foot. She finally found the first section and bent over to get it.

"I'm going to read your paper, asshole," she called out. Then she went to a plush chair against the wall, sat down, and pulled the paper up in front of her eyes. She checked with her peripheral vision to make sure there were no sight lines for a hidden camera, then flipped the paper to page 7.

There was another note taped there.

I'm terribly sorry for what I put you through today. You probably want to kill me. But I'm NOT one of the rogues. I couldn't set things straight earlier without being captured myself. It was the only chance I had to save you.

Why do they think I'm one of them? Because Rodgers was originally. I'll tell you about it later. But here's the best part: I was wearing a wire when Crowley was there. We've got his confession on tape!

She read through it three times, trying to get herself to believe it. If this was another trick, she would go completely insane.

She heard Jack coming out of the bathroom. She wasn't sure she could look at him, but she had to. She lowered the paper just enough for her eyes to see. He was leaning against the wall, his arms crossed, with the most beatific smile Ellen had ever seen.

"More tricks?" she said quietly.

He shook his head.

Ellen pulled the paper up again. She could feel a rush of emotion coming on. She didn't know if she could keep it in—didn't want to keep it in. She wanted to run to Jack, but they were in a fish bowl surrounded by guns.

"There's a good piece on page 13," he said. "Want any food?"

It took her three seconds to find page 13. In big letters, the note said: ESCAPE PLAN. The first item read: *Order champagne!*

She laughed and pulled the paper down. "Yeah, since Brendan is paying for it, let's have champagne."

While Jack called Room Service, Ellen went back to the escape plan. It was almost too simple. But at this point, she would follow anything. And it was a plan, something more than she had.

The champagne came, and most of it went down the bathroom drain. By now, it was after 3 A.M. Jack was propped up in one of the stuffed chairs. Ellen made stretching motions and moved toward the bed. Then she turned and walked to the small desk.

"Do you trust me with a pen?" she said.

Jack's eyes widened. "What are you planning to do?"

"Write a last note to my mother."

Jack seemed totally baffled. "You know they'll read it."

"That's okay." She gave him a quick smile.

It took her ten minutes to write down instructions for countering Barnett's computer attacks: detailing the existence of the logic bombs; listing the databases most likely to be targeted; and identifying back-up facilities and disaster recovery sites the militia cells might assault. She didn't know the methodology of Barnett's computer bombs, but if word was spread fast enough and far enough through the media, especially the Internet, then there was a good chance the geniuses who built these systems could figure out how to protect them.

She reviewed her instructions and said a silent prayer; it was in the rogues' best interests to follow them. Then she folded the sheet, put it in an envelope, sealed it, and laid it on the desk. She wrote URGENT on the envelope, then got to her feet.

"I'm going to sleep now," she said. "Can I turn out the lights?"

Jack looked up. "Yeah, but don't try anything funny."

Ellen stifled a smile and tried to quiet her racing heart. She turned off the light at the desk, walked over to the front door and switched off the hall lights, then went to the bed. She threw back the covers, kicked off her shoes, and turned off the last light. The room plunged into darkness.

She jumped onto the bed, fighting urge to roll in Jack's direction, to grab him, to hold him. She didn't know, given the rush of events, if she was feeling love, infatuation, gratitude, or relief, but it was the most alive she'd felt in too long.

And it was also not the time for such thoughts. She told herself that for the next hour as she lay quietly, her heart pounding all the way to her toes. If they were lucky, they'd both survive to explore the possibilities.

Finally, there was the lightest tap on the end of the bed. She cleared her throat to acknowledge. Moving very slowly, she bunched up the pillows in the bed, putting them into a line parallel to her body. When she was satisfied that they were positioned right, she cleared her throat again, then slid silently out of the bed. She found her shoes and crawled to the bathroom. She reached up onto the counter, found the champagne bottle, and waited behind the door.

Ten minutes later, Jack started coughing. Over the next five minutes, the coughing accelerated. Then Ellen heard his footsteps across the room. She saw the faintest outline as he passed, and heard him tap the bathroom door lightly. Then the door to the room opened and light spilled in from the hall.

Jack coughed again, then said, "Charlie, could you spell me for ten minutes. I've got to get some medicine. The woman is out cold in there."

Ellen saw a shadow bend into the light, peering into the room.

"Okay," the man said, "but hurry." The shadow retreated.

Jack coughed. "Thanks. You're not going in there?"

"Naw, I'll just leave the door open."

Shit! So much for the simple plan. If the guy wasn't going to come in, then she would have to go out. Unless Jack shot him or something. But Jack's feet moved across the carpet and onto the stone floor by the elevator. She could hear him coughing lightly. He wasn't going to leave her there, was he?

She moved forward, as slowly and silently as possible. A dash to the elevator or the stairs was out of the question; the man was armed and probably had a radio as well. She could try to nail him with the champagne bottle, but a blow to the face might not put him out like one to the base of the skull, provided she could even get a clear shot as she swung around the corner of the doorway.

She was close to the door now, her back pressed against the wall. From the sounds of the man's breathing, he was probably sitting down. Another six inches forward and she would be visible; another ten seconds and she would have to attack. She tried to slow her heart down and relax her limbs.

Just then, the elevator chimed and the doors opened.

Jack called out. " Charlie, come here! You've gotta see this!"

"Huh?"

Jack laughed. "Come here, you're not going to believe it."

The man snorted and got up from his chair. A second later, he passed, headed for the elevator. Ellen waited until he cleared the doorway, then stepped up behind him and swung the champagne bottle. It hit the back of his head with a sickening thud and he tumbled to the carpet, out cold.

Ellen stripped the man of his gun and his radio and dashed to the elevator. She spun in as the doors were closing and collapsed against the wall. "God, I thought you were going to leave me there."

"Never. I just wasn't sure if you were picking up my thoughts. I would have bashed him if you hadn't, though it wouldn't have been so clean."

Ellen smiled. "You're a piece of work, Jack Townsend."

He grinned. "Save it. We're not out of here yet."

"So tell me about Rodgers. Your note gave me nothing."

"He told me about this before we left on Friday. He was re-cruited six months ago along with several other SACs; something about strengthening the hand of justice. But he got disillusioned by the way things were developing, and became suspicious with the lack of explanation about the deaths of the Director and the Deputy Director. Then, with the blatant attacks on you and Mor-ton, he went ballistic. He knew Hailey was involved, so he ran that session with her as much to confirm his assumptions as to educate you."

"Why didn't anybody tell me? What was I, bait?"

Jack nodded solemnly. "It's kind of complicated. I don't have time to explain it right now."

The elevator reached the garage level and the doors opened. Jack stuck his head out to survey the area, then grabbed Ellen's hand. They ran to another bank of elevators fifty feet away, but went through a doorway instead. The sign said: "Plaza Level. Subways."

Jack closed the door behind them, then spun Ellen around.

"Nobody wanted to put you at risk like that, but we—Rodgers, Morton, myself—agreed that this might be our only chance to nail the big guys. We weren't sure about Potter, but we knew you'd be tapped somewhere along the way. That's why I came along, as protection."

"That's great," Ellen said, "I'm everybody's little toy." She pushed away from him and started down the stairs.

"Hold on!" He charged after her. "There's so much respect for you out there. You won me over when you threw me out that window. But we were on their turf, we had to let them dictate the course of things. Otherwise, you might never have been able to get those words out of Crowley." He stopped her. "You've got a rep for being headstrong, and we couldn't risk that changing the balance. I really am sorry for what we, what I, put you through."

Ellen looked up, her anger softening. "Okay. Let's just get out of here."

"Follow me." Jack sprinted past her.

Ellen rattled down the stairs behind him. "Where are we going?"

"Subway. I found us a place to stay, a change of clothes—I hope I guessed your size right—and other bits for disguise. Then, at 9:00, we're going for a make-over. Ever been a redhead?"

"And here I thought you were celebrating with the boys. I did want to kill you earlier. I laid on the bed trying to devise the most painful way to do it."

Jack stopped and gave her a lecherous smile.

"You are wicked," Ellen said. She brushed past him and pushed through the door to the Plaza level.

It was still empty at this early hour, except for the rag piles of homeless here and there. Ellen and Jack dashed along the corridor, cut to their left, and headed for the Metro station.

They were almost to the door, when Jack stopped abruptly. He ran back to a magazine stand, where a man was setting out the morning papers. He tossed some change at the guy and grabbed a paper off the top of the pile.

He walked slowly back toward Ellen, his eyes riveted to the paper. When he reached her, he turned the paper around for her to see.

The headline screamed: WATER DISASTER!

"They've hit the supply lines," Jack said. "Burst water mains, reports of explosions at multiple points around and outside the city —and the authorities only 'suspect' foul play?"

Ellen looked up at him, her heart racing. "It's started."

Tensions in the van were at a fevered pitch. Fear of discovery hung over them like a guillotine. Every car they passed was a major threat; every blind corner hid an army out to stop them. It was amazing they made it to Indianapolis without melting down, the Commander in particular.

It was now just before 9 A.M. They were parked on a street lined with car dealerships. Flags were flapping in the wind. Kevin was in the driver's seat, nervously watching the traffic pass; Barnett was in the other seat, checking the sidewalks. The Commander was nagging Harry unmercifully.

"Come on! It can't take that long to get cleaned up."

"Have you ever tried shaving without a mirror, with a five-day growth of beard?" Harry said.

"Just finish and change your shirt. You're putting us at risk."

"That's funny coming from you. Especially with this suitcase."

The Commander yanked on the handle and kicked the door open. He pushed Harry into the street and followed him out.

"Don't forget this," the Commander said, his voice harsh. He shoved the FBI credentials into Harry's hand. "Remember, I do all the talking unless we need to use your badge."

A scrawny young man bounded through the lot, clearly bent on intercepting them. His eagerness hit them thirty seconds before his mouth.

"Hey, some early morning shoppers! Just my kind of people." The guy shoved out his hand. "The name's Tony and I'd love to sell you a car today."

It was the kind of slimy, smarmy approach you wanted to punch.

"I'll make this easy," the Commander said. "Follow us, answer any questions, and otherwise keep your mouth shut. Do that and you'll have a nice fat commission."

"Whoa, okay! You're the boss! What are you looking for? A truck? Sport utility vehicle? I've got some great deals on——"

"I said, keep your mouth shut. Do I have to get someone else?"

The young man shook his head.

"We need a van," the Commander said. "A utility van. I only see white ones here. You got anything else?"

"In stock?" the salesman said. "No, that's it. Can you wait?"

"We need it now. Show me your best one."

"Size? Engine? How do you mean?"

"Just show me."

It took five minutes to go through the choices. Harry stayed in the background, watching the young man, trying to figure out how to get him alone. They had to be only ten hours away from Washington now, so this might be his last chance to alert Morton. Otherwise, he would have to find a way to wreck the van, and perhaps a certain amount of the state of Indiana along with it.

"Good choice," the salesman said to the Commander. "That's a fine machine. You'll be really happy with——"

"Let's take care of the paperwork," the Commander said.

They went into a small office with windows facing into the showroom. The salesman settled grandly behind the desk.

"Now, did you want to finance this or lease it?"

"Cash," the Commander said. He pulled out a roll of bills.

"Wow! This guy is amazing! You sure you don't need two?"

The Commander glared at the man.

"Right. Sorry!" He dug into the desk and started pulling out forms. "I'll need ID and stuff. I can see you're in a hurry."

"Is that necessary?"

"Well, yeah. I can't let you take that van off the lot without it." The salesman's eyes narrowed. "Is that a problem?"

The Commander frowned. "Of course not." He nodded at Harry.

Harry flashed his credentials. "FBI, Tony. We need to do the minimum possible for you to keep your job."

The man's eyes were fixed on the badge. "Wow, you're a real agent? I'll bet you wish you were in Washington right now. Is that where you're headed? Wait'll the boys hear about this!"

The Commander started to lunge across the desk, but Harry reached out and stopped him. Harry turned to the salesman.

"You can't say anything about this. You could be endangering national security. We'll arrest you if you do. Understand?"

The man slumped in his chair. He nodded nervously.

"What was that about Washington?" the Commander said.

"You haven't seen the news today? The water supply for D.C. was blown up last night; the FBI thinks it was done by some militia guys. I just skimmed the article at breakfast, but it seems they think a bunch more are moving on the city. They even put in pictures of guys to look out for. I've got the paper around here somewhere."

The salesman reached under the desk and pulled out a newspaper. He started to flip through the pages, but the Commander snatched it from his hands. Over the Commander's shoulder, Harry could see photos and sketches, eleven in all, including the Commander's and Barnett's. The sketches were so good, they could only have come from one source: Ellen!

It gave his heart a jolt. She was going to pull this out yet.

But they wouldn't know about this van, even if they knew about the blue one. He had to get through to Morton somehow.

Harry's eyes flicked to the Commander's face. Fury poured out of him as he stared at his picture; there was no mistaking the flattop. The Commander pulled the paper down and turned for the door, keeping his face away from the salesman. He stuffed the roll of bills in Harry's hand.

"Finish up here, Harper. I'll be right outside."

"Wow. Intense!" the salesman whispered. "Is he your boss?"

Harry nodded, his focus on the Commander, six feet away.

As the salesman filled in forms, Harry counted out bills. He added an extra thousand dollars. Whether this roll was illegal funds or the Commander's private stash didn't matter. Harry needed to get this man's attention, and there was one sure way to do that with a salesman.

"Okay," the man said. "These are multi-part forms. I need your signature where you see the Xs, and you'll have to fill in the address with something, even if it's just the FBI Building. Sorry, but I have to have it."

"No problem," Harry said.

"Make it fast," the Commander said, from around the corner.

Harry cast a quick glance at the doorway. The Commander's back was to them, his face buried in the paper. Harry put his finger to his lips, signaling the salesman to be quiet, then grabbed a spare form from the side of the desk. He flipped it over and wrote: *EXTREME DANGER! Call James Morton, FBI in San Francisco. Tell him about this van. $1000 extra for you in this pile.*

He added the phone number, then flipped over the form and pushed it back to the side of the desk. The salesman was wide-eyed, his mouth hanging open. Harry mimed raising his chin, then charged through the forms for the van. The man nodded and began tearing apart the forms.

"Aren't you done yet?" the Commander said.

"Just another second."

Harry grabbed the one form again. He added: *Page 3, second row, middle picture. Call SF ASAP. Tell Morton—*

The Commander burst into the room and snatched the keys off the desk. "You've had enough time. Let's go!"

Harry froze. His notes were in plain sight. If the Commander looked down and saw them . . .

But the salesman jumped up, grabbed the Commander's arm, and pulled him out of the office. "You've made a helluva purchase. I hope you'll be happy with it. Let's go pull the stickers off."

Harry exhaled sharply. That was too close.

Thirty minutes later, on the outskirts of town, the transfer of weapons between the two vans was completed. While they waited for Kevin to dump the blue van and steal some Indiana license plates, they followed the events in Washington on the radio. It was horrifying.

A rocket assault was underway against the Pentagon. The Roosevelt Bridge had been blown up by a truck full of explosives; similar disasters were narrowly averted at three other bridges. Car bombs had gone off at two traffic circles; others were thwarted and the perpetrators captured. The death toll was low at this point, but expected to rise. The city was in turmoil, ripped by uncertainty and fear. The President came on the air, pleading for calm.

"We are meeting this threat head-on with the finest forces in the world. Terrorism shall not triumph, it shall be crushed. The anti-terrorism bill, scheduled for a vote two days from today in a joint session of Congress, shall be our exclamation point to the villains of this country. I expect—No, I demand! —a unanimous vote."

The Commander snapped off the radio. "Did you tell him to say that?"

Barnett shook his head. "I wish I could take credit for it. I've got to get back to him soon. We need to set up a meeting."

"For what?"

"To make sure he's in town. We want him and the VP and some of the investigative heads, right?"

The Commander shook his head, fury building. "So much for the element of surprise. Fuckers! Here we are with the most sophisticated weapon ever—a goddamned guarantee that our efforts against ZOG will be successful—and they're blowing it for us!"

"Maybe not," Barnett said. "Maybe this is just the diversion we need."

"What?! The place'll be crawling with guns, twitching at anything that looks suspicious. What chance do we have of getting in there?"

"None right now. But maybe this will have blown over before we get there. Maybe there'll be this incredible relief and everybody's guard will be down."

"You're pathetic," the Commander said. "Our pictures are in the goddamned paper. They're going to be stopping every vehicle that comes into the city, I guarantee it."

Barnett grabbed the paper and flipped to the third page. He folded it back and held it up. "What's significant here?"

The Commander snorted. "You take a lousy picture."

"You're the one who's pathetic," Barnett said. "Who is missing from this collection?"

The Commander stared at it, his eyes narrowed. Then his eyes went wide and he looked up. "Kevin! Kevin's picture isn't on that page. He could get this van through! But what about us?"

"Let me see the map," Barnett said. He studied it for nearly a minute, then looked up, smiling. "It's perfect! It'll probably delay us until tomorrow for getting into the city, but that will give things time to settle down anyway. We'll need to buy a few supplies, including some Dramamine."

"What are you talking about?" the Commander said.

"We're going to come in on a boat!"

There was a huge explosion a mile or so west. A bomb? A rocket? A car? After hours of this, Ellen no longer jumped. But she raised her eyes, waiting for a blinding flash of light against the black and billowing skies. There was nothing but the hot, acrid rain of ashes. No nuclear blast, yet.

The tide had turned in the battle for D.C., according to radio reports, but fighting was still going on all over the city. That was clear just from the noise: sirens shrieking from every direction; helicopters thundering overhead; heavy military vehicles rumbling by; staccato bursts of gunfire echoing off the cement canyon walls. It was so loud it was painful. And layered over it all were the smells, a rancid mix of gunpowder, truck fumes, and smoke.

But none of that matched the fear on the streets: the churning desperation; the frenzied faces; the excruciating panic. People were being crushed in a race to find safety, to get away from the atrocities. Traffic was vicious. The whole scene was sobering, and laced with a tremendous paranoia which branded everyone a possible terrorist.

Even Ellen, with all her training, was not immune to these feelings. If she'd had a choice, she would not have been out there. But she had to be. Somewhere amid the frenzy was a suitcase and a face or two that were frighteningly familiar. For all the disasters and trauma now gripping D.C., the purest terror had yet to be un-leashed.

But it wasn't going to come in a blue van, she knew that. Maybe on rails or foot or in some other vehicle, but not like the rogues anticipated. So she and Jack had positioned themselves near a road block on C Street, close to Stanton Park and the Supreme Court. Ellen was armed with a video camera. Not to record any-thing, but to explain their presence there for several hours.

"They've got another one!" Jack called out. He was four feet away, but they had to shout to hear each other.

Ellen looked over at him. "Who was it?"

"The guy from West Virginia, by the White House. Dead."

"Shit! They've killed most of them, haven't they?"

"I don't think they want to bother with the courts," Jack said.

"How many total now?"

"Seven, if you count Ohio and Kansas, who stayed home."

"Any mention of the blue van or the Commander?"

He shook his head.

Ellen moved closer. "I have to take a break soon. I'm dying of hunger, I've got to find a toilet, and if I have to shout much longer, I'll be permanently hoarse. When are we meeting Rodgers?"

"Tonight, about 7:00. Morton should be with him, but if the cops don't start letting traffic through, we may never see them."

Ellen raised the camera again. Five more minutes and then they would have to hope the bad guys were on a break as well. She swung the camera back to the scene at the road block.

There was a burst of gunfire a few blocks away and everyone in the area dropped to the ground, collapsing like a pile of sticks. As people started to pick themselves up again, the car at the head of the road block suddenly leapt forward. The car behind it sped through, too.

Ellen watched them go by, cursing silently, and turned back to the road block. But something wasn't right. She pulled the lens into a tight zoom. Cops on either side of the road block were on the ground, motionless.

Her heart jumped into her throat. She swung the camera toward the two cars; they were crammed with men looking around nervously.

"Jack, come on!" she shouted, and took off down the street.

The cars were slowed by traffic from a side street, allowing Ellen to slow her pace and furtively scan the two vehicles. The traffic was so thick, she was able to pass the two cars and continue up C Street. Jack seemed to be matching her moves, from the sound of his footsteps.

At the next corner, she cut behind the building to wait for him.

"Something's up," she said. "Did you catch those two cars?"

"Yeah, but why?"

"They shot the two cops at that road block."

Jack stiffened. "There they are."

Ellen spotted them with her peripheral vision. She waited until they were just past, then raised the camera casually and started panning it along the line of cars. She zoomed in when she got to the first car; none of them looked familiar. The story was the same for the second car, though this time she saw the flash of a gun.

She frowned. A bunch of bank robbers who picked the wrong day? She decided to check them one more time, just in case. She went face by face, starting with the second car, walking slowly across the street to match their pace. She had worked her way up to the front seat of the first car, when suddenly the man on the passenger side turned, a drooping eye staring at her.

Ellen gasped and dropped the camera.

It was Tennessee! She knew that face anywhere.

Ellen was frozen in place. She saw the man raising his gun out the window, but the shock was so great she was powerless to move.

A hand grabbed her arm and pulled her to the ground, just as the first shots blasted from Tennessee's gun. Jack rolled over her into a kneeling position and returned fire.

The first car jumped out of line and lurched up onto the sidewalk, racing out of view. The second one cut sharply and accelerated toward them, guns blazing.

"Roll right!" Jack shouted. He went the other way.

Bullets flew everywhere as the car raced past. It was a wonder Ellen wasn't hurt. She scored hits somewhere on the car, but the whole thing had happened too fast to know what or where.

The car sped off, swerving wildly. It had gone a block, when there was suddenly an explosion. The car veered to the left and crashed into a building, erupting into a monstrous ball of flames and shooting scraps of metal in every direction.

Jack ran up. "Leave it. We've got to get the first one."

"It's the guy from Tennessee," Ellen said.

They rounded the corner onto C Street, changing clips. The view was chilling. The sidewalk was strewn with bodies writhing in pain. Ellen pushed up her pace, sprinting ahead of Jack.

At the next corner, people were hanging out of their cars, pointing to the right. "That way! That way!" they shouted.

Ellen turned the corner to see Tennessee's car swerving left around a corner two blocks up. "They're up here, Jack!"

"I'll continue on C," he said.

Ellen slowed her pace as she got to where the car had turned. The effects of gridlock on the street were almost complete, with cars backed up every direction now. The noise from honking horns was fierce. She could see the target car moving along the sidewalk, more slowly this time, being greeted by honks and furious fists as it went by the others. It made another left, back in the direction of C Street, and disappeared from view.

Ellen went back into a sprint. She did not want to lose that car.

She rounded the corner—the car was blocked at the next intersection! She moved in between cars stopped on the street, trying to hide her presence from the men in Tennessee's car.

Suddenly four men leapt out of the car, focused further down the street. They were jumping up on other cars, trying to take aim.

A scream escaped her. They were gunning for Jack!

She didn't freeze this time. In the milliseconds it took to set up, she picked her sequence of targets. Then she fired.

One went down, a clean shot to the back, his weapon spewing rounds into the sky. The next had been standing on top of a car. He took a bullet somewhere in the midsection and disappeared.

The third one alerted by her fire, suddenly turned her way.

"Get down!" Ellen shouted to the people around her. She ducked behind a fender as bullets raced up the pavement where she'd been.

There was another burst of gunfire and a body dropped.

Then everything went silent, not a horn, not a whimper. Ellen could hear her heart beating above the echoes of gunfire.

She dropped to the pavement and scanned the scene, trying to reconstruct who might be out there still. Her two known hits were definitely not the leader, the man with the drooping eye, and she was pretty sure the one who fired on her was not him either.

Ellen raised up just enough to see through the windows of the car she was behind. It wasn't fair to use these people as shields, but she didn't have a choice. "Everybody stay down!" she shouted. "We're not through yet."

Then she started moving toward the target car, staying low, cutting back and forth to disguise any trail. She got to Tennessee's car, on the driver's side, and noticed the third man sprawled out on the ground.

Jack had nailed him! She could go ahead with her plan.

She stood up. "Hey, Tennessee! It's Ellen, the Fed from California! Remember me? Come out, come out, wherever you are!"

She dropped to the ground just as a hail of bullets obliterated the windows of the car. She felt sharp little pains from the shower of glass, but nothing terminal. In a crouch, she moved to the end of the car.

Suddenly, there was a blaze of gunfire twenty feet away, but not directed at her. She scrambled up on the hood of a car, spotted her target, and set up. When he rose to fire again, she squeezed the trigger.

The militia leader from Tennessee crumbled to the ground.

Ellen stood there, numb. She surveyed the scene around her. Shattered glass everywhere, Tennessee's car riddled with bullet holes, bodies slumped and bleeding on the pavement, and a ghostly silence hanging over the sea of cars, seemingly empty but alive with fear. There was now one less threat, but nearly one huge tragedy.

She knelt down and rapped on the windshield of the car she was on.

"Hey, it's over," she said.

The man looked up at her, panic washing from his face. He leaned on his horn, and suddenly the whole area erupted with car horns, a continuous, cathartic chorus.

Ellen felt a tugging on her jeans and looked down to see Jack, his face beaming. "You sure don't do things in a subtle way," he shouted over the noise.

She shook her head. "I wish that was the last of it."

In One Flash

It was hopeless. Since that first glimpse of the Washington Monument through the narrow windows of the cabin cruiser. Just the top of it, still far away, but Harry knew it was over. They were going to slip into D.C. untouched with a weapon of catastrophic power. And he was chained to it.

What made it worse, staggeringly, was all the crowing on the radio. The rebellion had been crushed in one day. The forces of justice had triumphed magnificently and euphoria gripped not only Washington, but the entire nation. Harry's brain was screaming.

Wake up!

People were flooding the streets, anxious to view the scenes of devastation, even gather fragments of what nearly was Armageddon. They had no clue of the cataclysm motoring slowly up the Potomac. From the noises out of Warren Keller's mouth, the world was safe again.

Wrong!

In perhaps hours, the most destructive force ever created would be unleashed on a city giddy with relief. There were more people on the streets than normal, despite the horrendous traffic, in what radio reports were calling "the ultimate tourist attraction." The number of casualties would dwarf the hundreds from yesterday's warm-up.

And there was no way to stop it.

The rented boat they were on certainly didn't shriek "Nuke on Board!" There were so many other vessels streaming up the Potomac to view the wreckage that they were already lost in the crowd. With a blast radius of three miles, they could leave the boat, and him, in some marina close to downtown and no one would be the wiser.

Until the bomb went off.

The Rotunda of the Capitol Building was visible now and Barnett was grinning. It was really going to happen. Un–fucking–believable, but true. And what made it especially sweet was the Authorities creaming all over themselves about their huge victory the day before. Like they had really saved the world, never mind one missing nuke. Boy, did they have a surprise coming. It wasn't just poetic, it was inspired.

He looked over at the Commander, who was staring at the skyline as well. It was the first time in a week those beady little eyes didn't seem to be looking for a victim.

"I guess we have to thank those guys," the Commander said. "At least getting out of town will be easier. Nobody's gonna be watching the trains."

"Yeah," Barnett said, "but they totally ignored all the data centers and disaster recovery facilities. If they had hit those as planned, we'd have a 99% chance of success."

The Commander snorted. "Check the news. The whole damn world has banded together to stop the shit you started."

"We don't know it's failed. Somebody's tweaked the media."

"They've had more than a day! They can't all be stupid. Your half of this thing is coming up a big fucking zero."

Barnett started to react, but the Commander cut him off. "I'm sure you can worm your way back in again. Right now, you've got only one task, which you'd better deliver on: the President."

Barnett thought about saying "Fuck You" but the man would probably beat the shit out of him. Someday, someway Georgie had to suffer, big-time!

He almost had a way to get Ol' Flattop right now. In ten minutes, he would be online with the President, arranging for a meeting the next day to deliver CC's steamy video. Being that it was the Prez, he'd have an army of Secret Service around, so if Barnett could deliver the Commander to that meeting as well, the Feds could nail him on the spot.

But the first objective was to fry the government; he didn't want any Authorities coming after him again. That meant the Commander had to be free to set the charges and the Prez had to be in range when the mushroom cloud bloomed. The timer for the bomb would be activated a couple hours before the meeting, to give them time to get out of the area. Then Gordo would show up to get the video, all the snakes would be at the Capitol for the big vote, and poof!

Now, if he could somehow chain the Commander to the bomb. Nice idea, but the creep had the key to the handcuffs, not to mention all the guns. At this point, Barnett might have to launch his attacks from Tahiti.

He switched on his computer and shoved the thought to the back of his mind. Five minutes later, he was back into the White House computer system. In keeping with his standing order to the President, the entry procedures had not been changed. That was one annoyance he didn't want to have to deal with.

He brought up a new message and typed: GET THE PREZ. He went into chat mode and waited. A minute later, a response came back.

· *What do you want, Barnett?*

What the hell? How did he know? It was a logical assumption, since Barnett's picture and stats had been in the paper the other day. But it had to be pure speculation; there was no way to trace the calls to him. He attacked the keyboard with a vengeance.

· What are you talking about?
· *You're Jeff Barnett. You have to be.*
· "Jeff Barnett" . . . That hack? I'm insulted.
· *Turn yourself in before you get hurt.*
· What the hell are you talking about?
· *The militia rebellion. We got everyone except you and Pilkin.*

· Great work, Gordon! You really stuffed those morons. But the name isn't "Barnett" and the militia thorn in my side was not in your mug shots.
· *Who is it then?*

· You'll know tomorrow at noon. I'll meet you at the Washington Monument, by the flags on the east side. Bring all the friends you like. Maybe they'll enjoy CC's video as well. Shall I bring extra copies?
· *I've got a good mind to have you dragged off.*

· That'd be bad—for your kids and the people of this nation. Noon, Mr. President. And don't be late!
· *Go to Hell!*

Barnett closed the link and switched off his laptop. Screw the bomb fantasies, he just wanted out. Once they docked, he would slip away.

"Is he going to be there?" the Commander asked.

"Right on schedule. Want his autograph?"

The Commander smiled. "By this time tomorrow . . ." He gestured toward the panorama of Washington, stretched before them.

"In one flash, life will be changed forever. Totally, irreversibly. The most dramatic shift in history. Think about it. One moment, we're suffering under the most vile, corrupt, repressive government ever, then—" He snapped his fingers. "—all our problems are gone."

A crude laugh came out of him. "You know, this nuke is supposed to have a range of a couple miles, but we're not going to park it just anywhere." He turned to Barnett. "We'll put it in a place for maximum destruction. I don't want mere annihilation, I want these fuckers to melt. It's got to be dramatic, and impact people's brains all over the world, so everyone will know how cruelly these bastards paid for their crimes—and so no one will be tempted to tread on us ever again."

His eyes were blazing. "This is what we were meant to do. I knew it the moment I heard about the bomb. We had to do it, just because we could, even if it meant sacrificing our lives. Otherwise, this nation would be doomed to oppression for all time. That's why I rode you so hard. I wasn't going to let anything stop us."

The Commander thrust out his hand. "Nice going."

Great. The guy was getting all soggy on him. Barnett shook the hand and tried to smile, but that speech didn't win him over. The guy was still an asshole who deserved to suffer.

They cruised silently along, the Commander negotiating a path through the fleet of boats. Barnett wondered how things would look afterwards, what the effects of the bomb would be on the landmarks and monuments they glided past. No more cherry blossom festivals for a while, that was sure. Would the radiation last long? How much would be left standing? Talk about the ultimate tourist attraction! God, how many people were going to die? That was an interesting thought. Barnett couldn't see anyone years hence writing anthems to Torch Day, but anything was possible. It was going to be fascinating to see how this all worked out.

They passed the Kennedy Center and Watergate, motored around Roosevelt Island, and headed toward another bridge. Barnett was trusting they wouldn't end up stuck on this boat.

"Where the hell are we meeting him anyway?" Barnett said.

"There's supposed to be a yacht club or something up here. He said he'd meet us there."

"And you really trust Kevin to be standing on the dock?"

The Commander frowned. "I'm trying not to think about it."

Two minutes later, they saw him, standing at the end of a

dock, waving his arms in the air. Barnett looked at the Commander and broke into a huge grin. He lifted his arms over his head and applauded in Kevin's direction. It was a beautiful sight.

They pulled up to the pier and Barnett threw Kevin the bow line. "Way to go, buddy-boy!" he said. "Did you have any problem getting through?"

"Not really," Kevin said. "It just took forever. Two hours on the damn bridge alone. Traffic is ugly on the goods roads, and I didn't go near where the battles were. That may give us a problem tomorrow."

The Commander motioned them to the back of the boat. "Keep your voices down. We may have caught a reprieve from that shit yesterday, but let's not get cocky. We still have to get our cargo into the van and protect it until morning. Plus we've got this ZOG scum to deal with."

Kevin leaned in close. "Just leave him. Slit his throat or something and be gone. We don't need him any longer."

The Commander rolled his eyes. "Your brain doesn't work too fast, does it? First off, if someone finds his body in this boat, it'll get traced. Second, until we set the trigger charge, we might need him as a hostage. I'm not going to throw that away."

He reached into his shirt pocket and pulled out a small key. He handed it to Barnett.

"This is for the cuffs. Go unlock him and escort him to the van. I'm gonna handle the bomb. Kevin, you go on ahead and keep an eye out. Got a silencer on your pistol?"

The young man nodded.

"Keep it ready, but don't use it unless you have to."

The Commander disappeared into the cabin, with Barnett right behind him. The small key was hot in his hand.

He stood and watched as the Commander plied Harry–the–rat with more threats. Wouldn't that be a perfect pair to put together? A table for two at the epicenter! Talk about poetic. The only thing better would be if Ellen showed up with popcorn.

He rubbed the key with his fingers. Tahiti could wait. He was not leaving this party just yet.

The small hotel conference room was jammed with people, making it seem like they had a reasonable-sized force. It wasn't; anything less than a thousand wasn't enough. But Ellen flashed a hopeful smile at Jack, standing guard outside, then closed the door behind her and started toward the front of the room.

Every head turned toward her. Thirty pairs of eyes momentarily dropped their hardened, wary edge to make silent contact. The appreciative nods, the murmurs of support she got as she passed gave her a boost. It was nice to finally feel safe, at least for a few moments.

Up ahead were Jim Morton and Brett Rodgers, leaders of the hand-picked crews from San Francisco and Atlanta, most of whom had arrived in just the past few hours. Standing a few feet before them was Sonia Taylor, Ellen's friend and communications wizard.

Sonia gave her a sour look as Ellen walked up. "Nice hair. Do it yourself?"

Ellen picked at the short, red crop that had once been shoulder length and blond. "If you knew what I've been through lately."

"I've heard. You're a champ, El."

Jim Morton cleared his throat, quieting the crowd. "I understand you've all had a basic briefing of our situation, so we'll get into details now. For those of you who haven't met her, I'd like to introduce Special Agent Ellen King, who's been our point person in this investigation; she and her partner, Harry Harper."

God, what a thrill to hear that name again, knowing he was still alive, or should be. She nearly broke down when she got the news last night. It was the first thing Morton said to her. And it gave her a feral sense of purpose, to save this man to whom she owed her life.

"This won't be easy," Morton said. "In fact, it looks almost impossible, if you accept all the permutations. But we can't focus on that or we'll miss the few opportunities we have."

Rodgers stepped up. "To complicate things, we have to go it pretty much alone. We couldn't gather a larger force without drawing suspicion and we can't go to the Hoover Building to ask for help, which also means we can't go directly to District Police or the other agencies; they'll just call Warren Keller. A few of the people in this room have already been targeted by rogues within the Bureau, so I think you'll understand."

One of the agents raised his hand. "I understand Jack Townsend was wearing a wire the other day. Why can't we come forward with that and clean house?"

"No time," Rodgers said. "We've got less than eighteen hours to find this bomb and we can't waste it on a coup d'état, no matter how right we are or how threatening they may be to our efforts. It's just too much to get into, so until the nuclear threat has passed . . ."

"The case is even more difficult now," Morton said, "after what happened yesterday. So, we have a slight concern that the Attorney General might overlook some 'transgressions' of the FBI leadership in gratitude for their overwhelming victory."

Rodgers nodded. "We've got a case, we just need time to develop it."

Another agent stood up. "If you listen to their reports, the threat isn't here, it's in the Midwest. I understand there are a couple hundred agents out there beating the bushes right now. How do we know we're in the right place, not them?"

That brought a dark laugh from some of the agents.

"If by 'right place' you mean where the bomb is," Morton said, "we have information the rogues don't have. They believe the fugitives are in a blue van, which they've obviously tracked as far as St. Louis. But yesterday morning in Indianapolis, the fugitives switched to a white Ford van. We got this from Special Agent Harper, who is being held hostage by the fugitives—and, we hope, still alive."

"Can't NEST find them?" one of the agents said.

"The Nuclear Emergency Search Team was used, once," Rodgers said. "But then the rogues waved them off. From my brief experience 'inside,' I'm sure Keller doesn't want any more help than he absolutely needs. There's a huge land grab going on at HQ; after yesterday, their egos are obviously off the charts. If Keller says, as he does, that the two remaining threats—Pilkin and Barnett—have either run home crying or are hiding out in the wheat fields, then I'm sure he believes it."

"I tried to feed them this news yesterday," Morton said, "but Keller is refusing my calls. I was told to come in to HQ instead."

"How do we know our clock is eighteen hours?" an agent said.

Morton nodded at Ellen.

"We're not 100% sure," Ellen said, "but here's the logic: Barnett spoke many times about 'Torch Day,' which implies a specific event. Maybe something's tied to it, maybe not. But they moved up their timetable by a week, and a few days after that we got the news that Congress moved up their vote on the anti-terrorism bill by a week, at the urging of the President. We didn't put it together until last night, but it's the only thing that makes sense."

"Why is there a link?"

Ellen paused. "Barnett is blackmailing the President."

The crowd erupted, and Ellen had to hold up her hands to quiet them.

"It's legit," she said. "I can't tell you what it is, but I have no doubt that Barnett's pitch was successful. At least it does give us an idea of timing."

One of the agents stood up. "After what happened yesterday, what makes you think they'll go through with their plans? Do we know for sure that they actually have a nuke?"

"Short of actually seeing it ourselves," Morton said, "we have every reason to believe they have one."

"I spent a lot of time with them, undercover," Ellen said. "I know these guys well and have no doubt that they'll try to carry this through to completion. I also have great respect, if you can call it that, for their abilities. These were the guys, seven in total, who did all that damage in New York last month."

Morton shook his head. "It was three weeks ago, Ellen."

The room went silent, the weight of realization pressing down on them. Finally, someone raised his hand. "How are we going to find them?"

"We're looking for a white Ford van," Rodgers said. "The details are in your packets. We believe they'll keep the bomb with them until an hour or so before the vote on the anti-terrorism bill. Why Congress is running a joint session is beyond me, but it's scheduled for noon tomorrow."

"Why the van?" someone said. "Why not some other vehicle?"

Morton glanced at Ellen, then turned to the crowd. "Because we believe Agent Harper is still a hostage and they can hide him in that van. They used him as a cover in Indianapolis, so they'll probably keep him around to the end—"

Ellen winced.

"—or until they plant the bomb, if it's not going to be left in the van."

"The thing is," Rodgers said, "we don't believe they'll let it out of their sight until the last moment. If they plant it tonight and someone discovers it, their efforts would be wasted. They also aren't likely to detonate it before all their targets—Congress, the President, etc.—are in place, which means tomorrow, before or just after noon."

Morton walked over to a large map of Washington pinned to a wall. There were circles and arcs drawn on it, emanating from the center of D.C. like ripples in a pool.

"The devastation range of this bomb is roughly three miles. The two largest circles, in green, show the coverage if the bomb was detonated either at the White House or the Capitol Building. If the bomb is within the intersection of those circles, both buildings would be leveled. Sobering, isn't it?"

He started tapping points on the map.

"To the north, it could be in a parking lot at Howard Universi-ty. To the south, they could leave the van on the street at Buzzards Point. RFK Stadium is just outside the range of the White House from the east, but there are a hell of a lot of streets closer that would be prime territory. To the west, they could leave it on Roo-sevelt Island or at one of the marinas; maybe park it in the garage at Watergate or on some street in the eastern end of Georgetown. Are you getting the picture?"

"Forgive me, sir," someone said, "but we don't have the man-power to cover that large a territory."

"You're right," Morton said. "So we're not going to. That's why you see these other circles on the map. The blue ones show a two mile radius from the White House and Congress, the red show a one mile radius."

Ellen stepped forward. "These guys are fanatics. Their want a total destruction of the government. Given that, we believe they'll try to put the bomb where it can do maximum damage."

She walked over to the map. "In addition, none of these guys are experienced with this type of weapon, so they may not trust a wide blast radius. They've waited a long time for this chance and they're not going to waste it. We expect they'll place the bomb as close as they can to the mid-point between the Capitol and the White House."

She ran her fingers over the intersection of the two smallest circles.

"The FBI Building!" someone said.

Ellen nodded. "Right in the center. There are fast food restau-rants across E street; they could park the van out front like they're making a delivery, or put it in that short alley. Ford's Theater is just around the corner; maybe shove it in a bathroom stall? They could even come down to the Smithsonian and leave it under a bush at the Sculpture Garden. The field is a lot tighter, but that's still a frighteningly large area to cover."

"Or hotels," someone said. "If this thing is supposed to be in a suitcase, that would be a natural."

"We've distributed pictures already," Rodgers said, "but we really think they'll be in that van. Since Pilkin and Barnett were featured in the press, they'll probably want to stay as hidden as possible, even if they've changed their appearance."

"How are we going to cover this?"

Morton drew the boundaries with his finger. "Our target zone is less than one square mile, from 14th Street on the west to 3rd Street on the east, Constitution Avenue on the south up to K Street. We'll give the Mall a little coverage, since it's in range, but it's so wide open we don't think they'll be that blatant."

"So they could be parked right now in the garage below us?"

"Correct, but we expect they'll float around until morning. Scouts will be posted at the corners, looking for them to enter the zone, and coverage will increase as we move closer to the center, down to having people at each intersection around the Hoover and Justice Buildings. It'll be thin, but the area is tight enough that we can swing people into position quickly. These guys are not suicidal, according to Agent King, so we'll have a certain cushion before the bomb is set to go off."

A hand went up. "And if they don't enter this zone?"

Morton looked around the room.

"Then it's been an honor serving with you."

From the sounds outside the van, they were not parked in one of the better neighborhoods of Washington, D.C. No slam against the decent people who lived on that street, but it probably didn't get a lot of police coverage. The District cops were understaffed and underfunded in a city called the Murder Capital of the U.S. Where were their efforts going to go? Not here. At least the smells wafting through the window which Kevin had vented were interesting. Harry sat in the dark, trying to pick apart the ingredients.

The Commander had gone off with Barnett a couple hours ago. Kevin was up front, staring out the window, ignoring Harry's few attempts at conversation. If Kevin was to be his key to getting free, it wasn't working. Maybe Harry needed to be more direct?

"So, Kevin, what are you going to do when this is all over?"

The young man chuckled. "Go to Disney World."

Harry laughed. "Nice answer. I'd forgotten about your sense of humor. I haven't seen it when the Commander is around."

Kevin looked away. "He doesn't get my jokes."

"Or anything else about you."

Kevin's head snapped around. "The Commander is different than you and me. You still don't get that, do you?"

Harry could feel a rhetoric battle welling up. "Yahweh" was probably perched on Kevin's lips. Harry had to be careful or he'd totally lose the conversation.

"Don't you have a right to your own life?" Harry said. "In the time I've known you, all I've seen from him is nastiness and abuse toward you. Where's the respect, particularly from one's father? Look at how he treated you in that barn, setting you up that way. Remember? When he put that gun in my hand?"

Kevin glared at him. "Yeah, and you pulled the trigger."

"But I didn't aim at you. I was prepared to risk my life for yours. Want to know why?"

"'Cause you're a chump?"

"Because you didn't deserve to die. Whether anyone deserves to die is another question. By the way, you do know that millions of people will die if this bomb goes off tomorrow. Millions of innocent, unsuspecting people who have the same rights as you, all lined up like you were in that barn. Except they won't know it's coming, so they won't feel the humiliation you felt, or the betrayal at the hands of their own father."

Kevin was shaking. It was palpable in the darkened van.

"You can change that," Harry said quietly. "To save them. To give them the respect they deserve. To do something you know is right, not what you've been ordered to do."

He paused. "Isn't that what Yahweh would want you to do?"

Kevin turned away. "Fucking Yahweh." He sighed heavily. "Right now, I don't give a shit what happens."

"Yes you do," Harry said. "It's just been beaten out of you all your life. No respect, no loyalty, no consideration, no love——"

The door on the passenger side jerked open and the Commander stuck his head inside the van. He looked at Kevin, then at Harry. "What is this? True confessions? Babbling on about 'Yahweh' again, kid? Has he told you about the Arm Test yet, ZOG scum? He's a scream."

Kevin glared at him, then turned away. The Commander chuckled and climbed into the van. He glanced back at Harry.

"I swear, Betsy must've fucked somebody else, because this kid can't be my spawn."

Kevin snorted. "She's fucked everybody, *Dad*."

The Commander yanked Kevin off his seat and threw him onto the floor of the van. His hand lashed out and slapped Kevin across the face. The sound reverberated off the metal walls. Then he grabbed Kevin's shirt and yanked him up.

"If you ever talk like that again, I'll kill you. Understand?"

He dropped Kevin and bolted out of the van, slamming the door behind him.

Harry looked down at Kevin, sprawled out on his back. His eyes were raging, but the kid just laid there. Not a move for fifteen minutes, until the passenger door opened and Barnett slid inside, a bag of groceries under his arm.

"God, what's going on here?" he said.

"Don't ask," Kevin answered.

The door on the driver's side opened and the Commander climbed in. He glared at Kevin, then looked away.

"We'll take shifts guarding the van tonight; two awake, one asleep. At 0900 hours, I'll set the trigger charge, then we roll. If you gotta use the can, there's a fast food joint a couple blocks down. If

Harper has to go——" He picked up a plastic cup and tossed it at Harry. "—he can use that. I can't believe you lost the key to the cuffs, Barnett. You're as big a fuck-up as the moron here."

Barnett shrugged. "It's probably here somewhere."

"Screw it. Tomorrow, he can shit in his pants. He'll have a couple hours to stink up the place before the bomb goes off."

He chuckled, darkly. "By the way, Barnett, I didn't say this earlier 'cause I knew you'd freak out. Those Feds we spotted, staked out on the street corners? They're looking for us."

"What?!" Barnett dropped the bag, and cans rolled everywhere.

The Commander looked back at Harry. "I didn't get a good look at her face, and from behind in the dark I could swear she had red hair. But I'd know that voice anywhere."

Harry's heart soared. "Ellen?"

The Commander nodded.

"Shit! Where?" Barnett said.

"Over by Chinatown, walking with another woman and talking into her sleeve. I caught her again—went right by her—a few minutes later, just to confirm the voice."

"Jesus Christ, why didn't you tell me?!"

"Cause I knew you'd react like this."

"God, we're fucked. They'll find us for sure, parked across from the FBI Building."

The Commander chuckled. "Which is why we won't be anywhere near it. Maybe that car salesman reported us or maybe it's just a hunch by Ellen, but I'm not driving this van into their web."

"Where are you going to put it? On the moon?"

"Barnett, I'm fed up with your outbursts. There's nothing to worry about. Why did I have you meet me by the Smithsonian? For culture? There's a slew of parking spaces out front. We'll leave it there, and on the slim chance they do know about the van and actually find it, I'll have a special surprise for them."

"Which is?"

The Commander grinned. "The van will be booby-trapped. If they try to break in or move it, it'll blow sky high."

Torch Day

It was morning now. Slivers of light seeped into the cramped interior of the van, giving shape to the ominous suitcase next to him. Cool air leaked in, but Harry was drenched with sweat, flinching at every move the Commander made.

Rigging the trigger should be simple: detonator cord, enough to set off the nuke, around the bomb case; wires running from the det cord to a battery; wires from that to a countdown timer.

But the look in the Commander's eyes had Harry in a panic. The man was not all there. What if he sparked the det cord somehow? The way he was slinging tools around, the probability was high. What if he missed a step, left out a crucial break in the chain? What if the timer tripped accidentally, closing the circuit and setting off the bomb?

He took a long, slow breath and tried to relax. It didn't help that his hands were cuffed to the handle of the bomb case. Unless he could reach the components with his toes, he was going to have no chance to try to dismantle the trigger.

The Commander reached over and pressed the Start button on the timer. The red numerals switched from 03:00:00 to 02:59:59. The bomb was now "live."

"Is this added torture," Harry said, "setting it at three hours, not two?"

The Commander's head swiveled around like a rattlesnake.

"Haven't you wondered why I let you live this long? I want you to have as much time as possible to think about your death. To imagine it in every detail. The way your flesh will melt, the way your muscles and your heart will seize up. I want you to watch this count slowly down to zero."

"You give 'vindictive' new meaning."

"Don't push me!" The Commander's fist shot up, but then he pulled it back. "I want you alive until the end. I want you to get the most out of this."

Harry forced a smile. "If an extra hour means that much."

"That's not why I did it, ZOG scum. I want to make sure this thing goes off. If we meet resistance from your friends, I can't be worrying about activating the bomb. This mission will be successful no matter what, even if it means my life."

The Commander pulled out an assortment of items from a Radio Shack bag, including another timer. He held up a small device with two metal plates suspended microns apart. He wiggled it and the plates clacked together. He laughed wickedly.

"Ever seen a motion trigger? Once this is armed, don't sneeze too hard. The plates will make contact and you'll blow out more than your ears. Any little movement inside or outside the van . . ." He attached wires to the plates.

"What is this, a defense system?" Harry said. "Keep me from getting help? Maybe I'll sneeze once you get out of the van and take you with me."

"I'm ahead of you, ZOG scum." The Commander held up what looked like a dial. "A crude switch assembly, but it'll work."

"I don't follow."

"I need some way to activate the defense system after we leave the van. Otherwise you *could* blow us up." He turned the dial a few times. "This gives me a second break in the circuit. I attach this other timer to it, and once that hits zero, the switch flips and we're down to one break—the motion trigger. *Then* if you sneeze . . ."

"Clever," Harry said. "A short–sequence timer to arm the defense system in the van; another timer, set on three hours, to detonate the bomb. But you've got a problem."

The Commander nodded. "Normally, I'd set this at thirty seconds, but with a nuke, we'll need more time to get clear. But I can't leave you alone for fifteen or twenty minutes, so I'll have to gag you. Or kill you, if things are tight."

Harry watched him attach wires to the switch. Once the defense system was live, the van would be impregnable. The only window of opportunity Harry had was the countdown period on that short timer, provided he got help.

A few minutes later, Kevin stuck his head in the door and held up two sets of license plates. "What do you want? D.C. or Maryland?"

"Where have you been? I was ready to leave without you."

Barnett leaned in behind Kevin. "Have you seen this?"

"What?"

"Graffiti! All over the sides of this thing! Fucking vandals."

"God damn it! If you guys had paid attention last night." He went to the front of the van and stuck his head out the door. Then he went to the other side, looked out, and erupted with laughter.

"What's so funny?" Barnett said.

"It's fucking camouflage! Kevin, use the D.C. plates. Maybe we'll drive this tub up to the FBI Building after all."

The Commander settled into the driver's seat and revved the engine. "ZOG, here we come!"

There were white vans all over the city, crossing in and out of the zone, many of them Fords, but not the one they were looking for. It was impossible to stop them all with so much traffic, but the scrutiny in the zone was intense. Thirty agents, staked out in an area of less than one square mile, searching feverishly for the slightest clue to lead them to the bomb. So far, nothing.

Ellen couldn't help herself; she checked her watch again. 9:15. The bomb could be activated at any moment. Where was it?

She was running on caffeine now, having exhausted her stores of adrenaline during the night, as she cruised the zone on a mountain bike. Everything that could have been done had been done. The area was nailed down tight. Odds had to be on their side.

Unless the bomb never entered the zone.

A sharp thud rescued her from that thought. She looked across the command van. Sonia was deep into something at the communications console. Brett Rodgers was clenching a telephone. At the far end was Jim Morton, disgust on his face and a cell phone at his feet.

He looked at her and threw his hands in the air.

"They don't believe there's a threat. I've called everyone I know at the White House and it's the same story: Keller is doing a great job, so they're taking their cues from him. And since he believes the other militia leader is in the Midwest—nobody is using the word 'nuke' here—well, then it's business as usual. The President is said to be anxious to make a strong statement with this anti-terrorism bill, and he supposedly has a full agenda of other events in town today. Nothing will make him budge."

"And Capitol Hill?" Ellen said.

"Rodgers has been working that angle, but it's the same story. They're not going to be pushed around by some half-baked terrorists. And nobody seems to know anything about a nuke. I keep getting referred to Keller."

"You'd think he would at least give this a little credence."

Morton shook his head. "I have 24 hours to show up or face serious discipline. That's all the feedback I'm getting."

"What if you show up with the bomb?"

Morton chuckled, darkly. "He'd probably use it on me."

"Have you figured out how you're going to reel him in?"

"I haven't figured out how we're going to survive this day."

It felt like a thousand degrees in the van. Barnett was trying not to panic, telling himself he could bolt out the door any second. But the fucking nuke was live and the damned timer was fast! He'd been watching it for ten minutes, comparing it to the dashboard clock and to time checks on the radio. The dial was already under 02:20:00 when it should have read 02:25:00 or so. Barnett wasn't sure how much longer he could keep quiet. The Commander was weirding him out, but this was serious.

"Goddamned traffic!" the Commander said.

Kevin cleared his throat. "Sir, you expected it to be like this."

"Don't tell me what I said."

The timer skipped a whole minute, and Barnett jumped.

"Hey, Captain," he said. "Your fucking timer is fast. If we don't leave soon, we're going to be toast."

"What are you talking about?" the Commander said.

"The timer. It's fast! It's going to blow up earlier than we expected."

The Commander glanced back. "You're crazy."

"Fuck you! Look at the dashboard—9:36. That means this thing should read 02:24 or 02:23. And right now, it says 02:17:42."

The Commander exhaled sharply. "Forget about it."

"Forget about it?! What if this suddenly spins out of control? Do something, damn it! I don't want to die in a traffic jam."

The Commander pulled to the side of the road and threw the van into Park. "We're three blocks from the Mall. We'll be out of this thing within ten minutes. It's not going to be a problem."

"How do you know that? The other timer is probably fucked-up, too."

The Commander held up his hand. "Hold on!" He turned to Kevin. "Get out here. Traffic is slow enough; you'll catch us on the way back. You know what to look for?"

Kevin nodded and slipped out of the van.

"What was that all about?"

"I spotted a sentry last night up ahead on 7th Street, the other side of the Mall at Constitution. If he's still there, Kevin is going to take him out."

"What?!"

"God damn it, will you relax?"

"Relax?! We've got a nuke that could go off at any second, and you're out killing Feds? Why not just raise a banner and say 'Here we are!'"

"I've had about all I can take from you, boy."

Barnett wanted to lash out, but he throttled it.

He looked at the timer. It was already down to 02:14. "Excuse me, but can't you do something about this timer?"

The Commander shook his head.

"What?!"

"I disabled the Stop function. We couldn't let Harper or somebody else interrupt this after we left. It's set so that once it's rolling, it can't be stopped."

"Great! Mr. Electronics screws with the timer and now it's out of control. Didn't you test it beforehand?"

"There was no fucking time, thanks to your ZOG friend here. All my good stuff is back at the compound. I was lucky to find these bits at that Radio Shack in Indianapolis."

"This is a nuclear bomb! You just assumed everything would work okay? You were more worried about your money—"

"Don't push me, Barnett."

"You're a bigger fuck-up than your son! For all we know, that's not even a bomb in there; it's probably filled with dirty underwear." He applauded, derisively. "Way to go, Commodore, you're going to wipe out the government with a load of laundry. No wonder ZOG is so scared of you."

The Commander lurched out of his seat. He grabbed Barnett by the throat, lifted him up, and slammed his head against the wall of the van.

"One—more—word."

He dropped Barnett and went back to the driver's seat, put the van in gear, and moved into traffic.

Barnett rubbed his throat, his fury rising. The Commander

had to die—today! He reached into his back pocket. The key to the handcuffs was still there, and so was his dream of chaining the Commander to the nuke. Now all he needed was a gun, and the van was loaded with them.

They weren't coming. Ellen could feel it. It was already 9:45 and there was still no sign. The city would be obliterated while they sat, blindly, near the base of the Washington Monument. Was this plan her idea or did she just agree to—

Sonia's voice interrupted her. "El, I need your help. Would you go check on position #4? I can't seem to raise him on the radio."

Ellen's eyes widened. "That's Jack Townsend."

Sonia held up her hand. "I think the only problem is a bad unit. He hadn't seen anything at his last check."

"Shouldn't someone nearby go over?"

"I'd rather not lose that coverage, since the others are deeper in the zone. Besides, you look like you could use some exercise. Grab one of those spares out of that box."

Ellen checked the map for position #4—7th and Constitution —then picked up a radio and headed outside. She ducked back in for a pair of binoculars, then jumped on the bike.

Please let it be the radio.

Twelve minutes had passed—fourteen on the timer—and they had moved only two blocks. The trees on the Mall were visible, even from where Harry sat. If he remembered D.C. correctly, they had to be close to the Smithsonian, probably bottled up in bus traffic headed for the Air & Space Museum. He squinted at the clock— 9:48. Didn't the museums open at 10? God, all those people!

He couldn't think about it. Very soon, these guys would leave the van. Check that: the Commander was going to press the Start button on the "defense" timer, set for twenty minutes, and then they would leave the van. After that, Harry would have his one chance to stop this horror. His mind had to be clear.

The passenger door swung open and Kevin crawled in, a huge grin on his face. He gave the Commander a salute. "Mission accomplished, sir."

"You took long enough. Was it clean?"

"Perfect. Got the eye of an eagle."

"Spare us your ego. Here . . ." The Commander pulled strips of cloth from a bag and tossed them at Kevin. "Tie up Barnett and gag him."

"What?!" Kevin and Barnett said it together.

The Commander pulled out his gun and pointed it at Barnett.

"Drop that weapon—Now!—and raise your hands."

Barnett's hand *was* on a gun. Harry hadn't noticed it before. If it was set to fire, whether or not Barnett knew how to use it, there could be a battle with catastrophic results.

The Commander had the edge: his gun was up, aimed at Barnett's face. Horns were honking behind them, but inside the van it was deathly silent.

Slowly, Barnett set down the gun. His eyes were locked into the Commander's. "This is an outrage. We were partners."

"Not anymore."

Kevin cleared his throat. "What are you planning to do, sir?"

The Commander's eyes narrowed. "Gut him. I want him to bleed."

Barnett lunged forward, fury roaring out of him. The Commander swung the butt of his pistol, trying to fend off Barnett. Kevin was shouting and grasping at arms in a vain attempt to separate them.

The whole van rocked as the three men battled, bodies lurching forth and back. Were it not for the presence of a nuke and other explosives, the Commander would probably have shot Barnett. But Harry knew that was only a threat. There was too much commotion to get a clear shot.

In the midst of all this, Harry felt something graze his hand. His eyes flicked down and saw a small, silver piece of metal.

The key to the handcuffs!

If he could somehow reach it.

Ellen tried to stay calm as she neared 7th and Constitution. She couldn't see Jack, but he had to be there somewhere. Had to be. If he wasn't, there must be a reason. But there was no sign of—

Her breath stopped, her eyes fixed on a dark stream flowing over the sidewalk and into the gutter. It was on the other side of 7th, a short distance from the corner, coming down from a side entrance to a building.

Please, no!

She dropped her bike and darted through the maze of traffic on 7th Street, her heart out of control.

It was Jack. Crumpled in a doorway, eyes lifeless, blood pouring from his head. It looked like a single shot, from a distance; he would not have been caught off guard at close range. That kind of accuracy meant one thing:

They were here.

She grabbed her radio. "Man down! 7th and Constitution!"

She choked back her emotions and bent down to check his pulse. Then she raised the radio, tears flooding her eyes.

"Hold your positions. He's dead. Suspects are in the zone."

She raised her head, rage coursing through her.

Where are they?

The battle ended abruptly. Barnett was leveled by a vicious blow and lay slumped on the floor. The Commander waited to be sure Barnett was out, then put the van back in gear and moved the vehicle forward. The honking behind them tapered off.

The Commander glanced at Kevin. "I can't believe you tried to help that scum. That's as close to mutiny as you'll ever get, boy."

"Commander . . ."

"I gave you an order; don't make me repeat it."

"Sir, if you want to kill him, just leave him with the bomb."

The Commander slapped him. "Tie him up and gut him or you'll get the same. How I ever got you as a son . . . If it wasn't for your mother, I'd have thrown you out long ago."

He reached in a bag and pulled out a large hunting knife. He thrust the handle at Kevin. "Follow the goddamned order. Is that clear?"

Kevin nodded weakly and took the knife. He gathered up the strips of cloth and moved slowly to the back of the van. His eyes were spinning. He glanced at Harry, searching his face, but Harry looked away.

Harry was trying to appear calm, or bland, or worried— anything but energized. The key to the cuffs was in his hand now and his mind was soaring. Was it dumb luck or had Barnett tossed him the key? Regardless, he had a chance!

Timing was everything. Kevin was working on Barnett, tying up his hands, his back to Harry. That was the first opening, and it took surprisingly little effort to get the key into the lock. Harry waited, though. If it made noise, he was sunk.

He coughed. No response. The Commander was focused on the street and Kevin was still working on Barnett. Harry coughed louder and twisted the key. One cuff popped open. He waited several seconds and repeated the process. He was free, almost. He kept his hands in the opened cuffs, waiting.

Barnett began to rouse as Kevin put a gag in his mouth. Barnett's eyes, desperate, craned back to Harry, then flicked down toward cuffs. He *had* tossed the key! Harry gave the barest of nods.

"Aren't you done yet?" the Commander said.

Harry noticed the Commander was staring in the rearview mirror. Had he seen the nod to Barnett?

"Yes, sir," Kevin answered quietly.

"Well, what are you waiting for?"

Kevin took a deep breath. "I've never killed a friend before."

"I gave you an order!"

"Yes, sir." His voice were barely audible over the honking.

Kevin reached down and put his hand on the knife. His fingers curled around it hesitantly, then he raised it, his face tortured. Was he not going to do it? Maybe he couldn't decide where to start? Harry was mesmerized.

Kevin exhaled. "I'm really sorry, JB."

"Do it, you miserable shit!"

"Get off my back!" Kevin roared.

Harry yanked his hands out of the cuffs and lunged for the knife. He wrapped both hands around Kevin's wrist, then twisted it abruptly. There was a sharp crack and Kevin yelped with pain.

Harry threw an elbow up under Kevin's jaw. It snapped the young man's head back and the knife came free. Harry leaned over and started to cut into the cloth around Barnett's wrists.

"What the fuck?!" the Commander said. His head whipped around, his eyes wide with disbelief. He started to rise out of his seat, pulling out his gun. Harry dropped the knife and dove forward to block him.

With no one at the wheel, the van plowed into the car in front of it. There was a loud crash and everyone in the van tumbled forward, fighting to get the gun, to get the knife, to get the wheel, to get away.

Ellen jumped at the sound, her hand on her gun. She swung toward the crash, and cursed sharply. Fucking drivers! If they had any idea of what was going on. She pulled the binoculars to her eyes. A white van was involved in that crash! She grabbed her radio.

"Position 4. White van spotted on 7th heading towards—"

The van suddenly lurched to its right, jumped the curve, and swung onto the expanse of grass on the Mall.

"This may be it! White van, covered in graffiti, driving erratically across the Mall. I'm going to investigate."

She clipped the radio to her belt, swung her leg over the bike, and gave a last look at Jack. This wasn't how she'd remember him.

She raced passed the National Gallery and onto Madison Drive. The van was further down the Mall, swinging wildly. She hopped the bike onto the curb and sprinted forward. She was within two hundred feet when the van swerved sharply and crashed into a tree. Were these people on drugs?

Suddenly the side door flew open and somebody bolted out, heading down the Mall. Ellen jammed her brakes and pulled the binoculars to her eyes.

It was Barnett! His back was to her, but it had to be him. He was dashing toward the crowds in front of the Air & Space Museum. If he got lost in that mass . . .

A gunshot ripped her focus back to the van. Kevin was out now, aiming for Barnett. What was going on?!

She grabbed her radio. "Suspects on the Mall, near the Air & Space Museum! All units respond! Situation extremely dangerous. Barnett is headed west; Kevin is following, firing on him. I'm going for the van."

They were sprawled on the floor of the van, their fingers inches away from the second timer, the Commander straining to get to it and Harry trying desperately to stop him. But his strength was going, he could feel it. If the Commander hit the Start button, the bomb could go off in twenty minutes, not two hours.

The Commander's hands were just beyond Harry's reach, the fingers stretching, grasping—for the switch? He was going to bypass the timer and activate the motion sensor manually.

He was suicidal. The bomb could be detonated in seconds!

With his last bits of energy, Harry launched himself forward. He brought his fist crashing down on the Commander's hand, the one closest to the switch. The Commander howled and pulled his hand back. Then he spun underneath Harry and kicked him against the wall.

Harry landed on something sharp, but he kept his focus was on the Commander, going for the switch. Harry dove, but the Commander was ahead of him, his fingers reaching the metal, starting to grasp the lever.

In that instant, Harry knew he couldn't get the Commander's hand away in time.

But one of the wires connected to it was right in front of him, right below his hand. He curled his fingers around it and yanked, just as the Commander was turning the lever.

The wire came free in Harry's hand.

"Damn you!" the Commander shouted.

He lunged at Harry. They slammed into the wall of the van and tumbled out the side door, onto the grass. The Commander stunned him with a hard blow to the head.

When Harry's eyes focused, the Commander was leaning into the van, grabbing for something. Harry caught a glimpse of a gun as the Commander wheeled around. He dove for the Commander's knees.

The Commander sidestepped him and leveled the gun.

"You picked the wrong man to fuck with, Harper."

Suddenly, a shot rang out, spinning the Commander around.

Harry lunged, not knowing or caring who had fired. He drove the Commander into the ground, slamming his head back.

Several more shots exploded nearby. Harry raised his eyes.

Kevin. Aiming at—not them, but someone further away.

Ellen! She had found him!

Suddenly, Harry was thrown backwards. He pulled his head up to see the Commander on his feet, confusion on his face. A bullet ripped through the air near them. The Commander started to point his gun at Harry, then swung it toward the van. Harry's breath caught.

The Commander was going to fire at the bomb!

Another shot rang out and the Commander screamed. His gun went spinning away. The Commander turned and ran.

Harry was paralyzed. Should he stay with the nuke? Go after the Commander? What about Kevin? And Barnett?

The nuke was safe, at least for a little while; he had to trust that. Barnett was of no consequence and Kevin was Ellen's to deal with. He had to go after the Commander.

Harry spotted the Commander's gun, grabbed it, and took off in pursuit. He was jolted immediately—the Commander was headed straight for the Air & Space Museum.

Crowds were just starting to enter the museum. The lines stretched down the steps to the street in front. Harry spotted the Commander from the jostling and commotion at the far right side. He was pulling people out of his way.

Harry dashed up the steps, fighting his way through the mob pushing to get in. "FBI! FBI!" he shouted, as he snaked his way up to and through the smoked glass doors.

It was a madhouse inside. People shrieking and shoving, craning their necks and pointing to the right. For all the historical treasures around them, he knew what they were watching.

A circle of people near the right wall were bent over something. Harry moved in. It was a security guard, his body limp.

"He got the guard's gun!" someone said.

"That way!" another added, pointing around the corner.

He heard a scream and looked up. The Commander was just past the escalator, grabbing at a young woman. She was scrambling backwards, trying to avoid his grasp.

God, don't take a hostage!

Harry dashed onto the escalator, taking the steps two at a time until fatigue slowed him down. It seemed to take forever to get to the second level. When he stepped off, the Commander was near the far end of the floor.

The Commander spotted him and fired several shots. Harry dropped to the floor; screams erupted throughout the museum.

Harry rolled over to the elevator. There was a slight inset to it and he raised himself up along the doors. Another shot cracked into the wall a foot away, then Harry swung his gun up and returned fire.

The Commander bolted from his spot, headed for some stairs. Harry started running, trying to get a better angle, when shots exploded from below. He dropped to his knees and peered over the edge of the walkway.

It was Ellen!

The Commander continued up the stairs, then ducked into an exhibit space. The sign above it read: "Sea-Air Operations."

Harry ran to the opening, and was nearly knocked down by people trying to escape. Ellen reached him a moment later. "Thank God, you're alive!" she said. Harry could only nod.

They entered the exhibit area, and it was imposing. Planes were everywhere—above them, across the floor—like being on the deck of an aircraft carrier in a war zone. The room was dark, lit mainly by pin spots. Audio of planes, crew, and sea filled the air. Past the planes, on two levels, were exhibit rooms, with stairs at either end and several passageways. It was a daunting place to try to find someone with a gun.

"Let's wait," Ellen said. "He'll have to come out sometime."

Harry shook his head. "He might grab a hostage, and these places are riddled with exits. We've got to go in."

He nodded toward the right. "Go along that wall and protect the entrance. If you can get up onto a wing of one of those planes, that'll give you better coverage. Watch this emergency exit just to the left here, too."

"Where are you going?"

Harry pointed toward the exhibit rooms.

He dropped to a crouch and swung around the corner, his gun

in front of him, sweeping the length of the room. It seemed to be empty, but it was impossible to tell.

There were four openings to the exhibits on this level and two sets of stairs leading to the upper level. Plus a booth of some kind near the first set of stairs. Harry waited a moment, scanning for movement or shadows, then dashed toward the booth. He flattened his back against it and listened.

Someone was in there, breathing roughly. Exhaustion or fright? It sounded too light to be the Commander. Harry took a step and swung into the opening, his weapon leveled.

It was a young boy, cowering in the corner, his eyes frantic.

"FBI," Harry said quietly. He lowered his gun.

"He's on the stairs," the boy whispered. He pointed up.

Harry stepped through the booth, then swept around to cover the stairs. They were empty, bathed in an eerie red glow. Slowly, Harry made his way up the stairs, trying to hear, amid the sounds of takeoffs and landings, a noise which might guide him.

He paused at the top of the stairs. A railing on the left over-looked the planes on the flight deck. The railing continued around in front of him, with a six foot gap between that and a wall. On the wall was a steel rung ladder going down fifteen feet to the first level; decoration probably.

To his right was the upper level exhibit area. The Commander had to be in there somewhere, unless he had found an exit or the boy had been hallucinating. If he was still there, he was waiting— waiting for a clean shot.

As Harry tried to figure out his next move, he noticed a flash of something just to the side. In a mock-up of a flight control deck was a sheet of plastic that reflected images from the rest of the exhibit area—and in it he could see the Commander moving around an exhibit case and heading toward the other stairs.

"Ellen, heads up!" he shouted. Then he spun into the exhibit area, leading with his gun.

There was an exchange of gunfire, and Harry raced toward

the stairs. He was just to the opening, when the Commander leapt at him.

Harry was knocked off his feet, landing on his back as the Commander trampled over him. Harry rolled and squeezed off a shot, but all he hit was a shadow.

He jumped to his feet and raced forward, hearing thudding noises over the taped sounds. He got back to the railing in time to see the Commander burst through the emergency exit for the West Terrace.

"Down that ladder," Ellen shouted. "Get him!"

The Commander must have jumped to get to the ladder, but it was too far for Harry. He turned and hurried down the stairs.

He hit the first level and shouted, "Ellen, where are you?"

"Just go! I'll alert the field!"

He blasted through the exit doors—and a gunshot pushed him back. He stepped forward a moment later, but the Commander had vanished.

The door flew open behind him and Ellen hobbled through.

"He's gone," Harry said. "We'll have to get him later." Then he looked at Ellen. "Are you okay?"

Ellen nodded. "Just grazed. I got knocked off that jet and landed hard. Sorry."

He shook his head. "I wouldn't be here if it wasn't for you."

Ellen forced a smile. "I could say the same."

Harry put his arm around her waist. "Let me help you. We have to secure that bomb. The timer is fast and I don't know how much time we have."

They got outside and felt the first wave of relief in a long time. Even from a distance, they could see a crowd of agents and vehicles around the graffiti-covered van. At this point, it probably didn't need their help.

They sat down on the steps of the museum.

"Did you get Kevin?" Harry asked.

Ellen shook her head. "You were my first priority. You and the

nuke. He ran off after the Commander did. Let's just hope someone grabs him."

"What about Barnett?"

She shrugged. "I was occupied by Kevin. I'm kind of surprised he didn't hit me; he's supposed to be a great shot."

"I think I broke his shooting hand. He had to be using the
other one."

Ellen looked over, searching Harry's face. "What are we going
to do?"

Harry exhaled. "I know where to find the Commander and
Kevin, provided we get there in time. As for Barnett . . ."

Don't Die Like This!

First stop tomorrow: a Porsche dealer. Second stop: computer store. Third stop: Tahiti? Barnett tilted his head back, to the point where his eyes could just see the road, and let the wind rush over his face. Not a bad little car he borrowed, this dinky convertible.

Life was going to be good again. Once he got this bullshit out of the way, once he stripped that asshole Commander of whatever fortune lurked at his cabin, once he burned to the ground any vestige of what the man owned. Too bad Ol' Flattop wouldn't be there for the bonfire; more than anything, Barnett wanted to crucify the fucker. Somehow, someday he would finish the task, since the Authorities, in their blinding ineptitude, had not been able to capture the creep, or so said the radio reports. And once he had disposed of the Commander, as viciously as he could, then Barnett would be at peace. Life would be very, very good again.

It was easier to feel that way, the further he got from D.C. Getting out of there had been more nerve-wracking than difficult; airlines had planes going everywhere. And a few greedy hacker friends in San Jose had agreed to help out in exchange for some quick cash: a car from one; a gun from another. Now, Barnett was on a twisting mountain road, bathed in the warm glow of sunset, gradually recovering from so much pressure.

It had been a nice dream, burning down the government. Nearly pulled it off, too. But now the Authorities were slobbering all over themselves on the radio about how they saved the country from annihilation today. Nobody was giving *him* any credit, of course; the nuke would have blown up if he hadn't tossed that key to Harry–the–rat. Humans. Just couldn't count on them for anything unless money was involved.

Or videotapes! He had to remember to grab the original of the CC tape before he torched the Commander's cabin. Who knew when that might come in handy? Kind of a nice idea to have the Prez as your slave. Unless some rat took the copy out of the van and spread it to the media. Fuckers.

His eyes flicked to the rearview mirror. Still nothing. Not that he expected much traffic way up here, but lurking in his brain was the question of whether the Feds or Georgie-boy were headed this way. Maybe, but he had gotten out of D.C. fast and he would get away from this mountain merry-go-round as quickly as he could. Didn't want to tempt fate.

He swung the car off the paved road, onto the steep grade leading to the cabin. It was the only road in. He had memorized the route on the way out, knowing he'd be back for that stash of gold and a certain "personnel" file that Betsy was supposed to be holding. It was a rough road, but he barely cut his speed; it wasn't his car.

He was surprised at how much dust he was kicking up. Everything was so dry, he'd have to be careful when he torched the cabin —didn't want a forest fire to flare up and outrun him to the main road.

He cut his speed, realizing the dust could be a signal to Betsy. He planned to stop a mile or so short of the cabin anyway, but he didn't want to find her waiting on the porch with a shotgun.

Ten minutes later, he pulled off and parked behind a stand of trees. It was dark out now; no one would see it unless they were looking for it, if anyone even came this way. He took a large backpack out of the trunk and wedged a five–gallon gas can into it. The urge to hum was overwhelming.

He started hiking toward the cabin, staying away from the road as much as possible in case Betsy was out strolling. The weight on his back was heavier than expected and he was sweating like a mule, but it would be worth the effort: fry the man in absentia; rob him of everything in life except his wench of a wife; and someday decimate the creep in person. In the solitude of the dark forest, his rage blazed the way.

It was twenty minutes before he saw flickers of light through the trees. He picked up his pace, grinning fiercely.

Suddenly, he heard a noise behind him. Not close, but clear. And the smell of dust—someone was coming! He hid behind a tree and waited, unsure of anything now. If this was the Feds . . .

The sound grew louder, a car or truck bouncing up the last rugged parts of the road. Headlights swung across the trees and granite walls. In a moment, it would be close enough to—

It was the Commander!

How the hell did he get here so fast? Did he have a plane waiting? Barnett's heart rocketed out of control.

He took a deep breath. They didn't know he was there. He just had to proceed quietly; dump the fear, keep the fury in check. If necessary, wait until they were asleep before walking in. The Commander had to be tired.

In five minutes, Barnett was within sight of the cabin, and he didn't like what he saw. They weren't going to be spending the night there; the Commander and Betsy were motoring between the house and the Jeep, loading up belongings.

He set his pack down and watched them, planning his moves. He had to be calm about this or he would blow his chance. After the scene in the van that morning, this had to be an ugly, vicious death.

The Commander and Betsy continued their task, focused on the path in front of them, passing each other in mid-trip as they dashed in and out of the cabin, their timing consistent. And the Commander did not appear to be armed. Perfect.

Barnett moved to his left as Ol' Flattop was shoving the latest load into the Jeep. So nice of them to pack it for him! The Commander turned to head back to the house, and Barnett ran in a crouch to the front of the Jeep. He listened to the exchange of footsteps—the Commander's receding, Betsy's approaching. He took a breath to try to settle himself.

He pulled out his gun as she reached the Jeep, moving along the side as she dropped her load. When she turned toward the house, Barnett stepped up and grabbed her, one hand around her mouth, the gun at her head.

"Not a sound, bitch," he whispered in her ear.

Betsy's body jerked. A scream was stifled under Barnett's hand. Then the Commander's boots sounded on the porch. He got halfway to the Jeep before his eyes came up and grasped the scene.

"Well, for the love of God. I hoped you were dead."

"Guess again, asshole."

The Commander tossed his load of boxes to the side and started toward them, waving with his hand. "Give me the pea shooter, sonny, before somebody gets hurt."

Barnett snapped. "Pea shooter? Let's see." He pulled the gun down and fired, the explosion echoing off the canyon walls. The bullet tore into the Commander's left thigh, spinning him into the dirt, blood pouring from his leg. Betsy broke free and ran to him, screaming.

Barnett sneered at him. "A pea shooter? Maybe not. At least it got you and your wife together. She's usually off fucking someone else, isn't she?"

The Commander roared and lunged forward, his eyes blasting into Barnett, his fingers nearly covering the distance on their own. Barnett took a step to his right and the Commander tumbled past, unable to change direction. As the Commander pulled himself up to charge again, Barnett calmly pointed the gun at his other leg and fired. The Commander crumpled to the ground, raging in pain.

"You are so right, Private. This is a lousy pea—"

Betsy leapt onto his back, her fingers tearing at Barnett's face, trying to gouge his eyes. He swung his body wildly, but couldn't get rid of her. In a panic, he threw himself backwards. Betsy's body hit the ground first, air blasting out of her lungs, then Barnett's head cracked against hers. He was stunned, but free.

He struggled to his feet and looked at the two of them, sprawled in the dirt. The temptation was overwhelming—step up and put a bullet in the man's brain—but he didn't want to kill the Commander that way. The man had to suffer and die more slowly than a bullet would allow.

It was tough, but he and Betsy got the Commander into the cabin and onto the couch. Wisely, neither tried to attack him.

Betsy had her hands over the Commander's bullet wounds, a vain attempt to stop the bleeding. She looked up at Barnett, desperation in her eyes.

"Let me get him out of here. Please! You can have our money. Anything! Just let us go."

Barnett shook his head. "I want his life, lady. Earlier today, he was going to take mine—viciously. He deserves the same."

Betsy jumped to her feet. "Please! You can't do this! What will it take? You mentioned sex? Let's do it." She grabbed her shirt and ripped it off.

The Commander's head snapped up. Barnett's eyes went wide.

"In front of him? That's better than I had planned!"

Betsy was pulling down her jeans now.

"Hold on," Barnett said. "I don't have time for this. Even if I fucked you, I'd still kill him. Put your clothes back on."

He walked to the couch, holding the gun in front of him. He placed it against the Commander's forehead, then reached down and patted at his pants. "Where are the car keys?" He reached into a blood-soaked pocket, pulled out the keys to the Jeep, and stepped back.

"Thanks for packing this for me. Is CC's video in there?"

The Commander glared at him, his teeth clenched in pain. "I'm going to see that you die."

Barnett chuckled. "It's the other way around, Georgie."

His eyes scanned the room, and settled on a kerosene lamp on the dining table. Keeping the gun pointed at the Commander, he walked over, yanked the top off the lamp, and brought the base over to the couch.

Betsy was to the side, frozen. The Commander's mouth was open, but no sound came out. Barnett lifted the lamp and slowly poured the kerosene over the Commander's head, drenching him.

"You can pretend you're a monk or something," Barnett said. "Now, all I need is a match." He turned and started toward the kitchen.

The door to the cabin flew open just as Barnett passed it. Kevin charged in and slammed Barnett against the wall, then down onto the floor. He grabbed the hand with the gun and bashed it against the floor until the hand was bloody and the gun flopped away.

"Thank God you're here!" Betsy said.

She rushed over to him, but Kevin brushed her off and went to retrieve the gun. It was only then that Barnett noticed how Kevin was dressed—in a three-piece suit!

Barnett groaned and got to his feet. "You keep surprising me, buddy boy. I never thought you'd make it and look at you, dressed for success."

"Shut up. I should've killed you like I was ordered to."

"Nice work, son," the Commander muttered.

"I'm not your son!" Kevin shouted.

"Yes you are," Betsy said.

"Leave me alone, all of you!"

The kid was totally crackers. If they weren't careful, he'd probably drill them all. This was not how Barnett wanted to check out. Maybe chumminess would do? The kid's ego had been trashed.

Barnett smiled. "Where did you get the neat costume?"

Kevin exhaled and walked to the table. He dropped into a

chair, the gun in front of him. "I killed a guy for it. A politician, so no big deal. Got his credit cards, too."

"Why did you come back?" Betsy said.

"I thought for you, slut! Until I saw what you were doing with JB."

"Kevin, it's not what—"

"SHUT UP, ALL OF YOU!" He jumped to his feet, waving the gun across the room. "You've all fucked me over. You all deserve to die. Nobody gave a shit about me, especially not you!"

He pointed the gun at the Commander and fired. The bullet blasted into the couch, an inch from the Commander's arm.

"I don't even care anymore," Kevin said. "All that crap about being disappointed and shit?" He fired again, just missing the other arm.

"You know something, 'Dad'? Harper was right, about respect and stuff. I deserved it. And now this is what you deserve."

He swung the gun back and forth in front of the Commander's chest, each time shortening the arc, until he stopped, the gun leveled at the heart.

"Kevin . . ." Betsy whispered. "Don't do it."

He cocked the trigger.

"Kevin."

His eyes narrowed.

"Kevin!"

Barnett bolted for the front door. Kevin wheeled around and fired at the handle, driving Barnett back.

"Stay where you are!" Kevin roared.

Barnett looked at him, lost.

"Oh, fuck you. Go ahead and leave." Kevin turned the gun back on the Commander. "Say 'Hi' to the Feds on your way out."

"What?!" Barnett and the Commander said it in unison.

Kevin chuckled crudely. "You didn't see them? What losers."

"Hold on," Barnett said. "How do you know?"

"A bunch of 'em passed me nearby on Highway 49. I ditched

the rental car and hiked in. I'm sure they're waiting."

"Jesus Christ! How am I going to get out of here?"

Kevin shrugged. "You can hike out, though you'll never find the way. Or you can try to blast through their defenses." He smiled. "Good luck."

"You've got to help me!" Barnett said.

Kevin pointed the gun at him. "If you offer me sex, I *will* shoot you."

Barnett stumbled outside. It wasn't possible! How could the Feds know about this place? Or gotten here so fast, unless . . . Harry–the–rat? No, this moron had to be hallucinating.

Barnett ran to the Jeep, started it, and drove about twenty yards. Then he went back for his pack, the one with the gasoline.

There was a shot just then. And another one.

Barnett's heart went into overdrive. He pulled the top off the gas can and started running, pouring a trail of flammable liquid over the dry forest tinder as he made a big circle around the house. He half expected someone to come running out, but no one did.

He got back to the Jeep, sloshing gas as he went. He tried not to get any on himself, but that had been impossible. He threw the can to the side and hopped in the Jeep, pressed in the cigarette lighter, and moved the Jeep another twenty yards away.

The lighter popped out, ready. Barnett took a breath, sucking in some gas, and pulled the lighter out. Nothing ignited. He carried it quickly back toward the house and the ring of gas, and tossed it at the gas can.

A huge explosion erupted. He was pushed back by the heat and intensity of the blast. In both directions, the fire raced around the ring, encircling the cabin, and leaping—arcing—to trees on either side of its path. It seemed like the whole section of forest was suddenly one giant flame, streaking upwards past the tops of the giant trees.

Barnett backed up slowly, watching the blaze jump from tree to tree, the pace accelerating as the wall of fire widened. Then he turned his back and walked to the Jeep. He got a surprise when he glanced at the passenger seat: a woman's wig? So that's how the Commander got by the Feds.

Harry and Ellen dashed to their car at the first sharp echoes from the canyon. Harry revved the engine and they flew out of the woods, across the paved road, and onto the steep grade. A fleet of FBI vehicles followed them.

Earlier reconnaissance had determined that only Betsy was up in that canyon; there had been no sign of the Commander or Kevin at the turn-off where agents were staked out. Only two people had turned onto the dirt road all day: a woman in a Jeep, twenty minutes ago, shortly before Harry and Ellen arrived at the checkpoint; and a man in a Miata, a while before that. One of the agents thought it might have been Barnett, though why he'd come back after what happened that morning in Washington . . .

Regardless, waiting for the Commander to show up, even waiting for him to leave the cabin, in case it was booby-trapped, was no longer viable. He knew this area; he might have gotten in another way.

It was a tough road in the dark, particularly with all the ruts and rocks and steep drops off the side. It wasn't a road to speed on, and they had five miles to cover.

They came around a blind corner—to a panorama from Hell.

"Holy shit, look at that!" Ellen said, her voice hushed.

A ridge of flames swept across the vista, right in the direction they were headed. The whole forest seemed to be engulfed.

"If this is a defensive measure," Harry said, "we're screwed."

"And fried, if the wind shifts," Ellen said.

Harry cut his speed slightly, his eyes fixed on the inferno ahead. If he remembered this drive correctly, the cabin was probably on the other side of those flames. Or in the midst of them.

That thought was answered a minute later. A fearsome series

of explosions, like cannon blasts, battered the granite walls. There could be only one explanation: the Commander's arsenal was blowing up. What a horrible way to die.

Ellen put her hand on Harry's arm. "Turn off your lights."

Harry did so, then squinted into the distance. Up ahead, halfway between them and the fire, were two pin spots. Headlights! Was this the Commander making his escape? He must have been in that Jeep. Ellen picked up her radio and passed the word along to the convoy behind them.

Harry eased the car to a stop, then maneuvered it to block the narrow roadway. To one side was a granite cliff, to the other a steep drop off. They got out and waited behind the car, guns ready.

The lights approached, getting larger and more defined. It was indeed a Jeep. Fifty feet away, it rolled to a stop. It sat there, idling.

The wind shifted then, and Harry felt the first wave of hot, parched air. The fire had turned in their direction.

The Jeep started creeping forward. To get a better look? It stopped twenty feet away—and Barnett was inside! His face was clearly visible, looking from Harry to Ellen. He shook his head.

"Where's the Commander?" Harry shouted.

Barnett put his hand out the window and pointed behind him.

"Checkmate, Jeff," Ellen shouted.

Barnett stuck his head out. "Can we bargain? I've got a nice video the President would like." He held it out the window.

Harry reached into the car and pulled out a box. "Got one of my own! The one you left in the van. Want it back?" He held it in front of him.

Suddenly, there was the roar of tires on gravel. The Jeep rocketed backwards, swinging wildly as it raced up the road in reverse.

Ellen turned to the line of agents. "Hold your fire! We need him alive!"

They jumped in the car. "Do we?" Harry said.

"If we hope to find his computer targets," Ellen said. "The lab techs will have a rough time with that laptop in the van."

Harry cranked the wheel around and stomped on the accelerator, the tires kicking up dirt as the car fishtailed and took off. The Jeep was a hundred yards in front of them, careening side–to–side as Barnett tried to keep it on the road.

"He can't go as fast in reverse," Harry said.

"He'll try. I know how he feels about going back to prison."

They were gaining on him.

"Is he suicidal or does he know some exit from this road?"

"He's got a four-wheel drive," Ellen said. "Maybe he'll make one."

Harry's eyes flicked toward the drop-off. "Hell of an exit. The terrain has to flatten out up ahead, but the fire may be there already. He's got to stop."

The Jeep disappeared around a sharp bend, leaning hard on the outside tires as they skirted the edge of the road. Harry stabbed the brakes, skidding the car around a curve, then accelerated toward the bend where the Jeep had last been. Harry moved carefully through the turn—and stopped the car.

A wall of flames obliterated the view, less than half a mile away. It ran from the valley floor to the tops of the trees, in furious shrieks of red and yellow and black. Hundreds of feet high and filling the width of the canyon. Heat blasted through the car, burning what little breath Harry had left.

The Jeep had slowed. Barnett was weighing his options.

"Will we push him over if we continue?" Ellen said.

"I'm not sure I want to go further, the way that fire is moving."

Ellen squinted at the area of flames Barnett was approaching. "If he could get through that first wall, could he get away? If everything past that is already burned out?"

"How should I know? And I don't feel like trying it out."

The Jeep had stopped a hundred feet short of the flames.

"Come on, we've got to get him," Ellen said.

"What if he's armed? What if he wants to take us with him?

If he's not suicidal, he'll come back this way."

Ellen turned to face him. "Maybe he is suicidal. I don't want to see him die this way. I'll walk up there if I have to, Harry."

He groaned and pressed on the accelerator, moving ahead slowly.

"Thanks."

As they got closer to the Jeep, the heat became unbearable. Flames hurtled from tree to tree, leaping up over the roadway in long, vicious streaks. Harry was hypnotized. It wasn't until they were almost to the Jeep that he finally looked at Barnett. His eyes were frantic.

Harry turned to Ellen. "Don't get ou—" She was already gone. He grabbed his gun, opened the door, and propped his arm against the roof of the car, his weapon zeroed on Barnett's face.

Ellen stopped between the two cars. "Come on, Jeff. Let's go."

He sat there, his head swinging side–to–side.

"Come on! We don't have much time. Get out of the car."

Flames roared up beside her, driving Ellen away from the edge.

Harry glanced to his right. Fire in the valley had already moved past their position. They could be trapped in minutes.

Ellen ran to the Jeep and slammed her hand on the hood.

"Come out of there, damn it! Don't die like this!"

The Jeep suddenly shot backwards, leaving Ellen grasping at air. In fifty feet, it reached the first edge of the fire. They stood in shocked silence as the flames inhaled the Jeep, blurring its lines, covering its path, reducing its image to formless motion, rocketing deeper into the molten core.

Ellen's shrieked, "Noooooooooo!"

Then a massive explosion thundered through the canyon, the force knocking Harry and Ellen off their feet. A white-hot ball of fire shot skyward.

Behind them, Harry heard the rest of the convoy lurching into gear, heading off. It was going to be a hellacious ride—downhill, backwards, racing the flames—but there was no time to get nervous. He ran to Ellen and helped her to the car, then dashed back to the driver's side. He started to get in, but stopped.

His eyes were on the videotape, the one of CC. He glanced up at the fire. Then he grabbed the video and ran to the edge of the road. With a roar, he hurled it toward the trees and the cauldron of flames below. It ignited like a piece of flash paper.

Harry flew back to the car and jumped on the pedal—and prayed that the fire wouldn't cut them off.

Good News?

The sun was high in the sky now, baking the dusty landscape. Traffic rumbled along the state highway outside, crossing in front of the diner, past the booth where Harry had been parked for hours, past the motel they had checked into late in the night, when fatigue threatened to pull Harry off the road, past whatever room Ellen was still snoozing in, past . . . everything.

It had been a fitful night's sleep, crowded with flames and noise and furious, frantic motion. Faces appeared and dissolved—melted—poking him every time he tried to find a corner of stillness in his head. The morning light was a relief, despite his exhaustion. He dragged himself into the shower, back into rancid clothes, and out across the parking lot to the diner.

Despite the hour, whatever it was, he was still only on his second cup of coffee. He was mesmerized by the traffic. It was mostly commercial, big rigs and such. People whose lives were focused on the moment: get this shipment to Sacramento before noon; pray the tires hold out another thousand miles; find a gas station fast. No worries about madmen or murderous rogues or nukes or catastrophic disasters. Maybe how to make the next house payment, but not how to stop the world from melting down. It must be nice.

The door to the diner swung open, accompanied by an annoying little bell. Harry glanced over and saw a rumpled figure shuffle in, short chopped red hair, dark sunglasses blocking her eyes. Ellen paused to look around, spotted Harry, grabbed a cup of coffee from a passing waitress, and shuffled over, slumping onto the bench seat opposite him.

"Where are we?" Her voice was an octave lower than usual.

"Does it matter?"

She shrugged. "Been here long?"

"Long enough." Harry returned his gaze to the window. "I've been watching people drive past, trying to pick apart what's going on in their heads. Family, boss, money, sex, TV, food, sports—in some kind of order."

Ellen chuckled darkly. "Any Commanders?"

"That's just it. You wouldn't know it if you saw him driving by. Who knows what horrors lurk behind the faces I've seen today?"

"Feeling morose, are we?"

"'Bludgeoned' is more like it."

Ellen stretched, stiffly, and let out a groan. "I hear you. I've never felt this bad, except maybe after one particular drinking binge in college."

Harry laughed quietly. "Don't try to one-up me."

A buzzing from inside Harry's coat stopped him. He pulled out his cell phone, raised it to his ear, and listened quietly for several seconds. Then he said "Thanks" and put the phone away.

"That was cryptic," Ellen said, her voice still in the basement.

"It was Morton, calling back with some details. I've been on the phone with him twice already; he's still in D.C."

"And . . ."

"And there's going to be a memorial service tomorrow for Jack Townsend. It's in Washington, but he figured you'd probably want to go."

Ellen turned her head away, then nodded slowly.

"Yeah. I'm not wild about getting on a plane again, but I have to be there." Her voice softened. "The one time I reconsider my ban on getting involved with another agent . . ."

Harry reached out and squeezed her hand.

Ellen squeezed back, then let go and pulled off her sunglasses, tossing them on the table. "So, did Morton have any good news? What disasters await us now?"

Harry chuckled. "Actually, he did have good news. Warren Keller, Brendan Crowley, and half a dozen others are in custody, with more arrests expected. It'll be a while before all the details come out, but the Attorney General is anxious for a full disclosure."

"Crowley's a snake. What do you bet he gets off again?"

"That's occurred to me."

"What about the nuke?"

"Alleged to be safe and sound with the military."

Ellen shook her head. "Do you believe what we've been through?"

"Barely."

"I swear, we've got to get something less toxic to work on, Harry. I can't take another one like this." She leaned back and stretched her arms over her head. "I'd like to do something slow and boring and—"

She stopped, looked at Harry, and started laughing. "I know, don't say it: Be careful what you wish for . . ."

Thanks!

I hope you enjoyed *Torch Day*. If you *really* liked it, please help spread the word. Tell your friends and family. Give it a rating on Amazon. And post a short review, too!

Follow us on Facebook at www.facebook.com/torchday

And you'll get longer-form content at www.torchday.com

Among the things you'll find there are chapters from works-in-progress, starting with updates to my first novel, *Remote Control*. That book introduces Harry and Ellen, and Brendan f'n Crowley. It's a fun, fast, absorbing read.

Best Regards,
John

www.ingramcontent.com/pod-product-compliance
Lightning Source LLC
Chambersburg PA
CBHW071202250626
47159CB00001B/171